DEAD RICH

LOUISE FENNELL

**SIMON &
SCHUSTER**

London · New York · Sydney · Toronto · New Delhi

A CBS COMPANY

First published in Great Britain by Bedford Square Books, 2012
This edition published by Simon & Schuster UK Ltd, 2012
A CBS COMPANY

Copyright © Louise Fennell, 2012

3 5 7 9 10 8 6 4 2

Simon & Schuster UK Ltd
1st Floor
222 Gray's Inn Road
London WC1X 8HB

www.simonandschuster.co.uk

Simon & Schuster Australia
Sydney

Simon & Schuster India
New Delhi

A CIP catalogue record for this book is available
from the British Library

ISBN: 978-1-47110-192-2

Printed and bound by CPI Group (UK) Ltd, Croydon, CR0 4YY

For my beloved family
Theo, Emerald, Coco, Mum
and, of course, for Susan

ACKNOWLEDGEMENTS

From the moment I showed Ed Victor my first scribbled pages he has been herculean in his support and enthusiasm for *Dead Rich*. His faith in me has brought me more joy than I can ever convey – I will never be able to thank him enough. Huge thanks too to my magnificent editor Susan Opie whose tact curbed my worst excesses and whose warmth and humour made the editing process such a pleasure. I have my wonderful daughters to thank for all their enthusiasm and encouragement, Emerald for her wise, patient and perceptive editorial advice and Coco for her creative design skills and my fabulous, funny husband Theo, for the life that we have together and the inspiration that life has brought me. My boundless gratitude goes to Susan Boyd for her lifelong friendship and encouragement and a particularly huge thank you goes to Garry Blackman and Tesco for taking on *Dead Rich* – a fantastic dream come true for me. Thanks also to Ian Chapman, Maxine Hitchcock, Hannah Corbett, Rumana Haider and James Horobin at Simon & Schuster. Vociferous thanks to the team at Bedford Square Books, who have all been incredibly supportive; Edina Imrik, Maggie Phillips and Linda Van. Then Mark Hutchinson, Christopher Jenkins, William Boyd, Sally Woodward Gentle, Jennine Carpenter, Poppy Cotterell, Hazel Clukas and Jenna Housby who have all played their part in the journey of this book. I also have Bear Grylls to thank for the Everest inspiration and my lovely, kind, indomitable mother, Jenny MacGregor, for demonstrating to me that tenacity usually gets you there so never give up!

Celebrity is a mask that eats into the face.

JOHN UPDIKE

CHAPTER ONE

The black Mini hit the kerb and ground to a halt with a jolt.

Valentine Robinson flung the car door open and leapt onto the pavement. Music and laughter pumped out after him as he reached back into the smoky car and pulled out a very dishevelled young girl. His Oxford friends, Charlie and Art, helped him by pushing her from behind. Dusty stumbled and Valentine caught her gently. He gave her a brief hug. Then, in a blur of Dolce & Gabbana velvet and floppy blonde hair, he jumped back into the Mini and it sped off into the clear spring dawn.

Turning unsteadily, Dusty gave a desultory wave, then bent down to pull off her vintage Terry de Havilland shoes.

Dusty March didn't really look her age; she could have been even younger than fourteen. Skinny, with long, untidy blonde hair, she looked like a child who had raided her mother's makeup and wardrobe, which, in fact, she had. Her eyes were large black smudges in her delicate face. She looked wasted because she was. She set off down the London street, her bare feet padding softly through fallen cherry blossoms that littered the pavement like marshmallows.

The day was beginning fresh and bright. The same could not be said for Dusty, who was feeling distinctly queasy. As she walked past the grand, dazzlingly white-pillared houses of Hollywood Road in Chelsea, she rummaged in her large Chloe handbag.

'Fuck, fuck, fuck!' she muttered, unable to find her keys.

Gently sinking onto some polished granite steps, she pulled out a pack of cigarettes, lit one and took a deep drag, trying to decide whether this made her feel better or worse. She had another listless look in her bag, noticing the time on her watch said 5.15a.m. Finally finding her keys she stood up, turned wearily, and opened the huge front door.

Once inside she dropped her shoes to the floor and walked quietly through a massive open-plan room. It looked as if it had been decorated by a colour blind lunatic: eclectic and expensive, it was a monument to Contemporary Art. One wall was completely covered with Damien Hirst butterfly pictures. The space was dominated by numerous huge sofas; in red, pink and yellow, with a coffee table by Philippe Starck, and a Mondrian kitchen. It was as if a neglected colour might some-how be offended if it was left out.

The only sound that Dusty could hear was a baby crying. She set off up the wide, ornate staircase, which led straight off the main room. Taking one last drag of her cigarette she casu-ally stubbed it out in a precious orchid pot as she passed.

The baby was really bellowing by the time Dusty got to the

nursery door. She pushed it open and found her little sister standing in her cot wailing, taking huge gulps of air, then wailing again. The baby held her arms out and Dusty scooped her up.

'Hey, Willow, what's up? Calm down. Dusty's here, Dusty's here. It's OK – let's find Mama, shall we? It's OK. Good girl.'

Dusty held the baby tight, stroking her soft curls, kissing her head. The baby pushed her snotty tear-stained face into her sister's neck and gradually her juddering tears subsided. They set off up the next flight of stairs to the top floor of the house, where double doors stood slightly ajar. Dusty gently shouldered them open. The room was dark and messy in the gloom. Putting the baby down onto the bed she went to draw back the curtains. The early morning light flashed as it hit the framed gold and platinum albums that lined the walls.

She spoke softly. 'Mama, Mama, morning. Time to wake up. Willow needs you and I need some sleep before school, Mama.' Then, more loudly: 'Mama – Georgia! Come on, wakey, wakey!'

As she turned towards the bed she saw that the baby had climbed onto her mother's back and was bumping her cheek against her shoulder, quietly saying, 'Mum-ma, Mum-ma.'

Dusty swiftly crossed the room and bent over her mother's sprawled body. Georgia's face was turned away from her. As Dusty leant across she felt her mother's skin, cold against her wrist. She looked down and saw the face she loved – distorted, bloated, dark and dead. Dead. Dead. Dead. In horror, she pulled her baby sister from her mother's back and sank to the floor. She could feel the floorboards beneath her, but Dusty continued to fall – down into darkness and despair. Her eyes closed.

And so it began there, just like that. With Georgia's last little exhaled breath, a cool breeze had begun to whisper amid the charmed lives of 'Britain's Favourite Family'.

CHAPTER TWO

The early-morning sun was streaming into the vast library, spotlighting an old leather chair. Sprawled in it was a comatose man. His handsome face crinkled uncomfortably against the worn leather, his nose nearly touching an almost-empty glass of whisky. He wore a white shirt, which was crumpled and damp against his brown skin. An overflowing ashtray was precariously perched on his denim-clad crotch. Jake Robinson wasn't looking his best.

A solid mahogany door swung open and crashed into a small table, but Jake didn't stir. An exquisite but angry-looking woman stormed across the room towards him. She had obviously just tumbled out of bed; her pale silk dressing gown swirled around her. Jake glimpsed a flash of her perfect long brown legs as she leant over him. He pretended to be asleep – he sensed trouble. He was used to it, because frankly he was often in trouble.

Zelda Spender, his beautiful, famous, furious wife was not sounding happy. 'Jake, Jake! Wake up, wake *up*! Oh, for fuck's sake . . . Jake!'

Jake wisely remained lying doggo. When he didn't open his eyes Zelda became even more livid. She leant closer and grabbed a handful of his thick dark hair and pulled it, quite hard. Jake decided to pretend to wake a little, see how the land lay. He bravely reached out to put his hand on Zelda's tempting thigh. She slapped it away. 'Jake, you prat, wake up!'

Jake groaned, beginning to realise that this didn't sound quite like the usual bollocking from his wife. Somewhere, through the haze of his hangover, he detected something else in her voice, something that made him feel that he should make an effort to struggle back into a semblance of consciousness.

'Your bloody sister has finally done it! Can you hear me, Jake?' Her voice was softening, not something that would usually happen in these circumstances. Alarm and panic began to hum in his befuddled brain. He started to pull himself up in the chair.

Looking at his wife wildly, he tried to make sense of what she was saying. 'Wha . . . what? What're you . . .' he mumbled. The ashtray tipped from his lap onto the worn, but priceless, Persian rug. Jake flinched as if he was expecting a slap. But Zelda just put her hand gently on his forearm and quietly said, 'The Daily Mail just rang. Woke me up. She's been taken to Chelsea and Westminster hospital.'

'What? Who?' Jake was really beginning to feel panicked and sick. What was she saying?

'Georgia, Jake, it's Georgia.' Zelda was speaking very quietly now and Jake could see her eyes were starting to brim with tears: a sight so unusual and unnerving that he almost screamed. He just managed to respond weakly, 'Is she OK?'

'No, Jake, I'm sorry, she's not OK. She's . . . she's dead, Jake. I'm so sorry.' She moved to hug him but Jake pushed her away, slurring slightly. 'That's a hor . . . horrible thing to say – just because . . .'

Zelda straightened up and walked over to the monumental fireplace, took a packet of Marlboro Lights from her dressing-gown pocket, lit one and inhaled deeply. She turned to look at her husband. No matter how dissolute he had become she was sometimes surprised when she noticed how very beautiful he still was, after all these years.

He ran his hands through his hair and looked up at her with his 'vulnerable child' face, which usually made her want to kick him – but today she couldn't help feeling a momentary wave of compassion for her wayward spouse.

Zelda knew that Jake really loved his sister, Georgia. She was arguably even more of a fuck-up than him. But they had shared a familial charisma, humour and talent that had brought them both fame and fortune and endeared them to millions. Well, it had to Georgia, anyway. Jake had long ago left his talent under a bar somewhere. Zelda suddenly felt furious with both of them for all the pain and chaos they had caused.

Taking another sharp drag on her cigarette she said, 'Jake, she bloody did it when Dusty was out, so that poor baby was left alone and crying. Thank God Dusty came home when she did – imagine if she had stayed with her friends for a few days?

Christ, this is unbelievable, even by Georgia's appalling standards.'

Jake struggled to sit up. 'God, Zelda, what are you saying? She's dead? Are you sure? For Christ's sake, are you sure?'

'I spoke to Dusty, Jake. I'm sure, OK. I'm sure.' She looked despairingly at him as he sank to his knees on the floor, and let out a sob.

'Oh Christ! Georgia, Georgia!' He stared up at his wife with a desolate plea. 'What happened?' His voice was husky with emotion and hangover.

Zelda crossed the room and gently touched his shoulder. 'We don't know yet, but I think we can probably guess, can't we, Jake? We'll know more later. I need you to tell Ed, OK? I have to get dressed. Tell him we are going to the hospital to collect Dusty and Willow now. Jake, come on, we need to get going. I'll drive.'

As she swept out of the room Jake heard her mutter, 'Jesus, still pissed, fucking hell!' not quite under her breath.

Ten minutes later Jake came out of his bathroom, vigorously rubbing his hair and face with a towel. He walked along a wide landing, past a sculpture of a child by Jake and Dinos Chapman. He draped the towel over its grotesque phallic features and knocked on a door marked 'Fuck Off'. No reply. He knocked again, harder this time. 'Ed! It's Dad, I need to talk to you. Please, Ed ... open the door, mate. C'mon.' Jake tried the handle but the door was locked. 'Ed ... Ed!'

The door opened a couple of inches and a sweet-faced teenage boy peeped out sleepily. 'What time is it?'

Jake looked bemused. 'Christ, I don't know, um, but there's a ... something ... Ed, Georgia's had an accident ... er ...' He was lost for words, unable to break this terrible news to his youngest son.

But Ed only had to look at his father's face to know what was wrong. 'Oh God – Dad! She's dead? She's dead isn't she? Shit.' Ed paused, letting the door fall open. 'Where are Dusty and Willow? Are they OK? Are you OK?'

'They're ... they're at the hospital. Mum and I are just going to get them.' Jake turned and started downstairs, as if he had suddenly been reminded of his mission.

He called back up to Ed. 'Stay in the house, do not answer the phone.'

Ed moved to the edge of the banister and leant over. 'Dad, Dad!' But his father didn't hear him. Ed turned forlornly and disappeared back into his bedroom, quietly closing the door behind him.

Jake ran down the wide staircase of his home, a massive converted church, St Bart's, in Chelsea. It was irreverently known in the media, and therefore by practically everyone, as 'God's'.

He had always felt that the founding fathers would be turning in their graves if they knew what a truly godless future their beloved church was destined for. The Spender family had bought it in the early 90s, when godliness was at an all-time low. No expense had been spared to turn it into the most lavishly comfortable home. God's House was very luxurious indeed.

Jake had always felt it was an insane place to live but it suited the family perfectly, not least because its stained-glass windows, set so high into its towering walls, afforded them the privacy and security that they craved; it was their sanctuary. God's House was this godless family's home, an irony that was mostly lost on their adoring fans.

Zelda was already waiting outside, sitting in the driving seat of a sinister black Porsche 4X4 with blacked-out windows, watching as her security guy, David, remonstrated quietly, but very firmly, with a few of the regular paparazzi who were always waiting at their gate. They were fairly subdued today but as Zelda opened her window the cameras started to click frantically.

Zelda ignored them. She knew she was looking vulnerable, not in full makeup. She hoped her huge Gucci sunglasses helped to give an impression of the grieving sister-in-law. She felt completely naked without lipstick. Her lucrative contract with Fabulous, the largest cosmetics company in the world, stipulated that she must never, ever be caught out in public without being fully made up in their products. But somehow she felt they would have to make an exception today; surely 'vain and heartless' was not a look they were trying to promote?

As David approached the car, Zelda felt the little thrill she so often experienced when she was in the company of her security team. Like her very own personal cast of the Chippendales, all tight uniforms and taut muscles, they were always burning to serve. David was the Head of Security and the finest example of his type (ex-SAS) she had ever employed. Zelda opened the car window a little further and David leant in towards her. She spoke softly: 'David, do you think we should get some more of the guys to help today?'

David looked at her over his Wayfarer sunglasses. 'They're already on their way, but they won't be here for fifteen minutes or so. I think it would be wise to wait till they get here, then I'll leave them in charge and come with you to the hospital.'

Zelda shook her head impatiently. 'No, stay here, David, I'll have Jake with me.' She pulled her legendary beautiful mouth into a tight, somehow sexy, grimace. 'We'll be fine ... but more than ten fucking photographers – call the police.'

Jake emerged. Slamming the front door, he flinched slightly at the noise and sprinted down the wide stone steps. The photographers went berserk. Zelda closed her electric window abruptly when she heard him coming.

As Jake plonked himself into the back seat, Zelda turned to him crossly. 'Get in the front, I'm not your bloody chauffeur!'

He hopped out again and into the front. 'Sorry, I thought David would be driving.' Zelda gave him a hard stare, which he couldn't really appreciate, what with the darkness of her sunglasses and the fuzziness of his vision.

David stepped back adeptly and watched admiringly as Zelda sped out of the gate, her hand pressed hard on the car horn. The paparazzi had to scramble out of her way, like rats running from a burning building.

Lana turned away from her small bedroom window as the car sped off. Tears streaked her pretty young face as she wearily pulled a heavy suitcase onto the bed. She clicked the catches and it sprang open, revealing a jumble of clothes. She began to unpack the things that she had hastily stuffed into her case only a few hours earlier.

She didn't hear Ed until he burst through her door calling her name. He stopped on the threshold, suddenly embarrassed, feeling thirteen, shy and in need of a hug. A hug from his lovely Estonian au pair, in particular, was something Ed needed really badly. She didn't disappoint him. She put her arms around him, murmuring sympathetically, 'So sorry, Ed, so sorry.' He let her hold him. Unsure of where to put his hands, he lifted them tentatively and lightly touched her back; the soft cotton blouse she wore felt warm, comforting – and something else too . . .

'Is OK, Ed, is OK,' she said soothingly and kissed the top of his head. He began to feel better. He even managed a tiny smile. Then he noticed the suitcase on the bed and stepped away, distraught again.

'What's that, Lana? You're not going away, are you?'

She shook her head and sadly replied, 'No, no, Ed, just sorting some things out is all. I am here, I am here, no worry.'

*

Zelda drove fast and well through the London streets, occasionally glancing in the rear-view mirror, to make sure that the press weren't following.

She turned to look at Jake. 'Is Ed OK?'

'What do you think, Zelda? His favourite aunt just died. Of course he's not OK. He's only twelve. This is fucking awful – he is going to be so freaked out.' Jake took a deep breath. 'And his cousins have been orphaned – well, as near as dammit.' Jake gazed miserably out of the car window before he continued accusingly, 'You should've told him. You're his mother, it was your job. I didn't do it very well . . .' His voice trailed off.

'You surprise me. Well, let's be clear, she's *your* sister so I think it was your job to tell him – and he's thirteen, *thirteen*!' Zelda looked exasperated.

'Really? Christ – how did that happen?' Jake, mystified, rested his head against the side window and closed his eyes.

'Wake up, Jake, you need to get hold of Elliot. Poor Dusty. Now all she has left is that irresponsible prick for a father!' She prodded Jake's thigh. 'Jake.'

Jake shook himself and pulled out his phone. 'OK, Christ. Elliot, yes. Where is he? Where is he!'

'Stop panicking. Jesus, I think he's in Iraq or – um – Afghanistan, Libya? Oh, I can't remember. Just try his mobile.' Zelda accelerated fast through a red light.

'What if he doesn't answer? Shall I leave him a message? What shall I say? Zelda! Fuck! What shall I say?' Jake's eyes were wild and really very red.

'Just ask him to call you urgently, for God's sake. Jake, are you still drunk?'

Jake looked a bit sick. 'I need to stop at a shop. I . . . I need some fags. I do really, Tiger, please stop for a minute. I'm sorry about last night, I don't know how it happened – can't remember much. Sorry.'

'Not now, Jake, we both know if you were sorry you wouldn't do it. We are going to the hospital to collect your dead sister's children. So you can forget stopping at a shop. Christ!' Zelda jammed on the brakes; a bus narrowly missed them as it swept past blasting its horn.

Jake furiously punched the buttons on his phone, squinting at the screen. He put it to his ear and, not for the first time that day, a look of panic crossed his face. 'Sssssh, ssssh, Elliot's phone is ringing . . . definitely abroad. Shit. Answering. Elliot, Elliot – can you hear me?'

He could only just hear Elliot's faint reply through the static. 'Hello, Jake! Can you hear me?' There was a pause, and then both men tried to speak at once.

Jake: 'Yes, yes, I can hear you.' Which wasn't strictly true, but he could vaguely make out, 'Heard this morning . . . rang' from Elliot's reply. So he ventured, 'Oh God, they got hold of you?' He could just hear some tiny snatches of phrases: 'Terrible . . . devastated . . . details . . . get back.' But the rest was crackle and buzz. Jake just had to improvise his responses. 'OK, I know, man, I'm sorry, God, mate. I know, it's a shock.' He could just understand, 'the girls' and replied, 'Yeah, yeah, we're on our way to the hospital. Don't worry. We'll take them back to ours.' He didn't hear the next thing Elliot was saying because Zelda butted in, 'Where is he, when's he coming home?' Jake, very stressed, demanded, 'Where are you?' as Elliot shouted, 'Top secret ... lines too bad, Jake ... landing tomorrow ... spoken to Dusty ...' Jake heard the line go dead but he still said, 'OK, man. Be careful, Elliot. Bye.'

'Where is he?'

'He said he couldn't say.'

'Christ! Elliot March, international man of mystery! God help us. Did he say how long he'll be home for? Will he take responsibility for Dusty now? And Willow? Who will have her? Elliot? I mean, what a mess – I hope your stupid moron sister has left instructions – like who Willow's father is for a start. So typical, so selfish – where on earth are they going to live?'

'Whoa there, Tiger, they can live with us, can't they? That huge bloody house. Lana's got nothing to do. It'll be fine.' Jake started to look rather pleased with himself – problem solved!

'You are unbelievable. What about ... ?' Zelda's voice trailed off. Up ahead was the entrance to the hospital. She could see that the main area had been blocked by a seething mass of photographers and rubberneckers. As Zelda ploughed through them there was a terrifying noise as cameras and fists banged on the car roof and windows. Zelda was used to it. She ignored them and screeched to a dramatic halt on the double red lines of the hospital forecourt.

She turned to Jake. 'Ready?'

They both reached for their door handles. 'Yep – go!'

Jake and Zelda flung themselves out of the car and raced up

the steps, just as the first few photographers pursued them. Fortunately they were then intercepted by hospital security, stopped and pushed back into the unruly crowd.

Zelda and Jake tumbled into the main foyer of the hospital to be greeted by the surprised faces of staff and patients who clearly couldn't quite believe their eyes ... because there, standing in front of them, was Zelda Spender and her husband Jake What's-his-name, the most famous actress in the world – well, almost – and her husband. Just like that! Right there.

Later they would proudly, but not at all originally, observe to everyone they knew that, 'Zelda and Jake are much taller than they look in their pictures, odd really, because we thought famous people were supposed to be smaller in real life!'

Zelda and Jake walked briskly up to the reception desk and whispered that they were there to speak to the doctor dealing with Miss Georgia Cole and to collect her children. After a certain amount of panicking from the receptionist they were shown upstairs by an orderly who seemed very relaxed, until they realised he had no idea who they were. Which was a novelty that made them both smile. They thanked him as they left the lift and found themselves being greeted by a harassed, slightly sweaty-looking man who introduced himself as Dr D'Angelo.

Only two hours earlier, when Dr D'Angelo was coming off the night shift, all hell had broken loose at the hospital with the arrival of the body of Georgia Cole. Everyone was in shock –

she was the most famous person, alive or dead, any of them had ever seen. They just couldn't wait to tell their families and friends.

Dr D'Angelo had been very unpleasantly surprised when he caught one of his junior doctors trying to take a photograph of her naked body. The intern justified himself by claiming that he didn't feel good about it, but he knew the photograph would be worth tens, no, maybe hundreds of thousands of pounds. As he was trying to struggle by on next to nothing a year, well ... ?

Dr D'Angelo could see his point but nonetheless he confiscated the intern's phone disapprovingly and told him sternly that he would deal with him later.

Although he wouldn't describe himself as a fan, Dr D'Angelo did have some of Georgia's albums, and he had even been to one of her concerts a few years ago. He was shocked and saddened to see the condition of her poor, lifeless body as it lay before him on the gurney. Although she couldn't have been more than late thirties, she looked older. He noticed that her white-blonde hair was dark at the roots. 'Rich and famous counts for nothing in the end: dazzling, vibrant superstar to corpse,' he thought to himself, gloomily.

But the doctor, a credit to his Italian ancestry, was proud to call himself a chivalrous man. In his opinion, the press had not afforded Miss Cole much respect during her life, and he was determined to protect this poor lady from any more unscrupulous people now that she was dead. Having reinstated her dignity by covering her body with the green hospital sheet, he gently patted her shoulder and left the morgue.

He completed his preliminary report and instructed the orderly on duty to ensure that her body be placed securely under lock and key. No one should be granted access without his permission. In the meantime he went up to his office to await the toxicology reports from the lab. This was going to be a long day, and although he was officially off-duty he intended to see it through.

No sooner had he slumped down at his desk than reception called to say Zelda Spender was on her way up. His heart rate doubled. He went out to greet her at the lift and was mortified to find that he broke into a sweat and started stammering as soon as she appeared.

Jake noted, with familiar resignation, that Dr D'Angelo was clearly a fan.

The doctor's office was small. Having politely insisted that Zelda and Jake go in ahead of him, he realised that the space was too cramped and that, embarrassingly, he would have to squeeze himself past Zelda, 'Sorry! Sorry!', to get to his desk. This only served to increase his awkwardness and he finally plopped into his chair, feeling hot and slightly humiliated. Why was his office so small, he thought glumly, and why hadn't he noticed it before?

He tried to concentrate, pull himself together.' I am so sorry, Miss Spender, Mr Spender, Mr, Mr and Mrs um? So sorry!' The doctor shuffled his papers and took a deep breath 'I . . .'

Jake interrupted him. 'Robinson – it's Mr and Mrs Robinson.'

Dr D'Angelo continued, 'Yes, yes, of course – I'm sorry.'

Zelda leant forward in her chair, saying sweetly, 'Doctor,

thank you so much for looking after everything so brilliantly, we are very, very grateful. Do you know what Georgia took? Obviously with the press pounding at the door it would be helpful if we could give them some sort of statement soon.'

The doctor took a deep breath, remembering that he was there to do a job and if he wanted to impress this ... this goddess, then he really needed to get a grip. 'Well, it is too soon for us to be able to tell exactly what caused her death. But I am sorry to say, it does seem likely that Miss Cole has perhaps died from an overdose of alcohol, sleeping ... anti ... well, um ... and possibly some other substances, we cannot be sure yet but ... I'm sorry.'

Zelda took off her huge sunglasses, and gazed directly at the doctor. He tried to gaze back but found himself dazzled. Very self-conscious again he looked away and desperately started to rummage amongst the files on his desk.

Zelda was all too familiar with this sort of behaviour, as it was something she had experienced for years. Whenever she was out in the 'real' world, everyone she met behaved like a lunatic. If she hadn't been used to it, she might have seriously doubted Dr D'Angelo's sanity and competence. But his behaviour was par for the course, with a little bit of extra 'fan-crazy' thrown in, and she knew this was all good, since he would be vulnerable to her charm.

She pressed on. 'Well, Doctor, it won't really surprise anyone who knew her.' She smiled tightly. 'Half the world! The truth is, I'm afraid she recently became involved with a doctor who diagnosed her as bi-polar, which suited her just fine as it gave her access to even more drugs. I can see that you are a very professional person and we, her family and particularly her poor children are very grateful for your help. That reminds me, where are the children? Jake, can you go and find them?'

Jake, very pale, was relieved to be offered a release from the stuffy claustrophobia of the doctor's office. Scrambling across Zelda, his jeans somehow got caught on her chair leg and he almost fell.

The doctor waved vaguely in the direction of the corridor. 'The Duty Matron should be able to find them for you.'

Jake scuttled off gratefully, murmuring, 'Matron, yes, of course – thanks, Doctor.'

Zelda called after him, 'I'll meet you there in a few minutes – do *not* wander off.' Then, turning back to the doctor, she continued sweetly, 'Where was I? Oh yes, we – I – would be so grateful if you could keep the substances involved simple, accidental overdose, prescription drugs and so on ... the press will go berserk with this as it is ...' Zelda then surprised and thrilled the doctor by leaning across the desk and kissing him gently on the cheek, he looked as if he might faint, and Zelda felt confident that she needn't say any more.

Dusty was extremely pale. Matron had wiped all the makeup, ravaged by tears, from her face, remarking as she did so, 'I don't know why you young girls have to put all this muck on your faces, in my day we had natural beauty.' Dusty thought this seemed unlikely, because Matron was huge and had been hit, quite hard, with what her father would call the ugly stick.

Nonetheless, she had been kind to Dusty, giving her a warm hug, after a doctor had brought her into Matron's office – a sobbing girl, with a howling baby in her arms. Matron ordered one of the nurses to change Willow's nappy, give her some milk and put some new clothes on her. The nurse had managed the nappy and milk, but couldn't find anything for Willow to wear. So she returned her, wrapped in a blanket, looking very sweet. Willow smiled and held out her arms to her big sister.

Dusty gratefully took her from the nurse and hugged her tight. Then, numb with shock, grief and exhaustion, she stood where she was told and waited patiently for someone to come for them. She was used to waiting.

Jake wandered about, confused by a number of identical-looking corridors, which seemed to disappear in every direction. He couldn't see Matron anywhere but he was faintly aware that he needed a lavatory. He just wanted somewhere to sit and collect his thoughts. Then, thinking about it, he realised that his stomach was threatening a revolt. He really needed a loo. He set off down the passage with his buttocks clenched, but he couldn't see any 'Gents' signs anywhere. He started a sort of skipping run. Where the fuck were the loos? The conveniences? Not very fucking convenient, he thought desperately.

Turning a corner he saw a 'Ladies' sign. He knew it would have to do. He had no time to find another. He rushed in and plunged straight into a cubicle, just managing to get his jeans down, before a hideous cacophony of lavatorial histrionics burst from his beleaguered bum. He rested his head against the cool tiles on the wall and let out a relieved sigh.

He opened the cubicle door to find three pretty young trainee nurses standing at the basins, giggling. He muttered, 'Sorry!' and kept his head down. But as he pushed his way out into the corridor he heard a sniggering voice say, 'You know who that was, don't you? Only Zelda Spender's husband!' then he flinched as he heard the others' disgusted response, 'Ehew!'

Jake vowed, not for the first time, that he would never, ever drink again.

As Zelda left the doctor's office she turned back to say softly, breathily, 'Thank you again, Dr D'Angelic – you are a wonderful man. I am so grateful to have found myself in your capable hands. Let's speak soon. Bye-bye.' She blew a kiss over her shoulder and firmly closed the office door.

Dr D'Angelo was now totally besotted and in her thrall.

Zelda smiled to herself, took out her phone and made a call.

She listened, frowned and left a cross message. 'Valentine! It's your mother again. I need to talk to you. Call me back the moment you get this – please!'

She turned a corner and almost bumped into Jake. Her eyes narrowed ominously before she put her sunglasses back on. 'Jake! Where are the girls? What have you been doing? Do I have to do everything?'

'I've been looking for Matron everywhere, couldn't find her and then I just had to nip to the ...' Jake tried to look sensible.

Zelda glanced over his shoulder and pushed past him impatiently. 'There she is, are you blind? Come on, we need to get going.'

She approached the nurse's station smiling warmly. 'Matron, hello, I wonder could you be an angel and help us ...' She proceeded to give Matron the full benefit of the 'fabulous Zelda' experience.

As Zelda and Jake set off to find the girls, Matron turned to a group of nurses and remarked, 'What a lovely, polite, charming woman that Zelda Spender is – just goes to show, doesn't it?'

One of the nurses raised an eyebrow and replied, 'The husband on the other hand!' All the others burst out laughing, much to Matron's annoyance.

One of the nurses pulled out her phone to update her Twitter account just as Jake was thinking, 'Christ! I hope the nurses don't have time to Tweet.'

Jake scampered after Zelda as she headed down the long hospital corridor, towards the exit. They could see Dusty in the distance. She was clutching Willow, still wrapped in the hospital blanket. To Jake they looked like tiny refugees – which, in a way, he realised sadly, they were.

He started to run towards the girls, still somewhat balance-impaired, he slipped about on the highly polished floor. When he reached his nieces he clumsily hugged them both, his eyes brimming with tears. 'I'm so sorry, Dusty, girls. So, so sorry, it's OK now, we're here.'

Zelda put her hand on Dusty's shoulder. 'We're taking you home with us. Dusty darling, give me Willow, OK? It's OK, just give the baby to me – Dusty!' There was a hard snap in Zelda's voice as she demanded, 'Give her to me!'

A small struggle ensued before Dusty reluctantly relinquished Willow and Zelda swept triumphantly out of the hospital.

They were immediately surrounded by security. Zelda clutched Willow, whose face she had tried to cover with a part of the blanket. Pausing deliberately at the top of the steps for an impromptu photo call she then hurried, quite slowly, towards the car. She had to concentrate hard to make sure that her face looked sad, but still somehow beautiful.

Her antics did not go unnoticed by Dusty. Jake frantically pushed his niece into the back seat and jumped into the front, locking the doors behind them, which he then had to unlock hastily, for Zelda to get in too. She only just managed to manoeuvre past a photographer who was trying to pull the blanket from Willow's head. 'Jesus, Jake! Thanks for the help,' she fumed. Then she promptly, if unwittingly, slammed the photographer's hand in her door. He narrowly managed to pull his hand free before she yanked the door again hard and locked it firmly.

Jake looked contrite. 'Sorry, Jesus! We should have bought David with us, this is insane!'

'Shit! We haven't got a bloody car seat.' Zelda plonked Willow unceremoniously into Dusty's lap and told her, 'You are going to have to hold her, darling. I'll be done for reckless driving or "doing a Britney" and that's all I need right now! Jake, can you phone Kate? I've been trying her all morning. Tell her to get a car seat organised.' Zelda had to raise her voice as the roar of the crowd outside was deafening and the children were beginning to look terrified.

Starting the engine with a loud revving noise, Zelda began to push through the throng.

If she had bothered to look in her rear-view mirror she would have been gratified to see that the photographer was hopping about on the pavement, shaking his fist in pain. Not so gratifyingly for Zelda, he was dialling his lawyer with his other hand – assault charges were a much more lucrative source of revenue than paparazzi shots these days. He was quite pleased with himself.

Jake listened to his mobile and turned to his wife. 'It's going straight to voice mail – do you want me to leave her a message?'

Zelda looked livid. 'No, no, I've already left her a stack of messages – that fucking girl – Personal Assistant, pah! She's supposed to bloody assist, not disappear when I really, really need her. Can you ring the office then and get them to start crisis managing? Now, Jake!'

Jake's head fell forward. He looked beaten.

Zelda continued crossly, 'Just ring Dark Artists, speak to Lucien, he'll know how to keep a lid on it.'

'What? Have you gone mad? If you want Lucien to deal with it, you speak to him. I can't believe you would ask me to. Jesus!'

'Get over yourself, Jake, this isn't just about you. We need his help now – he's the most powerful agent in the world and this is what he excels at.'

'You know bloody well why I won't speak to that bastard, how dare you!'

'Oh, shut up, Jake.' Zelda turned to her nieces. 'Sorry, Dusty darling, are you two OK there? We'll be home soon. Look what you've done now, Jake,' Zelda hissed, 'they're crying!'

Tears of despair were rolling silently down Dusty's cheeks and Willow had begun to wail.

When they arrived back at God's the crowd of photographers had grown. David and his team, with the help of a few policemen, had managed to get them back behind some hastily erected barriers. A few of these were kept stored in one of the garages, since the last debacle with the press, which had got so out of hand that people were injured. The insurance company now insisted on 'barriers being available at all times'.

The crowd went wild as David and the security team helped everyone out of the car. Jake tried to shield the girls with his body as they moved towards the front steps. The press were shouting. He could hear certain questions, which rose cruelly above the clamour:

'Did she kill herself?'

'Dusty! Dusty! Did your mum take drugs?'

'Was it because of Johnny and Lily in LA?'

'Are the kids going to live with their dads?'

'Who's the baby's father?'

'Dusty, Dusty, did your mum give you drugs?'

'Dusty, Dusty . . .'

Jake pushed the girls and Zelda through the front door, and then turned back towards the crowd. Ducking past David with surprising agility he ran across the gravel and smashed into the photographers, kicking and hitting out wildly with his feet and fists. He felt a stab of pain in his ankle as he accidentally kicked the metal barrier.

His face was bright red, eyes bulging, as he screamed, 'Fuck off, you fucking . . . blood-sucking, fucking bastards. Where's your sense of decency, have some fucking respect, you cunts!'

David managed to push in front of Jake and pulled him gently away, saying firmly, 'OK, that's it – show's over.' Then he led him, hobbling and moaning, 'Ouch, I think I've broken my ankle, fuck!' back to the front door.

Jake hopped into the main hall, still seething with fury. 'I want to get a gun and just shoot those fucking animals.' He glared at Zelda accusingly. 'Why haven't I got a gun?'

Zelda looked at him vaguely. 'What? What gun? What are you talking about? God forbid! You? A gun . . . you'd only shoot yourself in the foot anyway.'

Jake hobbled across the room and lowered himself painfully onto one of the sofas. He lifted his agonisingly sore ankle onto a cushion, a look of martyrdom etched on his tired face. His pain, he noted resentfully, was completely ignored by his family.

He felt dwarfed, not for the first time, by the scale of his own home.

From its exquisite inlaid floor to the vaulted ceilings soaring above, it was sublime. The living room at God's was known as the Great Hall. To call it simply 'the living room' would utterly misrepresent the spectacular nature of its vast and magnificent proportions. It was showing off on a wildly unnecessary scale, with a decorative lavishness far above and beyond what even the public might expect from this family who were often dubbed by the press 'The Big Spenders'.

The internationally renowned interior decorator Robert Kime had arranged the furniture so that there were different areas for different uses, all configured artfully within the same massive space. Familiar paintings, ancient and modern, soared up the walls. Large sofas, chairs and an ottoman stood in front of a vast fireplace. A long dining table, which could seat at least twenty-four, ran down the west aisle, beneath the arches. Wide French windows led into a beautiful walled garden. *Interiors* magazine had featured God's on their cover a number of times.

Ed was lying sprawled on a sofa, surrounded by crisp packets, clasping a bottle of Coke and watching TV. His dark hair was grubby and dishevelled, his young face serious and sad. As soon as he saw his cousins he jumped up and hugged Dusty, wordlessly taking Willow from her. He jiggled the baby in his arms, squeezing her and making faces at her until she smiled. She was an adorable child.

Lana was busy in the kitchen area. She looked at Dusty sympathetically, a small frown marking her pretty face as she tilted her head and asked softly, 'Dusty, you are hungry, no? I make toast for you.' Dusty didn't answer. She slumped down onto a chair and lifted her arms over her head; hiding her face she struggled to keep calm as another wave of grief rushed over her.

Jake tried to catch Lana's eye, but the au pair ignored him, glancing over at Zelda who was on her mobile, texting her PA Kate.

Petulantly throwing the phone down onto a chair, Zelda asked crossly, 'Lana, has Kate rung here this morning?'

Lana was buttering toast – she licked her fingers, which didn't go unnoticed by Jake or by Ed. Their private joke was to call her the 'ohhhh-pair!'

Jake limped over to the island and asked sweetly, 'Can I have some of that toast, Lana?'

Lana ignored him, picking up the plate and whisking it past his nose. Looking calmly at Zelda, she said, 'The telephone has been ring and ring but I have not answered it like you say to me.'

'Yes, yes, fine,' Zelda replied absently, vaguely wondering why Lana's English wasn't improving at all, despite the fact she had been with them for ages. 'Bloody Poles,' she thought to herself, 'they never quite get the hang of the language.' Anyone from Eastern Europe was always Polish as far as Zelda was concerned.

Lana leant towards Dusty, gently touching her arm. 'Dusty, come see your room. I have toast. Come with me.'

Dusty raised herself up and allowed Lana to lead her upstairs.

Jake threw himself back onto the sofa with a groan while Ed carried Willow over to the French windows, cooing fancifully, 'Let's look for a kitten in the garden, shall we, Willow – or a little bird, eh?'

Zelda was banging about in the kitchen area. 'Oh, don't worry about me, I'll make my own coffee.' She looked vaguely about, 'Typical, no bloody staff when you need them. Where the hell is everyone?'

'They are probably being sensitive towards us, the family, giving us some space in our darkest hour,' Jake mumbled from the sofa.

'Christ!' Zelda frantically punched her mobile, leaving another blistering message: 'Kate! Where the fuck are you?'

As she yelled loudly for her housekeepers, Ed felt the baby flinch in his arms. He knew how she felt, so he kissed her head and gave her a reassuring squeeze.

Gazing out of the window Ed suddenly saw Zelda's mother, Cleo, walking towards him, from her own house across the garden. 'Uh-oh. Look out! Granny's coming over, has anyone told her?' Ed turned to his parents.

Zelda bit her lip and Jake made a 'yikes' face at her. Zelda smiled at him for the second time that day, not that he was counting. They both looked like naughty children.

Ed felt, not for the first time, that he was the parent when he asked crossly, 'Christ! Mum? Dad? No?' Ed took one look at them and stomped out in a huff, carrying Willow with him.

Cleo Spender entered the room like a whirlwind. The veteran actress and 1980s superstar looked ravishingly beautiful, in full makeup, her mane of dark hair caught back loosely in a glittering diamond comb. Although she was now in her early (or allegedly mid-) seventies Cleo was obviously incredibly fit, and this was accentuated by her outfit: trainers, tracksuit bottoms and a tight black T-shirt bearing a picture of Julie Andrews and the slogan 'Climb Every Mountain' writ large.

She swept past Zelda as her famously violet eyes spied the top of Jake's head disappearing behind the sofa.

'Oh Jake, darling. I am so, so sorry. Poor you, poor Georgia, poor, poor girls! Where are they?'

So she had heard the news.

Cleo tried to hug Jake but it was too awkward, as he was still lying down. God, he felt ill, and his ankle was definitely broken. Not that anyone cared. That's what you got for trying to be heroic, he thought to himself bitterly.

'What did the hospital say?' Cleo straightened up and looked across the room at her daughter Zelda, who had found some instant coffee and was pouring far too much into a mug.

Her gorgeous mother went on, 'There are photographers swarming everywhere. Max caught one climbing the garden wall! But luckily your father, the hero, managed to push him off with a broom. He said there was a very gratifying crack when the creep hit the ground! Hah! Has anyone spoken to Elliot?'

Weakly, Jake managed to reply. 'Yes, C, I have, he's on his way, he'll be back tomorrow.'

'Oh, I might miss him then, damn! I love Elliot!' She sighed theatrically. 'Oh well. But Everest waits for no one! We heard from base camp last night. They say we have to be there to start our ascent by the end of the week or we will miss the window for another year. I can't risk that after all our training, and the production company has all the crew out there already, so – I'm so sorry, Jake darling, I know you understand but I will miss the funeral. Will you be all right? Elliot and the girls can always stay with us, well with Max anyway, while I'm away. Is the baby here too? Who is going to look after her now?'

Jake sat up a bit to answer his mother-in-law. 'Ed just took her upstairs. Don't worry, Cleo, they can stay here till we decide what to do.' He stood up and hobbled unsteadily across the room. He realised that the funeral would be chaos – so many people would want to be there, mostly for the wrong reasons, he thought bitterly. He wasn't sure that Cleo would be missed at all but he was tactful enough not to say so. Grabbing a large bottle of water from one of the drinks fridges which were built in under the kitchen island, he took a huge swig. 'C'mon, C, I'll take you up to find them.'

Zelda watched as Jake led her mother out, leaving her alone. Then she slammed about, opening and closing cupboard doors before petulantly pouring boiling water into a cup. The kitchen area was uncharted territory to Zelda; in fact it was only ever used by anyone to make coffee or toast, and in the event of any real cooking being required there was another kitchen, for staff, hidden away in a small crypt concealed behind a faux bookcase. This was a brilliant idea, design-wise, but a total waste of space because the family never made use of it. Zelda had her own organic shakes made up specially, just for her, and they were delivered daily. Jake and the boys just ordered pizza whenever they were hungry or when they got bored of toast.

Zelda found herself reaching for a biscuit from a packet that had been left lying next to the kettle. She ran her hand across her washboard stomach, suddenly flinching with surprise when she felt a warm, dry hand placed over hers. One finger ran provocatively along the top of her low-rise jeans, stopped at her hip and lightly squeezed. Then she felt her hair being gathered up and pulled to one side, and the touch of warm, dry lips on her neck.

Picking up the packet of biscuits she petulantly threw them into the rubbish bin and slammed the lid shut with a bang.

'Christ, Milo, be careful!' She wriggled away from her mother's ridiculously handsome personal trainer. Clasping her by the elbows he gently turned her to face him. Zelda wouldn't catch his eye. His strong brown arms held her firmly. She tried to resist looking at him. It wasn't easy – no mortal could keep their eyes off Milo Denovitch for long. He was a properly beautiful man. Tall, with leonine features, he had been blessed with a sort of animal grace. His charm and presence were irresistible and everyone he met responded warmly to him. These were gifts that Milo rarely failed to exploit.

He now looked concerned. 'Are you OK? I'm sorry, Zelda, what a mess, how are the kids?'

Zelda wriggled away from him, 'How do you think they are,

Milo? Not really your problem though, are they? No! They're mine, as bloody usual. I'm the one who has to clear up the unbelievable mess this family leaves wherever they go. It's so stressful. Jesus, Milo! And Mum tells me you are leaving any minute – great bloody timing, thanks!' Zelda was beginning to feel sorry for herself, which made her very cross indeed.

Milo let his hands drop and leant towards her, his voice low and husky. 'I'm gutted too, Zelda, but you know this is what your mother employed me to do. What she, we, have worked so hard for. I can't let her down now. You know this Everest show is the best thing she has been offered for ages, we have to go, she would be furious if I blew the whole thing.'

Zelda glared spitefully at him. 'Not the first thing to be blown by you, or my bloody mother for that matter, and certainly not the last!'

Milo looked disappointed. 'Oh, Zelda! You've always known we were leaving this week. What excuse could I give for cancelling? Eh? Be reasonable – I'm going back to the house now, we'll speak when you feel better.'

'Oh, fuck off then – mother's little helper!' Zelda stuck her beautifully manicured middle finger up at Milo's back as he stepped out into the garden.

Cleo and her 'Rich List' husband Max Spender lived in a massively grand house, which backed onto the same garden as God's. This wasn't a coincidence. In fact it was Max who had originally found out that the church was for sale.

Max's father had made a vast fortune in property, after the war. The trustees of his estate had always encouraged him to take an interest in the family business. Predictably, the monumental wealth that the estate had endowed Max with hadn't really inspired him to get involved in any gainful enterprise. But the trustees always kept him appraised of the activities of the estate. They had notified him when they heard that St Bart's was to be sold.

He had been toying with the idea of buying it for his beloved Cleo, to give them both a bit more space. But in a moment of madness, he had carelessly mentioned it to Zelda and, before he knew what had hit him, almost his entire family was living at the end of his garden. It hadn't seemed like such a bad idea at the time but, after years of such close proximity, he was getting pretty fed up with them all. Though it did please Max that living next door to God's had inevitably meant that his house became known as 'Devil's'. This was, in truth, quite apt. Beneath Max's charming exterior lurked some surprisingly dark and, some might say, dirty little secrets.

Milo strode purposefully across the garden. Max watched admiringly as he jumped gracefully over a small hedge and landed lightly on the path. Max himself was partially concealed behind a huge bush, which he had been pruning in a fairly desultory manner, wearing his battered straw hat at a rakish angle.

Milo, lost in his own thoughts, was startled when he heard

Max's voice from behind the bush: 'What's going on in there, dear boy? Is it safe?'

He poked his head out and looked mischievously at Milo. 'I don't think I can quite bear to see those darling girls yet. It's all too stupid for words. Just when the bloody press have quietened down a bit too. God, Georgia was always such a selfish, crazed creature. It will be unbearable here now. Really, darling, no wonder you are running away to the mountains with my beloved. If it wasn't the most beastly place on earth I'd come too.' Max leant towards Milo conspiratorially. 'Niagara Falls next, I s'pose? Actually, perhaps you could arrange that, darling boy? Cleo in the first barrel – ladies first! Then you could come back and have proper adventures with me, here. Now wouldn't that be heaven?'

Milo seemed annoyed. 'Not now, Max, I'm really not in the mood for your bollocks.'

Max smirked. 'That's not what you said last ...'

A shout rang out across the garden; it was Cleo calling from one of the towers. 'Max, Max, come up and see Dusty, she wants to talk to you.'

Max called back, 'Yes, yes, my darling, coming! Coming!'

Max sighed. As he set off across the garden he couldn't help wondering to himself that Milo might be Man of the Month in his dysfunctional family today, but how long could this state of affairs go on without someone getting burnt? Although he and Cleo had always had an 'understanding', he couldn't help but feel that they might both find they'd bitten off more than they could chew with Milo. He might look like just another Hunk of

Burning Love but Max hadn't failed to notice that Milo was nobody's fool.

Max and Cleo's marriage had always been one of convenience for both of them. It afforded Cleo the jet-set lifestyle that she had aspired to from the formative moment, aged ten, when she read a magazine article about Howard Hughes – before he went crazy. Even at the height of her career as an actress she couldn't possibly have maintained such vaunting levels of extravagance without Max's inheritance. For Max it had been essential to get married and remain married because, put quite simply, his homophobic father, suspecting his eldest son's sexual proclivities, had stipulated in his will that in order to reap any benefit from the estate Max must marry and remain married. Until death they did part. This had not proved to be such a hardship for Max. He was bisexual and although his preference might be for beautiful young men, he adored and had sometimes even desired his wife. She was a surprising and exciting woman. Her iconic status as 'The Most Glamorous Woman in the World' had always appealed to the camp side of his nature.

He waved gaily up to Cleo and repeated, 'Coming, my darling, coming!'

Dusty was lying on a huge bed, wearing a little embroidered smock that Lana had insisted she borrow, after she had gently persuaded her to eat some toast and have a bath.

Unfortunately Cleo thoughtlessly remarked that Lana would

make someone a lovely mother. This inevitably made Dusty start crying again.

Cleo had always been better at tactics than tact. So, faced with a sobbing Dusty, she decided Max might be more useful in such a delicate situation. She was very relieved to see him in the garden when she glanced, slightly desperately, out of the window. Having summoned him, she blew Dusty an unappreciated kiss and left the room.

Max arrived to take over. He settled himself onto a corner of the large bed and gently patted Dusty's shin as he waited for her tears to subside.

'There, there, Dusty darling. Poor you. So sorry, darling...' he soothed.

He looked around at the beautiful bedroom. The walls were papered richly with delicately painted birds and flowers. A large chest of drawers, inlaid with mother-of-pearl and silver, reflected the light in glittering starbursts, on the walls and ceiling. It always pleased Max that one of the many things Zelda had inherited from him was his fabulously good taste.

Eventually Dusty spoke. 'Why did this happen, Max?'

Max was bewildered. 'Horrid accident, darling, so sorry. Awful for you.'

Dusty sat up slightly. 'Max, I need to ask you something, but you have to swear not to tell.'

'Oh, darling girl, you know you can ask me anything.'

Dusty's voice sounded faint, cracked. 'It's just that ... I'm not sure Mum only took the pills the doctors gave her, I think she took something else too.'

Max squeezed her leg. 'Like what, darling?'

Dusty took a deep breath. 'I think she took heroin, Max.'

Max shook her leg gently. 'Oh darling, I doubt it. She was an idiot, sorry, darling, she was, but not that mad. No, no, Dusty, I'm sure not, you mustn't worry. I hear the doctor said it was definitely an accidental overdose. Pills and booze. He's a doctor so he knows what he's talking about.'

Dusty sat up slightly. 'But Zelda "spoke to" the doctor, so I don't think anyone will ever get to know what Mum had in her blood. I don't want anyone else to know either – it's horrible. Mum always promised me that she never took hard drugs, ever! So I need to find out who gave her that stuff, it's their fault she's ...' She started to sob again, throwing herself back against the fine embroidered pillows. 'I loved her so, so much. She would've been OK, we were doing well, she was happy.' She looked at Max imploringly. 'You have to help me, Max. Please, please? You see everything, know everything.'

'Dusty, Dusty. Of course I will help you, darling – if I can. But I don't really understand what makes you think this.'

Dusty mumbled, 'I just know, OK. I just know.'

Although Max was sceptical about Dusty's suspicions he realised it would be wise to encourage discretion, and so he patted Dusty kindly. 'This family is a leaky boat and we don't want the press, you know – so let's just keep this between us, eh? Sssh, sssh, Dusty darling. Your father will be home tomorrow and everything will be ... well ...' He stopped as Dusty curled up into a ball and her shuddering breaths seemed to subside.

Max stood up and pulled the beautiful embroidered bed-spread loosely across the grieving girl before he crept from the room. He hoped that his words would comfort Dusty and get her to sleep for a while, thinking to himself that there really was nothing more fertile than a teenaged girl's imagination. Max had always felt that Georgia had been her own greatest threat.

As soon as Dusty heard the door close she pushed the cover aside, sat up and slowly slid off the bed. She took her handbag from the floor and tentatively looked inside. After a moment she took out her evidence – a syringe, which was sealed in a plastic bag. After a bit of a struggle she managed to hide it behind the heavy chest of drawers. She couldn't share this with anyone yet. She hoped she could trust Max – but she had to be sure.

CHAPTER THREE

Kate's flat was small and cluttered. The sun shone brightly through the unlined Cath Kidston curtains that her mother had made for her bedroom. Clothes were scattered about in an abandoned fashion. Hanging on the brass bedpost was a military velvet coat.

Kate stirred, reached for the bedside clock, squinted at it and then cried out, 'Oh my God, oh my God. Val, Val … Valentine! Wake up! Oh Christ! She's gonna kill me!'

She rummaged on the floor searching for her phone, eventually finding it under her pants. She peered at it and squeaked, 'Dead, dead! My fucking phone is dead. Shit, but …' Kate traced the cord to the wall and saw that Valentine had unplugged her phone to plug in his iPod.

'God, Val, if I get sacked it will be your fault. Shit!' She looked across her bed at Valentine's adorable sleeping face – the face of an angel.

When Valentine had turned up on the doorstep at dawn she had, pathetically she realised, still been pleased to see him,

41

despite the fact that he had promised to be there at midnight – 'Straight after the film premiere,' he'd said. When he had failed to show up at one, two, three a.m. she had been cross, disappointed and unable to sleep.

She had just managed to doze off when he finally rang her doorbell. Opening the front door, to her dismay she found that all her resolve to tell him to push off dissolved. He was smiling broadly and looked ecstatic to see her; she momentarily forgot that he was probably literally 'ecstatic'. He was offering her a half-drunk bottle of milk and someone else's newspapers, pinched off their doorstep. She knew that she should dump the milk over his head and send him on his way but . . .

Valentine woke up. 'Shut up, Katie! Stop yelling, for fuck's sake – God, I feel horrible, horrible. I'm sleeping here today, OK?' Not so angelic. Getting no response from Kate his voice softened, his smooth tanned arm reached for her across the rumpled bedclothes. 'Come back to bed? C'mon, Katie.' Imploring, seductive.

Kate pushed his hand away, 'Val, pleeeese, get up! I have got to go. I am in so much trouble.'

'Oh, you push off and run around after my lovely mother then – go on, I don't care! But I'm sleeping here today.' Valentine was a petulant boy.

Kate had plugged in her phone. 'It's my job, Val. You know? A job? Christ!' She was looking at her phone. 'There are twenty-two missed calls! Shit, I am so done for. And some texts too! OK, OK, here goes.' Kate pushed back her tumbling auburn hair, listening to her messages, then she gasped, 'Oh! Oh no, oh God! Val, Val, something terrible has happened!'

Valentine had disappeared under the duvet.

Kate gently pulled it back. 'Valentine, I'm so sorry. Georgia has, Val! Can you hear me? Georgia's, er, she's died. I'm so . . .'

Valentine, beautiful, dishevelled and bewildered, raised himself up and looked at Kate. His blond hair was wild. His almost freakishly bright blue eyes were screwed up against the light.

Kate thought for a moment he was going to cry but he just slumped back onto the bed and moaned, 'Please! Just shut up! I can't deal with this right now, OK? I really, really can't. Don't tell them you've seen me – tell them I've died too. I feel like I might be dying. No, no, now I come to think about it – just say nothing.' He was rambling, almost talking to himself.

Kate leant over and kissed him softly. 'This is a horrible shock, Val, you're not thinking straight. I know how much you adored Georgia, she was a wonderful person. Don't worry, you can stay here – but I have to get to work. Zelda sounds furious.'

Valentine looked at Kate vacantly and then said, unkindly, 'Georgia was bonkers! Mum always said something like this would happen. Jesus! Mum will go crazy if she finds out I'm sleeping with the Help,' he continued unpleasantly, 'and she's bad-tempered enough as it is these days. God, this is a night-mare!'

Kate ignored him. She pulled on her clothes thinking, The Help! Charming! God, Valentine. You bastard! But she resisted the urge to retaliate. After all, she told herself, he had just lost a beloved aunt. What with the shock and grief, exacerbated by the drugs that she knew would still be pumping round his system, she couldn't really expect him to be his usual enchanting self.

She hadn't noticed yet that Valentine's 'enchanting self' was reserved for when he wanted something, and for charming the press and public.

Kate sighed, picked up her phone and popped it into her bag. She stood over the bed for a moment. Images flashed through her mind of the few joyous, licentious hours she had just spent with Valentine. She knew she wouldn't be cross with him for long but she still tried to sound a bit cold as she said, 'Goodbye, Valentine.'

Valentine remained oblivious, locked in his own selfish little Val world. He only whispered to her as she left, 'Not a word, Katkin, this is just between us. Our special secret!'

Kate didn't reply. She shut the door to her bedroom gently then darted into her tiny bathroom where she quickly brushed her hair and cleaned her teeth, spitting into the basin with a strong satisfying spurt that expressed her indignation. Her pretty face stared back at her from the mirror – she looked as tired as she felt. She slicked concealer over the dark circles under her eyes and whacked on some bronzer as she quietly considered her increasingly complicated position in the Spender family.

Kate knew that her job was finished if Zelda ever discovered that her PA was having an affair with her son. Not because of the age difference – Kate was nearly twenty-eight and

Valentine was just nineteen – Kate knew that Zelda had never applied those ageist principles to her own romantic life, so that wouldn't be the problem. Nor, as Valentine had just so kindly pointed out, was it because Kate was Staff. Although in Zelda's eyes, as Staff, Kate was indeed very much a second-class citizen.

No, the real reason Zelda wouldn't want Kate to be involved with her son was simply because she knew far too much about her boss's life. Therefore pillow talk with Zelda's beloved, mercurial Valentine might be very dangerous indeed.

When Kate arrived at work, in the basement office at God's, she was very relieved to find it empty. Hoping she could just pretend she had been there for ages, she ventured up into the heart of the house to face her boss.

Finding Zelda alone in the Great Hall Kate ducked expertly as a mobile phone narrowly missed her head and smashed into the wall, shattering dramatically. She knew there was no hope of avoiding the tirade of abuse that was coming her way next.

Zelda looked especially terrifying today as, incandescent with rage, she screamed, '*Where the fuck have you been?* You are *fired*, Kate, do you hear me? I can't believe you could let me down like this.'

Kate was very embarrassed. 'I am so, so sorry, my phone . . .' She hesitated.

To her surprise her boss appeared to falter. Sitting down hard on an upright chair and placing her hands over her face,

Zelda continued in a barely audible voice, 'I haven't time for your excuses now, Kate. Before you go I, um, I need you to do a few things ... ring Dark Artists – get hold of Lucien, he knows about Georgia already, he's doing damage limitation but I need him to get someone to re-organise my shooting schedule next week. We have to start a guest list for the funeral.' She waved her hand airily at Kate. 'Very important; get in touch with Johnny, tell him to stay away – it will be enough of a circus without Georgia's ageing runaway ex-boyfriend grabbing all the limelight with that grubby little child/model girlfriend of his. Just another photo-op for her! Christ!'

Zelda began to ramble and rant. Clearly the stress and exhaustion was beginning to take its toll.

Kate quietly filled a glass of water and gave it to her boss. Zelda drank deeply and pressed the glass to her forehead, and then seemed to rally. 'Oh, and get some choices of venue for the after show – er – wake. Get Lucien over here now, I need him.'

Kate frowned slightly. 'OK, but ... is Jake here?'

Zelda looked exasperated. 'Don't question me, Kate, I can't worry about Jake and his sensitive soul now, just get Lucien here – fast.'

Unfortunately Jake overheard this exchange as he came downstairs, and Kate beat a hasty retreat, expertly gathering up the pieces of the shattered mobile phone as she went. She would replace it immediately from the supply of new phones, which were always kept in the office for these eventualities.

As she left the room she heard Jake, uncharacteristically indignant, say to his wife, 'I've told you a thousand times, if that bastard crosses this threshold I'm leaving. That's it, Zelda, I mean it.'

Zelda remained seated, appearing fragile and vulnerable. She was as good an actress in life as in her occupation. She gazed innocently up at her husband. 'Look, Jake, I'm sorry, I really am. But I – we – do need his help, need him to manage this situation, otherwise it could blow up in all our faces. Couldn't you just keep out of the way while he's here? I need you – the children need you – to be sensible. Please, Jake?'

Jake looked suddenly deflated, hurt. 'I can't believe you could let that scum back into our lives, after all he's ... it's too much, Zelda, you know, too much.'

'I'm sorry, darling, but he is the only one with the power to control this for us. I'll make it up to you, one day ... I will, I promise. But you have to let me ... you know?' She looked imploringly at her husband. 'We need to handle this and Lucien is the only chance we have to keep it down.'

With a tragic sigh Jake turned on his good leg and tried to hobble out of the room with dignity, not altogether success-fully. As he set off downstairs he heard Zelda call out, 'Oh! I can't find Val – can you try to track him down for me?'

It could be noted he was limping slightly less when out of sight of his wife.

Jake wandered downstairs to the office, searching for Kate.

Zelda's office was impressive: a large, windowless space, painted in a vivid pillar-box red. The walls were lined from floor to ceiling with framed magazine covers of Zelda. On one wall a huge, glass-fronted cabinet was filled with BAFTAs and numerous other awards. But, as often mentioned in the press, no Oscar.

When Jake came in Kate was fielding calls. 'No, I'm sorry, no one in the family is available for comment at present – no, I can't! A statement will be issued through the family's representatives later today. No! Goodbye.' She slammed the phone down.

Jake stared blankly before him. For a moment he forgot why he was there . . . oh yes. 'Kate, have you seen Valentine?'

Kate anxiously tried to look innocent. 'No.'

Jake didn't notice; he really wanted to lie down. 'I've been trying his mobile but it's switched off. Can you try and track him down? God knows what he'll be up to.'

Kate raised an eyebrow and smiled to herself as she turned away to answer one of the phones.

Jake almost jumped out of his skin when Dusty appeared suddenly from behind him. 'Dusty! Hello, darling, are you OK?'

Dusty looked at Kate then back to Jake; she had obviously overheard what they were saying. 'Valentine was with me and Charlie . . . and Art, last night. He dropped me off at home this morning . . . I don't know where they went then. Has anyone looked in his room?'

Jake put his arm round her. 'Good point, Dusty, Zelda must've checked, or maybe not? The bleeding obvious after all! C'mon, let's get something to drink.'

Catching Kate's eye he thought it best to elucidate. 'A Coke or cup of tea. C'mon.'

Kate put her hand over the phone and called after him, 'Don't worry, Jake, I'll find him.'

But Jake had already forgotten about his missing son. He was looking after Dusty, getting her a drink ... and a little something for himself, he thought, just to take the edge off.

CHAPTER FOUR

A matt-black Range Rover with blacked-out windows sped along the King's Road, travelling at a speed that showed a blatant disregard for the safety of the 'StreEtonians' who were sent scattering and swearing in its path.

Inside the plush customised interior, a fox-faced fifty-nine-year-old man was on his telephone, speaking very quietly. Lucien Dark always spoke in a quiet voice, his tone never straying far from a hint of menace, no matter how bland the conversation. He scared everyone. That was his intention, his modus operandi. It had always served him well.

He was saying, 'Tell her that everyone in the office is onto it, Kate. I'm on my way. I'll be there in ten.' He hung up abruptly, without saying goodbye, a nicety he never bothered with when talking to his inferiors, a category that included pretty well everyone he had dealings with. There were a few exceptions; unsurprisingly they tended to be people who would be described as rich, famous or powerful, preferably all three.

Only the Chosen Ones got any semblance of courtesy from the most powerful agent in the world.

Lucien was in a very bad mood. A surfeit of drugs and alcohol was still poisoning his system from the night before. There was a blur of half-remembered images; the premiere, that dreadful business, an aspiring starlet, two hookers, a hotel room. But, what had once been a wild thrill for him was becoming an effort, no matter how many drugs he took or how 'special' the women were – was he losing it? He was famed for his beastliness and misguidedly proud of it, thinking people envied him his debauched lifestyle when, in fact, he was despised for it. And now he was coming down and feeling horrible.

It hadn't helped that he'd had an altercation over breakfast with his young, pregnant wife ...

Christ! Wife! What was he thinking? He still couldn't quite believe that he had married Kristina. God knows, she knew what his preferences were when they married – he had met her in her professional capacity, after all. Now she was acting up, asking where he'd been ... crying even, when he asked her what she expected? He'd told her he found her physically repulsive pregnant, pointing out that a baby was her idea. He had never had children and he didn't want them now.

He thought he might have gone a bit too far, but he hadn't hit her. He prided himself on his restraint. She really made him want to thump her just to shut her up. She was turning out to be a very moody cow, not what he'd signed up for. God, he felt furious!

He spoke brusquely to his driver: 'Louie, there's a change of plan. Take me to Miss Spender's first.'

He pressed auto-dial on his phone to bark instructions at Anna, his shockproof PA: she answered with 'Dark Artists International'. Lucien just spoke over her, rudely, 'Ring Universal and tell them I have to reschedule, OK? Yes, what? Hang on!' He peered out of the car window. Whatever he saw appeared to catch his attention – made him hesitate. Then he instructed his driver firmly, 'Louie, stop the car, stop! Over there! On the right.' He hung up, cutting Anna off. Winding down the electric window he called out to Zelda's son, 'Hey, Valentine! Do you want a lift home?'

Valentine was sitting outside a coffee shop, smoking, looking very handsome and shambolic, with his long blond hair and eyes so blue – in fact on this particular morning they were a bit red. His lightly tanned skin showed little trace of his debauched night and he still turned heads. Pretty young girls were pointing and giggling as they passed.

Two girls of about fourteen stopped and asked if they could have their picture taken with him – their favourite model whose picture adorned almost every poster site in London. He was studiously ignoring them – always so cool – when he heard someone call out to him from a car. He glanced up.

He vaguely recognised Lucien. So, without any hesitation he jumped up and quickly ducked past the girls, diving into the back seat of the Range Rover.

The girls looked surprised and hurt. The prettiest turned to her friend and said bitterly, 'What a fucking loser. He doesn't look nearly as hot as he does in his photos anyway!' They lit cigarettes and pulled out their phones to share their story, soon to be much embellished, with everyone they knew.

As Valentine leapt into the back of the Range Rover Lucien sounded almost friendly. 'Come on, come on, mate. Get in. That's it.' But then he found himself unaccountably over-whelmed by a surge of jealousy for this clever, beautiful young man. Valentine represented everything Lucien wasn't, and had always felt, chippily, that he never could be.

The sudden unexpectedly close proximity to the over-privileged 'golden boy' son of Zelda and Jake brought out the very worst in Lucien and he couldn't resist saying spitefully, 'Gawd, you look rough. Not so much the brilliant Oxford scholar today, eh! Where've you been? You need to cool it, Val, mate, don't want to end up like your dad!' He chuckled in a very unpleasant way.

Valentine remembered, too late, that it was wise to keep clear of his mother's agent. Lucien was a notoriously nasty piece of work. He knew that his father loathed him, although he didn't know specifically why. He thought it might be something to do with Jake's career, or lack thereof, as a screenwriter. Until Lucien's recent reinstatement as Zelda's agent, he had been out of their lives for years. Valentine had probably only seen him a couple of times since he was about ten years old.

He felt cross with himself. He shouldn't have got into the car, but those girls ... Ugh! He just wasn't up for all that today.

Feeling a combination of antagonistic and claustrophobic,

he decided to get out again. He pretended to ignore Lucien's remark and addressed the driver directly: 'Could you stop the car please? I want to get out. I can walk.'

Lucien put his hand on Valentine's forearm. 'Hold up, Val, your mum needs you home, something bad has happened.' It had suddenly dawned on him that Valentine might not know about Georgia, and so he tried to look sad. For once he wasn't quite sure how to proceed.

Valentine shook off Lucien's hand dismissively and said stiffly, 'I know about Georgia. So you can drop the insincere sympathetic crap! Now let me out please.'

Lucien looked at Valentine coldly as he spoke. 'Stop the car, Louie, the charming young man would like to walk.'

'Yeah, I need some fresh air.' Valentine didn't know what had come over him; righteous indignation wasn't usually his thing. Maybe last night's cocktail of drugs and booze had given him a personality disorder!' Or maybe he just had an adverse genetic reaction to this person, in sympathy with his dad? He reached for the door handle.

Lucien leant forward and said quietly, 'Oh, I think you'll need something a little stronger than fresh air to sort you out.' He took a tiny package from his pocket and pressed it into Val's hand. 'Here, have this on me.'

Valentine considered it, just for a second, as he jumped out of the car.

Then he thought, 'Nah!' and, turning quickly, he threw the wrap back into the murky car interior – where it hit Lucien, surprisingly sharply, on the nose.

Valentine slammed the door with all the arrogance and swagger of youth. As he walked away from the car he felt a little worm of doubt – he might not have handled that too well. But, then he thought, 'Fuck it', and hailed a cab to take him home.

Lucien leant back in the plush leather seat and lit a cigar. Like father like son, he thought to himself, a chip off the old block. Zelda had told him that Valentine was in his second year at Oxford, so, he was clever – like his dad. But Lucien could see his father's weakness in him too – hardly a worthy foe and still only nineteen.

He could afford to leave it a bit, let him rise, feel the power. Then take him down. He had done it before, after all. It still gave him pleasure to think of it.

A slight was never, ever forgotten, forgiven or left unpunished by Lucien Dark.

CHAPTER FIVE

The pressure was beginning to build back at God's.

Siege conditions were being discussed and prepared for. Extra staff were being summoned, to bring in all the supplies that the family would need to survive: Kate was calling in makeup artists, stylists, masseurs, a friendly doc with 'happy pills', a few more PAs. A nutritionist. Zelda was overheard saying crossly, 'Fuck! Who ordered a nutritionist? Send her away! Jesus!'

There were a few people from Lucien's office, including the girl who had 'looked after' Georgia, but she was in floods of tears and not much help at all.

Extra drivers and security were under David's iron control. The street had been closed off for all the TV lorries and vans wanting to cover the story. The neighbours were not pleased and they certainly weren't the sort of people who would – or, truth be told, could – answer any of the press's impertinent questions about the Spenders or Georgia Cole.

The atmosphere in the Great Hall was relatively calm. Jake

was sprawled on the sofa again. Resting his leg. Max was making coffee when Cleo flounced in, hissing, 'God, I'm cross, can you hear that noise? That bloody helicopter?'

'We're not deaf, Cleo, of course we can hear it.' Max rolled his eyes.

'Well, I thought the production company had sent it to whisk Milo and me to the airport. I was rushing like mad to finish packing. Milo says it's only those maniacs trying to get pictures of Dusty and Willow. Apparently we still don't leave till tomorrow. I nearly broke my leg running upstairs!'

Max raised an eyebrow. 'Doesn't bode well for your Everest attempt if you can't even manage the stairs! A broken leg – imagine that, darling? Stuck back here, confined to social climbing again, what misery that would've been for us all. A lucky escape, I'd say.'

Cleo laughed; she had always chosen to ignore her husband's barbed wit. It was among so many things that went unacknowledged, unspoken. She had instinctively known that feigned obliviousness would be the only way to sustain her long and 'happy' marriage.

She looked at her husband playfully. 'Oh, come on, Maxi, you know you will miss me dreadfully when I'm gone! Milo and I were just saying how much we both wished you were coming too, at least to base camp.'

Max sipped his coffee, and his eyes twinkled with what could have been fun or might have been malice – it was often hard to tell. 'Oh yes, I can just picture my poor, frail little body hurtling into thin air, down a crevasse, with you and Milo sniggering up above. It's treacherous enough living here with you, my darling. I think those grim, remote spots would just be too much of a temptation for you!'

Zelda swept into the room, cranking up the static electricity a few more volts. Jake couldn't help noticing that she looked ravishing. She had changed into a tight black Balmain dress with high Gucci platform shoes. God, she looked good in mourning, Jake thought to himself glumly.

Zelda looked at her parents, and said firmly, 'Give it a rest, you two. Mum, before you go, don't forget your PR lot need to issue a press statement to explain why you can't be at the funeral.'

'I know, I know, I've told them, it's all under control, don't worry.' Cleo looked a bit vague.

'Anyway, more exposure for your TV programme, the producers will be pleased!' A little note of spite crept into Zelda's voice. 'We might have to say you are halfway to base camp already, that'll sound less heartless!'

Jake's head appeared over the back of the sofa. 'But she's here! And so are half the world's press. How would we get her out? I mean, c'mon! Get a grip.'

Zelda looked stung. Her eyes flashed darkly, not for the first time that day, and she responded provocatively, 'Well, Lucien will be here in a minute and I'm sure he'll be able to think of something. Let's face it, it'll look pretty shabby if my mother buggers off to climb Everest when one of the most famous, or the most infamous, member of our family is being buried!'

Jake slumped back onto the sofa, feeling defeated and

upset. He really wished everyone would piss off so he could get himself a fucking huge vodka.

Cleo responded to her daughter in much the same way that she would to her husband. 'Oh, I don't think they'll notice me leaving, darling. Nobody notices me these days. I'll probably have to die halfway up that bloody mountain to get their attention.'

This was a fantasy that Cleo sometimes rather enjoyed, envisaging a massive state funeral, with fans hurling flowers – and themselves – at the cortège, à la Lady Di, and reruns of all her old films and TV series playing on a prime-time loop . . .

Her reverie was rudely interrupted by Max complaining to Zelda, 'The phone's been ringing off the hook at our house too, you know. The tabloids seem to be desperate to know if Johnny is coming back from LA for the funeral, and the speculation over who Willow's father is, is back to haunt us all. Has anyone spoken to Georgia's lawyer? Did she leave any information about the girls? Instructions? News about Willow – the one thing we are all burning to hear?'

Jake sat up. 'As far as I know there's nothing, no will, no paternity news, nothing.'

'I don't believe it, what, nothing at all? Christ, she really was fucking bonkers.' Zelda lit a cigarette and started pacing around the room, and there was plenty of room to pace: almost the length of a cricket pitch.

Jake ignored her and went on, 'Apparently Johnny had been requesting a DNA test – he thinks Willow is his. Georgia was adamant that she's not. So, I don't know, we'll have to sort it out when Elliot arrives. Dusty and Willow will have to stay together whatever happens.'

Zelda puffed on her cigarette, in fact she positively fumed, smoke pouring out of her exquisite flaring nostrils. 'What? Jake, how will that work? One person who definitely isn't Willow's father is bloody Elliot March. He doesn't even have anywhere to live. He's always away playing War Stories. So he's going to be a fat lot of use!'

'He does have a perfectly good flat in Battersea, Zelda, you've seen it, remember?'

'Christ, has he still got that horrid little flea pit?' Zelda had to pretend she could only remember it vaguely.

When, in truth, it was one of the few places she felt she'd ever been truly happy. But that was all a long time ago. Taking another deep drag, she made a concerted effort to push those memories, so long suppressed, away.

Jake was watching her closely, so she pulled herself together; looking him directly in the eye she said bluntly, 'Don't be mad, the girls can't possibly live there, it's vile.'

Max was languidly sprawled in one of the huge armchairs. With his slickly groomed silver hair and his slim frame clothed in well-cut jeans, a Navaho belt and a crisp linen shirt, he looked like an elegant escapee from a Ralph Lauren advertisement. His perfectly pedicured feet were bare; Max only wore shoes if he had to go out, and then they were the most stylish ones that were hand-made for him by Berluti. He sipped his coffee, calmly, astutely observing his family.

Jake lay down again, wincing as he lifted his 'broken' ankle back onto a cushion. He spoke softly, to no one in particular: 'Well, they've got Georgia's house, even without a will it still belongs to them. As long as there's enough to pay those death things and tax stuff. I haven't got a clue how much dosh G had.' Jake paused. 'I s'pose the beastly lawyers and accountants will be able to sort it, for an extortionate amount of remuneration for themselves, of course.' His voice was muffled by the unbearably loud noise of the helicopter, which sounded so close it might be landing in the garden. Cleo went to look out of the window.

'Fuck that helicopter. God, I wish I had a gun!' Jake repeated crossly.

Dusty wandered in and Max sprang up solicitously. 'Come and sit down, darling, here, next to me.'

She perched on the edge of a solid kelim-covered armchair, its rough fabric prickling the backs of her pale, bare legs. She looked particularly young and vulnerable, still wearing Lana's little embroidered smock.

She glanced over at Jake. 'Willow and I will go home. I can look after her. We'll be fine.'

Zelda looked up from her phone – she had only just noticed that Dusty was in the room. 'No, no, darling, you are staying here. Don't worry, we will sort everything out when your father gets back tomorrow.'

Jake piped up, 'Anyway, you can stay here with us forever if you need to. We'd love that, wouldn't we, Zelda?' Zelda remained tight-lipped, and she simply raised one perfect eyebrow at her husband.

Cleo chipped in: 'You can always stay with us too, or with Max at least.'

Max didn't look thrilled. 'Yes, yes, of course you can stay with me, darling.'

'There you are, we are all fighting over you already!' Jake smiled warmly at Dusty.

Zelda changed the subject. 'Dusty, is Willow awake? Get Lana to organise her some lunch. After all, she's nothing else to do,' she added, unjustly. She was rather pleased with herself for remembering to tell Kate to send someone to get all the baby things that Willow would need. 'Lucky someone has their head screwed on!' she thought to herself and gave a little self-congratulatory sigh.

Dusty really wanted a cigarette – she felt exhausted, numb. She looked at Zelda with guarded gratitude. 'Thanks,' she said, 'I just looked in on her – she's still sleeping.'

Dusty had woken from a short sleep to feel the full force of what had happened. In a panic she stumbled into Willow's room to check on her baby sister. Willow lay fast asleep, in the old travel cot that Lana had found, blissfully adorable and oblivious to her tragic situation. She was loosely wrapped in soft cashmere blankets. Seeing her tiny sister, so vulnerable, Dusty was instantly overcome by a surge of grief and sorrow for herself and for her beloved Willow. She clutched at the edge of the cot and sobbed. She knew that the baby would never remember their mother, never know the wonderful person whom Dusty had loved so, so much.

Georgia was – had been – like a really loving big sister, rather than a mother. Always up for some fun. Naughty and irreverent, she shared everything with her daughter, not only clothes and makeup, but all her secrets too. Sometimes very lurid details of her complicated love life. Often, it could be said, far too much information for a child. But Dusty loved every moment they spent together. She became very knowing, emotionally far more developed than her peers, almost the adult to her mother's child.

Georgia had missed out on her own childhood. Her parents had her working as a model from an early age.

Everyone remembered Georgia as the 'Cowgirl Ice Cream Child' from the '80s ads. Then she graduated to singing and dancing her way to stardom. At the age of fourteen she had her first hit single, 'Please Love Me', an apt anthem for her life as it turned out. Her career took off from there.

It had only really slowed down in the last few years. This had given her much more time to spend with Dusty.

They had both been overjoyed when Willow was born, sharing parenting duties equally. Perhaps Dusty did slightly more, with the help of a daily live-out nanny. Georgia refused to have a live-in nanny after the first one sold her story to the tabloids. The girl had dished all the dirt, mostly fictional, when the 'Rock and Roll' Johnny/Georgia affair ended sensationally, but heartbreakingly for Georgia, a few months after the baby was born.

Johnny Toogood, lead singer of The Bastards, and stereotypical bad boy. Ran off with the supermodel Lily – the media's darling, and a very bad girl indeed. The sorry tale provoked a feeding frenzy in the press and Georgia's humiliation was public and very painful.

Not even Dusty knew if Johnny was Willow's father – Georgia liked to keep an air of mystery around the baby's lineage. Johnny might, or might not, have been on tour when she was conceived – he was too dazed and confused to know, and Georgia had her own reasons for keeping schtum. It wasn't something that had ever bothered Dusty.

She always felt that they made a very happy little family unit just as they were. Anyway they didn't want or need to have to share their precious child with anyone. Until now, perhaps, when even Dusty had to admit Willow's future was more precarious than anyone could have ever imagined.

Kate stuck her head around the corner of the entrance to the Great Hall and announced nervously, 'Zelda, Mr Dark is in your office to see you.' She ducked back out and disappeared, feeling a bit like she'd thrown a grenade into the room.

At the mention of Lucien's name Zelda glanced warily at Jake, and was relieved to see he was pretending to be asleep. She swept out and almost collided with Valentine, who was trying to sneak in unnoticed. He was annoyed to be caught by his mother.

Zelda grabbed his arm, taking him by surprise, scaring him even. He had to suppress an instinctive urge to pull away. Thinking to himself, 'Show no fear, show no fear.' He was looking very much the worse for wear now, still in the velvet coat, his shirt crumpled, undone and untucked – showing an unnecessary expanse of his smooth bare chest.

Jake looked on, amused. His eldest son was about to get the 'Jake Treatment' from Zelda. It made an entertaining change.

Valentine had always been Zelda's most beloved in the family.

Jake would have denied it if anyone had asked, but he had sometimes been a little jealous of Valentine's easy relationship with Zelda. He often found himself feeling in awe of his eldest son. Valentine's self-assurance was unnerving and not a characteristic he shared with his father, who was a mess of insecurities. So the impending fireworks that promised to head his son's way were rather thrilling.

Zelda was very angry. As she grabbed her errant son's arm she fumed, 'Where the hell've you been? I've been going *mad*. I've told you a thousand times to keep your fucking phone charged. Haven't I? Haven't I?' She glared at him. 'If I ever need to get hold of you urgently? Eh? And now, I did! Or, if the worst happens? It has! What do I find? No you! No fucking phone call, text, nothing! Honestly, Val, I am really, really cross.'

Valentine bit the bullet and flung his arms around his seething, frightening mother. He gabbled a bit. 'I know, Mummy, Zelda, I am so, so sorry. I think there's something wrong with the battery. I really am sorry. Sorry about Georgia. Poor you. Are you OK?' He looked directly into his mother's eyes then he hugged her again. His magic worked fast. Jake could tell Zelda was already mollified. Damn, the boy was good!

Valentine looked sympathetically at Jake, over his mother's shoulder. He crossed the room, and flung his arms around his father. Their eyes welled with tears. Valentine spoke softly into his father's ear: 'Dad, Dad, I am so, so sorry.' Jake felt comforted. He noticed immediately that his son smelt of sex and cigarettes, with a little of hint of dope too. He felt a stab of envy and pride for this golden boy of theirs.

Then the golden boy left the room, seeming distressed. As soon as his foot hit the first tread of the stairs, out of sight of his family, he composed himself and took the steps two at a time. He didn't notice that Dusty had appeared from the basement and was following him silently, lightly.

As they came to the second landing she spoke out: 'Val?'

Valentine spun around. 'D! You gave me a shock! I was just looking for you,' he lied easily, giving her a brief hug.

Putting his hand to his forehead, he looked pained. 'Shit, I'm so wasted, sorry, Dusty, I'm crap at this. I know there are things I should say, do? But I just can't, you know? I really feel like hell! How are you though? Have you had any sleep?' He looked tenderly at his lovely cousin.

'No, not really, but I'm OK. Tired and, well, um, I ...' Dusty was, momentarily, lost for words.

Remembering something, she glanced inquisitively at Valentine. He did look terrible. She whispered, 'I wasn't keeping up with you and Charlie last night, what had you taken? You were so out of it when you got to The Box – Charlie and

Art didn't know where you'd been. We were all a bit worried. You are OK, aren't you, Val?'

Valentine looked around to make sure no one was coming. Grasping Dusty by her delicate upper arm, he pulled her into a bedroom and shut the door.

They found themselves in the beautiful room that Dusty had been given. The bed was still crumpled from her rest. Her bag lay on the floor. The long, fantastically theatrical curtains were almost closed against the clear late-morning light and, of course, any stray long-lens cameras. Dust danced in the shafts of sunlight and bathed them both in a golden glow.

Valentine gazed at his beautiful young cousin and almost felt he was seeing her for the first time. Though he wasn't particularly surprised to feel a strong surge of desire for her – she was beautiful, female – he almost forgot what he'd pulled her into the room for. 'God! Get yourself together,' he told himself firmly. He lit a cigarette, calmed down. Then Dusty moved to sit on the bed, blissfully unaware of the inappropriate thoughts that were galloping through her beloved cousin's mind.

Valentine sat down next to her and said quietly, 'The thing is, D, I don't want the crazy parents to know where I was last night, OK? They won't be OK with it. So I need you to say I was with you and Charlie and Art all evening. Sorry, do you mind? I cleared it with C and A. Mum would go ballistic if she found out . . . um. I can count on you, my favourite coz, can't I? No big deal really. It just helps someone else out too, if I keep it down, you know?'

Dusty didn't know what he was talking about, to be honest. Being there, with him like this, so close, she could hardly breathe.

If he was asking her to keep a secret she would. Luckily he didn't know it, but Dusty would do anything Valentine asked her to do. She had been madly in love with him since she was six. Something that hadn't really been a problem for her until she was older and discovered that the cousin thing might get in the way of her plans for them to marry.

She looked at his perfect profile. His strong, fine hands held a cigarette in an odd but familiar way that somehow made her feel weird. Her heart was pounding. Worried that Valentine would hear it in the silence, she spoke. Her voice came out a bit too squeaky: 'It's OK, of course, whatever you want. But Val, there's something else I wanted to ...'

They both jumped guiltily when the bedroom door swung open. Kate's head appeared. 'Oh! What are you two up to?' She peered curiously at them, feeling a stab of jealousy. She asked herself, 'Could Valentine?' then she quickly answered herself, 'God no, surely not?' but she felt slightly sick.

'Valentine, your mother is looking for you,' she said stiffly. She noticed that Valentine jumped up hastily, too hastily?

He turned and smiled sorrowfully at Dusty as he followed Kate out, closing the door gently behind him.

Kate tottered after Valentine down a flight of stairs. Trying to sound casual, unsuccessfully, she whined, 'What was that all about?' She just couldn't help herself – why, oh why couldn't she be more cool?

Valentine didn't look back. 'Nothing, Katie. Just covering our tracks.'

By making new ones, Kate thought bitterly.

Valentine disappeared round a corner and Kate was even more annoyed when she followed him, only to find that he had vanished.

As she passed the door to the linen room, a hand suddenly reached out and grabbed her. Valentine pulled her in after him, pushing her roughly against the shelves of fresh laundry. She squealed as he put his hand over her mouth and pulled up her skirt. Why, why couldn't she resist him, she thought weakly. But if she had known exactly who he was thinking about as he made love to her so urgently – she might have found him very easy to resist indeed.

When Dusty came downstairs a few minutes later, she walked past the laundry room. Hearing something strange, she stopped, listened. Stricken with shock and disgust as she recognised the unmistakable noises from within. The last name she wanted to hear being moaned with pleasure was Valentine's. Yet there it was.

What was left of her tender young heart broke then, she couldn't bear it, couldn't think. As she ran on, down the stairs, she wept some more desolate tears.

She found Jake slumped at the bottom of the last flight of stairs. His head was in his hands. To her dismay Dusty realised that she couldn't get past without climbing over him, which didn't feel like an option.

Suddenly, she felt very weak, feeble. She just slid down the final steps, almost collapsing on top of her uncle Jake. He caught her and put his arms around her. They both sobbed gently for a while. They had much to share, to feel sad about.

Georgia had always told Dusty that she loved her brother Jake very, very much.

From their teens, they had lived alone together, after their parents were killed in a horrific car crash in Spain. Jake was a scholarship boy at Westminster School at the time.

They both agreed that their happiest home had been the little mews house that Georgia had bought with the proceeds of her early recording career, when she was just fifteen.

The siblings had so much in common: they were beautiful, funny, clever and increasingly popular. They went everywhere together, to all the wildest, most decadent parties of their day. They dressed extravagantly, travelled extensively, and threw the most notorious parties in London. Georgia became known as 'the Muse', a nickname bestowed on her by one of the gossip columnists who wrote a bitchy piece about her, Jake and their hedonistic lifestyle. Georgia was one of the first celebrities to have all the designers vying for the honour of calling her their muse and dressing her exclusively. Georgia played hard to get, never really committing to any of them but accepting the never-ending deluge of exquisite clothes that were sent to her as 'gifts'. This antagonised the green-eyed columnists more than somewhat.

It was in the tiny study at the Mews that Jake had written his first collection of short stories. These had some success when they were published just before his twenty-second birthday. He was then commissioned to write for a succession of television dramas. The most successful of which, 'Wild World', was where he first met Zelda. The rest was tabloid history. Jake and Georgia always felt very nostalgic about those years. Neither of them had known such carefree happiness since.

Dusty looked at Jake through her tear-lashed eyes. She was about to speak when, to her horror, she realised that the footsteps she heard thundering down the stairs were probably Valentine's. She couldn't face him seeing her like this.

She wriggled from Jake's comforting embrace and ducked into a downstairs loo, locking the door firmly behind her. She could just make out Jake's husky voice: 'Hey, Val, there you are. Come and talk to me, man. Christ! I am so depressed.'

Valentine sat down next to his father, unaware that he was being overheard. 'Dad, your sister died a few hours ago. You're supposed to be depressed.'

'My only, favourite sister,' Jake said sadly. 'Val, what will I do without her?' Overwhelmed, he lay back uncomfortably on the stairs. Opening one eye he slyly asked his son, 'Have you got anything to ... you know?'

Valentine reached into his pocket and gave his father a pill. 'Just don't tell Mum.'

Jake looked at the pill suspiciously. 'What is it? Looks like Haliborange!'

'Just take it, Dad, trust me, you'll feel great in no time.'

Jake knocked the pill back with a swig of vodka from a glass that he'd sort of hidden under his leg.

'There you are, that'll perk you up a bit.' Valentine sprang to his feet. Moving on. He didn't want to bump into Kate when she came downstairs.

'Oh Dad, sorry, I forgot to say,' he sniggered as he wandered away, 'it might make you a bit horny!'

His father called after him glumly: 'Oh, great! Thanks, Val, thanks a lot.'

'Do you want me to let Mum know?' Valentine added mischievously, as he disappeared from view.

CHAPTER SIX

Zelda had pushed all the extra staff out of her office so that she and Lucien could talk in private.

Kate had disappeared again. 'Where is that fucking girl?' Zelda wondered crossly. She asked a pretty temporary secretary to get some coffee for Lucien and noticed him eyeing up the poor little thing in an all-too-familiar, unpleasantly predatory way. When the timid creature placed the coffee on the desk in front of him, he took pleasure in her nervousness, watching her like a buzzard.

Zelda could see that the girl couldn't wait to get away and dismissed her firmly. 'Thanks. We can manage.'

Lucien really is a dreadful old goat, Zelda thought grimly. Most women felt extremely uncomfortable in his presence. Of course, he believed he was God's gift. He really was a deluded psychopath. But, he headed up the most powerful agency and management company in the world, and when Zelda had needed to get out of a contract earlier in the year she knew that Lucien was the only person with the power and ability to pull it off without seriously damaging her career.

Zelda didn't like to admit it, particularly not to Jake, but she knew exactly what Lucien was really like – what lay beneath – and if she hadn't needed him to save her from such an impossible situation she would never have allowed herself to have anything to do with him again. What Jake loathed him for, well, it wasn't even the half of it. But Zelda had a career to maintain, she needed Lucien to do it, and there would a price to be paid for that. But then, wasn't there always, she thought bitterly.

The girl shut the office door behind her. Lucien turned his attention back to Zelda. 'So, what was I saying? Oh, yeah. Apparently one of the paps was arriving for his door-stepping day, when the ambulance and police arrived. That's how the press got to you before I could. Dusty didn't ring me for a while. Turns out Georgia had told her, if anything ever happened to her, to call me first.'

Ah yes, Zelda thought; Lucien, everyone's fixer.

'So I don't know why she waited, not that there was much I could've done. But I'd like to have told you myself, rather than have you learn it from the press ...'

His mobile rang, and he answered it gruffly: 'Yeah. Hello ... Tony, yep, yep, yep.' Zelda could see his brain working, as his eyes flickered with what she instantly recognised as anger. She watched him closely as he went on, 'Well, you could print that, mate! You could! But I think you should bear in mind that if you did you'd never get another fucking story from my office as long as you live! So, Tony, you might want to throw that small consideration into your editorial decision-making process.' He listened for a moment. 'Sounds wise, mate, yeah – accidental.' He hung up.

Zelda had forgotten how easily he exploited his power. He had even placed himself firmly in her chair – automatically assuming the role of boss in her office! The vivid red walls glowed behind his head and Zelda was given the disquieting impression of an audience with the devil. She was reminded, with a chill, that she had sold her soul to him a long time ago. Now, here he was again, invited back in, by her. If she sensed the danger in that decision, she didn't show it.

She must play the game.

So she looked at Lucien admiringly, the actress always. 'God, I love watching you in action, Lucien. I am so grateful to you for keeping the dogs at bay.' There was truth in that. 'I'm so glad you took me on again – I really need your protection now. I can't afford to have my family secrets splashed all over the papers when two of the biggest films of my life are on the go.' She smiled warmly.

She seemed grateful. Lucien thrived on grateful.

'I've got the office rearranging all your press for the film promotion – it won't be seemly for you to do anything till after the funeral. The studio and distributors ain't pleased, but can't be helped.' He looked smug. 'What are we going to do about Jake, Zelda?'

'Oh, don't worry about him, he'll come around. He just hasn't worked for so long. Maybe you could put in a good word for him?' She wondered if she was pushing her luck.

'Oh, he'd like that! Maybe I will!'

'Really? Could you? Of course he'd never know. His pride, you know?' Zelda raised an eyebrow at Lucien. She felt a little twinge of guilt conspiring with him over Jake. But she hoped it was for her husband's benefit.

'Anyway, Zelda, we need to talk about the kids. As I say, Dusty didn't call me for a while after she found Georgia. What held her back, do you think?' Lucien watched Zelda keenly.

'Did it occur to you that she wouldn't call you because she's a bit scared of you?'

'What! Are you crazy, she's known me all her life – she loves me! Where is she? I'll go and talk to her.' He smiled reassuringly at Zelda. 'Look – the press are gonna have a field day. But they can only speculate and I've locked down the worst of it. Accidental overdose – anti-depressants etc – it will be official in an hour or two then the office will issue statements to the press.'

'Thanks, Lucien, do you think you could you speak to Johnny in LA? I think he should stay away. I've asked Kate to call him, but he might need to hear it from you. I think we should make double sure he doesn't fly back for the funeral, don't you?'

'Don't you worry about that little bastard – I'll make sure he stays a million miles away.'

Just then, Kate put her head round the door. 'Zelda, Johnny's here!'

Zelda spun round, astonished. 'Shit! I don't bloody believe it! When did he call?' She noticed that Lucien's complexion had darkened ominously.

Kate replied, 'No, I mean here – he's here, now!'

'Jesus! That was quick. Christ! Who let him in? Lucien, we really need to think of something now – come on!' They both stormed past Kate in a blast of hot air.

Johnny was making his way around the Great Hall, expansively hugging everyone in turn. When he got to Dusty, she buried her head in his leather jacket as he stroked her hair with his diamond-skull-encrusted fingers. His dark hair was artlessly tousled and spiked. He was every inch the rock star – yet somehow warm and cosy at the same time. Max always described him as 'that pikey pop star' and Dusty had been very fond of him until he'd upped and left Georgia. But now, being held by him, all his misdemeanours seemed to fade from her grief-worn mind. Johnny felt comforting and familiar, and she clung to him tightly.

They all looked up nervously as Zelda and Lucien swept into the room.

Zelda went straight up to Johnny, air-kissing him stonily. 'Johnny! What the hell are you doing here? You're in LA! Really, you might've rung. You being here now is all we need – did the press see you? What am I saying – of course they've seen you. Shit!' She was clearly very annoyed. 'You'll just have to go straight back to LA again ... Lucien, tell him!'

Johnny lit a cigarette. He looked a bit shifty as he replied, 'Er – no can do. There was a bit of bother there as it happens, had to make a quick getaway, been hiding out back here –

well – till this happened.' He took a deep drag. 'Anyway, here I am.' He noticed Jake sitting up and waved his cigarette vaguely in his direction. 'Sorry about your sis, Jake, mate.'

Lucien was watching them both beadily. Looking directly at Johnny he asked, 'Did Georgia know you were here?'

'Yeah, yeah, she did. But she wouldn't let me anywhere near. Told her I wanted to see her – sort stuff out, you know? But she wasn't having it – quite pissed off as it happens. Thought she might be over it, but, well ...'

'So when did you speak to her?' Lucien asked.

'Week ago – few days ago – dunno. But this was nothing to do with her and me, she was hacked off with me that was all.' He turned to look at Dusty. 'I loved your mum, you know that – but she and me, well, stuff. Seems stupid now.' He hung his head. Then he looked about vaguely for an ashtray, and not seeing one he plopped his cigarette into an open can of Coke where it sizzled and died. Looking up at Jake he offered, 'She said everything was going great. What happened – what the fuck happened?'

Zelda replied hastily, 'Just a horrible accident, Johnny, too many sleeping pills, anti ... well, you know, anyway. When are you off again? No need for you to stay for the funeral.'

Johnny looked surprised. 'Course I'll be there ...'

'No, Johnny – tell him, Lucien. We all agree it will be even more out of control if you are there, with the press and so on ...' Her voice trailed off.

Jake was unsteadily getting to his feet. He interrupted his wife. 'Zelda will be leading the mourning, Johnny, we can't have you there stealing her thunder now, can we?' He smiled and turned calmly towards Lucien. 'Oh and Lucien – get out of my fucking house!'

Lucien looked completely unfazed. 'I am here to help *your* family sort out its mess, so shut up, you pathet . . .'

Dusty silenced everyone with a shriek. 'Stop it! Stop fighting. My beautiful mother is dead – *dead*! And all it's about for you is PR and . . . and you, you, you. Just stop it!' she sobbed. 'Why can't we be like other families – just normal and nice. She only wanted you to love her, she just wanted to be loved, have a normal life . . .' Her voice trailed off. Johnny tried to put his arm around her again, but she pushed him away. Everyone looked embarrassed.

Max stepped in through the French windows and remarked, unsympathetically, 'Normal and nice is all very well, darling – but dull, dull, dull. Your darling mother was a lovely, brilliantly talented woman – but her thrill-seeking and pill-popping killed her, not this family. You need to accept that, my angel, because we are your family now and we are all you've got, for better or worse. Well, us and Elliot of course.' He shrugged and looked around at the others, but no one would catch his eye. He carried on regardless. 'Sorry, darling. I know it's sad, but it's true, and there is nothing any of us can do to make things different for you.'

Dusty's heart sank. She was shocked by Max's dismissive duplicity – he obviously wasn't going to be any help to her after all. Pale and fraught, she crossed the room and asked Lucien, 'Can I talk to you? In private.'

Lucien glanced at Zelda. 'Yes, of course – c'mon – office OK, Zelda?'

Zelda answered distractedly, 'Yes, yes, fine.'

Jake yelled after them, 'Then fuck off , Lucien,' and then, under his breath, 'Cunt!'

Everyone felt shattered. Nobody spoke.

Johnny hopped from foot to foot, almost dancing with discomfort on his skinny, black-jeaned legs. He tried to sound natural. 'Well, I'd better be off – if you don't ... I'll ring later, when everything, you know ... calms down.'

Max called over to him, 'Bye, dear boy – lovely to see you,' and stepped back out into the garden. He couldn't wait to get out of there – couldn't even remember why he'd popped over to God's in the first place. Honestly, what a madhouse!

Johnny left the room with Valentine hot on his heels. 'Hey, Johnny, can I get a lift with you?' he whispered.

'Yeah, mate, sure, where you going?'

'Fuck knows – just out of here. Maybe I could come and meet Lily?' He was doing up his shirt, running his hands through his hair as they left through the front door.

Johnny looked at him and smiled. 'Yeah, OK, c'mon – back to mine.'

They jumped into Johnny's limo as the crowd outside went wild.

Johnny turned to Valentine. 'Hold on tight, my driver guy will have to lose this lot.' The sound and smell of burning rubber tyres as they sped off gave Valentine a rather sick feeling. He slumped back into the plush leather seats just as his mobile rang. He groaned then answered it: it was his girl-friend. 'Hi, Indie.'

She sounded sweetly sympathetic. 'Val, I'm so sorry. Are you OK? I've been trying to get hold of you for hours. Where are you?'

He grimaced at Johnny. 'At home!'

'Oh, I spoke to the house, they said you were out. Didn't know where you were . . .'

'Really? Who said that?'

'Kate.'

'Well, she obviously didn't look properly, you know how thick she is. Don't know why Mum doesn't get rid of her, to be honest.' He stretched his long legs out across the limo floor. 'Nah! I'm just here, in the den, crashed in front of the TV all night. Then all this crazy shit to deal with. I'm knackered.' He rolled his eyes at Johnny.

'Shall I come over?' She sounded concerned, sweet. He almost relented, then he looked across at Johnny who was lighting a joint and offering it to him.

'No, no! Don't come over now, it's a bit – you know – but thanks, babe, maybe later, I'll call, yeah?'

'Val, are you sure you're OK?'

'Just need a bit of quiet, y'know, speak later, love you.'

'I love you too, Val, I'm so sorry.'

Valentine hung up as Johnny popped open a bottle of champagne. 'Hey, man, that's so cool. You're going out with that beautiful India girl! She is hot – grrr. She was so great in "Festihell" – God, I loved that movie!'

Valentine looked very pleased with himself as he took the bottle that Johnny was offering and had a long swig. He gasped a bit. 'Yeah, yeah, she's very cool, sweet. You know she's in the new Vortmore movie with my mum. They are filming at the moment. Scares the shit out of me, to be honest. Prefer to keep all the girls apart. India and Mum get on like a house on fire – literally – they fuckin' hate each other! But somehow that makes going out with India – just – well . . .'

'You are a piece of work, Val, mate – respect!' Johnny laughed as he sprawled out across the back seat and happily took another drag of his joint.

In the basement office, Dusty had perched herself against the edge of Zelda's desk.

Lucien thought how pretty Dusty looked, vulnerable. He hadn't seen her in ages. He couldn't help noticing, with a small pinch of excitement, that she was no longer a child. Perhaps he hadn't become as jaded as he feared. He felt quite cheered up. Dusty was asking him if he knew who Willow's father was. He didn't.

'Well, she did tell me it wasn't Johnny. I believed her. To be honest, she had no reason not to name him if he is her father. Maybe it's best left, Dusty, eh? You want to keep her with you, don't you? So . . .'

'Well, yes. Um, Lucien?' Dusty looked up at him anxiously. 'Do you think Dad could live with Willow and me at Hollywood Road?'

'I'll see to everything, Dusty, you don't need to worry. As your trustee I am not sure about you and Willow moving back there yet. I mean, Elliot is away a lot and, unless he is prepared to give up his wanderlust for you, to look after you ... Well, we'll just have to see about all that, when he gets back.'

Dusty looked crestfallen.

Lucien took her fragile arms in his huge hands and squeezed a little too hard. Dusty could smell stale alcohol undisguised by his strong aftershave. She felt trapped, slightly sick.

Lucien sensed her discomfort but did not release her. He said, quietly, 'Don't worry, D, it will all be sorted. One day at a time, eh?' He was rather pleased with himself for remembering to use the infuriating Rehab expression, so beloved of all his clients.

'Thank you, Lucien. I just don't think we could survive if we had to live here.' She bowed her head, and was relieved to be able to wriggle away when Lucien loosened his grasp.

As she scampered back upstairs Dusty felt furious with her mother, unable to believe Georgia would make Lucien her trustee when she knew Dusty couldn't stand him, knew that he gave her the creeps. What was she thinking? She realised sadly that Georgia obviously hadn't been thinking – she always did whatever was easiest and, for reasons Dusty had never been able to understand, her mother had always insisted that it was easiest for her to have Lucien manage her affairs. But now she had left her daughters in his hands, and Dusty instinctively felt that was a very un-easy place to be.

*

Back in the kitchen area, the entry-phone was buzzing frantically. Lana answered it with Willow balanced neatly on her hip.

She turned to Zelda. 'Miss Spender, Shona is arrive with
clothes from designers. Oh! I forgot to say – hair and makeup
is here. They went up already.'

'About bloody time – God, I need them desperately today.
Tell Shona to … oh, never mind, I'll do it! Christ, I'm knackered, where are my … ?' Zelda picked up a massive Hermès
handbag as she left the Great Hall and rummaged about until
she found a bottle of pills. As she walked upstairs she tipped a
few Adderall into her mouth and swallowed expertly – she
needed the energy and the appetite-suppressant effect. She
knew that Shona, her stylist and best friend, would be pleased
with her; she had already lost a few pounds this week.

Jake was lying doggo. Opening one eye, he realised he was
alone with Lana.

Without moving he spoke softly: 'Sorry about this La-La,
can't be helped though – will you be OK to stay for a while?'

She crossed the room silently and placed Willow gently onto
his chest. Jake stiffened as she whispered, too loudly, 'This is
what our baby feel like …'

Jake sat up and shoved the baby back into Lana's arms,
hissing, 'Christ, Lana! Look, I am really sorry. I know it's terrible for you to have … you know? But Lana – one night? Just
one, drunken night? I am so sorry but, you know, I don't even
fucking remember it, no reflection on you, but we have been
through this and I am truly, truly sorry. I know this is hard for
you, but it's difficult for me too. I've said I'll look after you –

and I will. But, you know how things are with Zelda and me – it's all very precarious, you know? I have to try to keep things together. I need you to be OK – OK?'

Jake jumped to his feet and, without the hint of a limp, strode over to the island and poured himself a large vodka, which he knocked back with a shudder. Glancing across at Lana, he continued imploringly, 'Thank you, Lana, you are an angel, an angel.' He was close to tears. Jesus, this was a nightmare. Downing another vodka he gave Lana a beatific, if slightly deranged, smile.

She looked away sadly and, hugging the baby tightly, she left the room.

CHAPTER SEVEN

Johnny Toogood was crashed out on an enormous L-shaped sofa in his cinema room at his vast house in Richmond. Fashion TV played quietly on the massive screen, beautiful girls marched like automatons up the catwalk. He lay, spread-eagled with a burnt-out cigarette still in his mouth, a velvet cushion clasped to his chest. One skinny leg dangled over the edge of his resting place; his R. Soles cowboy boot was planted in an overflowing ashtray. Johnny was clearly out cold; he looked dead – in fact even when wide-awake he appeared dead anyway, it was his 'look'.

While Johnny lay sleeping Valentine was upstairs, casually taking advantage of the opportunity of a little late-afternoon entertainment with Johnny's enchantingly degenerate girl-friend Lily. They had been joined by a young friend of Lily's who, even Valentine was surprised to note, seemed to be hur-riedly pulling on her school uniform before briefly kissing Lily and rushing from the room. As she went she muttered some-thing about being grounded and her GCSEs.

Valentine's recollection of how he had come to be in this potentially compromising position was hazy. He languidly called 'Bye!' after the schoolgirl and turned his attention to Lily. She was so different, in the naked flesh, from her exaggerated supermodel persona. A tiny, fair-skinned Lily was stretched out unselfconsciously in front of him. Her golden hair was tangled, matted with a charming 'too gorgeous to have to brush my hair' look. She casually lit a cigarette and smiled mischievously at him. Then she crawled across the bed, put her cigarette to his lips, leaning in to kiss him as the smoke wove between their perfect mouths. The annoying sound of a ringtone caught Valentine's attention and he reluctantly pulled away from Lily. Groping on the floor, he looked at his phone, swore, and jumped up off the massive bed.

'Shit! What time is it?' He grabbed his clothes and began to pull them on. Lily watched him, without a word. She leant back against the headboard and continued to smoke and simmer. Valentine glanced at her and felt an overwhelming urge to jump back onto the bed, onto her.

But then he noticed a massive, iconic Mario Testino photograph of Lily and Johnny. It loomed accusingly on the wall above her head. He vaguely remembered seeing Johnny, passed out, downstairs and realised he might be wise to make a move.

'Nice to ... you, Lily, um, I'd better be off – before Johnny ... you know,' he said inarticulately, reluctantly. Lily's eyes shone softly in the gloom. When Valentine turned to go, she shrugged her delicate shoulders, stubbed out her cigarette and got off the bed, before disappearing into the bathroom, silently closing the door behind her. Valentine was free to go, dismissed.

He felt confused – girls were never this cool with him. He was tempted, for a moment, to go and knock on the bathroom door, to call out her name. Then he got hold of himself, grabbed his pride and left the room.

Taking the staircase two steps at a time he virtually flew out of Johnny's house. As the front door slammed Johnny woke with a jolt. The cigarette stub fell from his lips and he stumbled up off the sofa, to be greeted by Lily, looking ravishing in a Japanese kimono. She silently took him by the hand, kissed his cheek and led him down to the kitchen to make something to eat.

As they walked downstairs he asked where the others were.

'They left hours ago, don't you remember? You told them to "fuck off", then you passed out,' Lily lied casually.

'Oh yeah, right! Didn't take me seriously, did they?'

'Nah, they did just what you told them to do!' Then, whispering smugly to herself, 'Well, the fuck bit of your command anyway!'

'What's that, babe? Eh?' Johnny looked tired and bemused as he sat down at his kitchen table.

'I said, they said goodbye and went on their way.' She turned on the iPod. Then she poured Johnny a glass of whisky and softly kissed his forehead as the music soared around them.

It was dark outside. Valentine ran to the corner and hailed a cab. He settled back into the seat looking thoughtful. He sent a text. Having given the cab driver his address at God's he remembered that he wouldn't be able to get through the crowds unnoticed, so he leant forward and asked the cabbie to drop him outside Max and Cleo's.

His grandparents' house was less likely to be overrun by paps. He was relieved to be proved right; a few desultory clicks from a couple of stray chancers and he was in, through the emergency basement route, then out across the garden. He had to knock on the kitchen window to be let in. Luckily Lana was there making up a bottle for Willow. She let him in silently just as his mobile began to ring again.

It was India telling him she would be over in ten minutes.

He ran upstairs. Pulling off his clothes as he went, he leapt into his wet-room, soaped himself lavishly with Dior Homme from head to foot, dried himself, threw on some fresh clothes and ran down to greet her.

As he opened the front door he was temporarily blinded by the flashes from the photographers at the gate. David propelled India through the door where she almost fell into Valentine's arms. He held her tight, happy to see her now. Her sweetness always comforted him, calmed him. Yes, he realised happily, he felt genuinely pleased to see her, to hold her. She kissed him warmly and hugged him again. Valentine looked up to see Kate standing at the top of the basement stairs. He looked right through her and, taking India by the hand, led her upstairs to his room.

Dusty was on an upstairs landing, looking for Ed, when she heard Valentine and India approaching. She overheard

Valentine telling India that he was exhausted because he'd been at home all day looking after everyone. She knew he had only got back home about ten minutes before India arrived and couldn't help feeling shocked by his brazen ability to lie. Particularly to girls she thought, glumly.

Zelda had decided on an early night.

Jake felt this was his opportunity for an attempt to make amends. He found Zelda sitting naked at her magnificent, flatteringly lit dressing table. A surge of desire ran through him. One look at his fabulous wife could often make him weak with lust and longing. He realised that the pill his son had given him earlier was probably still having an effect; it had certainly made him feel better, less sad. Now he was trying to work out which way to play this. Should he petition for a sympathy fuck or maybe catch her off guard with some warmth and laughter? Both seemed unlikely as potentially successful strategic paths to success. He decided to play it by ear, or maybe just pray.

Zelda was rubbing cream into her perfect skin as Jake disappeared into his bathroom. He would have been surprised and pleased to know that she had already made up her mind to make love to her husband that night. She had been feeling so many conflicting things about him today. Pity, anger, guilt, a little sympathy, quite a lot of frustration and a tiny bit of amusement. He was just so endlessly maddening. But he had had a beastly day. She hadn't been very nice, she knew, she sort of owed him one really.

Particularly after this afternoon, in the home gym, with Milo putting her through his 'special' exercise routine. It was all very invigorating and satisfying but she always felt a bit guilty after their sessions. Today's had been particularly intense. They both knew it would be their last for the foreseeable future. Zelda felt angry with Milo, almost bereft at the thought of being deprived of his physical attention for ages. She had deceived herself into thinking he was at her beck and call – but the intensity of her desire for him was beginning to mean that he was the one with the power. Perhaps it was for the best that he was leaving. Anyway, she intended to have some sort of revenge by sleeping with Jake tonight. Killing two birds with one stone, she thought to herself, as she gazed admiringly at her reflection in the mirror.

When Jake crawled sorrowfully into his marital bed a few moments later he was thrilled to find that Zelda was warm, welcoming and naked. His body was fresh, fragrant and invigorated by the shower and he was soon happily making love to his almost-enthusiastic wife. Things really were looking up. He was also proud of his sustained ability to keep things going for much longer than usual. Was it the pills, he wondered, or his sense of his own mortality at the death of his sister? He tried not to think about that – stick to the point, concentrate. He was dimly aware of Zelda murmuring encouragement. 'Jake, Jake!'

'Yes, Tiger, yes . . .'

'Jake, Jake!'

He felt her go limp beneath him.

He looked down at his beautiful wife. 'What, Tiger, what . . . are you OK?'

Zelda looked up at him and said, coldly, 'Come – or get off!'

So that was it, no amount of pills would get past that level of discouragement.

Zelda felt instantly remorseful. That was not what she had intended at all, and so she reached out as Jake jumped out of bed. She said quietly, apologetically, 'I'm sorry, Jake, I'm just so tired and I wasn't expecting a . . . .a marathon, I'm sorry – come back to bed, you're tired too.'

She watched helplessly as Jake threw a sarong around his waist. He looked at her darkly, clearly hurt and furious. 'You are such a fucking bitch, Zelda. What happened to you? To us? It never used to be like this.' He stormed across their bedroom. She heard, and felt, the bedroom door slam shut. She almost cried.

What a horrible day.

She reached into her bedside table and pulled out a bottle of sleeping pills. Pouring a few into her palm she considered them for a moment then poured a couple back into the bottle, thinking of her sister-in-law's untidy demise. She downed the rest, turned off the light and punched her pillow for a while before slip-sliding into a peaceful, narcotic-induced, sleep.

Jake meanwhile, had gone downstairs and got himself a drink.

Ed wandered into the Great Hall. 'Oh, hi, Dad, I thought you'd gone to bed. Dusty and me are about to watch a movie. Do you want to come?'

'Love to, what're you watching? And it's Dusty and I, Dusty and I.'

'Yeah, Dad, whatever, come on. It's an oldie, like you, you'll love it. Let's go.'

They entered the den. Dusty was already fast asleep on the wide velvet banquette. Father and son slumped down and Ed switched on 'Random Harvest'. Jake turned to Ed and made a sobbing face, Ed sob-faced back at him. They both lay back and smiled to themselves. Dusty slept on.

CHAPTER EIGHT

Kate arrived early the next morning. She had been unable to sleep, tormented by visions of Valentine and India together, and furious that she had allowed herself to fall into such a compulsive, romantic entanglement. She was hooked and she knew it. She was a fool, she knew that too. But the buzz – oh, the buzz! Just knowing that he was there in the house sent a dark thrill through her. She knew that India couldn't stay there forever.

In fact she knew India would be leaving soon because the film shoot had been rescheduled to allow Zelda a few days at home, until after Georgia's funeral, and so Kate had useful inside information on exactly where India would be – and when. She took some comfort in that.

Having checked the office computer she groaned when she saw a hundred and ninety-eight e-mails, most requiring a response.

It was still early so Kate decided to pop upstairs to the Great Hall and see if anyone was around yet.

At God's, someone's early was often someone else's late and it wasn't uncommon to find a person who had just got home making toast with someone who was just leaving. Quite often these people could be complete strangers, or strangers to Kate anyway. So she was always prepared to find anyone or anything.

On this particular morning-after things were relatively quiet. Zelda was in the Great Hall kitchen, glugging water from a huge bottle of Evian. She was clearly just back from an early-morning workout. Kate noted that her boss still looked great, hair scraped back, no makeup, a Stella McCartney tracksuit flattering her hard-won, firm and fantastic figure. She looked up sharply when her PA approached her.

'Ah Kate, early today!' she huffed. 'I need to talk ...'

She was interrupted by the loud ring of the front doorbell.

Kate was relieved to be able to avoid Zelda by springing out of the room to answer it. Although she opened it cautiously, the bright early-morning light and the clamour and flashing from the paps outside momentarily blinded her and made her hesitate. When her eyes had adjusted she saw a very tall, well-built, untidy man standing in front of her. She didn't recognise him immediately. But then he said, 'Hello, Kate', and she recognised the deep, dulcet tones of her favourite family member, apart from Valentine, of course. She flung open the front door and pulled him into the hall, slamming the door on the rabble, and led him into the Great Hall.

Elliot March strode into the room and threw his arms wide. 'Zelda! I'm home!'

Her boss looked shocked and flustered, Kate noted, as she left them to it.

Zelda regained her composure, took another sip of her water. 'Elliot! About bloody time, the prodigal father, hurrah!' She sat down, casually she hoped, on a kitchen barstool. Elliot bounded across the room towards her. He bent down and kissed her warmly on the cheek.

She wrinkled her nose. 'You need a bath.'

'Lovely to see you too! Just got in, came straight here, sorry, yeah . . .' He looked down at himself. 'Came from the front line, wanted to get here, see Dusty, could've gone by the flat, but the water won't be on . . .'

'Ah ha, still living like a student then?' She couldn't help smiling. 'Oh, Elliot, it's fine. You're here now. No one's up yet . . .' She looked at him directly. His bright blue eyes sparkled with emotion. His mane of hair was dirty and matted, and his face looked brown and healthy despite the two-day growth of stubble. His clothes were khaki, crumpled and not at all clean. He looked like an action hero who had strayed onto the wrong film set. Zelda felt a huge surge of relief at the sight of him; gratitude that he was here to rescue Dusty and hopefully Willow too. But she also found herself wondering, would he, could he, rescue her, too?

She jumped slightly when Jake walked in.

'Elliot, Elliot. So glad you are here, mate. So glad.' Jake hugged his ex-brother-in-law with one hand while clasping his low-slung sarong in the other. 'Dusty's still asleep, she and Ed stayed up late watching movies. She won't be up for a while. I'm just going for a shower.'

Zelda raised an eyebrow and turned to the newspapers on the island – the lurid headlines featured Georgia, Elliot, Johnny, Lily, Dusty and Willow. But, she was very peeved to note, nothing about her. She delved further.

'God, I need a shower too, or a bath would be great – can I come up? Might need to borrow some . . .' Elliot looked down at himself with his strong hands spread wide in the universal gesture for 'what do I look like?'

"Course you can – c'mon, follow me.' Jake put his naked arm across Elliot's broad shoulders and led him away. Full of bonhomie.

As they left the Great Hall Elliot thought he heard Zelda mutter quietly, 'What's mine is yours.'

Cleo was knocking impatiently on the garden door. Zelda slipped off her stool to let her in.

'Morning, Mother.'

'Just heard, darling, we are off today! This afternoon, all confirmed – I am quite excited.' Cleo looked gorgeous, in full makeup as always. She was wearing a black tracksuit, her hair pulled back by a sparkling velvet band. With mother and daughter dressed almost identically, it wasn't hard to see where Zelda had inherited her fabulous body. She and her mother were more alike than either would care to acknowledge; not only in their famous good looks, but in their ambitions and desires too. They were a formidable pair.

Zelda was annoyed by her mother for all the reasons that women are often annoyed by their mothers, particularly a mother that lives at the end of your garden. She tended to forget that, technically, she lived at the bottom of Cleo's.

Her mother was competitive, tactless, popular, very high-profile and generally quite selfish. She had always treated Zelda as a sort of mini-me until she realised that Zelda had a massive career and had become a maxi-me; then the gloves came off. Whenever one of them got new work she couldn't wait to tell the other. A lifelong game of trumps had made them, almost, forget their familial relationship. They were rivals first and foremost. Perversely, although this had caused massive tension and tiffs between them, it had, in fact, supplied the fuel for their perpetual drive towards greater levels of fame, notoriety and success.

But this new idea of Cleo's was straying into different territory altogether, literally: signing up for a reality TV show that involved famous contestants pitting themselves against the elements, in an attempt to do things that most sane people wouldn't consider doing in a million years. This celebrity challenge show was breaking new ground. The public were no longer content to see famous people eating witchetty grubs or sleeping on rainforest floors. They wanted them out there in real danger.

So, when the Everest show was first mooted Cleo jumped at it. She was fit, she was feisty, she had spent much of her life on the slopes of St Moritz and Gstaad. 'For God's sake,' she'd said, 'How hard can it be!' And before even her agent could blink, she was signed up for the show.

The prize, if she made it to the top, was £1,000,000. But she wasn't doing it for the money. In fact, she had managed to draw even more attention to herself by promising to donate the money to charity. She knew that this would be it; the show that would give the public an opportunity to see the kind of person she really was.

She had already imagined herself sticking her flag into the snow at the top of Everest, while her crew lay, almost dying, at her feet. She could picture herself standing there, looking quite lovely in her Chanel climbing suit, which was already packed for that triumphant moment.

Then she imagined the avalanche of praise and adoration for her, when she returned to distribute funds, at photo-shoots with cute little AIDS orphans. This would be her finest hour, she was sure of it. She felt fitter than she had ever been in her life. Milo had helped with that. Her steely determination would win through. Of that there was no doubt in Cleo's mind . . .

So now she was somewhat put out to hear her daughter asking her rudely, 'Cleo, are you sure about this, I mean really, I know you are fit and everything. But Everest has beaten people a quarter your age, and that's just the blokes. I mean, you could get out of your contract, couldn't you? It's not too late? I'm sure Lucien would help.'

Cleo looked furious. 'Why would I do that, have you gone mad? Honestly, Zelda, I sometimes wonder if you know me at all.'

Lana came in with Willow in her arms. 'Oh! Sorry to inter . . . but I hear the girls' father is arrive, so I bring the baby.'

Zelda snapped at her impatiently, 'Mr March is here, Lana,

but he is not Willow's father, is he? He is only Dusty's. I know you don't speak English very well but surely you have grasped that? It's all anyone has been fucking talking about for the last twenty-four hours, for Christ's sake!'

Lana's pretty cheeks flared pinkly as she took the baby into the kitchen area and got a bottle of juice out of the fridge. Max chose that moment to arrive from the garden. Stepping jauntily into the room, he exclaimed brightly, 'Morning, darlings. How are we all today? Any exciting new developments in the night?'

Cleo and Zelda ignored him.

Zelda lit a cigarette, took a sharp drag and said petulantly, not for the first time, 'Jesus! Endless fucking staff and you can't even get someone to make a cup of fucking coffee. I can already tell this is going to be another hideous day.'

Lana calmly poured some coffee and placed it quietly in front of Zelda who grudgingly mumbled her thanks.

Max went to join his family at the table and squeezed his daughter's shoulders kindly. 'Are you all right, Zelda darling? Anything I can do to help?' Zelda still didn't bother to acknowledge her father. He withdrew his hands and made a small strangling gesture behind her head. No one noticed him do it, but it cheered him up anyway.

When Max sat down, Lana asked him if he could hold the baby while she made breakfast. Max liked babies, and he dangled Willow expertly on his knee, tickling her until she squeaked.

Zelda looked at him sharply. 'Dad, stop it! It's far too early for that din.'

Art and Charlie appeared out of nowhere, casually lifting the freshly Marmited toast that Lana had made. They mumbled, 'Thanks, bye!' to no-one in particular.

Max called to them, 'Boys, Boys! Don't go out through the front, go through ours, there are fewer paps over there. If anyone asks who you are, you can say you are my godsons.'

Cleo and Zelda both raised an eyebrow – always quite an achievement considering the amount of Botox they had in their foreheads. Then they returned to the absorbing task of scouring the papers for a mention of their respective names. Art waved vaguely, and both boys left through the garden doors.

Kate appeared. She whizzed through the Great Hall and out into the garden, chasing after the boys.

She called out and they turned towards her. They had the raffish, slightly shifty and intimidating aura of their peer group. Kate faltered, momentarily embarrassed. 'Charlie, Art! By the way – just wanted to remind you – nothing you have heard – you know – Mum's the word.' The boys looked inscrutable, but then they both smiled winningly at her and Charlie replied, 'Yah, we know, Kate. Sure,' and 'We're cool.' Which, Kate had to admit, they really were.

They turned away from her, slightly dismissively she felt, and set off nonchalantly to get out of God's the 'anti-pap' way. No one had seen them arrive. Kate wondered where they had sprung from, and indeed when.

With a sinking feeling, she also knew, from something in the way that they had looked at her, that Valentine – so keen to keep their trysts a secret – had clearly told them that his relationship with his mother's PA was not purely platonic. She tried to console herself that this was a good sign.

As she was about to re-enter the kitchen she could hear Valentine's distinctive voice, answering his mother's killer question, 'Where is your lovely girlfriend, darling, I haven't seen her here for days. You haven't broken up, have you?'

Valentine's reply was not a surprise to Kate, but it still hurt when she heard him say, 'Why would I break up with her? She bloody loves me!' He continued disingenuously, 'She had to leave really early, she's shooting today. They had to switch her days around to accommodate you, Mummy darling, didn't you know?'

Zelda looked slyly innocent. 'Really, darling, I didn't know. That is so sweet of her. Does she mind?'

'Well, she's not thrilled. I had promised to take her to Paris this weekend. But all this has fucked that up anyway,' he sighed, 'and she will be shooting some nights too. But you know how lovely and understanding she is, Mummy. She'll do anything to help you. She idolises you. You do know that, don't you? But we all do, don't we!' He bent down to hug and kiss his mother. He tickled her and she laughed for the first time that day, pushing him away softly. Zelda had cheered up a little.

Kate remained outside, leaning against the doorframe, with her eyes closed.

So, Little Miss Cute would be shooting nights too – this was good news indeed. Kate felt a shiver of anticipation and delight. She ran her hands through her hair, mussing it up a bit, took a deep breath and stepped back into the Great Hall.

But, to her dismay, Valentine had already disappeared.

CHAPTER NINE

A cleaned-up Elliot knocked gently on Dusty's bedroom door. He wore a fresh linen shirt and a pair of Rag & Bone jeans borrowed from Jake. His hair was no longer matted, dirty brown but 'John Frieda fresh' blond, the thick waves curled against his tanned neck. The crisp white shirt, also belonging to Jake, was slightly tight on his muscular arms and torso. He looked anxious as he prepared to see his bereaved daughter for the first time in ... 'How long since we've seen each other?' he asked himself. 'Months – fuck! How many?' He winced guiltily when he realised he didn't even know.

He entered the bedroom, crossing the floor stealthily, to gaze solemnly at his daughter as she lay sleeping. Seating himself tentatively on the edge of her bed he looked down at his beautiful, fragile child.

Reality hit when he realised with a jolt that she was his now and his alone. She and Georgia had always been such an inseparable little unit he had never really seen Dusty as his. It wasn't that Georgia had ever deliberately excluded him, she had never been mean-spirited in that way. It was just that their marriage had disintegrated so fast, when Dusty was so young and, what with his frequent work overseas, somehow it was always just them – Georgia and Dusty together, a little unit of two – with him the outsider, dipping in and out. 'Hey, Elliot – you're back! Come over, see Dusty, hang out here with us ...'

And so he would just drop in, now and then, everything very friendly and fun. No pressure, nothing required of him. Just 'Dusty, look, it's Daddy!' and then off again, into the world he understood, where things were dark and dangerous but he felt free. His only real dependant was his editor, always voraciously demanding copy.

No one else relied on him, expected anything from him – especially that something he had, so far, proved spectacularly incompetent at delivering; something called love.

As Elliot looked down at his sleeping daughter, she seemed particularly small and delicate in her opulent surroundings.

He was disturbingly reminded of the moment that the call came through to him about Georgia; he had been standing looking at a young Afghan girl of a similar age to his daughter. She had also looked unbearably vulnerable, but in contrast she lay in the filthy, blood-spattered hell that was a hospital bed in Kabul – when was that? Yesterday? Elliot shook his head to try to clear the image, but it wouldn't budge – and the girl was as thin and fragile as Dusty. She had lost her mother too, but in a bomb blast in the local market; she was in deep shock with some superficial shrapnel wounds and burns.

The doctors assured him that she would recover physically,

but there had been no sign of any family to claim her; when she was released she would have to fend for herself. A fearsome future awaited her in that hellish place. Ostensibly, his daughter had entirely different prospects; she had a father – ha!, an extended family and vast wealth, but would any of these things guarantee that she would flourish?

He asked himself anxiously: what did he really know of Dusty, of her life? He knew that many of her peers in London were falling into the abyss of drink and drugs or anorexia, the statistics were terrifying ...

So here he was. With Georgia gone, Dusty and her baby sister would need something from him now; that could not be denied. But could he deliver? He felt a knot of fear in his gut as Dusty stirred and opened her eyes. Seeing her errant father looking anxiously down at her she burst into floods of tears, flung her arms around his neck and sobbed until both of them were completely drained of emotion.

'Can we go home now?' Dusty asked, gasping for breath.

Elliot felt panic rising ... home, what did she mean – the flat? 'Um, er – home?' he answered uncertainly.

'Hollywood Road, Dad? Willow and me? Our home – and yours now too.'

'Yes, yes, sweetheart, of course. I've only just arrived, so not sure what has been sorted out about ... well, um. We will probably have to stay here for a bit till we can work out what's what, you know?'

'But all our stuff is there, everything – why can't we just go back there now?'

'Well we can ... to get some of your stuff. Sure, let's do it! You get dressed and you and I will scoot over there. OK?'

Dissemble. Buy time. Elliot thought weakly.

Dusty looked at her father and said perceptively, 'We can't live here, you know, Willow and me, they don't want us and we don't want to be here. So you are not going to try to fuck off and leave us here, are you, Dad?' There was a flash of steely determination in her voice that Elliot hadn't heard before.

He smiled his most reassuring smile and stood up. 'Don't worry, everything is going to be OK, sorted. Hurry up. I'll go down and see about a car.'

He left her and leapt down the stairs two at a time, the deep red carpet on the staircase juxtaposed in his mind with images of a blood-slicked stairwell in a bombed-out building he had gone into with his photographer, only days ago.

He was feeling suddenly tired, overwhelmed as the enormity of what had happened began to sink in. He couldn't be the observer on this one – it was his and his alone. He slumped down onto the bottom step and put his head in his hands.

He felt a hand on his shoulder. Looking up he found his ex-brother-in-law standing over him.

'On the naughty step already? Didn't take long!' Jake laughed and continued kindly, 'C'mon, mate, let's get you something to sort you out.' He leant forward and gently pulled Elliot to his feet, leading him into the Great Hall.

Lana was lifting Willow up from one of the huge armchairs, and the baby was chuckling as the au pair cooed, 'Let's go, baby – time for nap? Eh?' Turning to see Jake and Elliot enter she looked flustered.

'Oh, Lana, hi! This is Elliot.' Jake waved airily and headed for the drinks fridge.

Elliot froze for a second, unsure how to proceed. Then, quickly composing himself, he smiled broadly. 'Hello, hello – Willow.' He tentatively reached out and gently squeezed the baby's arm. Looking at Lana, with his astute reporter's eye, he took in everything: her soft, glowing skin, slim hips in skinny jeans, a loose cotton top which maddeningly disguised her upper body but showed her firm, golden arms. Her fair hair sprang loose from a slightly tangled ponytail. He was entranced.

She pushed the baby towards him with a look that seemed to be saying, 'Take her, it's OK!'

But Elliot and baby-holding? He backed off, muttering nervously, 'No, no, don't worry – if she needs a nap . . . you know – I'll see her later, um, hold her . . . later!'

Lana smiled. Elliot wondered if he could detect a tiny hint of disapproval in that smile. He was trying to think of a way to redeem himself as she left the room, speaking soothingly to her small charge.

Jake watched this scene with vague interest and amusement.

'So, what can I get you, Elliot – eh? Vodka, coffee – both?' Jake had already poured a very generous neat vodka into an empty coffee cup. 'I'm having both.'

'Coffee, great, thanks . . . no, actually, fuck it! Vodka would be good.' Elliot sat down on one of the Philippe Starck barstools. With his long legs extended and elbows resting on the bar he watched as his charming, dissolute ex-brother-in-law poured him a massive pick-me-up, which might just turn out to be a knock-me-down, it was so strong.

'Jake, so sorry about Georgia, what's been going on? She was fine last time I saw her ... everything seemed to be going better. I know she was cut up about the Johnny thing but she was talking about going back into the studio and she was, or she seemed, sorted. What the fuck went wrong?' Elliot began to feel angry, with Johnny, Georgia and, if he was honest, with himself. He had been a useless husband to Georgia and a worse than useless ex. He knew it and he felt ashamed. 'I should've been there, looked out for her more.'

'We can't both beat ourselves with that stick, Elliot. You know, I've been thinking – maybe ...'

Kate walked into the room. Realising there was a private chat going on she tried to back out tactfully.

'Kate, you know Elliot.' Jake, always polite, gentlemanly. 'Elliot, Kate – Zelda's PA – poor Kate.'

Kate responded patiently. 'We've seen each other already, Jake. I know Mr March anyway. I have worked here for a while now!' She rolled her eyes and smiled conspiratorially at Elliot. 'Is there anything I can do for you – get for you? A hotel? Car?'

Jake looked bemused.

Elliot was grateful. 'Oh, yes, yes, a car would be great. Dusty is just getting up – I said I'd take her over to Hollywood Road to get some stuff for her and the baby. Thanks, Kate, that would be great. Oh, and a hotel would be good too, somewhere nearby ... my flat is, um, rented at the moment so ...' Elliot didn't mind Jake knowing what he hadn't wanted to admit to Zelda, that he was still so broke he had to let his flat whenever he was away on assignments, which was in truth all the time. He knew she would not have been impressed.

Jake interrupted: 'What? No, no, Elliot – you are staying here with us. Christ, coming and going from here is fucking impossible with that rabble outside – anyway, we need you here. The girls will need you too. Wouldn't hear of you staying anywhere else. Nor would Zelda. Particularly not Zelda.' Jake's face was inscrutable as he said this.

Elliot often wondered if Jake knew, or even suspected, about his affair with Zelda. It was impossible to tell. On the numerous occasions that the men had been alone together since then, Elliot often felt that Jake was hinting that he knew, but he never said anything directly. He never seemed particularly ruffled when he dropped those ambiguous remarks, so Elliot didn't feel he had any choice but to ignore them. But he always felt a bit uneasy when they were alone together. Of course it had all been a very, very long time ago ... he had a sudden flashback – Zelda arriving at his flat and taking off her coat, she'd been wearing nothing underneath. He felt thrilled but guilty at the memory ... to his horror he almost blushed, quickly pretending to look at something on his phone to hide his shame. He needn't have worried. Jake was preoccupied pouring himself another drink.

He heard Kate say, 'Well, if there's anything else you need

just buzz me, I'll be in the office. I'll tell David to make sure there is a car on standby for you.'

Elliot composed himself. 'Thank you, Kate, and Jake, very kind.'

'Where's Zelda, Kate?' Jake asked.

'She is just doing a quick interview about the film. Mr Dark said the film company insisted. They are in the office. Should be finished soon. I'll tell her you are looking for her.' Kate turned to leave.

'What, Kate? Is Lucien downstairs too? That fuck – he'd better not be here for long.' Jake was very cross.

Elliot wondered what that was about. Lucien Dark? He was a rave from the grave. What was he doing back in the fold and why was the implacable Jake pissed off about it? So, Zelda had let the wolf back in? She had balls – he had to admit that. More balls than Jake, or himself for that matter, he thought, regretfully.

As Kate left the Great Hall she passed Dusty coming in. She could see that the poor girl still looked shattered, with dark circles under her eyes. She appeared to be wearing Ed's clothes.

At the same moment the garden doors were flung open and Cleo emerged with a squeal. 'Elliot, oh my God! How heavenly – I thought I was going to miss you!' She flung her arms around his neck and kissed him, leaving a livid red lipstick mark on his cheekbone.

Dusty looked on in furious disapproval – how typical that Cleo should be inappropriately happy on a day when everyone else was at least attempting to behave in a slightly subdued way. Unusually, Cleo picked up on this vibe and calmed down, giving Dusty a gentle hug. 'You must be pleased to have Daddy here now, darling, what a relief.'

Elliot smiled winningly at Zelda's lovely mother. 'Cleo – you look marvellous, so fit and well. Longing for a catch-up, but Dusty and I are just off to Hollywood Road to get some of the girls' stuff. Shall I see you later?'

'Well, I hope I'll still be here, darling, but I may be gone – off to climb Everest actually!' Cleo looked smugly pleased with herself.

Elliot was suitably amazed. 'What the . . . !'

Dusty grabbed his arm and pulled him from the room. 'Bye everyone – we won't be long . . .'

As they opened the front door all hell broke loose. Dusty put on a huge pair of sunglasses and Elliot put his arms around her, while David protected them as best he could. The cameras were going crazy and the press and fans were shouting, roaring like a bloodthirsty crowd at the Colosseum.

The car had drawn up close to the bottom of the front steps. Elliot pushed Dusty in first, and then David slammed the car door firmly behind them. The blacked-out windows made the dark car interior alive with starbursts from the flashbulbs popping outside; it was like being trapped in a tiny, demented nightclub. Their experienced driver sped calmly between the barriers. Motorbikes peeled off after them.

'Did she say Everest?' Elliot was incredulous.

''Fraid so – yep.' Dusty smiled at him. 'Good, eh?'

'Fuck me! I mean, what is she thinking? What for? I mean, she could die . . .'

'Fame game, Daddy-o. Cleo can't get arrested these days and Zelda's career has been going stratospheric. So reality TV, it has to be, for Cleo – she'll get a lot of attention for this one. To be honest I don't think she would mind if it killed her. "Better to die dramatically than to live drearily," I think she said – or something idiotic like that.' Dusty leant her head back against the leather seat and looked over at her father, reaching out to wipe Cleo's lipstick off his cheek. It looked like a smear of fresh blood – she realised the press had just taken hundreds of pictures of him and she wondered if they would make something of it.

She wondered correctly; the pictures were already being sent to the papers – perfect front-page shots: 'Georgia's ex leaves her brother's house, bloodied but unbowed, with their grieving daughter Dusty, looking painfully thin.' Linking the pictures to yesterday's shots of Jake going berserk with the press. 'Has Georgia's "over-emotional" brother got into a fight with his sister's ex?' And so on . . .

David had called ahead to the security team outside Hollywood Road, but the crowd was huge, unmanageable. Stretching all the way up the street, the railings and pavement were covered with flowers, candles, teddy bears and pictures of Georgia. The car managed to inch through the unruly crowd.

The security guys attempted to hold everyone back while Dusty and Elliot sat silently stunned in the car. Elliot took his daughter's hand. He tried to decide whether they should just get the driver to turn back.

But Dusty suddenly leant forward and the car door was open – she was out.

When she emerged the crowd fell silent, stood still. She walked up the steps, a small, dignified figure, and pulling a key from her pocket she quickly opened the door and Elliot followed her in. As he closed the front door behind them there was an almighty roar from outside. Dusty threw herself onto one of the sofas, her hands over her ears. The crowds were shouting hysterically, chanting, 'Georgia, Georgia!' 'Dusty, Dusty'!'

Elliot was shattered and shocked. 'What the fuck? Who are these people? Jesus Christ.' He pulled out a cigarette and lit it, taking a deep drag.

'Can I have one?' his daughter asked faintly. 'They were bad when Johnny left – but this is . . . really scary. When will they stop?'

He handed his cigarette to her and lit another. 'Jesus, I don't know. They make me ashamed to call myself a journalist. These are not my people . . .' But thinking to himself he wondered, 'or are they?' Was his story about the girl in Kabul going to be any less prurient, any less of an infringement of her privacy? He felt sick.

He was jolted too by the familiar Georgia-ness of her house. He hesitated, almost expecting her to appear; laughing, holding a fag and a glass of wine, waving her arms about; so warm and familiar – so alive. He wiped a tear away and looked at Dusty. She was watching him through a thick cloud of smoke.

'Dad, I think it's too soon for me to be back here – I don't want to go upstairs. Can we go back to God's now?' He could see that she was shaking.

'I am just gonna call them and get more police over here before we try to get out again. Tell me what you need, baby – I'll nip up and get it. OK?'

When he had bounded off upstairs Dusty quietly finished smoking her cigarette, stubbing it out in an already overflowing ashtray on the table. She realised that the maid hadn't been allowed in to clean the house. Pulling her knees up she arranged herself in the foetal position, and as she slid her hand under a cushion she found a scarf and hugged it to herself. She smelt it and pulled it out to get a proper look. It was soft cotton, pale blue. She frowned at it. She had seen it before – often – it was Valentine's favourite. Something about it bothered her, but she wasn't sure what. She sat up and, putting the scarf around her neck, she waited for Elliot to come back downstairs.

She heard him shouting from the landing: ' . . . trainers, iPod, Kindle, makeup, T-shirts – got them! Everything off the floor too . . . anything else?' He bounded back down. 'Sweetheart – fuck me, you have got a lot of stuff up there . . . maybe we should send, what's-her-name? Lara? over to get things for you and Willow later . . . Oh! Hang on.' Elliot dumped a big bag of stuff in the hall and disappeared back upstairs.

He went into Georgia's bedroom tentatively – the smell of her scent made him dizzy with sadness and nostalgia. He steadied himself and looked around. Nothing had been touched since the ambulance had taken Georgia's body away. He searched the room quickly, diligently, unsure of what he was looking for. An answer, certainly, to the question that had been tapping in his head since he first heard the news. That question was now pounding at him as he stood in the place where she had died: why, why, why? What went on here two nights ago? Oh, he knew Georgia's weakness – God, how he knew. But there was something that didn't feel right – just a tiny glimmer of an instinct, and he had learnt to trust his instincts; they had kept him alive, too many times to count.

On his way back downstairs he popped into the baby's room and grabbed a little toy lamb from her cot. Dusty was waiting for him, sunglasses back on, scarf over her head.

She looked at him and then at the lamb in his arms. 'Well done, Dad, that's her favourite! Ready?'

'Yep. Let's go, baby.'

They flung open the front door and ran the gauntlet to the car. The element of surprise allowed the extra police to hold the crowd back for a moment. But once they were safely in, with the doors locked, the screaming began. Cameras and fans' fists banged on the roof and doors. The driver crept slowly, carefully but determinedly, through the throng. The noise was deafening, terrifying.

'Fuck, Dad, what were we thinking?' Dusty started to giggle, slightly hysterically, and then Elliot succumbed too. 'This is as scary as a fucking war zone, Christ – it's scarier!'

They laughed till they cried, all the way back to God's.

CHAPTER TEN

Zelda sat alone in the Great Hall. She could hear the doorbell ringing constantly. The housekeepers were desperately trying to keep up with the deluge of flowers that were arriving, with commiserations from everyone in the business. The Great Hall already looked as if it had been decked out for a wedding, with massive bouquets from the brilliant florist Rob Van Helden. Zelda loved flowers but even she had to admit they were becoming overwhelming. Every room in the house was full of them. She asked Kate to redistribute any more that arrived; some went over to Max and Cleo's and the rest, God knows where ...

Zelda sat quietly texting, although she had decided not to tweet apart from a brief line to say she was 'too saddened by the tragic loss of my beautiful and beloved sister-in-law to tweet anything for the foreseeable future.'

She sighed. At last she had a few moments to herself – a chance to collect her thoughts. The hair and makeup artists had left for the day and Zelda looked lovely. Her dark hair fell in soft waves, glowing with health. Her face was picture perfect. She wore a tailored grey-and-black Alexander McQueen day dress, which emphasised her fabulous figure. The interviews had gone well this morning – the journalists were almost deferential, not the usual snide questions. She felt good, powerful, in control, desirable.

Her thoughts strayed to Elliot. God, he'd looked wonderful when he'd showed up earlier that day. The strength of her feelings for him still surprised and annoyed her whenever she saw him – dirty and tired though he'd been, she had felt his pull as strongly as ever.

They had seen each other very rarely over the past few years. But now here he was, back again, and staying in her house – or so she had been told. Not a great idea perhaps, but nobody had asked her opinion and it would seem churlish to turn him out now. Anyway, she understood that it was Jake who had asked him to stay – which was interesting.

So, what next?

Realistically: Elliot taking charge of Dusty and the baby? His own child, maybe – at a push – but someone else's? Giving up his nomadic life to settle down in London? He hadn't been prepared to do it for her, she thought sadly, so would he do it for the girls? Dusty was almost grown up but the baby really was another thing altogether – and not a thing Zelda wanted to find herself lumbered with. She realised that Willow's paternity needed to be established, and soon.

Perhaps she should look into it herself to see if anything

interesting came up? She knew that no one else would be prepared to take any real action, or nothing more than half-hearted attempts, anyway. No, she would have to do it herself, as bloody usual. But how – DNA? Fuck, yes! But how did you go about that without anyone knowing?

Milo stuck his handsome head round the door. 'Is this a good time?' He seemed apprehensive, almost nervous.

Zelda smiled radiantly at him. 'Hey, come in. Where have you been? I've been missing you.' She stood up and kissed him warmly on the mouth, running her hands through his hair. He flinched. 'Ouch!' he protested softly.

'What? My kisses hurt you now.' Zelda was peeved.

'No, my hair, something caught in my hair.' He pulled her towards him.

Zelda stepped back. 'Not here, Milo.' She looked down at her right hand. Her huge diamond ring with its claw clasp had some of Milo's golden hair caught in it. She looked at him, smiled sweetly. 'So what's the ETD? I am going to miss you soooo much.'

'Half an hour – that's why I'm here, I came to say goodbye. Can we go somewhere?'

Elliot and Dusty walked in.

Milo went straight into professional mode. 'So you just have to keep your back flat when you do that move, Miss Spender, otherwise you can do damage. You don't want to do damage, do you?'

'No Milo – no, indeed I don't. Well, good luck, be careful.' Zelda smiled tightly and Milo knew he was dismissed.

Zelda closed the garden doors behind him, noticing his hair caught in her diamond ring. It suddenly dawned on her: hair. That is what they used for DNA testing. Yes, of course.

So . . . Who was she going to test for their DNA? Everyone Georgia had known in the last two years? How could she find out? Even though Georgia had lived the narrow, closeted life of the super-famous, it would be impossible to trace and track down all her romantic entanglements, surely? She thought hard . . . who was around at the right time? Well, Johnny certainly . . . She watched Milo's retreating back as he crossed the garden. Milo? No! She tried to remember if he had even known Georgia. Christ! What was she thinking, of course! How could she have forgotten – her sister-in-law had introduced him to this family and now that she thought about it, she recalled that Georgia was quite pissed off that they had instantly monopolised him, indeed taken him over completely. And, now that she was thinking about it, Milo never, ever mentioned Georgia . . . Hmm, so he was on the list and she had inadvertently, fortuitously retrieved his hair sample already. Nice work, she thought to herself.

Elliot had switched the kettle on and put some toast in the toaster. 'Anyone else? Dusty? Zelda?'

'No thanks, Dad, I'm going to put my stuff in my room, find Ed – give him his clothes back.'

'Toast! Fuck, no – I haven't eaten bread since 1995.' Zelda felt incredibly hungry.

Elliot tapped her lightly on the bum with the breadknife. 'You poor baby, how you have had to suffer for your art.'

Zelda couldn't always tell when Elliot was being facetious, so she responded with her default reaction and laughed.

'I still drink coffee though – so if you want to make me some . . .'

'Coming up. Sit yourself down, stop tapping at that bloody phone for a moment. Let's talk.'

Jake walked in. 'Yes! Let's talk!' He sat down on the stool next to Zelda. Her heart sank – she could tell he was already a bit pissed. He looked at them both, blearily, asking, 'But what shall we talk about? So much to say, so little time . . .'

There was an urgent tapping on the garden door. For once, Zelda was quite relieved to see her mother. Things felt a bit uncomfortable.

Cleo didn't sense a thing. She looked gorgeous in her black Chanel snow-suit with a fabulous, luxurious fur trim and large diamond Cs on the breast pocket. She gave a little twirl.

'What do you think? For the summit?'

'The summit! Mum, don't you think you should be managing your expectations a bit?' Zelda said archly. 'Anyway, why are you wearing that now?'

'Manage your own expectations, Zelda, mine are fine. And I'm wearing it because Milo and I have just done a press call at mine, thank you very much.'

'Ah, fame at last!'

'What do you mean? I was fucking famous long before you were even born, darling daughter.'

'Not you, Mother, I meant Milo.'

'What, Milo, famous! I don't think so.'

'Mum, he is climbing Everest with you and a film crew ... prime-time TV! Photogenic!'

Cleo pretended not to hear, turning to Elliot. 'So, darling Elliot, where have you been for so long? I have missed you.'

'Just messing about abroad, Cleo, you know the usual. But nothing, *nothing* compared to what you are attempting on the bold and brave front.'

Cleo giggled proudly and hugged Elliot to her firm, enhanced bosom. 'Oh I wish I could see more of you – but I really do have to go ...'

Max stepped into the room, saying, 'She's off, she's off, she's off!'

'Thanks, Max darling – you could try and contain your joy at my departure, at least till after I've gone!' Cleo smiled thinly at her husband.

Max grinned back at her and bounced across the room with a jaunty spring in his step that belied his years. Throwing his arms wide he boomed, 'Elliot, I heard you were here, how wonderful to see you dear, dear boy.' He hugged Elliot warmly. 'I just came over to ask if you'd all like to come over to Devil's tonight for dinner. I'll ask a few more to cheer us all up a bit – what do you think?' He looked around happily, confident that his wish was their command.

'Yes, thanks, Daddy, that would be lovely,' Zelda answered quickly, before anyone else could demur. A diversion would be a good idea – they were all beginning to go slightly stir-crazy at God's.

Cleo looked hurt. 'What, a party? After I've left? Thanks a lot!'

'No, no, my darling, not a party, of course not, no – just supper, a change of scene for everyone, to console us after you have gone, otherwise we will all be feeling too, too sad,' Max kindly reassured her, kissing her cheek spontaneously. She pushed him away playfully and was mollified.

Valentine swept in. 'Morning all, hi, Elliot! Did I hear someone say party? Can I ask some people?'

'It's afternoon – where have you been?' Zelda demanded in exasperation.

'Of course, the more the merrier!' Max was looking bucked.

'No, no. Not too many, Valentine, we can't have the press thinking we are having a knees-up when . . .' Zelda trailed off. Dusty had re-entered the room, with Ed.

'What . . . ?' She looked around at everyone. The room went quiet.

'Nothing, darling, just saying supper at mine tonight,' Max said casually. 'Do you want to ask someone? A girlfriend? Boyfriend?'

Ed immediately cheered up. 'Yes, c'mon, Dusty, ask your friend Scarlett!'

Dusty gave Ed a withering look. 'So she can spend the evening with you drooling all over her! Maybe not.'

'Aw, come on, Dusty, I won't, I promise. Come on – she's your best mate. She should be here with you anyway. Text her, text her now.' He put his hand into Dusty's pocket and pulled out her phone. 'Go on, you know you want to.'

Dusty smiled at him, took her phone back and quickly sent a text.

Ed put his iPod earphones back in and slumped down onto a sofa, turning on the massive wide-screen TV with a flourish. Dusty threw herself down next to him and they lost themselves in a soap, watching, texting and listening to music all at the same time.

'Tell anyone you ask to come in via mine, not through here, OK?' Max left with a fey wave. 'See you at about eight. Come on, Cleo darling – your sleigh awaits.'

Cleo pranced around the room, hugging and mwah-mwahing everyone.

'Be careful.' 'I love you.' 'Bye, Gran ... Cleo!' 'Bye, darlings, bye, bye ...'

Until, finally, she was gone.

'Wow! Gotta hand it to her – your mother is one hell of a woman.' Elliot laughed and shook his head.

'With the emphasis on hell!' Zelda muttered.

Valentine realised that Kate had slipped quietly into the room, and that she was good at insinuating herself into a situation without anyone really noticing.

But he was noticing her now. She was wearing a very short little jersey dress, which clung to her body, catching his attention. He felt an overwhelming urge to cling to her body too. She felt his eyes on her and glanced slyly over to where he had slumped into an armchair. Having caught his eye she nodded imperceptibly when he made a discreet upwards gesture with his hand. She slipped out of the room and scampered upstairs.

Valentine said, 'I'll ask some people tonight. India won't be able to come though, Mummy – she's shooting. I know you'll be very sorry not to see her, and catch up on all the set gossip!'

He didn't bother to catch his mother's reply; he was off upstairs, bouncing after his mother's PA. Desire sent his blood surging, pounding through his veins. Kate was a very, very tempting, convenient girl to have around the house. As he slipped into his room, he was delighted to find her standing naked, trembling before him.

She made a small, slightly embarrassed, 'Ta-da!' gesture. He looked at her, growled and pounced. All thoughts of India, Lily and even Dusty were, momentarily, banished from his dirty little mind.

Half an hour later, Dusty stood quietly outside Valentine's bedroom door, and knocked on it gently with her free hand. In the other she clasped the soft blue cotton scarf that she had retrieved from Hollywood Road.

'Valentine, are you in there?' She knocked again.

Valentine's voice came to her faintly, through the vast deep-panelled door. 'Er, yup! Um, just having a ... little ... nap. Um, can I catch you later, Dusty?'

Dusty hesitated in disappointment.

As she turned away she had heard a feminine, barely suppressed, giggle from Valentine's room. A nap? she thought bleakly. What a fool she was. She walked away along the passage, and as she buried her face in the soft, sweet-smelling scarf, her eyes filled with tears.

CHAPTER ELEVEN

Lucien Dark had spent the afternoon in his office, catching up on some of his other clients' work. Zelda and her family were proving to be very time-consuming. But he was managing to juggle people with his usual skill; skill that his staff described as practising his 'Dark Arts'. The manipulator and master – always.

A meeting had been called at God's, for the following day. To be attended by all the interested parties.

Lucien had briefed Craig Sanderson, the senior partner at Sanderson & Co (Dark Artists' accountants) to an exacting extent, on what he was to say and, most importantly, what he was not to reveal about Georgia's circumstances.

Craig Sanderson had protested weakly. His firm had somehow managed to become hugely dependent for the vast bulk of its business upon Dark Artists International and its high-flying clients. A mistake that frequently compromised the unbiased advice that they were legally obliged to supply.

Although the majority of the accountants employed by

Sanderson & Co were unaware of the complex accounting arrangements that allowed Lucien to take extraordinary liberties with his client's funds, Mr Sanderson knew only too well; he also knew the lengths Lucien would go to, to keep control of everyone and everything.

So his firm was in deep – way too deep to get out.

This business association with Lucien gave Craig Sanderson many sleepless nights and, it could be noted, a simply beautiful house in Provence.

Jake had taken Elliot up to the library to do some work, as he had copy to file. Jake kindly set him up at his somewhat redundant computer. Which prompted Elliot to ask how Jake's screenplay was going.

'Novel, um, novel, I've put the screenwriting on hold. Quite enjoying the novel – bit of a block at the moment but . . .' Jake smiled at Elliot, almost apologetically. He ran his hands through his hair, looking tired. He crossed the room and opened a false cupboard in the bookcase. He peered in. 'Can I get you anything? Vodka, whisky?'

'No, no thanks, Jake. Maybe later.' Elliot watched as Jake shakily filled a glass.

'I am so sorry about Georgia, Jake. She loved you, man, more than she loved any of the rest of us put together. Well, with the exception of Dusty and Willow of course . . . but them and you.' He took a deep breath, feeling uncomfortable, inadequate, but pressed on. 'I am really so bloody sorry this

happened to her, you, Dusty ... God, what a fucking mess.'
Elliot leant back in the surprisingly comfortable Eames chair:
Jake's chair, where he spent so much of his time fruitlessly
searching for inspiration from the bottom of a bottle.

'It will all be OK though, we'll work it out together. I'm sure.'
Elliot was sincere.

Jake looked justifiably sceptical and taking a deep swig from
his glass he wandered towards the door. 'Yeah, sure, thanks
Elliot.'

Elliot saw the tears that filled Jake's eyes as he shuffled out.
God, he thought, that poor fucker has deteriorated since I last
saw him. He wondered how things were between him and
Zelda. Not because of any vested interest, of course, he lied to
himself. God knew, he still found Zelda almost unbearably
attractive. But they had established, a long time ago, that any
future for them was doomed. Why was nature so perverse, he
wondered, to make a person so physically attracted to someone so utterly incompatible in every other way?

Stupid nature; stupid Elliot. Damn! He felt sad now, sorry
for himself. He even considered raiding Jake's booze stash.
But he pulled himself together, shook off the old ghosts, and
started his piece for The Independent. It shouldn't take
long – that other kind of hell was still vividly present in his
mind.

Zelda had e-mailed her new pal, Dr D'Angelo, for his advice on
her DNA plan.

Strictly *entre nous*, she'd said. Knowing that it would be just that. She used her secret e-mail address, which fortunately she had set up for clandestine communication with Milo while he was away. Well actually he had set it up – such expertise was beyond her. Now she was chuffed with herself for finding another use for it, and very glad to have a way of communicating privately. She was not exactly a technophobe but she did feel, justifiably, a bit nervous about technology and all the added scope for potentially dangerous intrusions into her already practically non-existent private life.

She began to feel apprehensive about the dinner at Devil's that evening. Lucien was coming over late afternoon for a quick debrief on funeral, film and her personal PR stuff. He would undoubtedly sniff out that they were all having dinner at her dad's. He didn't like being excluded from the social lives of his clients – it was the perk of his job as far as he was concerned. He was always wanting to be 'in', and a social equal. She knew his weakness stemmed from a massive chippiness. Lucien felt a huge egotistical resentment towards anyone who he considered had snubbed him socially even in the most tiny, inconsequential way. When crossed in that respect, he could get quite awkward. Careers had been destroyed for less. She remembered Anna Knight and shuddered.

Yes indeed, she would have to be careful. She was on the up and up again, so she really needed to keep him sweet – but Jake? Oh gosh! What would he say?

Tonight was going to be complicated. Maybe she wouldn't

mention Max's to Lucien, it was only a family supper after all, but still she felt a bit stressed. Reaching into her handbag Zelda pulled out a bottle and necked a few pills.

Dusty and Ed were both giggling softly and asking a few friends over to Max's for supper. They were in the den and Ed was on Facebook. Dusty seemed to have recovered some composure in the momentary reprieve that sometimes comes with the shock of grief.

'I've got five.' Ed peered at his screen.

'They'll never notice – I've got . . . two, no, three. So eight – that's OK. They are mostly boys anyway – Max will be thrilled.' Dusty giggled again.

It was an open secret that Max had an insatiable appetite for young men, but the younger members of the family were still unworldly enough to think his interest was mostly just a fun little flirtation, 'Nothing really yuk,' they always reassured each other. Anything more than that would be weird, and Ed felt pretty uncomfortable about the whole idea. So he made light of it, if he had to acknowledge it at all.

They slumped back on the wide velvet banquettes, cocooned in the most comfortable screening room in the world, or in their world anyway.

Ed put on a DVD of 'Fantasia', his favourite childhood film, hoping its familiar charm would comfort his cousin. He was a thoughtful boy.

*

Lana was making tea in the Great Hall, balancing Willow on her hip. She had been such a sweet baby all day, Lana was feeling attached to her already. She really loved babies. She sighed softly and gave the child a gentle squeeze.

Elliot wandered into the room. Pleased to find Lana there, he saw Willow and was reminded of something. He ducked back out and reappeared a few moments later with one arm behind his back. He approached Willow and Lana in a playful, goofy way. Lana looked slightly alarmed.

'Willow, I have something here I think you might recognise,' he grinned.

Willow's face began to crumple. She was going to cry.

Lana watched Elliot curiously.

Elliot whipped something from behind him and waved it in front of the baby's face. She looked stunned then burst into an adorable smile. She reached out for Lamby and gripped him tight, burying her little face in his toy fur. She squealed with joy.

Elliot burst out laughing. Lana did too. Her eyes were twinkling at him. Elliot felt pleased with himself. 'This girl is so lovely,' he thought, 'innocent and sweet – uncomplicated.' He also found himself wondering why Zelda would employ someone this attractive, since she was always off working and Jake was therefore home alone. Could he resist this tempting person? – Jake, he meant – could Jake resist this tempting person ... or he convinced himself that that was what he was thinking. He felt quite cheered up by her sweetness. Would that he could be Willow, cradled in those arms.

Lana was used to this stuff. Everyone in the household had hit on her at one time or another. She was usually unmoved – but this one? He certainly had something going for him. She found herself blushing and turned away to fill the teapot.

CHAPTER TWELVE

Max waved Cleo off from the front steps of Devil's. They had their own little gaggle of photographers, snapping away at her, for her official send-off.

There was much hugging and kissing of his wife from Max, and a certain amount of gurning for the cameras.

At last, Cleo set off towards the Bentley, smiling and waving, looking fabulous in dark Prada sunglasses and an Hermès scarf.

She noticed, out of the corner of her eye, that Milo was smiling and waving too and, to her chagrin, she heard some of the photographers calling, 'Milo, Milo, here!'

Stepping lightly into the car, her driver closed the door and Milo ran around to the other side. Grinning and waving he jumped nimbly in beside her.

The car sped off. Cleo turned to her trainer, lover and now she realised resentfully, potential co-star. She said sharply, 'Milo, please don't push yourself forward so, it's embarrassing. Nothing the public hate more than a pushy, fame-seeking person, you know? Be careful, you won't like it if they turn on you ... and they always do, particularly if you are not a proper star.'

Milo's face remained implacable. 'Of course, I'm sorry. I forgot my place, Cleo. Thank you for your advice – you are always just so ... right.'

Cleo looked out of the window, feeling uncomfortable – Milo had taken her criticism well, too well? Could she detect something in his tone, a little sarcasm perhaps? Oh, well, she thought, fuck it – she couldn't be worrying about his hurt feelings now. She must keep focused. Cool. Determined. Victorious.

Max waved until the car had disappeared. Then, thanking the photographers, he turned to go inside.

His butler held the door open. As he stepped across his threshold, he heard an insolent voice call out, 'Hey, Max – c'mon, you old poof, give us something on Georgia, will ya? What was it then – they say she topped herself?'

Max turned to the journalist who had shouted at him. All trace of the genial husband had disappeared. The look he gave the man was one of pure unadulterated revulsion. He held the man's gaze – his eyes were as sharp as a knife, shafting deep into the man's soul. The journalist turned away, almost ashamed.

Max walked briskly into his sublimely beautiful, empty house and his butler closed the door.

Turning to him, Max said, 'Jamie, OK – so! Let's get this party started!'

Jamie smiled broadly at his beloved boss. 'Yes, sir!'

Jamie was happy to see the back of Milo – too much competition for the boss's favour. He didn't trust that bugger at all.

Elliot opened the French windows. It was a lovely afternoon. Gazing up he saw soft clouds scudding across the sky, and felt it was a crime to be cooped up inside. Turning to Lana he asked if she wanted to bring Willow out into the garden, where the baby could play on the grass.

Kate overheard his suggestion when she walked in. 'Sorry, Elliot, no one is allowed into the garden. Especially not the baby. There are photographers' lenses trained on every bit of outside space, so we have to be extra careful, extra vigilant.' She looked at Lana. 'Have you seen Miss Spender?'

Zelda arrived on cue. 'Kate! I've been searching for you everywhere. Mr Dark is arriving for a briefing at six. Please show him into the office. Get Shona on the phone, I need all the designers to get their stuff over here tomorrow to sort out the um, you know, clothes for …' Zelda suddenly felt a bit embarrassed in front of Elliot. Even she realised that sorting out designer clothes for a funeral seemed frivolous, irreverent. She blushed slightly.

Lana spotted this immediately; cannily, she could see that she wasn't the only one susceptible to Elliot's charms.

Kate was too discombobulated by her furtive session with Valentine to notice anything. 'I'll get straight onto it.' She left the room with a little skip. Elliot noted that she had great legs. Hadn't she been wearing black tights when he'd seen her earlier? Now her legs were bare. He noticed these things.

Well, well, he thought. He wondered who? Hardly surprising really – everyone under siege in this place, day in, day out, with almost nothing to do . . . He had observed this before; the very, very rich and the very, very poor had always had that in common. 'Nothing else to do but drink and fight and screw', wasn't that how the song went?

Lana had gathered up Lamby and all the baby's things as she was leaving the Great Hall. When she brushed past Zelda, Elliot couldn't help noticing the contrast between these two beautiful women: one darkly, richly exciting; the other, charmingly innocent, pale and pure. Both very, very desirable . . . Oh, yeah! Elliot thought, there it was – the stir-crazy thing was getting to him already.

As Lana left the room a strong shaft of sunlight suddenly burst through the stained-glass windows and illuminated Zelda in a spectacular multi-coloured light. Mother Nature was drawing Elliot's attention dramatically back to her and he felt weak with desire.

Zelda was, momentarily, blinded by the light. So she missed the unmistakably lascivious look in her ex-lover's eye. By the time she had stepped out of that dazzling natural spotlight, Elliot had composed himself.

'Elliot, has anyone shown you your room? Where you're sleeping?' Zelda was messaging on her phone as she spoke. She went to sit down at the island, but accidentally brushed against Elliot as she passed. They felt a familiar, hard little shock of desire, which they both chose to ignore.

'Yes, Zelda, thanks, it's lovely – very, very luxurious in fact –

not at all what I'm used to. Thank you for letting me stay. Um, look. It's not easy, even after all this time ...'

Zelda didn't look at him, just raised her hand in the international sign language for 'enough already!'

Elliot instantly changed tack, with a sigh. 'Well, I've still got a bit of work to do so I'll see you later – at Max's?'

'Yes, yes, later – great,' Zelda answered vaguely, 'great.' Her attention was completely taken up by a message and Elliot knew he was dismissed.

Zelda was pleased with herself. She had just read the charming, informative and helpful e-mail reply from the devoted Dr D. Maybe this DNA thing could be sorted quite easily after all. Contacts, she thought, that's all you needed really to get on – and a bit of star-fucking-induced loyalty often went the rest of the way. Excellent. She was well on course to get the household and its inhabitants back to normal. The idea of being lumbered with those children for any length of time had made her feel quite panicked. And having Elliot under her roof was ... well, what was it? Torture, yes, that's what it was – fucking torture.

Kate stuck her head round the door. 'Miss Spender, the masseur is here – I have sent him up.'

'OK, I'm on my way.' Zelda slipped gracefully off the stool and disappeared upstairs to her personal spa, her salon.

Jake found the Great Hall empty when he came down moments later. He wandered aimlessly into the vast space, breathing in the heavily flower-scented air. He thought how ironic it was that this place – their home – had been built as a sanctuary for a multitude of lost souls. He imagined all the hundreds, no, surely tens of thousands, of people who must've knelt here and asked for comfort or salvation. Now here he sat, alone, and the scale and history of this vaulted room just made him feel overwhelmingly small, sad and lonely.

God's was all too much – it really wasn't suitable for this sort of use, as a home. Since the family had come to live here nothing had seemed to go right, at least not for him anyway. He felt cursed, overcome by a dark sense of doom.

He slumped down into his favourite chair, and thought back to his life with Zelda before the boys were born.

They had fallen spectacularly in love the moment they met, on the set of his hit show, 'Wild World'. Zelda and Jake were in heaven. Neither could believe their luck. They were both on a roll, at the very beginning of their successful careers, beautiful and full of joy and laughter. All they had needed to complete their happiness was this fabulous love affair. And so it arrived, with perfect timing . . . and they immediately bound themselves together, joyously high on their love and a relatively small amount of pharmaceuticals.

Zelda soon moved in with him at his favourite home, the Mews, just off Gloucester Road. Georgia had been away on tour at the time, so they had the house to themselves.

By the time Georgia had returned from her US tour, they were already married.

Georgia was thrilled. Not least because she had been worried how to break her own news to her beloved brother.

She'd got married too. To her wildly badly behaved lead guitarist, Nat Cole.

So the Mews was sold and before the first 'Wild World' series finished filming Jake found them a wonderful house in Milner Street in Chelsea – Zelda, and life, had been sweet ...

Jake fell asleep, the sudden unexpected sleep of a dipsomaniac, with a tiny smile on his face.

Elliot was surprised to find Dusty and Ed in the library. They were giggling and messing about on Jake's computer.

'Hey, hey, you two – I'm working on that! What're you up to?' He tried to say it nicely, but really, he asked himself, what the fuck did they think they were doing?

Dusty and Ed looked slightly guilty.

'Come on, move over! Anyway, shouldn't you be getting ready for supper? Having a bath? Or whatever,' Elliot suggested, hopefully.

'A bath?' Ed exclaimed. 'Fuck, no way – I had one, um ...'

Not for a while by the look of him.

'Well, I had one this morning and Scarlett is coming over.' Dusty looked at her watch. 'Shit! Any minute now.'

'Maybe I will have a bath.' Ed made for the door.

'Ed! You said you weren't going to drool over her,' Dusty admonished.

'I'm not!'

'Well, please don't, it's so embarrassing, and she doesn't like it. People are always fawning all over her because of her dad.'

Elliot suddenly realised who Scarlett was. Her father's stratospheric fame made this lot look B list – well, almost.

The kids wandered out.

He sat down at the computer to finish posting his copy, studiously ignoring all the e-mails from other publications. Since Georgia's death he had been bombarded with requests to write the definitive 'My Life With Georgia Cole' article – the fees they were offering were eye-watering. But he had resisted the temptation of that capitulation when she was alive – so, no matter how broke he was, he remained adamant that he would not crack now.

The Kabul article was weak and he knew it. He sent a covering e-mail to his editor, explaining the reason for his sudden return to London, hoping to evoke sympathy and to discourage any requests for rewrites. He didn't feel up to writing now. A bit jet-lagged and still in shock, perhaps? He longed to go upstairs and fall into that heavenly bed. They would be the first proper sheets he'd slept between in a long while.

But supper at Max's was always a three-line whip. Elliot looked down at the clothes he was wearing that Jake had lent him earlier; they would have to do. He glanced at himself in the exquisite 18th-century looking glass that hung between the two largest bookcases on the long wall. He looked crumpled, a bit scruffy, not by his own standards, but for Max's dinner party, certainly. Perhaps he should just nip along and see if he could borrow something else from Jake.

Elliot wasn't completely sure where the master bedroom

was, but set off along the wide landing. He passed a cabinet containing a frozen head made of blood, which he recognised as a Marc Quinn. He shook his head in disbelief. Knocking on a couple of doors, receiving no reply, he opened them, stuck his head round and discovered a vast spare bedroom: empty. A laundry cupboard: also empty.

Then he came to a massive pair of double doors. He hesitated. As there was no response to his knock, he opened one of them a fraction and nearly fell into the room when Zelda pulled the door wide open from the other side. She stepped back and exclaimed, 'Oh Elliot!' She was wrapped in a tiny white towel. Her naked skin glowed with massage oils, she looked soft and slippery.

'Christ, you gave me a shock – I was looking for Jake.' She smiled.

'Um, me too! Just wanted to ask him if I could borrow some clothes for tonight.'

'Oh, right, come in – his dressing room is down here.' She turned and led him down a dark passage, lined with Allen Jones drawings. Elliot was barely aware of his surroundings, he was so distracted by the riveting image of Zelda's sinuous back and long, agonisingly familiar legs. He felt an almost overwhelming desire to tackle her, to land her soft slithery body on the hard floor. Tear off that tiny towel ...

She flung open a door, said casually, dismissively, 'There, help yourself – Jake won't mind, he's got far too much stuff anyway.' Which was fine coming from her, whose closet took up two normal-sized rooms.

Elliot recovered his composure, remembered where he was and who he was.

Zelda slithered off. Leaving the sensuous, heady whiff of luxury and privilege in her wake.

Elliot suddenly felt very much like the poor relation. Which he indisputably was. It served to remind him how truly deluded the idea of Zelda and him was; his ardour cooled as suddenly as it had been aroused. That he'd ever thought they could have had any kind of future together – utter madness! God forbid, he could've found himself in Jake's position. Except worse – at least Jake had had an acclaimed and successful early career. What was his own achievement? he asked himself glumly.

Elliot felt secure and confident when he was in the field doing his job but here he was just another hack. OK, he realised, a different sort to the ones that terrorised this family. But a hack nonetheless, not esteemed here, not really wanted here either. Just a mess of uncomfortable associations, for everyone, and then there was Dusty and a baby, for fuck's sake! He felt the return of that familiar little germ of panic in his gut.

And so, here he was, about to pilfer his ex-brother-in-law's clothes. Just like he had tried to pilfer his wife. Nice. Although borrowing Jake's clothes perhaps wasn't too beastly on the scale of his past crimes.

Elliot scoured the perfect sandalwood shelves that reeked of money and were laden with hundreds of neatly laundered shirts. He was just helping himself to a particularly beautiful Prada shirt, when Jake walked in.

'Oh! Hi, Jake – sorry, hope you don't mind – um, Zelda said . . .' Elliot looked very sheepish.

'No, no! God, no – of course it's fine. Just help yourself to anything you need any time. I've got far too much of this shit anyway. Trousers are here – and shoes, what size?' Jake was a generous man.

'Eleven.'

'Yay! We are the same size – well, waddya know. Almost interchangeable!'

Elliot cringed inside. 'Thanks, Jake – so much. I really appreciate this.' Elliot grabbed the gear and pushed off.

He was almost hyperventilating.

CHAPTER THIRTEEN

Max's butler, Jamie, was in his element. There was nothing he adored more than arranging a party. Max always left everything to him, organising the caterers, choosing the flowers, the menu, the cocktails – and his favourite bit: choosing the waiters. He decided not to go too wild this evening. It was meant to be a casual, subdued mourning supper after all. So he had kept everything simple.

The first guests to arrive were a very famous film producer and his lovely wife, followed by Zelda's friend and sometime walker, Rocco – an actor who had been huge in the '90s but whose career as a leading man waned when he was outed by a disgruntled ex-boyfriend. He arrived with Shona – Zelda's stylist and best girlfriend. They were followed by a group of teenagers, most of them instantly recognisable as the sons and daughters of an international group of rich and/or famous parents.

They were all offered drinks as they arrived, from trays held by the most stunningly beautiful male waiters. Then Jamie showed them through to the Black Drawing Room where Max regaled everyone with funny stories about Cleo and her Everest adventure, an idea that he found hugely amusing even before it had really begun.

The Black Drawing Room looked its best at night. The walls and woodwork were all painted matt black. The furniture was dark too – the only splashes of colour came from a gruesome Francis Bacon triptych and a bookcase, where all the books had been covered in red fly-leaves, each with its title and author meticulously printed in black. Giant bowls of white orchids were lit from above and the room throbbed with decadent, luxurious beauty.

When Max's interior decorator had suggested a black room, Cleo was aghast – she had preferred peachy tones that, she felt, flattered her complexion. But the decorator reassured her that the dark walls and fabulous lighting would have the same effect as the lighting in Tramp, the old Jermyn Street nightclub where Cleo had spent many late nights looking ravishing, and so she agreed to give it a try. She was thrilled with the result and she always liked to conduct any press meetings and interviews in that room, confident in the knowledge that not only did it make her look her very best, but it also managed to be quite daunting, intimidating even, in its dark grandeur.

She always liked to intimidate her interviewers a bit, keep them on the back foot – it made it so much easier to bowl them over with her wit and charm. Which she could turn on, or off, with the same disconcerting effect as the strobe light on the dancefloor at Tramp.

*

But Cleo had gone. She was on her way to Kathmandu.

It had already been quite a challenging day for her. She and Milo barely spoke on the flight. The production company had placed him in First Class too, completely unnecessarily she felt. On their arrival at the airport they were greeted by a young girl from the production team and Cleo found her off-hand, almost rude. Then a very erratic driver had taken them all on the longest, most dangerous and frightening road she had ever been on, for hours and hours (actually half an hour) with the production girl and Milo chattering inanely, until she was almost mad with boredom.

She realised Milo had flirted the entire way with the horse-faced production girl just to annoy her. It had worked. By the time they reached the hotel in Kathmandu late that night, Cleo was absolutely spitting with rage. She stormed off to bed without even acknowledging Milo. He smiled to himself and spent an energetic night with the production assistant, who he didn't think looked horse-faced at all.

The following morning he knocked on Cleo's door. She let him in.

'Cleo, are you OK? I have just heard from the director. He wants us to meet in the foyer in an hour. The Mayor of Kathmandu wants to show you round and the producers want it filmed.'

Cleo had woken up in a better mood and the sight of Milo this morning, in all his handsome glory, had cheered her up.

Yesterday was gone, forgotten. Such was the capriciousness of Cleo's nature. She was going to be filmed in the romantic market places of Kathmandu and she had just the thing to wear, a Matthew Williamson beaded flowing thing – very 70s, perfect for this old hippy trail. She couldn't wait to get started. She could be up and dressed in full makeup in an hour. She skipped into the somewhat rudimentary bathroom – she prided herself on being accommodating about such things. She wasn't spoilt at all! She called out gaily to Milo, 'Great, I won't be long – tell them I'll be ready in an hour.'

Three hours later she arrived in the lobby. Everyone rushed about and gushed over her, 'How beautiful, how fit, how fabulous . . .', until she felt quite bucked up. She could already tell that this show was going to give her career the boost it needed. She could always tell, straight away, when something felt right. She had very finely tuned instincts about these things.

CHAPTER FOURTEEN

The previous evening at dusk, the occupants of God's had trickled glamorously across the lawn to Max's supper.

It was warm and the garden looked beautiful, laden with blossom, and a vast magnolia was in glorious early bloom. Zelda looked ravishing in a tight black McQueen dress; she had decided to wear his clothes in loving memory of him too, although she had only met him twice.

As she stepped out into the garden she wobbled on her high red Charlotte Olympia platform shoes. Elliot had to hold his hand out to steady her. He had forgotten that she was sometimes quite clumsy and felt a small stab of compassion for her; she never, ever showed it but he knew that there was huge vulnerability behind the coping façade.

They had both been a bit embarrassed when they found they had come down to the Great Hall before everyone else. So, rather than wait for the others, in uncomfortable silence or strained small talk, Zelda had suggested they go over to Max's and get a drink.

As Elliot followed Zelda through the garden, he tried to keep his eyes away from her tiny waist and her rather jolly, bouncy walk, which he had always found amusing, charming and frankly very sexy. Oh God, he thought to himself, why couldn't he stop this? He needed to stop following her about; that was the thing, but he wasn't doing it deliberately – fate somehow just kept throwing him behind her. He resolved not to talk to her or be drawn to her in any way for the rest of the evening.

So Zelda was slightly hurt when Elliot moved away, without a word, as soon as they got to Max's. But she soon found herself sidetracked by Rocco and Shona when they dragged her into a corner to ply her with questions about Georgia, bombarding her with their whats, whys and wherefores, most of which Zelda hadn't honestly given any thought to at all, and so couldn't give them any satisfactory answers – much to her two friends' annoyance.

The thing was, Zelda was never really very curious about other peoples' lives, or indeed death, in this case. It was only the effect they had on her life that interested her. Not that she was selfish or anything, she always told herself; she just had a lot to think about, worry about, always so much to do, so much to be – being Zelda Spender took a lot of concentration and energy. She wasn't going to waste any of it thinking about things that didn't directly concern her.

She noticed Dusty arriving with Ed and was reminded of something that really did concern her – her mission on this particular evening.

DNA.

She was to gather specimens from any likely, or frankly unlikely, candidates and send them off to Dr D, a.s.a.p.

Zelda was pleased with her plan. She didn't really expect to find the baby's father among her friends and acquaintances but she was still chuffed with her idea, excited to be playing the sleuth. It appealed hugely to the calculating side of her nature – she might discover something interesting, something that no one else would know, even something useful? She was quite excited.

The Black Drawing Room was beginning to get very full of people, not quite the tiny, quiet supper that Max had promised. Dusty and Ed were talking to Scarlett or rather Dusty was talking and Ed was just opening and closing his mouth like a fish. Valentine was in a corner laughing with Charlie and Art.

When Johnny arrived with Lily, Valentine noticed they still had the schoolgirl in tow. He was relieved that India had a night shoot and couldn't come to the party. Could've been fucking awkward, he thought.

Lily was looking irresistible. She wore a tiny kimono held casually with a wide leather belt. Her brown legs were bare, her hair was loose and dishevelled. Her kohl-smudged eyes caught his for a moment then she looked away.

Dusty looked on in horror. She couldn't believe that Johnny could be so heartless, to bring that cow Lily to the dinner – the creature who had destroyed her mother's happiness ... and now, what was happening? Her eyes swung between Valentine and Lily ... she looked on helplessly as Valentine left Charlie and Art mid-sentence. He crossed the room and pulled lightly at Lily's belt as he brushed past her and went on, out into the hall.

He felt Lily follow him as he went upstairs. He didn't look back, but disappeared into a bathroom on the second floor. She followed him in and without saying a word they kissed, almost drawing blood as their teeth and lips clashed. He noticed her hands were shaking slightly as she undid a diamond phial she was wearing around her neck; she snorted its contents then pushed it under Valentine's nose.

She was the most thrilling, filthy, beautiful girl he had ever met and he wanted to fuck her all night. Sadly it was not to be because a) he was too excited and b) no sooner had he come and he was about to suggest they start again than someone knocked on the door.

They were both relieved to find it was only the schoolgirl looking for Lily and her drugs. But then Valentine felt annoyed, as his interest was entirely focused on Lily and he didn't feel like a rerun of their threesome now. Anyway, he knew it was a bit risky – after all, the house was full of people. He ran his hands through his hair as he looked admiringly at his reflection in the bathroom mirror. The sight of his own gorgeous face momentarily distracted him and cheered him up.

He did up his Tom Ford belt. 'I'm going back down,' he informed the girls, his voice cool. Lily stared blankly at him and then she smiled enigmatically. Valentine was even more pissed off when he realised Lily was not going to follow him – she had started kissing the schoolgirl instead! He was used to girls following him everywhere, doing his bidding, and so he felt quite pissed off as he stomped off downstairs, alone.

He was met by Dusty at the bottom of the stairs. She looked very young and pretty in a vintage sequined tunic over jeans. He failed to notice the furious look on her face – he was distracted by the fact that she was wearing his scarf around her neck.

'Hey, that's mine, you little thief, my favourite scarf.' He went to pull it off her neck, just a bit too roughly.

Dusty watched him closely as she said, 'Yeah, I thought you might want it back, I found it – at Mum's.'

Valentine felt himself go cold. He grabbed Dusty, hugged her to him, squeezed her a little too tightly, spoke too fast. 'Thank you, little coz, I wondered where it had got to.' His mind was racing frantically and he hoped the coke would come up with something for him – it was meant to sharpen your fucking mind after all. But nothing – he couldn't think of an explanation at all. Shit, she was starting to wriggle.

Then inspiration struck. 'I must've left it there when I borrowed the Mini last week.' He smiled sweetly. 'Thanks, Dusty.' He wandered off, pleased with himself.

Dusty felt sick with dread, having been certain Valentine had been wearing the scarf on his way into the premiere – she had checked the paparazzi photos online earlier that evening, and sure enough there he was, posing on the red carpet with the scarf slung loosely around his neck. So, he must have been to her house on that fateful night – why? And why would he lie about it? She felt herself begin to unravel. This was unbearable. Could the boy she had always adored have supplied her mother with the drugs that killed her? She couldn't bear to think about it – it wasn't possible – surely? And now he was fooling around with that slapper Lily, it made her want to weep.

Confused and heartbroken, Dusty grabbed a large cocktail from a tray held by a charmingly fit young waiter. She didn't register him at all – just downed the drink, put the glass back on the tray and took another.

If Dusty hadn't been so preoccupied she might have noticed that the waiter, Alex, had been instantly, totally stricken by her. His eyes followed her longingly as she tottered into the darkness of the drawing room, which was now filled with noise, smoke and people.

Alex felt weirdly anxious for Dusty. He knew who she was of course, but she seemed even more of a fragile girl than her press pictures showed. He realised too that she was probably only a couple of years younger than him. Alex thought she looked like a beautiful, dishevelled angel and, as she entered the Black Drawing Room, he had an unsettling vision of her disappearing through the gates of hell. Then he found himself imagining rescuing her – pulling her back into the real world ... But she hadn't even noticed him, he admitted to himself, glumly. He had been doing these 'waiter' jobs for long enough to know that you became invisible to everyone, so he shouldn't have been surprised. Anyway, a girl like that probably didn't want to be rescued, particularly not by a boy like him. He went to restock his tray as more guests arrived.

Supper was what Max described as 'a moveable feast' and he gaily summoned everyone in to help themselves.

The vast dining room was looking stunning. Max was pleased. He thought that Jamie really had outdone himself tonight. The 'little' supper was laid out on the huge dining-room table. The food had been themed to match the decoration of the room, which had dramatic blood red walls and black woodwork. The vast candelabra were filled with white candles, which bathed the room in a rich, romantic glow.

The food was predominantly red and black. There were huge trays of lobster and fillets of beef – cooked to perfection, black on the outside, livid red within. Smoked salmon and caviar. Tomato and red pepper salads and vast dishes of pasta – black, made with squid ink. This was a particular favourite of Max's and was regularly flown in, especially for him, from Harry's Bar in Venice. Even the bread had been made black by the brilliant chef. There were also huge piles of fruit – more as decoration than anything. Watermelons, straw-berries, peaches, raspberries ... if it was red or black and edible, it was there.

Not that anyone ever ate much on these occasions, but it was the show that was the thing – the spectacle. It was very camp indeed, and Max was thrilled.

Jamie was such a treasure and Max had really enjoyed their time alone together earlier that afternoon; he had forgotten how uncomplicated things could be without ...

'Max – this looks amazing, you are brilliant.' Zelda's remark to her father froze on her lips when she saw Lucien crossing the room, heading towards them – nodding a cursory greeting to everyone as he passed.

'Max, Zelda.' He kissed her coldly, on both cheeks, then said pointedly to Max, 'Thanks for inviting me, Zelda didn't mention this little get-together when I saw her earlier!'

'I didn't know about it myself till after you'd left this afternoon.' Zelda looked innocently at him.

Lucien didn't appear convinced as he turned coldly away from her and made a beeline for Dusty and her beautiful friend Scarlett, who were languishing decoratively on a huge black velvet sofa. Ed was hovering near them, half-on, half-off a seat cushion; he was trying to pluck up the courage to speak to Scarlett when Lucien rudely plonked himself down in between them. He introduced himself to Scarlett, instantly spotting that both girls were already quite drunk – exactly how he liked them, although Dusty appeared a little too far gone. In fact, she looked as if she might be sick. He turned to Ed and quietly but firmly suggested that he needed to take his cousin home.

Ed wasn't happy at the prospect of leaving Scarlett, just when he was about to pull. But he could see that Dusty was getting pretty out of it. He could just whizz her back to God's, quickly hand her over to Lana, it wouldn't take long . . .

So he reluctantly dragged Dusty to her feet and, putting his arm around her waist, he half-carried her to the garden doors. He managed to get her down the steps – she was protesting weakly but incoherently. She slipped on the last step, twisted and fell out of his hands. He looked up to find a waiter trying to help him to pull her back onto her feet. Alex had seen them both leaving and had gone to their rescue. Surprised by how very light she was, Alex lifted Dusty up and carried her.

Looking at Ed he asked, 'Where to?'

'Oh, um, thanks, it's just across the garden – here – um, follow me.' Ed was relieved not to have to cope with this alone.

When they reached God's Lana was in the kitchen. She was shocked. 'What is gone wrong with Dusty?'

'She's just had a bit too much – you know . . . she's very sad. I think she needs to go to bed . . .' Ed looked anxious.

Elliot appeared. 'There you are, Lucien told me Dusty was sick.'

'No, she hasn't been sick,' Ed said.

With that, Alex gently let Dusty's legs down. He held her upright for a moment then she leant forward slightly, and was sick all over Elliot's shoes. Or Jake's shoes, to be precise. Elliot was completely unfazed; he had had far worse things on his shoes, and so he leant down unflinchingly and flicked the Tod's off. Then he took Dusty from Alex, thanked him for his help, and carried his daughter upstairs, followed by a concerned Lana. Dusty had begun to cry.

Ed and Alex looked at each other, smiled shyly, and headed off back to Max's. As they crossed the garden, Ed said, 'Thanks for that – she's had a bad time . . .'

Alex replied, 'No probs. I've done work experience on the "Booze Bus" so that was like – nothing!'

'Respect, dude!' Ed looked at Alex and grinned.

But, back at Devil's, Ed was very disappointed to discover

that Scarlett had already left. He was told that she had been taken home by her father's security guy, who had not liked the look of the dodgy old character who was talking to her. 'So,' he thought crossly, 'I missed my chance, shit! Her own security guard?' Ed had been wondering about the strange guy in the corner watching them, but had just thought he was a bit of a weirdo.

He went to join some of his other friends and took them down to the screening room with some drinks, where they had their own little party away from the not particularly prying eyes of the rest of his family. He mostly kept his friends away from God's and Devil's – it somehow seemed dreadfully uncool that his family could behave far worse than most of his peers could ever have imagined behaving in their wildest, most rebellious, dreams.

Meanwhile, Zelda was attempting to gather evidence. Johnny was her main target. She had planned to use the claw ring to part him from some of his long locks. But when she had tried to kiss him earlier, he had ducked away with a maddening, 'Whoa!' She had decided to wait until he got really wasted – always only a matter of time – before she tried again.

Then Jake had accosted her, furious that Lucien was there. She tried to placate him, promised that she had not invited him, Max had. She swore she hadn't known he was going to be there. But Jake was not to be reasoned with, he stormed off and started knocking back cocktails as if his life depended on it. Zelda hoped nobody had noticed this ugly little scene. There were a few strangers in the room who could mention to the press that all was not well between Britain's Favourite Couple. But they had been very discreet – they were used to unpleasant exchanges delivered through smiling, clenched teeth.

Elliot had watched this evidence of marital disharmony with interest.

Zelda went back to her friends. Realising she hadn't seen any real food for days, she ate and drank too much, the evening flew by and she suddenly realised that Johnny and Lily were making a move to leave. She walked up behind him and put her hand on his shoulder. 'Johnny, I just wanted to say . . .' He turned and she felt the claw snag in his hair, result! She grinned hugely. 'Just wanted to say, glad you're here . . . sorry about earlier.' To her surprise, Johnny fell into her arms and burst into tears. 'I jush can' believe she's gone, it's jush so fucking horrible.' He hugged her tight and then turned, snuffling and shuffling, to be led away by Lily.

Zelda felt an unfamiliar surge of warmth for Johnny as she looked down at the ring, happy to see the few strands of hair that she needed. Mind you, she thought, not so sure of Willow's chances with that little slag Lily as her stepmother. She waved gaily at Lily as she left, sending her an insincere little air-kiss.

As she passed Lucien she noticed that he looked distinctly clammy. He was taking off his jacket, leaning in to talk to a very young girl whom Zelda didn't recognise. As she passed she took his jacket from him. 'Let me get that hung up for you, darling,' she said solicitously.

Lucien hardly seemed to notice her. 'Yeah, thanks.' He turned his attention back to the Schoolgirl.

As Zelda walked into the hall she noticed a dark hair on the collar of Lucien's light-coloured jacket. She thought for a second then decided, yes, why not? After all, they went back a long way – Lucien and Georgia. She picked the sample carefully from the collar and holding it firmly she dumped his coat on a chair and scampered back across the lawn to God's.

In her office she got a piece of paper from her private safe and stuck on the hair from the ring, marking it exhibit B. She had added it to exhibit A, the blond hair. Then she added Lucien's as exhibit C. And what a C ... he is, she thought to herself.

She had another piece of paper, which she would keep for her eyes only, marked with the key: A. Milo, B. Johnny, C. Lucien. She intended to make bloody sure that the DNA results would be anonymous to everyone but her.

She was enjoying herself. She felt quite powerful for a moment as she placed the papers back in her safe and spun the lock with a flourish. Then she put back the picture, which disguised the safe. It was a small, rare screenprint by Andy Warhol.

Upstairs Zelda almost bumped into Elliot as he was coming downstairs, followed by Lana. She glanced at them both with barely concealed hostility.

Elliot looked slightly flustered. 'Oh ... Lana was just helping me with Dusty – she has had too much to drink, I'm afraid, she was sick, fell over ...'

Lana giggled.

Zelda turned on her. 'Well you had better stay with her then, Lana. We don't want her choking in her sleep, do we? Off you go, thank you.' She spoke lightly but firmly; she knew how to deal with her staff when they got uppity. 'Oh, and Lana – check on the baby too please.'

'I already did it,' Lana replied, slightly petulantly.

'Well, do it again, thank you, Lana,' said Zelda, as she stalked off.

Lana knew she was dismissed. She stomped upstairs. That woman is such a bitch, she thought. Not for the first time.

Elliot was reminded of the other Zelda, the one that his exciting recent proximity to her had made him forget: the rude, imperious Zelda. He watched her as she poured a neat vodka and drank it in one shot. She looked at him defiantly and waved the bottle at him. 'Want one?'

'No, Zelda, thanks but no.' He looked at her disapprovingly and left, through the garden doors, to return to the party.

Zelda made a little hissing noise, and knocked back another vodka. Jake made her jump when he appeared behind her and said, 'Just passed Elliot in the garden, having a nice cosy little chat were you, reminiscing about the good old days?'

'What good old days would those be, Jake, eh? What good old days? I don't remember any at all. Just an endless succession of fucked up old days I'd say.' Zelda was furious and quite pissed.

'Have another drink, why don't you?' Jake suggested provocatively.

'Have another drink, me? Have another drink? *You* have another fucking drink.' She threw the vodka bottle at him and unexpectedly it hit him smartly on the forehead and shattered.

He fell to the floor with a loud groan. Zelda stumbled across the room to where he lay bleeding from his gashed brow. 'Oh, my God, Jake, Jake.' She burst into tears.

Jake realised she must be very drunk indeed – she never cried. He started to laugh. 'Ouch, you fucking bitch. Get me a doctor. My fabulous face is ruined, ruined.' And he laughed again.

Then Elliot was there. Mopping up the blood, wrapping Jake's head in a dishcloth.

Zelda snuffled gratefully, 'I thought you'd gone back to the party.'

'I just went back to get my coat,' Elliot replied, as he calmly turned away from Zelda's mascara-ravaged face and glanced down at Jake. '*Your* coat, Jake mate, actually – your coat now covered with your blood.' He grimaced, suddenly embarrassed. 'Sorry, shit – I'm afraid there was an accident with your shoes too. Dusty was sick on them. I'm sorry – hopeless.' He smiled apologetically.

Jake looked up at him and teased, 'Christ, if you're like this in Chelsea, what the fuck were you like in Kabul!'

They all giggled, tension dispersed.

Ed came back and made coffee for everyone. The evening had ended – they were all feeling a bit tired and overemotional.

Valentine sloped in, looking uncharacteristically subdued.

They all laughed at Jake in his bloodstained turban.

Elliot watched fascinated as the family gently fitted back into its own fucked-up normality. Zelda surprised him by kissing him goodnight, only lightly, on one cheek, but even that had been uncomfortable. Her ring caught accidently in his hair – he tried not to flinch, didn't want to seem like he had flinched from her kiss. But he saw something flicker in her eyes as she walked away. Something secretive, smug almost, what was that? He felt apprehensive again. Nothing with Zelda was ever quite what it seemed.

Everyone went up to bed, on seemingly rather good terms.

A few cuts and bruises – but nothing too bad. It could, and probably would, be much worse.

Max was still enjoying himself over at Devil's. Most of the guests had left. He noticed Lucien leaving with the Schoolgirl. 'Going to make sure she gets home safely,' he'd said.

Yes, indeed, I'm sure, Max had thought sarcastically.

Needless to say there were still a couple of very attractive young boys messing about in his own drawing room, so he was hardly in a position to disapprove of Lucien. Jamie was sorting them out. Max realised that he ought to get him to check how old they were. Not that he had always been so fastidious about such things. But these days he had learnt to be far more careful. Sometimes he longed for the '70s when naïvety and legal complacency led to far greater licence. But after Jonathan King – a perfectly charming person, Max had always found – things were never going to be quite the same.

The caterers and their staff had left. So it was just himself, Jamie and the boys – home alone. 'What larks,' he thought gaily, and no more Cleo for ages . . . he couldn't have felt more thrilled.

CHAPTER FIFTEEN

When Zelda leapt out of bed the following morning she was in a good mood. She and Jake had somehow managed to make some kind of drunken, damaged love before falling into a blissful un-narcotic-induced sleep. It had been good, the sex and the sleep. Although, she had to confess, she did have a tiny hangover. She couldn't wait to get downstairs to get on with her project.

She had added her sample from Elliot to the safe before she went to bed. She knew she was playing with fire when she decided to add him to the mix. There was one more sample she wanted to include. It had just dawned on her that she could get it from a hairbrush. Why hadn't she thought of that before all the crazy claw-ring stuff! Oh well, it had worked, hadn't it? None of the candidates had been remotely suspicious. She really must get that ring fixed.

Zelda walked naked into her pale stone and glass wet-room. The hot water flowed generously over her perfect body. She lathered her thick, dark hair with the French shampoo that was sent to her by the most celebrated hairdresser in France. He mixed it just for her. Her very own special 'Zelda' shampoo. It gave her hair the lustrous lift and shine that made her the perfect model for the hair products of the American company that had her under such a hugely valuable contract, as the 'Face of Fabulous' for both their hair and makeup products. In fact, she hated their shampoo, never used it. They would be furious if they'd known. But they would never know.

Like they would never know that her 'lightly tanned' body was not from the 'Kiss of Fabulous' self tan, but was the result of quite a few sunbed sessions and a fake tan called 'Golden Glow'. What you saw was not necessarily what you got with Zelda. But she told the world she used the Fabulous products and, as far as she was concerned, she had more than fulfilled her obligations to them. God knew, they only paid her $2,000,000 a year and after tax that was ... well, not that much really. She did a lot for them – in fact she had a shoot for them later on today. She must get a move on ...

Zelda was surprised to find Kate already in the office when she got downstairs. The girl really did have the most extraordinary knack for being in the wrong place at the wrong time. Just when Zelda needed the office to herself, to get into the safe, there was bloody Kate.

Zelda had just retrieved the final sample from a hairbrush upstairs. She felt she was now in possession of everything she needed but she had to get Kate out of the way. She thought fast.

'Um, Kate. Could you be very kind and go to the chemist for me – I'll do a list.'

Kate would normally have suggested one of the housekeeping staff do the job, as she had so much to do in the office this morning. But actually she was longing to get out. She needed to mainline Starbucks and try to calm down. She needed to think about what had happened last night and decide what to do.

So she took the list from Zelda, grabbed some petty cash and left the office by the side door. She would still have to run the gauntlet of the press, but they knew she was nobody – they had an instinct for these things. No cries of Kate, Kate, Kate, here, here, here. No indeed, not for her. She was nobody, and this morning she felt like nothing too.

As she left the house and all the madness that surrounded it, she suddenly felt an overwhelming desire to run. Once she got past the gate she started, and then found she couldn't stop running.

She couldn't stop crying either.

She finally ran out of tears and puff, just outside Starbucks. Going in and getting her coffee calmed her, made her feel part of the real world again and all the comfort that entailed.

Kate had made a huge mistake last night – she could see that now.

She had worked very late, while everyone was at Max's. She was about to go home when she found herself wondering why she was doing so. She knew India was working on a night shoot.

She had foolishly thought that Valentine would be pleased to return to his bed and find her there waiting for him, naked, ready and very, very willing. She had showered and dried her hair then jumped into his bed and, almost immediately, she had fallen fast asleep.

She woke to find Valentine's face very close to hers. She'd smiled at him, but he hadn't smiled back. As she blinked at the light she could see that he was furious, almost incandescent with rage. Her heart had stopped – she didn't know what to do. She moved to get up, intending to leave. She tried to tell him she was sorry, she had obviously made a mistake.

But he pushed her back onto the bed, roughly. He turned off the lights and she could hear him tearing off his clothes. He said nothing but she could feel his rage all around them. She froze with fear. Her blood ran even colder when she felt him grab her hair hard, jerking her neck painfully. He said, through clenched teeth, 'Right, you stupid little whore, you asked for this . . .'

By the morning Kate didn't love Valentine any more. She didn't love herself much either.

Zelda was pleased with herself. She had managed to order a bike messenger to go straight to Dr D with her hair samples and the anonymous list. Now all she had to do was wait. He had told her that it might take a while for the results to come through. She had included a sample from Willow, which she had gleaned from the tiny little hairbrush in the baby's room – the feel of it had given her a jolt of nostalgia for her boys when they were small.

She considered herself a good mother, oh, a bit absent because of her movies and stuff. But she loved her boys, they were close – they had no secrets.

She sighed. What next? Kate seemed to be taking rather a long time at the chemist – typical.

She looked at her Smythson diary. Oh yes, the meeting at eleven with Georgia's new lawyers, Lucien and all his people. Fuck, how dull. She had already had to sign God knows what for Lucien last night. Zelda found all things legal and financial incredibly tiresome; she was like many of Lucien's clients in that respect. It was something that he relied upon. It gave him absolute licence to handle their affairs in any way he thought fit.

Lucien was feeling very hungover as he got dressed the morning after the party at Max's. He wasn't looking forward to the meeting at God's much either. He was frankly apprehensive about the things that might come up.

Georgia had employed some new lawyers a couple of months before she died, and they had been asking some awkward questions, demanding release of some of her funds. He had to find £2,000,000 for them last month! Christ only knew what she suddenly wanted that for. He knew they would be asking more questions, probably demanding more answers again today. He had briefed Craig Sanderson extensively. But still, having to defend his position in front of Zelda, another of his clients, might be problematic.

Georgia had always left all things financial to her agency's management department. They paid all her bills for her. Occasionally Lucien would have a 'little chat' with her about her spending. But, in reality, she had always lived well within her means. In fact, Georgia had always been, unbeknownst even to her, a very rich woman indeed.

In truth it wasn't her overspending that sometimes required a holdback, but the reckless investments of her trusted agent.

Looking at himself in the mirror he took a deep breath and pulled in his stomach. He liked what he saw: immaculate Richard James suit, Hermès tie, Tom Ford shoes. He looked powerful, confident. Nothing ahead that he couldn't handle, he reassured himself, everything would be fine.

He was annoyed to find Kristina in the kitchen, sullenly picking at breakfast, when he came downstairs. His mood quickly darkened again.

He had got home at 4a.m. and Kristina had not been pleased. She had locked him out of their bedroom – *his* fucking bedroom. He couldn't believe it. He had screamed at her through the door, called her every name under the sun. Totally lost it, in fact.

Lucky for her that she had locked him out, as he had got home in an ugly mood. He'd had a very unpleasant experience with a young but deeply ambitious actress, who had managed to secure a promise from him for a contract with Dark Artists.

The girl had taken some compromising pictures on her phone – he couldn't believe he hadn't seen that coming. But, in his defence, he had been coming at the time and therefore wasn't fully compos mentis. But she pointed out – when she e-mailed the pictures to him half an hour after he'd dropped her at her family home – she was under-age, so a contract seemed cheap at the price. Anyway, he thought ironically, she had all the qualities required of an actress: ruthlessness, beauty, cunning; she might turn out to be a bit of a money-spinner for him. He suddenly realised something; he didn't know her name.

He didn't take kindly to being blackmailed by an unscrupulous, vicious teenager. Blackmail was his speciality and it was a fucking unpleasant sensation having it turned on him. No-name Schoolgirl was going to be a pain in the arse, he could tell. 'Christ! Women are vile,' he thought bitterly.

Now Kristina wasn't talking to him, which suited him just fine, as he wasn't talking to her either. He grabbed his coffee from the coffee-maker and slurped it as he left the kitchen – burning his mouth horribly. He hurled the cup to the floor where it shattered. 'Bloody bedroom-stealing, pregnant bitch!' Lucien yelled furiously as he stormed from the house.

Kristina flinched, then she smiled and muttered sarcastically, 'Good morning, darling. Have a lovely day.'

CHAPTER SIXTEEN

Dusty woke up feeling dreadful. For a moment she didn't know where she was – the light was streaming through the curtains, blinding her. So she slipped out of bed and pottered into the bathroom. She looked terrible. Her makeup was all over her face, with black rivulets smudged down her cheeks. Her hair smelt of sick. She thought she might throw up again. Stepping into the shower she washed away everything from the night before. She felt her body being purified but her mind was in turmoil.

She had been planning to talk to her father about Georgia's death: to ask his advice about the drugs. She didn't know why she hadn't done it before – there just never seemed to be a good moment yesterday, they had hardly spent any time alone together.

Now things were different. Valentine had entered the equation and, much as she longed for it not to be so, it was. She now knew that he had been in her house the night Georgia died. He had lied; he hadn't admitted to her, or anyone, that he'd been there. He did a lot of drugs. Georgia had taken an overdose of drugs.

So, guilty then? But, guilty of what? Supplying her mother with the drugs that killed her? Was that possible? Surely he wasn't into that stuff so deep?

Dusty couldn't believe it, couldn't bear to think of it. But then she remembered how wasted he had been when he caught up with her, Charlie and Art later that night. It didn't look good for him. But it would have been an accident – he could never have meant Georgia any harm, could he? Would he? No, of course not. He wouldn't do anyone any harm on purpose. He was a good person, she knew that.

So should she talk to Elliot about it? Confront Valentine?

She felt so feeble, so alone. She missed Georgia so, so much. How could her mother have been so fucking stupid?

She cried, desperately, sadly, but no one could hear her. There was no one to comfort her. She felt, justifiably, very sorry for herself. When her tears had finally subsided and been washed away by the shower she managed to emerge, dry herself with one of the huge white Hermès towels and get dressed.

Then she put on a brave face and set off downstairs to look for her father and her precious baby sister.

She didn't have to look far. She found Lana in the Great Hall being given instructions by Zelda. Lana didn't look particularly happy today, but Zelda was chipper; she even kissed Dusty good morning.

'Dusty, darling, are you OK? Get something to eat, for God's sake, you look like a ghost. Take some toast outside. Your father is on the lawn with the baby.'

Thoughtful, motherly Zelda? This was new.

In fact, Dusty realised she was very hungry – she couldn't remember when she had last eaten anything. Lana handed her a plate of Marmite toast. 'Have this, I make it for Willow. Take to her, you have some too, I bring out more in minute.' She didn't smile. So Dusty smiled at her. 'Thanks, Lana, lovely, just what I feel like too.' And taking the plate she stepped out into the garden.

Elliot lay sprawled out on the grass. Willow was banging him on the arm with a hard plastic elephant.

'Dusty, sweetheart. Thank God you're here! Lana insisted I look after the baby but I don't think she likes me, she keeps hitting me – look!' Willow whacked him on the arm again and laughed.

'It's OK, Dad. That means she does like you!' Dusty sat down next to them and started munching her way through the toast. She offered a piece to her little sister.

'Yeah, OK, women hitting you – that's a term of endearment in this family, right? Makes sense actually ... chip off the old block, eh, Willow?' Elliot tickled the baby and she laughed again.

He looked over at the house and asked conspiratorially, 'Kate isn't around, is she? She said we weren't allowed out here, but I can't see any paps anywhere. It's ridiculous to be cooped up inside all the time.'

'Just because you can't see them, Dad, doesn't mean they're

not there. You of all people should know that.' Dusty spoke with her mouth full.

'Ah well, if they are there, what'll they get? Just a lovely family group.' Elliot smiled winningly at his daughter.

'Yes, we are a family, aren't we, Daddy? You, me, Willow ... you are going to let us all stay together, aren't you? We'll be all right – as soon as we can get back home, with you there, everything will be OK. Won't it?' Dusty looked at him anxiously.

'Everything's going to be fine. We will work it all out, don't you worry, darling.' Elliot lay back on the grass, the sun warm on his face. He didn't want to look at his daughter. She looked so fragile, sounded so needy this morning. He didn't want to make promises he couldn't keep. It was all far too soon for him to commit himself to anything. What did he know about children? Being a father? And things weren't bad for them here. After all Jake was their uncle and there was Lana to look after the baby. Plenty of money. They would be much better off here really, he told himself. Yet he wasn't convinced; he didn't feel good about the idea at all, in fact. Guilt felt horrible – he knew it well, he had felt it a lot, one way or another. Spent most of his life running away from it, not always successfully.

Zelda called out to them from the house. 'You'd better come in, everyone has arrived for the thingy meeting. Downstairs, in my office – now!'

God, Zelda could be bossy. There were so many things about her that Elliot had forgotten. Absence ... and all that. He got to his feet. He was wearing his old combats and a battered white Aertex shirt. His filthy clothes had been retrieved from his room by one of the housekeepers and they had been returned to him this morning: cleaned, repaired and pristine – almost unrecognisable as his. He felt more himself, comfortable in them. Less of a dick than he'd felt in Jake's immaculate gear.

Dusty had picked up the baby and was carrying her expertly on her narrow hip. She looked like a tiny teenage mother – which in a way, he realised, she was.

She handed the baby over to Lana and they went downstairs to see what Georgia had left them with. Elliot had an uneasy feeling that it might be messy. But nothing could have prepared him for what was about to come his way.

The boardroom table in Zelda's office had been cleared. Kate had returned just in time to prepare everything: coffee, water, biscuits, notepaper, pencils etc. Then, when everyone had settled around the table, she tactfully disappeared. Nobody noticed that she had been crying.

The occupants of the room had all been introduced to one another: Zelda, Jake, Elliot and Dusty were there for the family; Lucien and Craig Sanderson for Dark Artists and its accountants respectively. There were also the new lawyers, Hugo Peterson and Giles de Winter. No one had met either of them before.

Hugo and Giles were both good-looking, in their early forties, Zelda guessed. 'Trust Georgia,' she thought. 'Bravo!'

Hugo cleared his throat. 'Firstly, Giles and I would both like to say how very sorry we are for your loss. Miss Cole came to us two months ago, not only to draw up her will but for help with her financial affairs ...'

Zelda interrupted. 'But I thought she hadn't made a will, you told us she hadn't! Jake?' She looked questioningly at her husband.

'Well, Kate said she hadn't – she said she'd asked Lucien ...' Jake looked daggers at Lucien across the table.

Lucien answered impassively. 'She always categorically refused to make a will when we were looking after her legal affairs. She said it was unlucky – maybe she was right!' he smirked. 'I just assumed she would still have felt like that – I didn't know she'd make one the moment she snuck off to Patterson and Winko here. How could I?'

'Peterson de Winter, thank you, Mr Dark.' Hugo Peterson cleared his throat with dignity and authority. 'Miss Cole came to us concerned predominantly about her financial affairs. We did suggest she wrote her will and she did not have any objections. It was drawn up with due diligence and if you would like us to begin, perhaps I should start with reading it to you now. It is the normal form in these circumstances,' Hugo said seriously.

Handsome but pompous, Zelda thought to herself, and said impatiently, 'Gosh, yes, please do read it. We haven't got all day.'

She felt Elliot glance at her somewhat disapprovingly. Jake was staring at Lucien quite menacingly. They should just get on with it. How complicated could it be?

Well, quite complicated, as it happened.

Georgia had left almost everything to her two children, Dusty and Willow: the house in Hollywood Road, all the rights to her music portfolio, her art, her shares and her cash.

She had also left a sum of money to be paid monthly to Elliot, if he was able to take over his full-time parental responsibilities. If he found he was unable to do that – then he would get nothing.

She had also bequeathed to her brother Jake a mews house, which she had instructed Peterson de Winter to purchase on her behalf when it came onto the market two months ago. Hugo mentioned that he was given to understand that it was a house that she and her brother had lived in when they were young. She wanted to give it to her brother, unentailed, as somewhere that would always be his, and his alone. Jake felt his eyes well with tears.

Zelda looked surprised and Lucien was furious as he realised that's what the two million had been for. 'Fucking hell!' he thought. 'The trouble I had to go to, to get that money, and it was for that fucking waste of space Jake. Christ, Georgia was an idiot.' He felt himself redden with rage as he fought to get his temper under control.

Hugo continued. In the event of Elliot finding himself unable to meet his responsibilities then Georgia asked that her brother Jake become guardian to both her girls. The named trustees of her estate were Jake and himself. So Lucien was no longer a trustee; Dusty was relieved.

The room was quiet, until Zelda broke the silence. 'You

haven't been given any indication of who might be held responsible for the baby, Willow, then?'

'No, indeed. Georgia made that quite clear. The father of the baby will remain anonymous. That was her wish. She insisted it was for the best, for all concerned,' Hugo replied emphatically, as if that was an end to the matter.

'Hmph!' Zelda accidentally let a tiny exclamation escape her perfect, pursed lips. 'We'll see about that!' she thought to herself.

'In the meantime we do have some concerns over the transparency of Miss Cole's financial affairs. As you know, Mr Dark, we have been requesting an up-to-date statement of Miss Cole's assets since she took us on. None have, thus far, been forthcoming. We wanted to know if you could explain the problem to us – the delay?' He looked questioningly towards Lucien.

Lucien replied patronisingly, 'You obviously aren't very familiar with the music business. Things can be very complex, we can't just deliver up-to-date statements on our clients' affairs overnight.'

'But we haven't asked for them overnight, Mr Dark – we have been asking for them for two months. We are not requesting an exact figure to the last penny. But I don't think it is unreasonable for her family to want to know roughly where they stand.' Hugo wasn't going to give up.

Zelda liked him. He was old-fashioned. Firm but fair – she liked that.

Craig finally piped up, 'We are just putting everything together now – we should have a statement for you within the next two weeks. Sorry for the delay, there has been a lot on and, you know ... fluctuations in the markets ...' He trailed off.

'Make it one week.' said Hugo. 'In the meantime we need funds to distribute. There will be funeral disbursements to be made and so on. So I would be grateful if you could transfer £100,000 to our client's account; here are the details.' Hugo pushed some paperwork across the table towards Craig. 'By tomorrow morning will be fine. Thank you.' He took a deep breath, closed his file. 'So, is there anything else?'

Dusty spoke. 'So you are saying that my dad will be paid if he looks after us and not if he doesn't?'

'Um, yes, Dusty, that is correct.'

'How much? How much will he be paid?' Her voice was rising slightly.

Elliot looked embarrassed. Panicked even.

'It will be £150,000 per year, net. All additional living or education expenses and everything for maintenance of the children will be paid, in addition to that, from Ms Cole's estate.'

Elliot looked shocked. Lucien looked inscrutable. Jake looked pleased. Zelda looked relieved. Craig looked very anxious indeed.

Dusty turned to Elliot. 'There you are – now let's go home.' She looked extremely relieved. All their worries were over.

Hugo and Giles de Winter got up to leave. Giles had not said a word, but he had been watching carefully. That was his job – Hugo spoke, Giles watched. They were a great team.

Kate appeared on cue and took the lawyers upstairs to show them out.

Jake hugged Elliot. 'You OK, Daddy-o? Looking after the girls? You'll do great! I can't believe she got the Mews back for me! How fucking sweet is that?'

He turned to Zelda. 'Hey Tiger, what do you think – we could move back there? How great would that be?'

Zelda looked at him sceptically and laughed. She was feeling pretty cheerful – it looked like her plan wasn't going to be needed after all ... Elliot would be in charge of both girls. Phew. And she could get back to her life, her work, normality.

She glanced at Elliot. His tan seemed to have faded and ... was that a sheen of sweat that she could see upon his handsome brow? Well, she had to hand it to her crazy sister-in-law Georgia – she had finally managed to clip his wings, more effectively than anything she herself had managed to achieve. Result! He was grounded. Ha! Why was she so pleased?

Zelda was scanning the morning newspapers for any stories about the family. The press had slackened off a bit today. The financial crisis was knocking all the Cole/Spender stories off the front pages. 'Thank God we have crafty old Lucien looking after our money. Or we could all be heading for trouble too!' Zelda thought to herself.

Somewhere in one of the papers Zelda noticed a small but glamorous picture of her mother arriving in Kathmandu the previous night. It was only in the Diary section. Milo was in the background smiling into the camera – God he was gorgeous. She was slightly surprised when she realised that she hadn't thought about him at all, not once, since he'd gone. She'd send him a text later, telling him she missed him, even though she didn't. Try to keep everyone sweet, that was Zelda's motto – well, it was her motto sometimes.

She wondered if Kate had organised that new personal trainer for her? She needed to get back to it. Didn't want the lovely bod falling apart when her career had just begun to take off again. OK, the reviews for the latest film weren't great – it was a bit of a stinker, she knew that, but it was a big-budget stinker with a huge-budget cast. She was back in the big time, with the big guys, and that's what counted. She was on the up and up.

Now Kate was back to remind Zelda that she had to leave for the studio for her Fabulous shoot. Christ, yes! She was looking forward to getting out of the house. To running the gauntlet of the press, even. Out into her world where everyone loved her, treated her with respect – or fawned all over her, as Jake would say! Back to fucking normal at last ... or almost. Only the funeral the day after tomorrow, then they could put all this behind them.

She took a couple of Adderall as she went upstairs. She couldn't believe how much she'd eaten at Max's last night; she'd suddenly found she couldn't stop once she'd started. God, that lobster was so delicious. Then again she couldn't remember eating anything at all for days before that, so it couldn't have done too much harm. She needed to watch herself though. Couldn't afford to let anything slip now. She went upstairs to get dressed and made-up for the press. She would then have to have everything taken off again, at the studio, to have more reapplied by the Fabulous makeup artists for the shoot. Tiresome, but there it was – her job. Anyway, she did rather love it. Today was coming along quite nicely for her.

Elliot was in the Great Hall with Dusty, having a slightly tricky conversation.

'No, no, Dusty, all I'm saying is I think we should all stay here till after the funeral – then we can go back to yours. It's just not feasible to go there now. There isn't the infrastructure for us – the press are still everywhere. We need to set up a proper staff to help, and then there is security and so on. We can't do that realistically until after the funeral. Apart from anything else we will need to fund it all and, I'm sorry, Dusty, but until the lawyers have sorted it I don't have the funds to support us. Hopeless, I know, but it's true. So you will have to be patient.' Elliot looked at Dusty fondly.

To his relief, she replied, if a little uncertainly. 'OK, but the moment the funds are cleared we are off – right? Promise?'

'Yes, OK, Dusty, I promise.' Elliot gave up; what could he do?

Dusty threw her arms around his neck and hugged him, kissing his cheeks madly. 'Thank you, thank you, thank you, Daddy. You won't regret it, I promise. You could write that book you talked about!' She kissed him again. He hugged her and let her down gently to the floor.

Ah yes – his book! Well, maybe he could, maybe he would.

He felt suddenly rather grown up. Dusty was very sweet and she needed him. What was wrong with that? he asked himself. Nothing, surely? Nothing wrong with that at all. Elliot thought he might just go out into the garden again with a cup of coffee – think things through. He was a man of means now. He had much to decide.

Dusty grinned. At last she would be able to get back to Hollywood Road, home. Maybe there would be something there to help piece together what had really happened to her mother. She felt hopeful as she set off upstairs to her room.

Dusty bumped into Valentine as he was coming downstairs. He looked awful, exhausted.

'D! I was just coming to find you – I need to talk to you, explain something, OK?' He looked at her and smiled his loveliest smile.

She led him back upstairs. 'OK, come on. Mine.'

He followed her, obediently, to her room. He had decided to come clean, or clean-ish anyway.

They sat side by side on her bed. Only this time Dusty didn't feel nervous, she felt cross.

Before she could say a word, Valentine had blurted it all out: 'D, I . . . I have a horrible confession to make. I . . . I was with your mum the night she died. Um, not for long . . . no. She called me, you see, before the premiere – said she was lonely. I couldn't face sitting through that fucking awful film again, so I slipped out as soon as it started and went to Hollywood Road.

I felt sorry for her, Dusty, you know? She and I always got along great. She was great. I loved your mum, you know that, don't you?' He looked at Dusty sincerely.

She looked away, got out a cigarette and lit it. He lit his own and continued: 'When I got there she was already quite far gone. She offered me some coke and I did a couple of lines. Fuck knows what it was – it knocked me for six. I could hardly fucking drive when I left! She had a huge amount of gear there. I'd never known her like that before, something was wrong, I could tell. But she didn't tell me anything. She was really out of it. I shouldn't have left her, Dusty. I am so sorry. I shouldn't have left. I am so ashamed, so sorry. I should've told you before but . . .' He looked as if he might cry.

He suddenly seemed very young and vulnerable to Dusty, and she reached out and put her arms around him. She was careful not to burn his hair with her cigarette. He buried his face in her neck and gave a juddering sigh. Then, suddenly, he was kissing her neck, her cheek, her lips.

Gently at first, then passionately, only breaking off to whisper her name, breathlessly, 'Dusty, Dusty!' Eventually, he pulled away, holding her at arm's length. 'Oh God, sorry, I can't help it – can't keep this a secret any more. It's just that I love you so much. I always have. I can't bear it that you are so young. It torments me. Makes me crazy with wanting you, Dusty. That's why I sleep with all those awful, disgusting girls. To stop me thinking about you, *all* the time. I know I have to wait. I know I do. But can you tell me you love me too, just a little bit? Give me some hope.' He looked at her passionately, pleadingly.

Dusty fell for it. 'I've loved you, since I was six! It makes me so unhappy to see you with India and Kate.'

He leant forward and kissed her again. Christ! He was tempted – but now that she was back onside, he knew it would be safer to play the long game. To give in and 'give her one' could cause a lot of problems. No, he absolutely had to restrain himself, keep her hanging on. In fact it might be quite fun, thrilling even. He never, ever had to restrain himself with girls – certainly not with Kate, although he thought he'd gone quite a bit too far with her last night.

Be careful what you wish for, Dusty, my innocent little darling cousin.

Yes, this holding back Dusty thing might be the sort of novelty he'd enjoy.

He held her frail body away from him dramatically, and feigned restraint. 'No, no, no, Dusty darling, you are far too young. Too pure and beautiful. I can't take responsibility for despoiling you, my darling, at such a tender age. No, no, only a beast would behave in such a way.' He wondered why he was talking like a character from a Georgette Heyer novel? Then he realised he was acting – rather well, it seemed, because unbelievably his tactic appeared to be working.

Dusty looked relieved.

They carelessly stubbed out their cigarettes in a Lalique pot. Valentine stood and smiled down at her. 'See you later then – OK?'

Dusty looked up at him, her eyes dreamy, her soft lips bruised. God, how the fuck was he going to manage to resist this?

She whispered adoringly, 'OK.' And Valentine fled. When he got to the Great Hall he found his heart was pounding. Jesus, that was a near miss! Then he nearly ran into Kate. Luckily, she left the room quickly without so much as a glance in his direction – thank God for that, he thought. He'd sort her out later. Then his mobile went off: it was India. 'Fucking hell!' He pressed 'ignore'.

He grabbed a cup of coffee and went out into the garden, where Elliot was lying on the lawn. As Valentine drew closer, Elliot appeared to be talking to a tree. Then Max's head popped out from behind the bush.

'Dear boy! Come and join us. Elliot and I are just having a chinwag.' Max was looking extra perky. 'Just had a text from your grandmother; they are filming in Kathmandu today then setting off to fly to Lukla tomorrow. Then the trial by Cleo will begin – pity those poor Sherpas, eh?'

'Wow, Max, you must be so proud.' Valentine lowered himself on the grass next to Elliot.

'I am proud, darling boy – positively bursting with pride!' Max chuckled.

'So, everything all right, Elliot?' Valentine asked, Mr Congeniality all of a sudden.

'Yes, fine, great in fact. I've just been telling Max. The will, Georgia's will, was read this morning and she requested that I look after the girls. So we are going back to Hollywood Road after the funeral.' Elliot was relaxing into the plan, or trying to.

Valentine was pleased. Thank God, only a few more days to get through with that little Dusty in the house. Should be able to make it. Might just ring India – get her over for a little R & R.

He sent her a text: 'Get here – now! I need you. X x V.'

He knew she would come. He couldn't wait. Slugging back his coffee he got back to his feet, looking down at Elliot as he did so, and realising that he was a good-looking bloke. He'd never particularly noticed before – yeah, handsome, Dusty's dad.

Jake knew Zelda had left the house when he heard an almighty roar from the crowd outside. People were screaming Zelda! Zelda! Zelda! The photographers went mad. She was probably posing for them. He sighed and smiled to himself; really, what was she like? She loved all that, no, she *really* loved all that. It was her life's blood. It invigorated her, thrilled her still, after all these years. Of course it was a love-hate thing . . . but when she was feeling good and they were calling for her she just fizzed and sparkled for them. She was out there, doing it now. Giving them what they had been waiting for.

Well, almost. In fact, what the press and public had been waiting for so patiently were sightings of the distraught, bereaved, suffering children. Dusty and Willow, devastated – that's what they really wanted.

But they had been waiting two days for nothing. No one famous, devastated or not, had come to the house, apart from that young actress India something ... oh, and Johnny the Bastard, but apart from them ... Nothing, nada, niente ... just an endless stream of nobodies: delivery people, hairdressers, stylists, makeup artists, agents, PAs, florists, lawyers, account-ants, laundry guys, postmen, DHL, Net-a-Porter, Selfridges, Harrods ... nothing to ogle or even laugh at. Very disappoint-ing.

So when Zelda emerged this morning in all her exquisitely turned-out superstar glory they all went completely, dispro-portionately, berserk.

Zelda did love the roar of the crowd – just as long as they didn't get too close.

David and the team could be relied upon to keep them at bay today. He was looking marvellous, she noted. She hadn't seen him for days. Had he even been into the staff room? she wondered. He was so conscientious. He was one man who could always be relied upon. Steadfast.

Until David had come to work for her, a few years previously, she had always felt nervous of the crowd. Some photographers, in the past, had given her some very nasty shocks; they had pushed her over to make her look drunk. Called her a slag and a whore to make her lose her temper. Tried to take pictures up her skirt ... oh, and plenty more besides. But David always managed to protect her from their worst excesses and she had started to quite enjoy the attention again.

David came to shield her as she got into the car. No matter how careful you were getting in and out of a car there was always the danger of a crotch shot for the paps – those cameras

could catch you out in the tiniest blink of an eye or the teeni-
est chink in a skirt.

In fact Zelda was wearing skinny jeans today. But that was
the kind of guy David was. Never one to take any chances.
Zelda thanked him and smiled up at him gratefully as he shut
the car door. The driver went off at speed – they weren't late,
but he had learnt that the more acceleration you gave it, the
more powerful and important the person travelling in the car
looked and felt. He knew that Zelda Spender like to look both
of those things and he wasn't going to disappoint her.

Jake was pleased to find Lana alone in the Great Hall; he had
been a bit worried about her. She hadn't looked happy when
he'd seen her talking to Zelda this morning and that had made
him nervous. He didn't think she was going to tell – was she?

Of course he could, would, just deny it if she did. Although
that was only something that would work short-term.

Zelda might even choose to believe him. She knew what he
was, after all; a bit of a boozer, certainly. A bit flaky on the
work front right now, indisputably. But she never would, or
could, accuse him of being a womaniser. Oh, he'd had a couple
of slip-ups here and there, but they meant nothing and only
happened when he was really, really drunk – so that didn't
count. He had never deliberately pursued any woman ... and
the Lana thing? He still felt very confused about that whole
episode. Very confused indeed.

No, Jake had always felt Zelda understood that he was just

too lazy apart from anything else, and of course he loved his wife – *loved* her! No, if anyone was guilty in the infidelity department, she would probably win that competition. But he wasn't absolutely sure about that, always preferred not to think about it ... God! What time was it? He felt like a drink. He hadn't had one at all so far today. He was quite pleased with himself.

He smiled warmly at Lana. 'Ah, ha, lovely Lana ... there you are! How are you? Not too tired looking after the baby all the time?' Yikes! He realised that was the wrong thing to say ... shit, shit, shit! Think of something else, anything ... 'Have you seen Ed this morning?' So, so fucking feeble.

He poured himself an enormous vodka. Lana watched him disapprovingly. She didn't reply. He splashed in some tonic and looked at her hopefully. But she just continued to ignore him in rather a stroppy way. This was unlike her. Lana was always sweetness and light. Oh, God. Jake didn't know what to do next.

Ed walked in. 'Hi, Dad, what's up? I was just going to watch "The Godfather" again – watch it with me, eh? You look beat. Poor Dad, getting old, can't take the heat ...'

If only he knew, Jake thought bleakly – he really couldn't take the heat.

He allowed himself to be led away by his young son.

They slumped in front of the telly. As the credits rolled Ed turned to his father and asked, 'Did you notice Lana is in a foul mood – for the first time ever!'

Jake looked non-committal. Ed continued: 'Well, Mum has

been having a go at her and I think she's had enough. Honestly, Dad – I found her with her bag packed the other day. She only stayed because of Willow. She's so great – you have to speak to Mum, get her to lay off. I need Lana, so does Mum. It's not like she can look after the baby herself if Lana goes! I mean, fuck! Imagine that?'

'Your mother looked after you perfectly well,' Jake responded loyally, relieved that the Lana bad mood thing didn't seem to relate to him at all.

'Yeah, right, Dad, Mum the perfect mother – dream on!'

Jake took another slug of vodka and they settled down to watch the movie.

Zelda's mothering skills, or lack thereof, weren't really something Jake had considered much. She'd done all right. He thought Ed was being a bit unfair; but, what was he thinking, of course Ed thought his parents were rubbish – he was a teenager! He'd soon grow up and realise how fabulous and fun Jake and Zelda had been. Wouldn't he ... ?

Valentine was getting really pissed off. India hadn't answered his text and her phone was switched off. He tried her PA, but she wouldn't pick up either – fucking infuriating because he knew the PA had her phone permanently glued to her face, night and fucking day.

Right! That's it, he thought furiously. He texted Lily.

Miraculously she had texted right back. Apparently, Johnny was in the studio, rehearsing with the band for their next tour.

She told him to come on over. She really was the perfect woman and – he realised suddenly – she hardly ever spoke! In fact he couldn't remember ever hearing her voice. Perhaps she was dumb! Even more perfect.

He went out through Max's basement. A pair of young boys were leaving at the same time as him and so the few photographers waiting there must've thought they were with Valentine – his pals! He wondered if Jamie had seen him crossing the lawn and timed their departure to innocently merge with his. Valentine couldn't help thinking what a brilliant aide-de-camp Jamie was for Max. He could do with a Jamie himself – well, not literally of course. God no.

A few desultory clicks from the paps, as Valentine passed, and he was in a cab and on his way – to heaven.

CHAPTER SEVENTEEN

Cleo was happy. The day's shoot in Kathmandu had gone brilliantly. The director was very kind, and quite handsome too, although he had a beard.

They had filmed her in the market place and then being shown around the sights of the town by the mayor, a tiny little man, but very sweet.

The tourists in the market had recognised her, of course – so there had been quite a lot of pointing and staring. That endless, stage-whispered, 'Did you see who that was?' that rolled along behind in her wake, wherever she went in public. All familiar, and quite gratifying, when witnessed by the producers, director and crew. She felt like saying 'Not completely forgotten, you see!' but she knew she didn't have to.

They filmed an interview with her that evening, on the hotel terrace. Bathed in the golden light of dusk Cleo looked extraordinary, like a sphinx, beautiful and darkly mysterious. She wore some fabulous Nepalese necklaces she had bought in the market. As far as Cleo was concerned you could never over-gild the lily. The director asked her what she had done in the way of training, climbing and so on. She had made them all laugh, quite a bit, as she breezily described her gruelling fitness regime.

At one point the director had asked Milo to join her, so that they could ask him to fill in the details of her training. But he tactfully declined, saying, 'No, no, this is all about Cleo – it is her achievement. I am just happy in the background – I'm just her trainer.'

The director looked a little peeved. But he wasn't going to get into a power-struggle right now. He couldn't help feeling there would plenty of opportunity for that stuff once they hit Everest. He had noticed that Milo was extremely photogenic. He would ask one of the cameramen to film him quietly while the other camera was on Cleo. He could cut him in nicely in the editing.

Cleo was pleased with herself and Milo too. He had obviously got the message.

They were all flying to Lukla tomorrow. They were to trek through charming Sherpa villages. Cleo was to be given a quad bike to conserve her energy. She had protested that she was perfectly capable of walking like everyone else. But she couldn't help being secretly pleased. She knew there were three days of trekking and acclimatising to be done before they even reached the Khumbu Glacier and then back and forth there, across the ice fall, for more acclimatisation. Then on up to base camp. She was beginning to wish she hadn't read *Into Thin Air*.

Milo walked her to her door. He grinned at her.

'Ready?' he teased.

'Ready!' she grinned back at him.

'Shall I come in? You should have a sports massage before we go, limber you up. Not sure we'll have much opportunity for another from now on. Too cold – tents and so on!' Milo looked mischievous.

Just the way Cleo liked him.

The day finished perfectly.

A lovely massage for Cleo – with a happy ending. She couldn't have been more pleased.

This show was her best decision ever.

Back at God's the florists had been in to redo all the flowers in the Great Hall.

Vast, spectacular arrangements of blossom filled the high stone vases that stood majestically on either side of the fireplace. All the central tables had stunning, loose arrangements of lilies, roses and wild lilac. The scent was heavenly.

The housekeepers had just left the room; it was the first time for days they had managed to get in to give it a really thorough clean. Now it looked perfect. They both agreed that all the rooms at God's were so much lovelier without people in them. They had been quite put out over the last few days with so many people coming and going ... extra laundry and cleaning and beds to be made and no one ever told them what was happening or when. They complained to each other– a lot – and went back down to the staff room for a cup of tea.

When Zelda got home from her shoot at nine that evening she was very pissed off to find Jake crashed out on the bed in his dressing room. She could smell the booze on him – he was clutching a picture of himself and Georgia when they were children. She took it from him and put it on the bedside table. Then she turned off the light and quietly closed and locked the doors that intercommunicated with their marital bedroom.

She had a quick shower, threw on a little Juliet Dunn kaftan and went downstairs to see if she could find anything to eat.

She found Elliot in the Great Hall, alone.

He appeared to making something ... a salad? Some pasta?

'Zelda! There you are. How'd it go? I'm making some food. Couldn't find much, do you lot ever eat anything but toast?' He grinned and poured her a glass of ice-cold rosé.

She took the glass from him gratefully. 'Actually, no, we don't, and I don't even eat that. But I am starving, I don't know what's the matter with me – can't stop eating.' In fact, she hadn't eaten anything since her mini-binge at Max's.

Elliot had found some pasta and pesto sauce in a cupboard and a few slightly tired-looking salad ingredients in the fridge. It wasn't exactly going to be a Jamie Oliver feast. It pained him because he was a good, quite creative, cook. But it would have to do.

He was glad to get Zelda alone. He had drunk a couple of glasses of wine before she'd appeared, and was feeling more relaxed and confident in her presence now. They were just relatives by marriage, he thought ... well – ex, of course. Nonetheless, they were here now and able to put the past behind them. To deal with all their family obligations in a grown-up way.

The little glimpses he had had of Zelda's less appealing characteristics since he'd arrived had reminded him of why they never had any sort of future together. He was over her; he knew that now.

He felt happy that they could proceed with their lives, unfettered by their past. They would, after all, be living in much closer proximity from here on.

They began a rather jolly evening. Elliot regaled Zelda with stories of adventure and disaster, always painting himself and his actions in a modest but comic way. Zelda told some stories of her own, all very showbiz and gossipy, but funny too – if told slightly less modestly than Elliot's.

The food tasted delicious to Zelda and she ate too much. She ended up rolling around on the floor clutching her belly and moaning.

By then, they had both drunk quite a lot, Elliot had just opened a third bottle of wine and they shared a joint. Zelda lit the huge, very realistic-looking fire and the flames leapt wildly over the massive fake logs. Elliot vaguely noticed that the lights were off; they somehow hadn't got around to switching them on when the daylight had faded.

Zelda sparkled and shone as she lay in the firelight, the sequins that were scattered across her kaftan catching the light like fireflies. Elliot had already become aware, quite some time earlier, that she didn't appear to be wearing any underwear. Something he had been trying not to think about until now.

Zelda sighed and stretched her arms above her head, carelessly knocking her glass. Elliot found himself hurling his body across hers instinctively, to retrieve the wine before it spilt. That little accident was averted but a more consequential one ensued.

Elliot found himself lying on top of Zelda and she was giggling, pulling his face towards hers. Her mouth was soft and sweet. This had been building up from the moment they had laid eyes on each other and there was no way they could or would stop now. Just as Elliot had suspected, Zelda was naked beneath her kaftan; it was all too easy, irresistible. Familiar, furtive and very, very quick.

Elliot was breathing heavily. 'Jesus Christ, Zelda. What have we done?'

'Well, nothing we haven't done before,' she said breathlessly, and laughed.

Someone was coming down the stairs. Elliot hastily pulled himself and his clothes together. He stood up, suddenly feeling very sober. Jumping for the light switch – all the lamps went on at once – Elliot thanked God for high-tech, high-spec electrics. Quickly crossing the room to the kitchen, he fumbled with the coffee machine.

Zelda coolly sat up. She shamelessly crossed her legs under the massive coffee table and nonchalantly opened a book of prints by her favourite photographer, the brilliant artist and singer, Bryan Adams.

Lana walked into the Great Hall.

She went into the kitchen, her head slightly bowed. 'Sorry! Just need bottle for Willow. She just wake up – not happy.

So ...' She grabbed a bottle from the fridge and disappeared back upstairs.

Zelda put her head in her hands and laughed again. 'Phew!'

Elliot looked annoyed. 'Not funny, Zelda, fuck! Really, not funny at all.'

'Fun though, the fuck, I mean, really fun ... fast fun!' She grinned shamelessly at Elliot.

'God,' he thought to himself, 'she has more balls than I will ever have. What now though, what next? Jesus, this is going to get complicated.'

He couldn't help feeling a rush of admiration for Zelda – a rush of admiration ... and the thumping pull of desire.

In a couple of graceful movements he was around the kitchen island and Zelda found herself being lifted and thrust urgently into the catering kitchen, which was so conveniently hidden behind the faux bookcase. It was the first time the room had been used since it was installed. Although it probably wasn't quite what the designers had in mind, the work surfaces proved very useful and adaptable to their new function. When Zelda and Elliot took their carnal trip down memory lane that night, it was something that blew both their bodies and their minds and, although their bodies would recover, as they lay in each other's arms on the shiny steel preparation table, Zelda couldn't help being seriously concerned that they had lost their minds.

Lucien had spent a very unsatisfactory early evening having crisis talks with Craig. It was the end of the day and, apart from his secretary Anna, he had sent all of the office staff home.

Lucien had been running a shadow company to Dark Artists for years, shifting clients' funds between the two companies, placing vast sums in high-interest, high-return hedge funds, keeping some of the profits for himself and letting his naïve clients bear the losses.

As with much of Lucien's reckless behaviour the risk of discovery and disaster was huge. But that risk was mostly to others, innocents – they just didn't know they were being exposed to it. Some clients had pressed for proper statements when they were informed that their accounts were empty – but they were fobbed off with talk of complex tax issues and accusations of their own profligacy. They were mostly artists with little or no grasp of what they had earned or indeed spent over the years, and they were soon silenced, confused and baffled by legal and technical accountancy jargon.

Failing the efficacy of that tactic, Lucien always made sure he had something compromising on all his beloved clients, just in case they proved to be difficult to subdue in the event of a public dispute. To find yourself in the pocket of Lucien Dark was to find yourself in a very murky place indeed.

He had managed to convince himself, over the years, that he worked far harder than any of his 'just got lucky, layabout clients'. So, with not a little envy or spite, he had begun to match their spending brazenly, like for like; if they bought a Bentley, he bought a Bentley; if they bought an apartment in Manhattan then so did he. A house in the South of France? Why not? Another on the beach in Barbados? Yes please.

This was all fine while it lasted. But when his clients' earnings dipped, or their tax liabilities became pressing, Lucien would conceal his losses by transferring funds from another client account to cover the amount. When that proved insufficient he began placing insane sums with his hedge fund chums. This had worked spectacularly successfully, at first. So much so that Lucien was able to build up a huge stash for himself in a Swiss bank account.

But recently the tide had turned; the investments were suffering spectacular losses. The financial world was in free fall.

Lucien was just about managing to juggle client funds without dipping into his own stash. He never intended to use that for anyone other than himself anyway. He had decided a long time ago that if push ever came to shove, he would do just that – shove off. But he didn't think it was ever going to come to that. Things were tricky, but he loved a challenge and was confident he could get around anything that anyone cared to throw at him. He'd always felt he was a survivor. He usually found that the people he came up against were amateurs.

But tonight he was not happy. In fact he was apoplectic with rage at one point, when Craig shook his head defiantly, insisting that there were no more client accounts to plunder, stating firmly, 'The cross-firing has back-fired; there is nothing left to be done.'

'Nothing left to be done, you fucking moron!' Lucien had screamed. 'Nothing left to be done – what the fuck are you talking about? I just gave you access to the Spender assets for a start.'

He'd had the foresight to nip over to God's the night of Max's dinner, to have Zelda sign some 'work contracts', one of which was a paper giving him absolute power of attorney over all her affairs. Of course she had no idea what she had signed – he had never known her to even glance at a formal document before she signed it. With one sweep of her pen she had given him access to a new and essential source of credit.

Lucien continued furiously, 'Start making those work for us – now! Jesus! I told you, all you need to do is transfer them to the Adventara fund and leave them there for a week or so, and all our troubles will be over. So just fucking do it.' Lucien was very red and looked as if he might burst.

Craig found himself imagining Lucien's blood and guts spattered all over the massive plate-glass window which so impressively framed the dramatic view of the London skyline. A satisfying image for Craig – a mental picture of the 'Death of Lucien', his nemesis, seemed very appealing right now. But life was never that simple, alas.

Craig pressed on. 'And I'm telling you, Lucien, that the Adventara fund is far from a safe bet – there are some very worrying signals coming from my friends inside. We have to stop now, before we lose any more. I can't be party to this any longer. I'm sorry, I'm out.' Craig looked grey and he was visibly shaking but his expression remained firm as he stood up to leave.

Lucien was around his huge desk and across the room like

a twister – darkly terrifying. He soon had Craig pinned, painfully, against the wall.

'Not so fucking fast, buster – you are in this way too deep. If you want to stay out of those striped jimjams you'd better do as I say. There is only one way out of here, you lily-livered fuck, and that's my way.'

Craig stared at him coldly and Lucien loosened his grip. Craig straightened his tie and left the office.

Lucien poured himself a large whisky. He went back to his desk. Revolving his chair to stare out at the view for a moment, he finished his drink before he slowly turned back. Picking up the phone he said quietly, 'Put me through to Tim Harper at Adventara – yeah.' He waited. 'Tim, hi, Lucien Dark here ...'

CHAPTER EIGHTEEN

Jake woke up early, in his dressing-room bed. He felt like death. The first thing he saw when he opened his eyes was the photograph of his boy-self and Georgia. What the fuck had happened to them? That bright-faced carefree boy seemed like someone else entirely – nothing at all to do with him. He felt so, so sad. Where was he? What was he now? A mess – God, yes, a mess, like Georgia. How had she come to that? She had so much to live for – her beautiful children ... but that was the thing, wasn't it? He had nearly come to that too ...

So many lost days and nights. What was the point? Round and round, and always needing a drink to steady the panic – or was the drink causing the panic? Someone had told him that once – some boring friend newly converted to AA. Could they be right? He didn't want to go on feeling like this, being like this, and then ... he gazed at the photograph and whispered sadly, 'Georgia, Georgia, I'm sorry ... my beautiful sister – don't go.' Tears were running down his cheeks. He staggered into the bathroom and ran the cold water, splashing it onto his face. He was only half-undressed – one sock was still on, his shirt was crumpled and undone.

He looked himself squarely in his bloodshot eyes, and told himself, 'This has got to stop, Jake, mate – or you are fucked.' Jake looked back at himself and grimaced, unconvinced. 'Yeah, right – you loser!'

He looked blearily at his Franck Muller watch – it said 4.20a.m. He drank some water, had a pee, and fell back into his dressing-room bed. He knew better than to try to rejoin his wife; he might wake her up – never popular. He knew when to keep his head down. God, he felt horrible. He had so much to do tomorrow – he had to write his tribute for Georgia's funeral for a start . . . oh God! He was never going to get back to sleep now. He heard a door close somewhere nearby. He rummaged in the bedside drawer. Ah! Yes, they should do the trick. He swallowed a couple of pills and turned out the light. But he still couldn't get to sleep, for what felt like hours, days, years . . .

Zelda woke with a start. Her bed was empty. Jake? Then she remembered . . . Elliot! . . . Shit!

Well, she wouldn't be bumping into either of them this morning; she had an early call – the film company needed her for a scene today and despite the fact that they had said she could have the week off, things had changed, with the usual dramas on set, and it didn't cost her anything to be helpful after all. So she had agreed do it, earning some Brownie points from the producers – always a good idea. But she wasn't really feeling up to it; she felt very rough. What was she doing, drinking that much? And ... she shuddered, she really couldn't think about that now.

She hauled herself out of bed. It was still dark outside, so she felt she could safely run the gauntlet of the photographers without full makeup. Sunglasses, scarf tied à la Grace Kelly, jeans, her Burberry mac that Christopher Bailey had so sweetly made specially just for her. Her Hermès bag ... and she was off.

On her way out, she went to grab a bottle of water from the fridge in the Great Hall.

She almost jumped out of her skin when a husky voice came from one of the armchairs: 'We need to talk.' Elliot was fully clothed. He obviously hadn't been to bed. He made no attempt to move.

Had he been waiting for her? Zelda wondered ... but he didn't know she had an early call. What was he thinking?

'Yes, well, sorry, but I can't stop now. I have to be on set. We can talk later. Though I don't think we have much to talk about, Elliot. Last night was a mistake.' Her voice sounded hard. She stood over him, her tone softening for a moment. 'A lovely mistake, Elliot, but a mistake. We both know that really, don't we?'

'A mistake that happens whenever we are near each other ... a mistake I have travelled the world aimlessly for fucking years to avoid making again. And now here we are. Going to be playing happy families, apparently ... and you and me in close proximity. How is that going to work, exactly? If I am near you I just don't seem to be able to control myself. There has to be a reason for that. I mean ... for fuck's sake, after all these years. Christ! Maybe we just love each other, Zelda? Hmm? Maybe that's all it is – love.' He looked up, and his ice-blue eyes pierced into her.

She looked away, sick with fear. 'I have to go.'

Her heels clicked across the Great Hall floor, even though her legs felt weak, she carried on. She couldn't ... she absolutely knew she couldn't stop now. If she went back ... no, she couldn't even think about it.

She opened the front door and David met her, with an umbrella – it was still dark, pouring with rain. He led her solicitously to the car.

The cameras flashed wildly through the windows as they sped out of the gate.

For once, Zelda was completely at a loss. What now? She needed time to think ... it was all so bloody exhausting. She felt something odd though ... what was that?

Shit! She realised she felt happy. Elliot loved her!

Dusty and Ed had been woken by the clamour of Zelda leaving. They lay amid pizza boxes and Coke cans, overflowing ashtrays and all the detritus of a teenage life lived in front of the telly – albeit a telly that was the size of a small cinema screen.

They had watched movies late, very late. Then fallen asleep. Now Dusty stumbled upstairs to go to bed. She was surprised to bump into Elliot as he was leaving the Great Hall.

'Hey, Dad, what are you doing still up?' She looked at him blearily, rubbing her eyes with the heels of her small hands.

'Well, Dusty, I've been thinking – making plans for us. Come on. I'll walk up with you. Tell you what I've decided. I'm pretty sure you'll be pleased.'

He put his arm around her and they set off upstairs.

A lovely little father-and-daughter team.

Valentine arrived home through the garden door just as Elliot and Dusty went upstairs.

So … he thought, Dusty was still up. Quite a little party animal! Maybe she would be worth waiting for after all.

He reached into the fridge for a bottle of Evian. He was completely exhausted. Like an idiot he'd fallen asleep at Lily's – about an hour ago. No sooner had he dropped off to sleep, Lily was shaking him and gesturing silently towards her dressing room. Johnny had come back! She had thrown his clothes in after him and pointed to another door leading from her dressing room to the hall. As he left he heard Johnny yell, 'Hey, baby, I'm home!' and then an almighty crash as he hit the bed. He could hear Lily laughing as he closed the front door.

She hadn't laughed with him. In fact he still wasn't sure whether he'd actually heard her speak. He thought back … she had pulled him through the front door the moment he'd rung the bell at Johnny's house. They had smoked weed and drunk rum – weirdly – and fucked a lot. But he still didn't think she'd spoken … was it possible? Oh, who cared – she was the perfect woman and her actions sure as hell spoke as loud as any words he'd ever heard. Lily was great.

India still hadn't texted him. He might have to dump her. That'd teach her.

He walked upstairs. As he passed Dusty's room he could hear her humming softly. He hovered for a moment outside her door. Almost knocked ...

No, no, no, he told himself firmly. To bed, to bed.

He wasn't going to have a shower – he'd take the smell of Lily to bed with him. A beautiful, heady mix of patchouli oil and sex.

Valentine felt almost happy.

CHAPTER NINETEEN

The flight up to Lukla was breathtaking.

As their small plane skimmed across the beautiful, ancient landscape of Nepal, Cleo felt excited.

They had got up very early. The call was for 6a.m. but she had to get up at 5a.m. – she wanted that extra hour to get her hair and makeup done. She was so glad that she hadn't brought hair and makeup people with her, she was perfectly capable of doing it herself; in fact she always thought she did it better than most of them anyway, as she had learnt at the hands of the old masters in Hollywood – real artists, not the silly girls they sent you these days. Anyway she had been told the production company's budget didn't stretch to hair and makeup.

As long as they hadn't made too many economies once the tough stuff started ... they had promised the best, the most state-of-the-art climbing equipment and tents. She hoped they would honour those promises. She might be able to do her own hair and makeup but she sure as hell couldn't pitch a tent or fix a rope up an ice wall. She preferred not to think about any of that now though. Cross that bridge or crevasse when she came to it.

She was told that the next few days would be relatively easy. They would be heading up through pasture to the Sherpa villages until they reached Namche Bazaar. They would be going slowly to acclimatise. Cleo would be able to use her quad bike for much of that time, as they wouldn't be doing any real climbing until they reached the Khumbu Glacier on the third day.

They would be sleeping in huts in the villages en route. Pretty basic but luxury compared to what they would expect when they got to base camp and beyond.

Cleo felt quite dizzy with excitement already.

She had noticed that Milo was becoming very chummy with the crew. Well, why not, she thought. He was one of them anyway – sort of. If he had any real aspirations for the limelight he should know that you always kept your distance from the crew. Even to some extent from the producers and director. Keep the mystery there and some respect. It never did to fraternise; Cleo never fraternised. She thought a bit of distance lent her the power, mystery and respect that she deserved.

But mostly, the people who worked with her just thought she was a cow.

Anyway, she was the last person to encourage Milo to take advantage of his situation. She was pretty sure he'd got the message, standing back whenever the cameras were rolling.

Yes, Milo was OK ... she could trust him.

CHAPTER TWENTY

Craig Sanderson took an EasyJet flight to Toulon, the evening after his meeting with Lucien.

The following morning he was found by his housekeeper.

He was floating face down in his pool – at his beautiful house in Provence.

Kate spent the day before Georgia's funeral in Zelda's office. As her boss was going to be filming all day, Kate had the chance to catch up with all her work.

There were still a lot of arrangements to be checked over before the funeral tomorrow; she was co-ordinating with a team from Dark Artists. They didn't know how many people to expect outside the church, the police would handle that, but nine hundred or so were included on the list for inside.

These were all people Georgia had known, worked with, slept with or been married to ... music business moguls, singers, designers, actors, artists and socialites, newspaper and magazine editors, in fact the very people who had deified and denigrated her in not particularly equal measure, for all of her adult life. Then there were the people who had worked for her . . . the list was endless. Everyone wanted to come because everyone loved Georgia Cole.

Ironic then, that she had been so lonely when she died.

Kate had made up her mind. She would be handing in her notice after the funeral. She had finally had enough.

She could hear someone coming downstairs. Valentine poked his head around the door. 'Can I come in? I got you something.' He'd got her a Starbucks. Actually he'd sent one of the drivers to get it for him when he heard Kate was downstairs alone. But she wasn't to know that. The driver even knew what she liked – perfect! Valentine couldn't help wondering if the guy had the hots for her too. She was quite cute – he wouldn't deny that. She'd just pissed him off when she'd forgotten her place.

Well, here she was, back in her place now. And . . . not speaking to him, it seemed. Ah well, he didn't give up that easily.

He had a plan. Blame the drugs. It was his usual failsafe excuse. He found that one of the many wonderful things about drugs was that you could blame the most awful, outlandish, disgusting behaviour on them and people would understand. Or usually they would.

Kate wasn't looking very understanding now as she furiously typed on her computer keyboard. She still hadn't looked at him.

In fact, as far as he could remember, he hadn't taken anything much at Max's ... whatever Lily had given him and ... oh, yeah, he'd smoked a bit of skunk. Otherwise nothing, a few drinks maybe ... but that was it. Hardly anything then, not enough to account for the torrent of rage and filth that he'd unleashed on poor little Kate. He almost cringed when he thought about it. Then he thought, 'No, fuck it! She was in my bed – uninvited. Teach her to be a bit more bloody careful in future!'

Valentine decided to go for it. He looked anguished. He began by sitting elegantly on the edge of her desk, not too close, and placing the coffee down next to her.

He spoke softly, his voice full of remorse. 'Katkin, I am so, so sorry. Can you ever forgive me? I don't know what happened ... I think someone must've spiked my drink.' (Ooooh yes, he'd only just thought of that – nice one!) 'Whatever it was, it was a vicious, horrible drug, should be banned.' (Inspired!) 'It made me crazy. I can't remember much, but I don't think it was very nice for you, was it? I feel terrible about it, honestly, Katkin.' He did manage to look quite plausibly distraught. 'You know how I feel about you. I would never ever want to do anything to hurt you, Kate, you know that.'

He was pleased. He was good. Maybe he really should consider following in the family footsteps and take up acting when he left Oxford next year?

Back to the job at hand ... he looked at Kate imploringly. 'Will you forgive me, Kate, please?'

Kate finally turned to look at him. What he saw in her eyes frankly scared him.

She quietly took the top off the coffee and took a sip. 'Mmm, lovely and hot – thanks, Val.' Then she threw it all over him. 'Now fuck off, you little shit!'

Valentine jumped up – he couldn't believe what she'd just done. 'Ow, ow, ow – that's fucking hot! You bitch.'

'Ooooh, sorry, Val, did I hurt you? How mean of me … someone must've spiked my drink! As I said, fuck off – I've got work to do.'

'Not for long – when my mother hears about this …' Valentine said pathetically, as he stormed out.

'Yeah, yeah, yeah … you run off after your lovely mother then,' Kate called after him. Oh yes, she was so over this lot. She realised she needed some legal advice – a nice big redundancy package would be good. Yes, indeed, then she could have a wonderful long holiday somewhere … Barbados maybe? Or Bali?

This was proving to be quite an effective day's work after all.

When Zelda arrived home that night she felt excited. She was looking forward to seeing Elliot. They would have to have a proper talk.

And Jake …

But when she got home there was no one there at all.

No one!

It wasn't possible. She had run around everywhere calling out. But God's house was empty.

She called David in from outside.

He was pretty informative.

He told her that Elliot, Dusty, Willow and Lana had all left, late morning. He understood they had moved over to Hollywood Road. He was surprised she didn't know – so she just tried, not very convincingly, to pretend she'd forgotten.

Valentine had gone out, alone, early evening.

Jake had left a short time ago, but he'd driven himself: a very, very rare occurrence. He'd taken his old Mercedes.

Kate had left the office at six thirty. The housekeepers had the night off, because they would be working overtime tomorrow, after the funeral.

Oh, and Ed had asked one of the drivers to take him to Richmond – David thought he'd said he was going to see someone called . . . Jade? No . . . Scarlett!

Well, there we are, Zelda thought miserably. David knows everything. She offered him a drink. He looked embarrassed and declined.

She let him go.

Fuck! This wasn't the homecoming she'd expected at all. She poured herself a stiff drink and slumped down into one of the massive sofas in the Great Hall.

What the fuck was Elliot playing at? Declaring his undying love . . . then running away? Felt familiar!

And Jake? Where the hell had he gone? Driving himself too! God help everyone else on the roads tonight. She tried to ring him. No reply.

She hadn't heard from Lucien today, which was odd, given how much was going on. She speed dialled him: also no reply.

So here she was – home alone. She was always moaning that she was never alone. Now she was and, frankly, it felt awful. She went to get another drink. She found a huge bag of crisps and furiously munched her way through them, knocking back a few glasses of wine.

She wondered where Max was. She needed her daddy. She called him on the house phone. Jamie answered. He told her that Sir Max had gone out for the evening, he didn't know where. Zelda knew that Jamie knew exactly where Max was – he always did, but he took his job and discretion very seriously indeed, did Jamie. So she wouldn't get anything more out of him. She rummaged in the cupboard again and found some biscuits. She guzzled her way through the whole packet while finishing off the bottle of wine. Then unwisely she moved on to brandy. She turned on the sound system and the music soared through the brilliant acoustics of the hall. At some point she hit her shin really painfully on a coffee table. She jumped about screeching 'Ow, fuck! Ow, ow!' then promptly forgot about it.

She suddenly wondered how Cleo was getting on ... and Milo! God, yes, Milo. She missed him – she'd send him a text. She was feeling quite drunk now. The text was extremely loquacious and explicit – it would almost make Milo blush when he received it.

In fact, when Milo opened it in his hut that night he was chuffed and flattered. but he was also a bit surprised. Zelda was usually so careful, very discreet. He would hang onto that – a bit of a trophy text!

Zelda tried to ring Elliot again, then Jake, then Lucien. She even tried Ed. But no one was picking up her calls. She felt quite angry now. She rang her best friend, Shona, who always took her calls. She gabbled and ranted down the phone to her for a while, repeating herself incoherently. Shona asked if she wanted her to come over. She did, she did want her to come over. 'Now, come over now . . .'

But by the time Shona got there Zelda had passed out. Shona had to ask David to help her get her to bed.

He carried her upstairs, carefully, with gentleness and deference. Shona noted that David was clearly a bit in love with his boss. He placed her tenderly on her bed.

'Thanks, David. I can take it from here.' Shona closed the bedroom door. 'OK, sweetie – I think you might feel better if you are sick before you go to sleep . . .'

Shona really was a very good friend indeed. Being 'Stylist to the Stars' involved a lot more than people realised.

Earlier that evening Jake had let himself into his old-new mews house. He'd felt very nostalgic the moment he walked down its familiar cobbled street.

He was surprised to find it furnished. He wondered if Georgia had bought it that way? Or furnished it herself? It was beige, he realised, so she had definitely bought it that way. She'd never owned anything beige in her life.

There was a bottle of champagne on the island in the kitchen, with a letter propped up against it – with his name on it. It was in Georgia's handwriting.

He felt sad and apprehensive.

Without touching the champagne, he sat down on one of the beige sofas, opened his sister's letter and began to read.

My darling, favourite brother, Jake,
I hope you like your present!
 I have asked my lawyers to give this letter to you if for any reason I am unable to give you the keys to the Mews myself . . .

Jake woke the following morning to a whole new world.

He was in the smart new master bedroom at the Mews. He had had plenty of time to think. He hadn't touched the champagne, or anything alcoholic, and he felt that he'd been able to think clearly for the first time in years.

His sister's funeral was today. He had a tribute to give. Everything had changed.

There was much to be done. He needed to get back to God's, back to his family. They were going to need him today, and he was determined to be there for them.

The news of Craig Sanderson's death had only made a small headline in the newspapers that day:

'English accountant found drowned in pool, at luxury holiday home in Provence.'

Most of the papers didn't even mention his name. No one at God's would notice it. Particularly not on this day of all days.

But Lucien had heard yesterday. He had been pleased, thrilled even. He couldn't believe his luck. This was pretty perfect for him. He could blame the whole mess – if it really was such a mess – on Craig.

After all, dead men can't fight back.

CHAPTER TWENTY-ONE

The day of Georgia's funeral began peacefully.

Zelda was still fast asleep when Jake arrived back at God's. He had avoided the hideous press and public scrum that was building up again in front of the house by nipping in through Devil's and the garden. Ed and Valentine were having breakfast in the kitchen. They were both already dressed for the funeral, and Jake had to admit they made a bloody handsome pair. 'Dark and light, light and dark,' he mused, as he made a cup of tea for his wife.

Up in their bedroom, it was pitch dark; all the blackout blinds were drawn. Jake stumbled over some shoes, managed to open a curtain to let in a bit of light and put the tea down on the bedside table. He sat down on the edge of the bed. Zelda was still sleeping soundly.

Christ, she smelt of booze! Was this what he smelt like, every morning? Shit! He wondered how she had put up with him for all these years.

'Zelda, Zelda!' he said softly. 'Darling, wake up, I've made you a cup of tea. We have to go in an hour – wake up.' Zelda opened her eyes, screwing them up against the light.

'Jake, what? Where were you? – I was worried. I was here, all alone. Everyone left. What happened? Are you OK? I was so scared – they said you'd driven . . . you haven't been in prison all night, have you?' She still sounded half-asleep.

Jake laughed. 'No, of course I wasn't in prison, or perhaps I should say thank God I wasn't. No, I went over to the Mews – sorry, I should've told you where I was. I just needed time to think about everything. And I have – thought about every-thing, I mean . . . things are going to be different from now on, Zelda. I'm going to be different.'

'Really, darling? Good, that sounds lovely . . .' Zelda seemed to be falling back to sleep. Jake couldn't blame her really. The idea of him being different, mending his ways . . . not really a novel idea. She'd heard it all before.

But this time, she didn't know it yet . . . this time everything really was going to change.

Everyone had gathered in the Great Hall.

Zelda and Jake had just joined the boys when Max arrived. 'Darlings, I'm so sorry I haven't been around as much as I would have liked – I've just been unaccountably busy for some reason.' Max looked contrite. 'Have you all been all right? Where's Dusty, Elliot et al? Have they gone on ahead?'

'They're going from Hollywood Road, Max. Elliot moved them over there yesterday, decided they might as well start as they meant to go on.' Jake lit a cigarette, and taking a deep drag, he continued, 'Now he has the means to look after the girls he's happy to step up to the mark.' Jake turned to Zelda, offering her the cigarette, which she accepted gratefully. 'I hope you don't mind, darling – I said they could take Lana, just till they get settled.'

Ed looked up from his phone. 'Well, I bloody mind, just giving away my gorgeous "Oooh Pair" without even asking me. Bloody cheek!'

Zelda looked at Ed and smiled indulgently. 'You are far too old for an au pair now. Anyway, Ed, you've got me to look after you.'

'Yeah, whatever!' Ed grinned.

Valentine was smoking quietly. He looked extraordinarily beautiful in his Prada suit, hand-made for him at their atelier in Milan. A bit pale but very handsome, his mother thought proudly.

Kate appeared. 'The cars are ready when you are.'

Jake looked around at his family. 'OK, everybody ready? Let's go.'

As they trooped across the Great Hall, Max remembered to tell them that Cleo had sent a message. 'She sent you all her love, she's thinking of us apparently, and I have no reason not to believe her. I'm sure she's missing us madly already – all that goat shit and dead bodies all over the place ...'

Zelda turned to her father, and said irritably, 'Daddy, what are you talking about?'

'Everest, darling. Apparently it's absolutely filthy – Cleo's not going to like that at all.'

'Oh, I don't know, Daddy. I'd always thought Mummy darling

liked things quite filthy!' Zelda's eyes sparkled mischievously at Jake. He smiled thinly. She couldn't help noticing he looked quite drawn. Poor Jake, she thought, he is really going to miss Georgia.

Then the front doors were opened and they all composed their expressions to look suitably sombre.

The press went wild about Zelda's outfit. She had to admit Shona had surpassed herself on the styling front: a black guipure lace Dolce & Gabbana suit, a Philip Treacy hat – just the right amount of attention-seeking crazy, but not too much, always a fine line. Exquisite and surprisingly comfortable Jimmy Choo shoes. Yes, much loveliness for the fashion press to discuss tomorrow. Zelda felt pleased: still very hungover, but pleased. She knew she looked fabulous.

Without Dusty and Willow in tow Zelda was getting most of the paparazzi attention. She knew it wouldn't be quite the same when they got to the church. Unless she managed to arrive or leave at the same time as Elton and David – she'd been told they were coming. If she was papped with them she'd definitely make the front pages.

Why was she thinking like this? She knew she had more important things to think about ... but old habits die hard.

The funeral cars pulled away from God's at a suitably sedate pace.

This was going to be a very long day for everyone.

Remarkably, the funeral went without a hitch.

Georgia still managed to cause a stir by having her bright

pink coffin covered in flashing, multi-coloured fairy lights. She had left this instruction with her stylist, or she'd mentioned it to her a few times, anyway – apparently.

The coffin was brought into the vast church to the sound of Mick Jagger singing 'You can't always get what you want.' This sent a warm and tender ripple of laughter through the congregation. Fortunately, the church had a most agreeable vicar – who, as it happened, was just as susceptible to being starstruck as the next man.

Jake's tribute was poignant and moving, inducing much laughter and some tears.

Dusty held Willow throughout and, although Dusty sobbed all the way through the service, Willow was quiet and good and smiled gaily at the people sitting behind her.

The family then went privately to Brompton Cemetery where Georgia was quietly buried among her peers. She had once been photographed for an album cover in the cemetery by Bob Carlos Clarke, and had always said it was one of her favourite London landmarks. The police had managed to keep all the paparazzi and public outside the gates, so that the final moment of her burial could be peaceful and private.

Until the papers were printed the following day when it became clear that at least one photographer had managed to get the pictures the media were after. The resourceful pap had paid some students for half an hour at their window in a top-floor flat on Ifield Road, which backed onto the cemetery. A number of his photographs were published: 'The Devastated Children of Georgia Cole Weeping at Her Graveside.' One particularly intrusive picture made the front page of every newspaper; it was of Dusty, bereft, holding an inconsolable Willow – they looked unbearably fragile and alone.

That was the 'money shot' – the photographer planned to take three months off on the proceeds.

The wake was held at Claridges, the beautiful Mayfair hotel, in the grand ballroom, which was soon filled and clamouring with the glamorous, rich and powerful, the famous and infamous. They were all there to be seen to mark the passing of one of London's most popular performing artists. Some of them had even known and liked her, although very few had known her well.

David managed to protect Dusty and Ed from the worst excesses of the press, shielding them with an umbrella as they came and went from the church, when it wasn't even raining. When they arrived at Claridges he guided them safely in through the back door.

Lana had taken Willow back home – she was far too young to be at the wake. They needed extra security and police for the driver to be able to get through the crowds that had been gathering in Hollywood Road again since early that morning.

Jake somehow managed to remain sober throughout that dreadful day. Zelda couldn't face anything to drink. She just took one tiny little Valium to get her through.

Valentine and India moved graciously through the crowd, side by side, reunited for this sad day. Everyone thought they made such a perfect pair. India had granted Valentine a reprieve and he seemed happy to have her on his arm again. Charlie and Art were pinned to the bar, trying to chat up a runner-up from last season's 'X Factor'. Valentine didn't fancy their chances much, and he knew his were non-existent with India glued to his side. He was beginning to feel slightly claustrophobic when he noticed Dusty talking to a very good-looking waiter. They seemed to be swapping numbers. Valentine felt a little stab of jealousy – which he convinced himself was just protectiveness of his cousin. He broke away from India and, giving the waiter a cold stare, he took Dusty firmly by the arm and said, 'There's someone you just have to meet. Come on!' As he pulled her away, Dusty turned back and, smiling over her shoulder, she mouthed, 'Sorry!'

Alex grinned and went back to work.

Zelda had only managed to speak to Elliot briefly in a snatched conversation, in the corner of the ballroom, where she had said crossly, 'Well, thanks for telling me you were running away again, Elliot.' Delivered through clenched, smiling teeth.

'I'm not running away, Zelda, far from it. I just have responsibilities now. I think you made your feelings, or lack thereof, perfectly clear yesterday. So just drop it.' Elliot moved away.

What, what the fuck was he talking about? . . . He'd declared his undying love and she'd, she'd? . . . Zelda thought back. Oh, yes . . . she'd just brushed him off and walked away. Oh God. There they were, misunderstanding everything about one another, all over again. Well, this clearly wasn't the moment to

try to resolve things with him. She'd speak to him properly ...
when?

She was leaving in the morning for ten days shooting in
Spain. Then her work on the film would be finished.

Oh, well. They'd waited this long ... and he sure as hell
wasn't going anywhere now.

Oddly, she hadn't spoken to Lucien at all. She'd seen him in
the distance with his visibly pregnant wife Kristina, a very
unusual sight, as he never usually took her anywhere. Zelda
couldn't imagine why not, she was very pretty and always
looked charming and smiley. It didn't really occur to Zelda
until much later that it was odd of Lucien not to have even said
hello. She was so busy greeting all and sundry – the great and
the good and the not so good – she hadn't noticed his behaviour. He did look rather red – she'd noticed that. 'Maybe he
should have his blood pressure checked?' she'd thought to herself with a tiny glimmer of uncharacteristic concern.

By the time they got back to God's late that afternoon they
were far from being in their usual drunken-car-crash state.
They were all going to go over to have a quiet supper with Max.

Valentine had a little chat with his mother, explaining that
he had got into a bit of a muddle about Kate. It was all rather
awkward. To his surprise his mother pre-empted him. Before
he had time to deliver his convoluted and somewhat implau-
sible reason for why she should be sacked, Zelda said simply,
'Don't worry, Val, she's going anyway. She's been a nightmare

this week – never in the right place at the right time. I need someone I can depend on. I'll deal with it. OK?'

Zelda went down to the office, where she was pleased to find that Kate was still there, packing up for the day. Never one to procrastinate, Zelda dived straight in. She knew quite a bit about redundancy laws, so she smiled very sweetly at Kate and said, 'Kate, so glad I caught you. As you know I'm away for a bit, finishing the film. I wanted to talk to you about your job before I leave tomorrow. The thing is – I'm not going to be needing anyone full time any more. I'm planning to scale back a lot actually. So if you wouldn't mind just putting everything in order while I'm away. Then you can take the rest of your redundancy time as a holiday. Just a brief handover when I get back. Then um ... off you go!' Zelda smiled, as if she had bestowed some fantastic gift on her PA. 'I'm sure you will do very well in your next job and I'll give you a reference, of course.' She got up abruptly and left the office, before Kate had a chance to respond.

Zelda put her head round the screening-room door and found Valentine watching MTV, smoking a joint. His mother smiled at him indulgently. 'Job done, darling! See you at Max's – he wants us there at eight.'

'Aw, thanks, Mum. Sorry about that ...' Valentine looked contrite. He was relieved and surprised that his mother had taken the whole thing so well and he sniggered at her parting remark, 'Well, I did warn you, darling, never fuck the staff!' as she closed the door again.

Her advice was a bit hypocritical, she realised. But that was different. She was a grown-up and knew what she was doing, how to handle people . . . yes, it was different for her.

She really wanted a shower and to get all her tight kit off. When she got upstairs she could just hear the shower going in the wet-room. Jake had put music on full blast – it was pumping around their bedroom and bathroom.

He had been great today. His tribute was brilliant and had made her remember what a good writer he was. A good man actually.

She peeled off her clothes and went to join him in the shower.

CHAPTER TWENTY-TWO

The next morning Jake lay in bed and watched admiringly as Zelda got dressed.

One of the housekeepers had packed her suitcase for her the night before, for the Spain trip, while they all had supper over at Max's. So she only had to get her makeup and clothes on. It was early, and the dawn light was soft. God, she is so beautiful, Jake thought. He felt overwhelmingly sad.

They had had a good night last night. So this was going to seem weird and Jake wasn't sure how Zelda would take what he had to say to her now. But it had to be done. He was determined that nothing was going to be 'just left' from now on.

'Zelda. I wanted to talk to you last night but ... Um, well, I've decided, I'm going to move over to the Mews for a while. Spend some time getting my head straight, getting myself straight. Things have been so complicated for so long and I just ... need some space.' He was watching his wife closely, but she just kept on getting dressed – she was doing up the buttons on a tight white cotton blouse, her hair falling over her face. He couldn't see her reaction. He ploughed on. 'I think we both do, to be honest, to give us time to think about what we want ... So that's what I'm doing ... we can have a proper talk when you get back. You'll have time to think too.'

Zelda was completely silent. She went into the bathroom. He could hear her rummaging noisily in her makeup drawer. Crashing about a bit. Then she emerged, wearing her sunglasses – making it more impossible to read what she was thinking.

'Right,' she said crisply. 'What about Ed, who'll be keeping an eye on him while I'm away? Since you gave Lana away so thoughtfully.' She sounded cold, sarcastic, furious – he knew that tone.

He hadn't thought about Ed. 'He can come with me, if he wants. Don't worry. I'll make sure he's looked after.'

'Well you obviously have everything perfectly worked out. Don't need me. Bye.' And she left. Just like that.

Jake wondered if he should go after her to try to reassure her – he was only suggesting a little space for them to sort themselves out a bit ... God, what did she think he'd said? He got up, grabbed a sarong, ran downstairs.

But her car was pulling away through the crowd when he opened the front door.

The press got a great picture of 'Jake Robinson, brother to Dead Georgia and husband to film star Zelda', looking very dishevelled and half-naked on his doorstep.

Zelda sobbed, quietly, all the way to the airport.

*

Later that week Hugo Peterson and Giles de Winter arrived at the Mews for a meeting with Jake.

They informed him that Craig Sanderson had sent a large box of documents to Peterson de Winter, which was delivered after he died. They threw considerable light on many of the pertinent details of Dark Artists' financial affairs.

So, Lucien was soon to discover that dead men did indeed fight back.

In a hunch that had paid off, Giles de Winter had buttonholed Craig Sanderson as he was leaving God's on the day of the reading of Georgia's will. Giles had correctly assessed the accountant's despair. He'd given him his card and told him to let him know if there was anything he could do to help.

Consequently, with the information that Craig had given, Peterson de Winter were able to subpoena Dark Artists and Lucien Dark to supply full and comprehensive details of all their clients' financial positions with immediate effect. When these were not forthcoming, they had put the matter into the hands of the Serious Fraud Office.

They both looked extremely anxious. Jake was unsurprised by what they had to tell him.

Hugo sipped tentatively at the coffee that Jake had made for him. 'We wondered when your wife would be available for a chat. She may have information that can help us too.'

Jake couldn't imagine what they meant. He pointed out that no one he'd ever met had a more tenuous grasp on how their finances worked than Zelda, well, with the possible exception of himself.

Giles said wryly, 'Well, sadly, I fear in this case, ignorance will not turn out to be bliss.'

'We are sorry, Jake. But, from the dealings we have had with Lucien Dark over Miss Cole's affairs, we are quite fearful for all the artists whose funds have been managed by Dark Artists International.'

Jake explained that Zelda was away for a few days finishing her film, but that she could be contacted by e-mail if they needed to ask her anything urgently. They just had to let him know what they wanted to ask, and he'd contact her.

He wasn't convinced that she'd answer – but it might be a good way of opening up the lines of communication.

Chapter Twenty-Three

The trek up to base camp had gone relatively smoothly, although one of the crew had already been left behind, suffering horribly from altitude sickness.

They had spent two days travelling back and forth across the Khumbu ice fall, which had been quite physically testing and frightening. The ice fall was in constant motion; enormous ice seracs, some larger than houses, dangled precariously over their heads, threatening to fall at any moment. They had to cross crevasses with the terrible, constant sound of creaking ice all around them. Cleo had managed well. In fact she was a bit annoyed about going back and forth to acclimatise – she didn't feel it was necessary. God knows she was used to the heady atmosphere of thin air; she lived most of her life in it. That was the sort of sound-bite she was giving to the film crew.

The director was pleased.

In the past, he had made a number of acclaimed documentaries in very inhospitable terrain, and he was an experienced climber. He had worked with Bear Grylls on a couple of his shows. But he had never combined a celebrity with something as challenging as this; no one had. He had to hand it to Cleo; she was one hell of a woman. Her level of fitness, for any age, let alone well over seventy – it was almost inhuman. She was entertaining on camera, with great one-liners that made for terrific television. She was fairly tricky off camera. Quite a few of the crew were scared of her. But he noticed she had the respect of the Sherpas and that would stand her in good stead when the going really got tough.

Bear was arriving at base camp tomorrow to do some filming with them.

Cleo was disappointed when she was told that he wouldn't be doing the whole climb with her. Apparently he had other work commitments. Damn! she'd thought when she heard. She loved Bear. So disappointing. But then again, all the more attention for her – every cloud had a silver lining.

This altitude made her feel rather cheerful, which was lucky because there was little to be cheerful about on the accommodation front. The pit toilets were absolutely disgusting. And as for the litter and filth that lined the track up to base camp, it was worse than the roadsides of Britain. Bill Bryson should bring his campaign up here. Clean Up Everest – yes, maybe she'd give him a call about it when she got back.

This was to be their last evening at base camp. They would be leaving the South-East Ridge at first light.

Cleo retired to her tent early. She wanted to conserve as much energy as possible. Milo sweetly popped in to make sure she was all right. He crawled in next to her and explained some of the last-minute advice he had been given by Bear, who'd just turned up unexpectedly early. Cleo was annoyed that she had gone to bed so promptly now; she'd missed a chance to meet him before the morning. Missed a chance to film with him around the campfire too; she would've looked good in that light – damn, how maddening!

Milo wriggled off out of the tent. Cleo put out her lantern and tried to get to sleep.

She could hear a buzzing noise – what was that? She could see a blue light flashing on the fur throw. She picked it up. It was Milo's phone. The screen screamed at her: Mick Silver.

She read the message from the worlds most infamous publicist: 'Tabloids very interested. Text evidence sounds good. Get more. The figures are promising. Think you'll be pleased. Best Mick.'

Cleo's hands were shaking. What the fuck! Well, clearly, Milo the fuck-over. Jesus!

But there was more and it was worse. She found Zelda's text first. What? – the bastard! – her daughter too?

But there was still more. Cleo's blood ran cold, it was hard to believe that it could run any colder but it did. A text to Max from Milo. It left no doubt in Cleo's mind ... although Max had had the good sense not to reply. (In fact Max never used his mobile. His butler, Jamie, checked it for him and gave him any important messages. He had deleted the one from Milo the moment he saw it. Jamie certainly wasn't going to mention that to the boss) The text said, 'Max. Missing you madly. Please send filthy thoughts to help sustain me through this trial.'

Entrapment too.

Cleo could hardly breathe and she felt sick, not with bloody altitude sickness either. Sick with rage. Oh God . . . She thought quickly: what should she do?

She wasn't a brilliant expert with phones, but she did know how to delete, and so delete she did. The text from Zelda and from Mick Silver went first. She scrolled down. There wasn't much else. Her family were quite savvy, thank God.

Except for Zelda . . . had she lost her mind? Clearly she had!

Cleo realised Milo wouldn't know about the Mick Silver message, now that she had deleted it without him seeing it.

God! How disgusting. Her entire family, for Christ's sake!

She furiously threw the phone out of the tent. With a bit of luck it would be destroyed. In fact, she instantly realised that she should've thrown it much farther away – it would have been so easily lost in the snow. Damn. She poked her head out of her tent. But she couldn't see anything. Except . . . was that Milo's retreating back? Damn, had he come back for his phone and found it? She looked desperately about in the snow. No phone. Damn it! God, what an idiot she was, maybe this thin air was getting to her after all. At least she'd deleted any evidence that the little bastard could use against them. Could anyone access things after they'd been deleted? She just wasn't sure. What a nightmare. How would she sleep now?

Cleo woke feeling frostier than the frostiest morning to find that Milo was calling her from outside the tent. She had resolved not to show that anything had changed between them, to carry on as normal until she could figure out what to do.

'OK, OK – on my way,' she called back brightly. She was an actress after all.

Bear Grylls turned out to be absolutely gorgeous. He was going to be climbing with them up to Camp One, up to 19,500 feet.

Apparently, the Sherpas would have stocked it in advance. How lovely.

The weather was good. Bear told Cleo it was the best he'd ever seen it. The forecast was promising too. Although, he warned, things could change very, very suddenly on the mountain. So they would have to be prepared to take each day as it came. After the morning climb he told Cleo that he was very impressed with her level of fitness. He asked her if she really was planning to try for the summit.

'Of course, darling,' she'd replied. 'I always aim for the top.' Cut.

The director knew that the producers had had an informal chat with Milo about the possibility of him doing his own show about training people in dangerous sports, or something along those lines. Milo had loved the idea.

The producers had been pleasantly surprised when Milo told them he had plans to do a big press drive when he got home, which he assured them would dramatically heighten his profile. It all sounded good to them.

They could only guess at the sort of thing he had in mind. But they realised that it would mean more press attention for this show and anything they did with him in the future. They weren't going to let their scruples get in the way of their ratings. They would turn a blind eye.

Anyway the producers had gone as far as they could go on this trip. They were very relieved to be off home to get some pre-sales of the show going. This was going to be a nice little earner. They were all very chuffed indeed. They were also looking forward to a nice hot shower and some real food.

The only person who was sad to be going home was the horse-faced production assistant. She had been having the time of her life.

Bear had to leave them after they reached Camp One. He told Cleo he would've liked to go on to Camp Two, only 1500 feet further up. But to get up to the Western Cwm was a slow climb and he daren't get caught up there if the weather turned – he had to get to the Arctic for another shoot, another show – so he reluctantly said goodbye to Cleo and her crew. He assured her that his old chum the director and their brilliant guide would look after her well. He told her he was sad but he really had to go.

Cleo waved him off, but she really wished he could do the whole climb with her. The first time he'd reached the summit he was the youngest person to do so, aged just twenty-three. If they had done it together, she would be by far the oldest woman to do it. Quite a good story, if anyone found out her real age, that was ... but that wasn't going to happen! Perhaps it was better that he wasn't going with her after all; the age comparisons might be quite annoying.

She crunched back across the snow to her tent. She wanted to finish getting her kit together and to put on some more sunblock, without completely destroying her makeup.

The cameraman had noticed that Cleo was still wearing red lipstick at all times. He'd done this climb before. Reckoned it wouldn't be long before the camera would be getting Cleo Spender in all her 'natural' glory. See what she was really made of.

Today was to be the first of the hard climbs.

CHAPTER TWENTY-FOUR

When Lucien had arrived at his office earlier that morning he was flabbergasted and enraged to find he was barred from entering. He was told that his entire office had been closed and sealed by the Serious Fraud Office.

After a lot of ranting at and threatening of the thugs that barred him from his company, then more fruitless yelling into his mobile at his lawyers, who informed him that the SFO had a court order to freeze all the assets of Dark Artists, Lucien was forced to admit to himself, reluctantly, that he was going to have to put Plan B into action.

He went to the nearest cashpoint. None of his cards worked.

That's when he'd decided to go home.

Kristina opened the front door to some very officious-looking men. They reminded her of the type of people who knocked on doors, at any time, day or night, back in her country. The sort of men who scared the shit out of everyone and often made people disappear.

But this was England and so Kristina remained calm when the men informed her that they were from the Serious Fraud Office. They told her they had a warrant to confiscate the personal computer and documents from the home of Mr Lucien Dark.

She felt her baby kick as she smiled and opened the front door wide, to let them in.

Lucien was already apoplectic with rage by the time he got back to his house, only to be told by Kristina that some men had just left – having taken his computer and many of the files from his home office.

'What, what the fuck do you mean? Who were these people? Who let them in?'

Lucien loomed over his fragile, pregnant wife. 'You did, didn't you? You stupid fucking bitch!'

He stood very close to her, placing his shoes over her bare feet and putting his face an inch away from hers, he pressed down hard on her toes. She didn't flinch, just looked right back at him calmly, letting his torrent of abuse flow over her and her pregnant belly, impassive and immune now to all his cruelty and violence.

He raised his arm to hit her. But something in her eyes made him stop – almost made him afraid. He turned away and stormed off upstairs.

Kristina went down to the kitchen and put the kettle on. She hummed a little tune.

She heard the front door slam just moments before the police arrived to arrest her husband.

CHAPTER TWENTY-FIVE

Valentine had gone to Paris for a few days, where he had arranged to meet India.

He had been missing her a lot. She was so adorable and good for him – he knew that now. He felt he was nice with her. India was what he needed, just her, and everything would be OK. She had turned up for the funeral, but she insisted that was only on compassionate grounds. She'd told him that she wasn't sure she wanted to go out with him any more. So, ironically, while he had been thinking about dumping her, it turned out she'd dumped him! Persuading her to come to Paris hadn't been easy – he'd almost been reduced to begging. She had played very hard to get.

He had booked a suite at L'Hotel, his favourite French hotel. The rooms were dark and sexy, all built around a circular hall that led from the ground floor to a glass-domed atrium. It was very romantic. Oscar Wilde had died there.

He had to pop into his agency's Paris office for a meeting anyway, so it all fitted in well. He had arranged for them to meet at the Café Flore at 6p.m. He hoped she'd like the romance of that old cliché of a place.

It was a beautiful evening. The soft, warm light lent an extra magic and beauty to his favourite city. Valentine had time to spare and so he walked through the Luxembourg Gardens, stopping to sit on a bench, to smoke an idle cigarette and watch the girls go by. The girls, in their turn, giggled with delight to be watched by him. He was in a mellow mood.

When he got to the café, at just after six, India hadn't arrived. He ordered a black coffee and Calvados. He tried to ring her at six fifteen in case she was lost. She'd said she didn't know Paris well. No reply. By six thirty he was quite pissed off with her.

He was staring petulantly up the Boulevard St Germain when his eyes lit upon the most beautiful girl, with tousled fair hair and bare tanned legs. She was wearing a tiny white Coco dress, with a massive tasselled shoulder bag swishing gently against her thigh. Heads were turning as she came swinging nonchalantly down the street towards him.

'Lily!' he called out, almost too loudly, too enthusiastically. He couldn't believe it. Without expressing any surprise at finding Valentine sitting alone in Paris, outside the Café Flore, Lily just plonked herself down on the chair next to him. Then she pulled out a Disque Bleu, lit it and handed it to Valentine, and lit another for herself. Lily smiled up at the waiter and ordered a Kir Royale in perfect French. Her voice was surprisingly light but somehow husky.

She took a deep drag of her cigarette, exhaled and leant

across the table to give Valentine the most exciting smoky kiss he had ever had.

He was lost.

So he didn't see India, as she ran towards him, up the boulevard.

He didn't see her stop and stare in disbelief. He didn't see her turn away with tears in her eyes and he didn't see her leave.

He had never really seen her and he would never see her again.

Jake and Ed had settled into the Mews.

Jake had been to his first AA meeting the night before. He had found it scary, enlightening and entertaining. The friend who took him had been sober for years.

They went to a small group in Chelsea. Surprisingly, a lot of the people there were very famous indeed. If that was a representative sample of the type of people who attended such meetings, then it seemed that addiction problems had to be a compulsory part of any sort of success in the entertainment or arts business.

Of course that wasn't the case. But his friend Andy thought he'd be more comfortable starting off in a social group that he was familiar with and one that was also 'safe' in terms of confidentiality. It had gone well; he was going to another tonight.

He was apprehensive when he told Ed, but his son responded with a supportive, "Bout time, Dad, it'll be good. All my friends' parents have done rehab – it's cool.'

And he went back to watching TV.

Jake wanted to hug him, so he did.

Ed pushed him off. 'Jesus, Dad! Get off – you're not going to get all weird, are you?'

'No, no – course not, sorry. But thanks, Ed – mate – thanks.' Jake looked tearful. This would normally have been a moment when he would have had a drink – would have ... he'd make a cup of tea.

'Oh, Dad, Dusty's coming over in a minute, to see the house.' Ed had only just remembered.

'Great, good.' Jake stood in the kitchen and looked around at the house that Georgia had given him – their lovely old house.

It looked quite different now, it had been owned by a lot of people since he and Georgia had lived there. The last were developers, who had added an extra floor – a master bedroom suite at the top of the house, quite state-of-the-art – and then all three bedrooms on the first floor were small but charming. The ground-floor kitchen, dining, and living area were all open plan, well designed but a bit bland.

The developers had converted the garage into a study. His study, 'for him to write in', as Georgia had suggested in her letter. He had to admit he liked the feel of it. He had collected his computer from God's earlier and now it was installed on his new desk: a fresh start.

God bless you, darling sister, he was thinking, just as Dusty arrived.

He made her a cup of tea and the three of them sat down at the table for a chat.

Dusty was looking eccentric. Jake thought he recognised some of her clothes as Georgia's old vintage stuff – an Antony Price dress over a long-sleeved T-shirt, Vivienne Westwood boots. Her mother had always been a massive hoarder and had kept clothes from as far back as her teens. They suited Dusty well. He told her so and she looked pleased.

'So how's it going at home – Elliot coping all right?' Jake tried to look hopeful.

'Yeah, I think so. He seems to be panicking about money all the time. I've told him Mum's got lots but he says there might be a problem. But he won't tell me what.' She looked a bit peeved.

Jake wasn't sure how much to say; he didn't want to worry her. But on the other hand she had a right to know. 'To be honest, Dusty, there do seem to be some problems with money. It's possible that quite a lot has been lost by, um, the agency and their financial advisors . . . we're not sure what yet. But everything will be fine, I'm sure. Between us we will have more than enough to go round. Not going to be on skid row yet. That's for sure!' He tried to look confident.

In fact, things were looking more alarming by the minute. Hugo and Giles had asked him to contact Zelda to ask her if Lucien had given her any documents to sign recently and if so, to ask if she had checked to see what she was signing.

She hadn't replied all day. Then a text message had come through with her answer: 'Why? I haven't inadvertently signed my divorce papers, have I? Everything comes as a fucking surprise to me these days.' She could still be funny, even when her heart was breaking.

Jake couldn't help laughing, as he texted back, 'Not unless Lucien has decided to divorce us . . . anything is possible with that bastard – but we all know he's never been my fave. Be assured that it gives me no satisfaction to tell you that he may have out-bastarded even himself this time. The lawyers really do need to know if you have signed anything for him lately. The SFO are investigating him and things look critical. Please reply. X Jake.'

His phone rang; it was Zelda. 'What the fuck's going on?'

'Hang on, just going upstairs.' He couldn't have this conversation in front of Dusty, or Ed for that matter.

'Jake, you are scaring me – what's going on?'

'We don't know yet. Looks like Lucien may have had his hand in the till, deep. But not just that. There have been massive losses over the last few months, years even. Nobody seems to know how much yet, but he is going to have a lot of explaining to do. I'll let you know when I know more.' Jake sounded strong.

'Are you saying he might have lost some of my money, um, our money?'

'Yes, 'fraid so – question is how much.'

'I did sign something.' Zelda's voice sounded tiny, like a child's. 'I did sign something without looking at it. Quite a lot of things. He came over with reams of paper the other day, said they were contracts – work stuff – money for me.'

'Well, chances are, he meant money for him,' Jake said wryly. 'The world is in total financial meltdown and he's been playing with fire. Let's hope he hasn't burnt us all to the ground.' He sighed. 'When are you back?'

262

'Not for a few days. I'll talk to the director. See if they can bring my scenes forward. I think I need to get back there. I'll call you. Bye.' And she hung up.

Just as Jake said, 'Zelda, I wanted to ...'

Just like that. There it was – that cold 'bye' again.

He e-mailed Peterson de Winter to warn them that Zelda had indeed signed numerous unspecified papers. Then he went back downstairs.

Dusty and Ed were sitting on the doorstep smoking. Much like he and Georgia used to do when they lived there.

He realised that he and his sister had only been a little older than these two were now when they had moved into the Mews. Far too young to be all alone.

Now, here was Dusty, in almost the same situation. She had her father Elliot, of course, but somehow that didn't feel quite right ... there was still something of the orphan about Dusty. He supposed Georgia really had been mother and father to both her girls. But now everything was different.

There was a lot of shit to be dealt with. He'd better get off to that meeting. They'd told him last night one AA meeting, every day, for ninety days – fucking hell! But they had also said 'one day at a time'. Which, in these crazy times, seemed like very good advice indeed.

He told the kids he'd be back at eight. Ed asked if he'd like them to get him a pizza when they ordered some. He said no, he was going to cook them something – just pasta ... but if Dusty wanted to stay?

She did. She would phone Lana to let her know that she wouldn't be home. Elliot was out with one of his editors.

'How is Lana?' Jake was ashamed to realise he hadn't given that poor girl a second thought. Pushed around from pillar to post, kindly, calmly doing everyone's bidding.

'She's fine. Dad says she's getting fat ... but she's fine. Willow loves her.'

Fat? Did she say fat? Shit! Jake really needed to have a proper talk with that girl.

CHAPTER TWENTY-SIX

They reached the Western Cwm at nightfall. The weather had turned and, within moments of getting to their tents, visibility was zero. There was a freezing, biting blizzard that tore at the canvas. The climb had been very difficult and tiring, particularly for the camera crew. They would be changing to helmet cameras tomorrow. Everyone was starving. The guide told them to eat the biscuit rations that they would find in their tents, as the weather was far too bad to move around in, and they wouldn't be able to get anything more nutritious together. Each person was ordered to get 'holed up' in their own tent, where they found themselves pinned, cold and lonely, for the next eighteen hours. They were all very hungry and grumpy by the time the storm had passed.

The next day only Cleo seemed chipper. She said she could go for days without food, and her feet were used to far worse than these boots. She'd walked around on Mr Freedom platforms, for God's sake! It was all part of the job, she said gaily. The director bloody loved her.

A couple of the crew wanted to strangle her.

Today was going to be big. They were to leave for Camp Four and climb up towards the Lhotse Face. The Sherpas didn't like to stay at Camp Three on the steep, shiny ice wall. They knew that if the weather changed, while on the face, it could mean death to the climbers. They preferred to push on across it, directly to Camp Four.

So that was the plan. Sherpas would be there to meet them with tea apparently, and Cleo thought it sounded like a walk in the park.

The guide looked grave. 'Now team, listen up – we will have to really push on today. Everyone use your oxygen, please. We don't want you passing out and falling off. The ice is very slippery but you know that already. Most of the wall is roped, so hang on and look where you are putting your feet. It's not easy while wearing the oxygen mask, but if you don't you might just drop off. I haven't lost anyone in a while and I don't want to lose any of you today. If we make it to Camp Four, I am happy to tell you we will then be in the Death Zone – so not so dishonourable for me to lose you there!' He was funny *and* Australian. 'Let's get to it!'

Everyone was roped to someone else. The guide was roped to the cameraman. They were to go first, to film Cleo from above. Then Cleo was roped to Milo – she smiled sweetly at him as they were clipped together. They were to be followed by the director roped to a Sherpa, then came the soundman, and another cameraman, with other Sherpas in between, to help anyone who got into trouble.

They would be climbing for eight to ten hours.

They were ready to roll. Oh. No, hang on. Cleo needed to pee. She unclipped herself and disappeared behind a boulder.

Then, they were ready to roll.

CHAPTER TWENTY-SEVEN

Lucien was arrested at Heathrow Airport, trying to board a plane to Switzerland.

A warrant had been issued for his arrest. The police had received an anonymous tip-off which enabled them to intercept him as he made his escape, rather than a triumph for the effectiveness of British border control, which was how it would be portrayed in the papers the following day.

He was taken to Chelsea Police Station.

His lawyer informed him that he had not yet been charged but the SFO had issued a restraint order against him. He was in for questioning and his lawyer told him that the police had the right to hold him for thirty-six hours, after which charges could either be made or not.

'What? What the fuck are they talking about? Get me out on bail or whatever, now!' Lucien screamed at his lawyer.

'That won't be possible I'm afraid; we have to await charges before we can apply for bail. Hopefully none of that will be necessary. But perhaps you could let me know where you might be able to locate the funds if you do need to secure bail. You are aware that all your assets have been frozen?' The lawyer looked slightly smug. Lucien wanted to thump him.

He knew he needed a better lawyer than this prat. 'I need your senior partner to handle this – get him! You're too fucking wet behind the ears. This is a big boy's job. I want your boss to represent me, someone who knows what the fuck he's doing. So fuck off and get him – now! – there's a good boy.' Lucien sat down heavily on the chair in the cell.

The lawyer picked up his briefcase and left.

The cell door clanged shut.

Lucien punched the table. He really hurt his hand.

The following morning the newspapers were rife with speculation. The financial press were all over the story.

Lucien Dark's wife Kristina was also said to be helping police with their enquiries.

And very helpful she was proving to be too.

Chapter Twenty-Eight

Things on the Lhotse Face were becoming very tough indeed.

They had been climbing for several hours. Word came down from the guide that they needed to move much faster. Everyone, including Cleo, was exhausted.

They continued, clinging to the ropes, kicking their crampons in with every step. Exhausting, boring stuff. Cleo was moaning. Everyone was moaning.

After another couple of hours they had almost ground to a halt.

The guide held back, and when they drew level with him he said, 'You're doing great. The good news is, we're almost there. Another hour should do it if we really kick arse. The bad news is, if we don't, the weather is coming in – so if we don't cut along we might die.'

Everyone's arse was kicked.

They pressed on – if not with renewed vigour, then certainly with renewed terror.

But they weren't fast enough. Cloud came down suddenly

and took out all their visibility. They had to keep going; but into what, they couldn't know.

They stumbled along like blind men. Clinging to the ropes, kicking into the ice. Trying to breathe through their oxygen masks.

Then Cleo slipped. She squealed – Milo could hear her, skidding towards him. He managed to catch her as she sped past. Holding onto the guide rope he threw his body on top of hers and they lay panting for a moment or two. Everything was deathly quiet. They couldn't hear any other voices at all.

Milo stood up, groping for the fixed line. Cleo struggled up too, looping her arm over the line, and began to pull herself up. She heard a sliding noise behind her and Milo saying urgently, 'Shit! Cleo! Hold on to something – *now!*'

She looped her arm and leg over the fixed line. Just in time – because she felt the line that attached her to Milo snap taut. It almost pulled her off the wall. It jarred her left arm and leg, and her back, very painfully.

She called softly. No shouting; they had been repeatedly warned that many more people were killed by avalanches than anything else.

Nothing. She called again: 'Milo.' She wondered where the other climbers had got to, the Sherpas who were supposed to be below them?

'Cleo, Cleo.' She could just hear his voice. 'Cleo, I have gone over the edge of something – can't see anything. I need you to pull me up.'

Easy for him to say.

She pulled rather feebly on the rope. Nothing. They were stuck. She didn't have to be Einstein to work that out, unless the others got here very soon, they were both fucked. Her back felt as if it was breaking. She looked around her. Called 'Help!' very quietly. She looked down at the belt that was cutting her in two.

There, she could clearly see it: the clip that attached her to Milo.

Attached her to the man who was planning to drag her entire family through the filth and mud of the gutter press. She felt a rush of blood to her frozen brain.

She reached down and unfastened the line. As she did so she called out chillingly, between clenched teeth, 'Oh, Milo . . . you can kiss and tell– from hell!'

She heard the rope as it went clip, slip and whip across the ice . . . then a very faint sound . . . aaaahhhh! Almost like a cartoon, she thought heartlessly. Then she felt a bit sick. Honestly, the lengths one had to go to, to protect one's reputation these days. People really were becoming like animals in their desire for fame. Cleo saw no irony in her justification for getting Milo out of the way. It was done now; no going back. She took a deep gulp of oxygen from her mask and started thinking fast.

The others appeared moments later, with their Sherpa. They found Cleo weeping hysterically. 'Milo, oh my God, Milo . . . I couldn't hold him. I just couldn't.'

Another Sherpa arrived. He indicated that he would stay behind to see if there was any trace of Milo. But everyone could tell from the Sherpa's faces that there was no hope.

The others told the stunned and sniffling Cleo that their Sherpa insisted they had to leave – now! Or they would all die. She pulled herself together and they all pushed on. Twenty minutes later by some miracle, or their Sherpa's good guidance, they arrived at Camp Four.

Camp Four wasn't what Cleo was hoping for at all, just a few scrappy tents. But at least visibility had improved; the wind had got up and the cloud was being moved on.

Cleo was given tea to calm her down. She had resumed her hysterical sobbing and kept saying repeatedly, 'I couldn't hold him, I just wasn't strong enough . . . couldn't hold him . . . oh, dear, dear Milo . . . I couldn't hold him.'

The guide sat next to Cleo. Freezing snow blew across them.

'Cleo, you need to get inside.' He pushed her into the nearest tent. Gave her a swig of rum from his hip flask. 'OK, Cleo, there you are. Now. We are going to pitch here for the night, obviously. Then we will head back down in the morning, OK?'

Cleo sniffed. 'What, what do you mean? Head back down? Why?'

'Well, Cleo, because of Milo.' He could tell her brain was getting a bit addled from lack of oxygen.

'What? No, no. Milo would want us to go on. Oh goodness yes. We must go on, in memory of him . . . to honour him. He was such . . . such . . . a special man.' She sniffed and started to cry again.

'Well, Cleo – if you're sure. We'll see how the weather looks tomorrow, eh?' He smiled. This woman really was something. 'Try to get some rest. Try not to think about what happened. It couldn't be helped. Anybody would've done the same in your position – it's textbook procedure, Cleo, textbook. So don't blame yourself, all right?' He left the tent.

Bloody hell, she was tough. He wondered if she had any Australian in her.

He went over to tell the director that, weather permitting, anyone who wanted to go on in the morning could do so. But he felt they should all be reminded that they were entering the Death Zone. No one should feel under any obligation to go any further. He offered to take Cleo on himself with a helmet camera, no worries.

But the director wasn't going to be left behind. Hell no, this was too good. He'd send the others back, as he could tell that they'd all had enough.

He and the guide and Cleo would be leaving for the Death Zone in the morning.

Weather permitting.

CHAPTER TWENTY-NINE

Valentine woke up and reached out across his huge, comfortable bed in L'Hotel. But his arm found nothing. No Lily. He sat up and looked over at the bathroom door, hoping to see her there. But she was gone. He could tell she was gone. He fell back onto the crumpled sheets.

'Zut alors!' he thought to himself. She could speak! But she only spoke French – she was French. Of course he realised she must be able to speak some English – she was an international supermodel after all – and her texts were always in English. She just chose not to speak it. How very chic.

They had made love all night and everything she said to him, every filthy, inspired command, sounded so much sexier in French.

Valentine was loath to admit it – but he was hooked.

Zelda finally returned home from Spain.

She hadn't managed to move any of her scenes, but the

leading man had suffered some family tragedy, so everything was juggled about for him. Her scenes were with him, so hers had to be postponed too. She couldn't believe her luck. Though she was rather peeved that they hadn't even considered her request for rescheduling for *her* family crisis.

Jake had texted her about Lucien's arrest; she was trying not to panic. She was home now, determined to sort her life out.

She was surprised to find that everything was quiet outside at God's.

A couple of the old 'regular' paps were at the gate and she greeted them both by name: 'Hi, Tony, John.' And she smiled at them. She knew them well. They had been standing there at her gate, practically every day, for years.

In fact they were called Terry and George, but it never bothered them that she'd always called both of them by the wrong name. They knew it was too late to try to correct her now.

They loved her – she was their livelihood and their life. Now they had her to themselves again, and they were thrilled. They hated those other rude paparazzi bastards, pushing and shoving, yelling obscenities at this lovely woman and her family.

It was great now, all back to normal again. They could get their shots in peace: Zelda going for a run ... Zelda coming home with a Starbucks ... Zelda going to a ball with her handsome husband. Zelda always beautifully turned out and in perfect makeup. She'd never get caught out like some they could mention, looking shit.

The circus had moved on.

David opened the front door as she approached. The driver had called him to say they were coming in.

'David, thanks. Is anybody home?' She was keen to see Jake.

'No. Jake came by earlier to collect some things for the Mews. Otherwise all quiet.' David tried to sound detached, but he was worried; he could feel that there was more awry than usual. He was worried about Zelda.

'Oh. OK, thanks, David.' He could hear the disappointment in her voice as she disappeared into the Great Hall.

'Oh! By the way, this came for you.' David handed her a brown package. It was marked 'Private and Confidential. Only to be opened by the addressee.' The addressee was Zelda.

She took the package. She put it down on the island and got a bottle of water from the fridge.

She was very, very anxious. She looked around her. Although the room looked ravishing, she didn't notice or care. Zelda felt merely very small, scared and alone.

She took a deep breath and opened the package. It had to be done. She read the results of the DNA tests. Her hands were shaking. She read them again – in disbelief. She was certain that she had memorised who each person was: A ... B ... C. Now she wasn't sure. This couldn't be right.

She ran down to the office. It was empty. Kate had gone.

She opened the Warhol safe door. Entered the combination. She was hyperventilating.

She took out her list. Compared it ... there had to be some mistake?

But in her heart she knew that there wasn't.

What the fuck was she to do now?

Earlier that day, Jake had gone over to see Lana at Hollywood Road. They had much to discuss. He had responsibilities and he needed to start facing up to them. Whatever the potentially dire consequences were to himself.

Lana was alone when he arrived; she told him that Willow was having a nap.

He could see that she had been crying. He asked her to sit down. He felt jumpy, nervous.

'Come on, Lana. Everything is going to be OK. I promise I will look after you.'

Lana looked surprised. She sniffed and gazed at him. 'No, no, I not cry because I am sad. I am happy. Well, happy and sad. I just hear from my husband. He is on way to England and we can be together.'

What? She had a husband? Was this good? Jake thought furiously . . . another Eastern European migrant? Would he be expected to support him too? Christ. Still, she obviously wasn't expecting him to . . . to what? He really hadn't anticipated this. He suddenly imagined a huge, angry Victor or Boris beating him to a pulp. Christ!

'I want to say to you, Jake, I am very sorry.' Lana sniffed again.

'No, no, Lana – I'm sorry . . .' Jake was confused.

'No, Jake. I have telled to you a lie, a very bad lie. It was stupid idea to get money from you. There is no baby. I was unhappy, wanted to leave – to go home. I was thinking to ask for money ... make you to help me. I am sorry ... we never – you know? You were drunk but you did not do nothing – I made it up. I felt bad when you did not tell me get rid of baby – you are good person. I am sorry, Jake. I was going to leave before but then ... Georgia happened so ...' Lana looked embarrassed.

'What? What – no baby! Thank God.' Jake was reeling with relief. 'But, hang on, you just said your husband was coming to England, so why did you want to go back to Estonia?'

'Oh no, he live here. He has been away, he had accident. I just hear he is on way back to here. He say we can be together now, he has a big insurance.' Lana looked very happy. 'I was thinking to leave him but I look after him now. I forgive, then he get well.'

Jake was incredulous, thrilled, gobsmacked. 'What the fuck. Lana!' He hugged her.

'I sorry, Jake, you will need to find nanny for Willow. I have to go to him at hospital tonight.'

'Right, right, no problem, Lana – no probs, don't you worry. I will sort it.' He kissed her loudly on the forehead. 'Mwah! Thank you, Lana – thank you!'

He jumped up and ran from the house. The street was empty.

The circus had left there too.

CHAPTER THIRTY

Zelda was sitting in her office, still thinking hard.

She knew in her heart that she had to tell Valentine. He had to know.

She had only added his hair sample as an afterthought. She'd always denied to herself the possibility of this truth. But something about the DNA tests, the opportunity of finding out for sure, once and for all, had made her slip into his room that morning, take some of his hair from the brush on the chest of drawers, and add it to the sample list.

Now here it was, the result, and all her fears had been realised . . . and more. Much more.

She heard the front door slam upstairs.

On cue, she heard Valentine call out to her, 'Mum, Zelda – I'm home! Where are you?' So, David had told him she was there.

She called upstairs. 'I'm here in the office. Come down – I need to talk to you.'

His heart sank. Summoned by his mother – he dreaded a

showdown. He thought she'd been talking to Kate. Shit! Well, he'd just deny it . . .

But that wasn't what she wanted to discuss with him. She had to tell him something else entirely.

Zelda was on her way over to Hollywood Road. She had texted Elliot to tell him to meet her there. They had things to discuss.

Her talk with Valentine hadn't gone quite as badly as she'd expected. He was a mysterious boy. He didn't even seem to be hugely surprised by any of the extraordinary things she had to tell him.

Some of it, yes; but not all.

He hadn't asked too many questions. Said he was meeting someone. Had to go. They could talk more, later.

He had asked, 'Does Dad know?'

And she had to admit the worst: that he didn't. God, no, Jake did not know.

But she would have to tell him. That could not be avoided now. She would have to tell him.

And then? And then it would be over.

Zelda found Elliot hovering just inside the front door of Hollywood Road when she arrived. He let her in and smiled uncertainly. 'Zelda, Zelda – come in, come in.'

She noticed his backpack at his feet.

'Going somewhere?' she asked. She was trembling.

'Yes, Zelda, I was going to ring you. Things have changed. Well, plans have changed – my plans have changed.' He looked shifty.

She let him speak. She almost didn't want to tell him now. Perhaps this was a mistake?

He continued, 'Yep. Thing is, the lawyers have told me there is no money. Georgia had no money left. Whether she spent it, or Lucien did, no one knows yet but, to be honest – I just can't manage them ... the kids, I mean, domesticity. I've tried the last few days, Zelda, I have. But I'm not cut out for this. I earn bugger all – I've been on the road too long. I can't just be in one place ... and without you ...'

She couldn't believe he was going to try that again. How could she have fallen for any of his shit, ever? She felt her blood rising.

Elliot stopped talking. He could see Zelda was beginning to boil, and he was pretty sure it wasn't with passion.

Zelda felt her voice rising. 'So, not going to be the perfect daddy, then? Not going to face up to any of your responsibilities? Not going to be a man at all, in fact?' She was incandescent with rage. How had she ever let this jerk touch her?

'There are different sorts of men, Zelda.' He looked determined. Put his chin up, defiantly.

'Oh, fuck yes, indeed there are.' She glared at him.

'I spoke to Jake. He said he was very happy for the girls to live with him at the Mews for the time being. He says there's plenty of room. He thinks it's what Georgia would've wanted so . . .' Elliot trailed off but he couldn't look Zelda in the eye. She had always scared the hell out of him – he realised that now.

'So you are just going to bugger off, then? Just like that.' Zelda was running out of steam. 'Fuck off and leave your children . . . all your children?'

'What do you mean . . . all my children? I've only got one, for Christ's sake.'

'No, actually, Elliot – you've got two.'

'What are you talking about? Willow is not mine. No way. I didn't even . . . I never. No way. You can't lumber me with that.'

'That! That? She's a child, Elliot, a person! Anyway I don't mean Willow.' She spat it out. 'I mean Valentine.' Her voice grew quiet. 'Valentine is your son.'

Dusty was coming down the stairs when she overheard those words . . .

She couldn't believe her ears. Jesus! Valentine . . . was Elliot's son! Her brother then? No, half-brother . . . She sat down on the stairs with a bump.

She was in shock. Then it slowly dawned on her: what might have been . . . 'Oh, my God.' She felt sick . . . but quietly continued to eavesdrop.

Elliot was looking at Zelda in disbelief. Why would she tell him this now? Did she think they were all going to play happy families? No, no. Christ. She couldn't!

To be honest he had always slightly wondered about Valentine. He was so blond and they were all so dark, for a start. But he'd denied it to himself; surely she'd have told him at the beginning if it was true. Wouldn't she?

But she hadn't. Because the truth was that she didn't really want him, happy families or otherwise. He'd always known that. She and Jake were 'the Ones'. Oh, they had had their moments, he and she. But it was all over now. Had she told Jake or Valentine about this yet? He didn't know. He realised he didn't care – it was her mess. She could clean it up. He felt himself go cold. This was his opportunity to get out and he was taking it.

Without a word, he turned, picked up his backpack and left the house. Forever.

Zelda hadn't even finished saying everything she had to say, and as she slumped down into one of the oversized sofas she realised it probably didn't matter any more anyway. She felt very small and alone. She almost jumped out of her skin when Dusty came downstairs, asking incredulously, 'Has he gone? My dad? What a wanker! He's been acting shifty for days, so I thought he might do a runner. Christ, Zelda – some dad he turned out to be.' For all her bluster she looked sad. 'And is that really true – Valentine is my half-brother?'

Zelda could see the understandable look of shock and disapproval on Dusty's face. She sprang to her feet and, looking very apologetic, she said, with a voice full of remorse, 'Yes, yes, it is true. I'm so sorry, Dusty. I have made the most awful mess of things.' And surprisingly she gave Dusty a hug. 'But don't you worry, everything will be fine.' She really wished that could be true.

Then Dusty looked directly into Zelda's eyes. 'And this thing about the money . . . Lucien and stuff. Do you think he has lost all Mum's money? Or stolen it?' She was astute.

'We just don't know yet, darling. Everyone is trying to sort it out. We just don't know.'

But Zelda couldn't help feeling it was lucky her career was on the up and up. There was always Max and the trust. They'd be OK whatever that scum had done.

'I have to go over to the Mews now, to talk to Jake.' Zelda gathered up her bag.

'Can I come too,?' Dusty asked. 'I have to see Ed.'

'Yes, I don't see why not. Yes, of course you can, darling.'

'I'll just tell Lana . . .' Dusty stopped. Lana had suddenly appeared, carrying Willow. 'Oh, Lana, I'm just going over to Jake's with Zelda.'

Jake's! Jake's? Zelda thought to herself glumly. So the Mews was already just Jake's. She felt panic rising.

Lana looked directly at Zelda. 'Well, you have to take Willow too. I tell Jake I have to go and he said he would organise. So here – you take her.' And she shoved Willow gently, but firmly, into Zelda's arms.

Zelda was really panicking now. 'What do you mean, you are going? What do you mean? You can't leave us!'

'Yes, I tell Jake I must go to look after my husband.'

'Your *husband*? What the hell are you talking about?' Zelda was amazed. More fucking secrets!

'Yes, Zelda, my husband – Milo.' Lana stared hard at Zelda. There was hatred there. Zelda knew hatred when she saw it.

She had to admit she had been seeing a lot of it lately. She couldn't help feeling that she would be seeing quite a bit more before this day was done.

Lana turned on her heel with some dignity, kissed Dusty on the head, and then she disappeared upstairs.

Zelda and Dusty were gobsmacked. Milo and Lana were married?

The baby smiled and pulled Zelda's hair.

'Ouch!'

CHAPTER THIRTY-ONE

At 27,000 feet the winds had dropped. They were still terrifying. But the day had begun clear and bright. So the all-important visibility was good.

Cleo was ready for action.

She, the director and the guide set off the moment it was light.

The guide warned them again that this was the altitude where most human bodies lost their ability to acclimatise. They would need a constant supply of oxygen to help them to push through the balcony and up to the Hillary step.

Progress was slow. Everything was painful and could only be done in slow motion. The guide and Cleo were moving on ahead. The director was slipping back. They pushed on through the morning.

Soon it was just Cleo and the guide and the tedious, repetitious sound of their boots crunching on the snow and ice. The guide pulled himself up the Hillary step first, using the fixed ropes up the side. Then agonisingly slowly he helped Cleo up, pulling her gently from above. It took the last of his strength, and when she got to the top, they both collapsed into the snow.

They were in danger of blacking out. The guide knew they had to get up or they would die. He nudged Cleo. She opened her eyes and he signalled upwards. They could no longer speak. She struggled to get up. Then, to her horror, she realised that the hump of snow she had been lying next to was actually a body. She got to her feet then, thinking to herself, God! How disgusting! She really would have to have a word with Bill Bryson about it, when she got home.

The guide was pushing on up the hill. Could this really be it? She felt a tug on the rope. He was encouraging her to follow. She started to move. Nearly there, nearly there. She felt so sleepy.

Then she could see him ahead. He had his thumb up – did he? Did he have his thumb up? Yes! He did!

She staggered the last few steps. Dizzy with joy ... dizzy, dizzy, dizzy.

The guide was gesturing to her to stand at the top. He was filming her. She stood swaying slightly in the wind.

He took a few steps back to be able to film her properly.

He looked into the monitor that was slung round his neck, which fed the images from the helmet camera. Oh God ... what the fuck was she doing? She had gone hypothermia-crazy.

Cleo was taking off her snow-suit. Underneath it, she revealed her lovely black fur trimmed version – from Chanel. She was hardly going to miss out on this endorsement opportunity now, was she? She pulled out her lipstick – not easy in those gloves – whacked on a flash of red and put her thumbs up.

She was ready for her close-up.

The guide was fucking impressed!

Now all they had to do was get back down. That was often the most dangerous bit. But something told the guide they were going to make it.

He had a good feeling about this one.

CHAPTER THIRTY-TWO

Dusty asked Zelda if they could go via God's, as she had something she needed to pick up.

David let them in again, surprised to see Zelda carrying the baby. She looked almost motherly. She went into the Great Hall kitchen, to try to find a biscuit for Willow, while Dusty disappeared upstairs.

It was no mean feat to find anything edible in that kitchen. But there was a place, a little secret stash she had, that no one else knew about. Somewhere that she could raid when she occasionally broke down and had to have sugar. Luckily there was still one biscuit left after that awful night ... but she didn't want to think about that now.

She gave the biscuit to Willow, who smiled happily at her. Zelda had to admit she was rather adorable. She looked out into the garden, where she saw Max sitting on his favourite Anish Kapoor sculpture, apparently miles away, dreaming. His trug and trowel lay discarded at his feet.

'Daddy! There you are.' She stepped outside, trying to sound as though she had actually been looking for him.

'Darling, you're back, hurrah! It's been like a morgue here. Where is everyone? I've missed you.' Max kissed his lovely daughter then Willow too.

'Missed you too, Daddy. A lot's been going on really. I'll need to talk to you later.'

'Me too, darling – everything has been dire over here this morning. My trustees came over.' Max pulled a face. 'Such a grisly, beastly, vile meeting. Apparently, they put most of my money into some hedge thing that's gone under. They say I'm broke!' He grinned. 'I can't be, of course – always had far too much to lose and they can't have been that idiotic. I sent them off with their tails between their legs. Told them not to be so ridiculous and sort it out! They said they'd send me a state-ment of affairs! Hope not! They can't know that much about my private life, can they?'

'I expect they mean your business affairs, Daddy!' It was sometimes hard to know when Max was kidding.

She smiled at her father. 'We seem to be heading for some financial problems too, Dad. I was hoping you might be able to bale us out.'

'Looks like we are all in the same leaky sinking ship then, darling. Oh well, don't worry, something will turn up.' He had led such a privileged life; something had always 'turned up' for Max and he had no reason to believe it wouldn't now.

Zelda turned to go.

'Oh darling, I almost forgot. Mum made it.' Max went back to weeding.

'Made what?' Zelda replied vaguely, as she began to walk off.

'Made it to the top of Everest! I just heard! It's all over the news – I thought you'd have seen it.' Max was grinning.

'You're joking, Dad! Oh my God, you are kidding?'

'No, darling – no, no, no. She has done it. I knew she would, she's an amazing woman, your mother. An amazing woman.' He was very proud. And not a little nervous, he had to admit to his gorgeous daughter, about how his fantastic wife would react upon her triumphant return, to find they were on skid row.

'She arrives back tomorrow. They'll helicopter her back from base camp, then she gets the plane from Kathmandu.'

'Wow, Dad. Wow.' Zelda was pleased. Weirdly – she found she was pleased.

'Gather the troops, darling. We'll have a lovely supper at ours to celebrate, tomorrow night. I'll get Jamie onto it.' Max thought sadly that it might be the last celebration Jamie would have to organise for quite some time. Ah well. He sighed. It had all been bloody good fun while it lasted.

Dusty called from the house. 'Hi, Max!'

'Darling! See you tomorrow – you're all coming to me for supper.'

Zelda followed Dusty back through the garden doors.

A few minutes earlier Valentine had bumped into Dusty on the way up to his room. They both stopped and looked at each other for a moment, uncertain what to do – then Valentine laughed, awkwardly, and said, 'Hi, Sis!' trying to break the ice.

Dusty glanced at him nervously. Then, shaking her head incredulously she just muttered eloquently, 'Fuck!' and disappeared downstairs.

Or not, thought Valentine. And even he had to admit, 'Phew!'

Dusty played it cool but inside she was mortified: she had fancied her brother! Ehew! In fact, she had begun to feel she didn't like him much anyway; after all he was demonstrably vile to all his girlfriends, and she wondered how she could have been so blind.

As Zelda and Dusty got back into the car they were both quiet, lost in their own thoughts.

Dusty was tired of secrets; she had just retrieved the syringe from its hiding place behind the chest of drawers in her old room at God's.

Willow was looking dozy. Zelda had forgotten how comforting, soothing, it was to hold a sleepy baby. She really needed all the soothing comfort she could get on this terrifying day.

Dusty was suitably impressed when Zelda broke their silence to tell her about Cleo successfully climbing Everest.

'Holy shit! Awesome!' was her articulate response.

Then she asked if they could go via Chelsea Police Station – she had something to drop off.

Coincidentally, Kristina was just leaving the police station as Zelda and Dusty pulled up. They almost walked straight past each other on the steps. Zelda didn't recognise her at first.

She blurted out, 'Kristina! You had your baby!'

'Yes, I did. A little boy. Ivan.'

Crikey! Zelda thought to herself. Ivan the terrible – rather a good name for the spawn of Satan that was Lucien's offspring.

'Congratulations!' Zelda kissed Kristina. She couldn't help feeling rather sorry for the girl.

A BMW pulled up next to them and Kristina opened the door. There was a Moses basket on the back seat. Zelda looked in at the baby.

'Look, Dusty, it's . . .' She was going to say Lucien's baby, but somehow she found herself unable to utter that bastard's name. She really did feel overwhelmingly sorry for Kristina. She kissed her again as she got into the car. She couldn't help noticing that the guy driving her was very handsome, and wearing an extremely expensive watch too. She wondered who he was; Kristina's brother perhaps? Oh, well. At least she had someone to look after her. Things were going to get very rough. And what the hell would the poor girl do for money? Lucien would have left her high and dry too.

What a nightmare. Yes, Zelda really did feel very sorry for her.

Although Zelda dreaded seeing Jake, when they got to the Mews she was disappointed to find that he wasn't there.

Ed greeted his mother fondly and made her a cup of coffee. Then he showed her round the house while Dusty played with Willow downstairs. He said Jake had gone to a meeting, 'not an AA meeting, a meeting with the lawyers.'

Zelda laughed. 'Blimey! That'll be the day. Jake! An AA meeting!' she scoffed.

'No, Mum. He is going to meetings. He's been going to them every day. He hasn't had a drink or anything since we got here. It's great. He's great. Wait till you see.'

Zelda's heart sank. This was all well and good. She was pleased. But how the hell was he going to cope with what she had to tell him? It would push anyone over the edge. Oh God! Oh God! Was this really happening to them? She tried to calm down. She needed a Valium. She had quick rummage in her Anya Hindmarch bag, but no joy, she realised all her bloody pills were at God's.

She tried to concentrate, following Ed as he showed her round upstairs. He did it so proudly.

'Isn't it lovely?' he said 'So cosy and homely.'

She didn't want to spoil it for him by reminding him that this had been her home once, her cosy, homely house; she knew it well. In fact, she had to admit it had changed a lot since then. The extra floor was spectacular. It had been really well done. She was impressed.

She heard Jake's voice downstairs and her heart stopped.

Ed called out, 'Dad! Mum's here – come up.'

Jake came upstairs. They faced each other.

Without taking his eyes off Zelda, Jake said, 'Ed, could you do me a favour? Take Dusty and Willow down to the shop and get us some milk.'

'But Dad, we've got mi ...' Ed suddenly got the message. 'Oh, yeah. Right. Will do,' and he disappeared downstairs.

Zelda and Jake continued to stare at one another.

'Right, let's go down, shall we? I'll make you some coffee.' Jake headed for the stairs.

'Oh, Ed already made coff ... that would be lovely.'

They were alone.

They sat at the table. Neither knew where to start. They both spoke at once.

'Jake, there's something I have to ...'

'Zelda, there's something I have to ...'

Jake tried again. 'Yeah, well obviously we both have to! Shall I go first or shall you?'

'You?' Zelda said weakly, playing hopelessly for time.

'OK. I'll try to keep it brief and to the point. Just got back from the lawyers – not good. As far as they can tell Lucien put everything you have into a fund that was going to "sort out his position" and it has gone spectacularly belly up. They don't know the figures yet. But he had used God's, and all the other properties, as collateral. Everything, including all the artworks, was used to gear up for his last push. He had already used up all your cash a while ago. It's nothing personal; he has done it to all his clients – everyone has gone down. Including Georgia. People are baying for blood. He's probably lucky to be banged up already or someone might have had a pop at him. I'm sorry, Zelda, but he has fucked you over big time.' Jake paused.

Zelda didn't seem surprised. 'Oh God. I have been such a fool. Signing those papers. You were right. If only I hadn't . . .' She was gutted.

'The only thing that the lawyers can say for sure is that this house is safe. Georgia structured it in a way that it is mine and cannot be considered one of the family assets – some foreign trust thing. Anyway, I think I should show you the letter she had left here for me. It explains more. But there is a bit of a shock in it . . . can you take any more? We could wait till later. Till all this has sunk in?'

'No, no, let me see it now, Jake.' Zelda felt exhausted, feeble. 'Oh, I just saw Dad. His trustees seem to have been caught out putting his money into some hedge fund disaster. So he's in the shit too.'

The world was in meltdown.

Jake had jumped up and disappeared into his office. He came back with Georgia's letter and placed it in front of his wife.

She started to read.

My darling, favourite brother, Jake,
I hope you like your present!

I have asked my lawyers to give this letter to you if for any reason I am unable to give you the keys to the Mews myself. So I hope you never read it!

I have been trying to put my affairs into some sort of order. Originally, I went to Peterson de Winter to ask their advice about dear agent Lucien. He has been very tight-fisted about funds for a while now and someone at my record company told me what I should've earned last year and I knew that even I couldn't have spent that much. This was before I bought your birthday present! Anyway, Lucien got really nasty when I asked him about it seriously – so I thought, fuck it, get the lawyers onto him. So I have.

Hugo and Giles are a bit concerned as they are not getting their questions answered in the way they'd expect. They managed to extract the money for the Mews with difficulty – so enjoy! I have made sure it is yours and only yours and can never be taken from you.

Jake, I just want to say, as your loving sister, I think you need to work again. And to do that I think you need to straighten out. I know I do too. I know.

You are a great writer, Jake. So I am giving you this gift to take you back to where we started. So you can begin again – start afresh.

Anyway, I don't want you to think I have bought it for you for any other reason, as a salve to my conscience or something. You might wonder why I would think that? Well, now I have to tell you.

This is very, very difficult for me. I am so desperately sorry to have to tell you this, Jake. It is such a terrible thing – I hardly know how I can begin write it down, but I know I must. I will completely understand if you and your family never want to speak my name ever again.

It's about Willow. There is a reason I have kept her father a secret from everyone, because it is a terrible, shameful secret.

A couple of years ago when I was very low, Valentine started coming round a lot, with Ed, to see Dusty. They all hung out here and it was really lovely, family fun. I was doing a lot of drugs and I could tell that Valentine was curious. He was already smoking weed and stuff. Oh, God, Jake. I am so ashamed. One night he came over when Dusty wasn't here. We got stoned . . . one thing led to another . . .

I didn't realise I was pregnant until quite late. Thought I was getting fat or early menopause – I was so out of it. Such a bloody fool. Then, when I realised what had happened, I didn't know what to do. Since that terrible abortion when I was very young, I knew I just couldn't do that again. Of course, knowing that Valentine was my nephew, I was terrified that there would be some hideous genetic defect. I felt I deserved that – but the baby didn't and, thank God, she was perfect. The doctors told me she was absolutely perfect and she is. Dusty and I are so, so happy with her.

Of course I have never told Valentine. Perhaps I never will. But I feel that someone else in this world should know the truth. I am so sorry, Jake, but I knew it had to be you. I knew that if anything ever happened to me you would have to know this – this terrible secret – about your stupid fool of a sister.

I do not expect forgiveness. But I beg you to take care of my girls if I am gone.

With so much love from me, I am so sorry.

Georgia.

Zelda put the letter down on the table. She had tears running down her face.

She looked at Jake. 'Oh, Jake – I'm so sorry.' Then she burst into more desperate racking sobs.

Jake reached for her hand across the table. 'It's all right Zelda, we'll sort it out ...'

'He knows ... he already knows ...' she sobbed.

'Who knows – what?'

'Valentine already knows about Willow. Georgia told him.'

'Jesus ... is he OK? How do you know – when did you know?' He was instantly suspicious. He let go of her hand.

'Now, I just found out now.' Zelda was feeling hysterical, but knew she had to continue.

'I ... I was trying to find out who Willow's father was. Because I ... I thought he should take responsibility for her.'

'What, rather than us, you mean?' He sounded annoyed.

Zelda pressed on; there was no going back now. 'I sent some hair samples off to Dr D'Angelo to see if any of them matched Willow's DNA and one of them did.'

Jake looked bemused. 'But ... what are you saying? Why would you send Valentine's off? Even your warped mind couldn't have imagined that scenario, surely?'

'No, no, that's what I have to tell you – what I've come to tell you. I had sent Elliot's hair to be tested too. I thought he and Georgia might've – you know, when he was over on a family visit. But then I put in Valentine's too. Not on a whim – but because I wanted to know something else – for sure.'

She didn't dare look at Jake. She spoke very, very quietly. 'I wanted to make sure that Valentine wasn't Elliot's son.'

Jake was quiet too. After what seemed like an eternity to Zelda, he asked her the inevitable: 'And what did the test reveal, Zelda?'

'Jake, I'm so terribly sorry. I should've told you from the start, I just couldn't bear to lose you – this is the worst thing. I am so desperately sorry. I didn't think it could be true, didn't want it to be true.' She covered her face with her shaking hands and said very, very quietly, 'Valentine is Elliot's son.'

'So let's get this straight. My sister probably died of worry for nothing because ... let me think ... she thought she'd slept with her brother's child – but actually it turns out he was her ex-husband's child. Nice, Zelda – very nice.' His voice was cold and hard.

Jake got up, grabbed his keys and left the house.

Ed came home with Dusty to find his mother sobbing help-lessly on the sofa. He tried to comfort her but she wouldn't tell him what was wrong.

Eventually she pulled herself together, put on her sun-glasses and went back to God's.

Dusty fed Willow then she and Ed ordered a pizza. Life went on.

*

Back at God's Zelda found Valentine in the Great Hall. He had the music on loud.

He seemed concerned to see his lovely mother so distressed. He got her a drink, sat her down. Told her he loved her. Then he asked what he could do to help.

'I mean, most of this is my fault after all!' he said.

'No, no, no, darling, it's my fault – it's all my fault. I am so sorry. You must think me such a disgusting liar. But I was never sure; and I do love your father ... Jake ... so, so much. I just couldn't tell him. Then it got bigger and more horrible, this lie. Now I have destroyed everyone. Particularly you, my darling.'

'Oh, don't get too over-dramatic, Mother. I'm OK about it. I always thought it was a bit odd. I am really different from Dad – Jake Dad. I mean, he is nice and kind, for a start!'

'You're nice and kind.' Zelda sniffed.

'No, Mummy, really I'm not.' Valentine put his arms around his mother. 'And what's more, I wouldn't be me if I hadn't got that, let's be honest, bit of a dick Elliot's genes. And without those genes I wouldn't be the face of all the biggest brands' ad campaigns and ... if what I've been hearing is right, we are going to need my modelling fees and every other bit of earning power any of us has, from now on.'

Zelda almost smiled. 'Thank you, darling. You are amazing, such a comfort. I have been a fool and very selfish, a deceitful, horrible fool and you are my wonderful boy.' She looked up at him in grateful admiration. 'And you are a good, strong person – and we are going to need all the strength we can get.'

'That's more like it. Fighting spirit. I mean, Granny just climbed Everest! Or should I say Great-granny?'

'What, oh my God – yes!' Zelda started to laugh. 'Oh, she won't be pleased, Valentine. Oh! Oh . . .'

Valentine was laughing too. 'She will be so pissed off with me. Giving her a lovely little great-granddaughter.'

They laughed, slightly too hysterically, for quite some time.

When they eventually calmed down, Valentine said sagely, 'Anyway, Mummy, I don't know what you're so worried about. Half my friends call the wrong person Daddy. Everybody knows. They're all just far too polite to talk about it!'

'Oh. Honestly, Val.' Zelda looked up at her son adoringly as he refilled her drink.

'That's all very well but our little secret is out now, and my marriage is over because of it.' Zelda felt so sad.

She really wanted to die.

When Jake arrived back at the Mews late that night, Dusty and Ed were already in bed, asleep. He looked in on Dusty, who had Willow in her bed with her; they slept like angels.

Having been to an early-evening AA meeting he'd decided to go for a long walk. He had much to think about, decisions to make. He thought long and hard about Zelda and his chaotic family life. He went over all the things that Georgia had written to him, again.

Although it was standard practice for lawyers to recommend that clients wrote a 'letter of wishes' to their nearest and dearest he still felt that Georgia must have had some inkling of what was to befall her – a premonition perhaps? She had often boasted that she was a bit psychic and he had always teased her about it, her sceptical brother. But still, no matter what, it didn't read like a suicide note, he felt certain of that. He had been thinking about the abortion she had mentioned in the letter.

Of course he had known about it and he had never been able to forgive or forget what Lucien, her agent even then, had done all those years ago. When Lucien found out that Georgia was pregnant with his child, he had insisted on her having an abortion. She was at the beginning of her promising music career – still just fourteen. Lucien had organised everything; indeed he had taken her to the clinic himself. When she had cried and protested that she didn't want to go through with it, he had forced her, by telling her that he would make sure her career was over if she did not do as he said. Then he had reminded her that without him, she and Jake would starve. So she went through with it. But when she confessed this to Jake, years later, she was still haunted by what she had done.

Of course, Lucien would hardly have wanted his crimes against Georgia exposed by the birth of a child; sexual abuse of a minor was not something that would have helped in his quest for world domination. So Jake hated Lucien for harming his little sister, a pure hatred that remained undimmed by the years.

Jake had wanted to go to the police the moment Georgia told him. But she had laughed bitterly, drunkenly, and replied,

'What, years after the event? No, Jake, I don't think so.'
Adding, with sad and slightly slurred resignation, 'Oh, anyway,
Jake – these things happen to people all the time. There is no
point in making a fuss. It was all a long time ago. I will never
forget what he did but he is, has always been, a huge part of my
life. He makes a lot of it easy and possible. If I can overlook it,
so can you.'

But Jake had never felt able to overlook it – least of all now.

He went downstairs to make himself a cup of coffee. There
was a knock on the door.

He opened it to find Valentine standing on the doorstep.

'Hi, Dad, can I come in?'

'Course, Val, come on. Need to talk, mate? Sorry – difficult
day.'

Valentine hugged Jake. 'You will always be my dad, Jake,
OK? Always. The perfect dad and the only dad I have ever
wanted. I'm OK about this – really, I promise, I said to Mum,
I always wondered – you know. It's OK. Everyone makes mistakes.'

Jake made them both strong tea, lots of sugar, and they sat
at the kitchen table.

'Mum is really upset, Dad. You know? Really sad.'

'I'm fucking upset. She should've told me.' Jake looked
tired.

'Yeah, but Dad, come on. You must've wondered. I mean, I
don't look anything like you and I'm an absolute bastard. It
must have crossed your mind?'

'If I'm honest, Valentine, it did. I just loved you, and your mother, so much – I didn't want it to be true. But it's not good for us to keep these things hidden. I am learning that now. I just need some time to adjust a bit, you know? I'm trying to knock the booze thing on the head. Maybe it's a good thing to get everything out in the open, once and for all. But it does hurt, Val. It does.'

'I love you, Dad. We'll be OK.' Valentine chinked his teacup against Jake's. 'There is something else I wanted to talk to you about. See what you think . . .'

Valentine lit a cigarette, took a deep drag and began. 'I went round to Georgia's the night she died. I know, I know, I should've told you before. But she had asked me to go round – she wanted to tell me something.' He looked directly at Jake. 'Yes, that Willow is mine. I know you know and I really am so sorry, Jake, seriously.' He looked away, embarrassed. 'I always liked that little baby – she's so cute.' He smiled wanly. 'Anyway, that's not the thing. The thing is Georgia had a lot, and I mean a lot, of drugs there – the table was littered with them. I must confess I took some and it was fucking strong stuff. I didn't think about it properly until all this Lucien thing started to get so heavy.' He tried to sip his tea, flinching when he burnt his tongue slightly. 'She told me Lucien had been round earlier that evening. She said she'd had some kind of run-in with him over the phone about money. After I left I was a bit the worse for wear, I ran across the road to get into the Mini – oops!' He winced. 'Sorry, Dad, I know I shouldn't have been driving! Anyway, a black Range Rover almost hit me. It stopped outside the house as I drove off. Thinking about it since all this, I'm sure it was Lucien's car. In fact I know it was – I was in it the next morning ... but that's another story.'

Valentine took a deep breath. 'So I just wanted you to know that Lucien was definitely at Georgia's twice that night. I think he supplied her with the drugs that killed her. Do you think we should tell the police?'

A sleepy-headed Dusty appeared from upstairs, looking shocked and bemused as she blinked at Valentine accusingly. 'Why didn't you tell me about Willow? Or that you knew Lucien had been at Mum's that night and gave her those drugs? You knew all this time and you didn't say!'

Valentine looked embarrassed. 'Oh, Dusty, I couldn't – I was too scared of what you would think, about Willow, about me and Georgia. I was so ashamed. I'm so sorry, Dusty. I should've told you – I was going to tell you – I just felt it was a bit too soon after your Mum ...' He looked very contrite. 'And I didn't think the Lucien thing was important until now. I'll give the police a statement tomorrow, I promise – we'll get that bastard for this.'

She glared at him sceptically, then she turned to Jake. 'I've already spoken to the police. Zelda and I went there today. I gave them a syringe I found in Mum's room.'

Jake tried to remain calm. 'Dusty darling, why didn't you tell us this before?'

'Well, I didn't want anyone to know that Mum might have done something so stupid! But now all I want is the truth.' Dusty was trembling with shock and indignation.

Jake gave her a hug. 'We all do, darling, and I am going to

312

make sure we get it, now go back to bed, OK? We can talk about this some more tomorrow.'

Dusty seemed very young, fragile and furious as she stomped back up to her room. Climbing back into bed she hugged her baby sister and cried herself into a deeply troubled sleep.

So, on top of everything else, Lucien was implicated in Georgia's death as her supplier; there couldn't be much doubt about that now. He was pure evil – Jake had always known that and he felt furious with himself, and guilty that he had not protected any of his family from that psychopathic monster.

Jake gazed at Valentine and thought about all the secrets there had been between them all. He lit another cigarette, then wondered if he should he feel angry with his son? 'Jesus, Valentine – and they say you never know what your kids are up to. You should have bloody told me about all this.' Valentine looked remorseful as Jake continued to scrutinise his, his ... almost son? 'And did I hear that your new dad, Elliot, has buggered off already? Nice. Did he speak to you before he left?'

'A quick phone call. Embarrassing. He's gone – that's fine. As I said, Jake, you are my dad. Always will be. I really am sorry about everything.'

Their eyes filled up. It had been a long, long day.

'Do you want to stay here, Valentine? There's plenty of room?'

'Not tonight, thanks, Dad. I can't. I'm meeting someone. But it's nice – the Mews. I'm glad you've got it. You deserve it.'

He hugged Jake warmly and disappeared out into the night,

up the cobbled street. As Jake closed the front door, Valentine heard him call out, 'Who the hell are you meeting at this time of night, you lunatic!'

Valentine might ask himself the same question. Who the hell was he meeting at this time of night? He had to admit she was an enigma. He didn't know who the hell she was, in fact. But she was what he liked, what he wanted, what he loved even?

Chapter Thirty-Three

Zelda woke with a start, alone in her huge bed. She had been hoping that this was just one big nightmare, but her aching heart told her that it wasn't; it was all horribly, grimly true.

It was early. She switched on the news. The financial markets were in free fall again – soon there wouldn't be anyone left with any money at all. She shivered. What the hell was she going to do?

Was it possible that out of all this she could lose this house? Homeless, husbandless . . . hopeless! She groaned.

But she could work. There was always that. Thank God, there was always that.

She stumbled into the bathroom. She could hardly see her eyes, they were so swollen from crying all night. She dug out an eye mask, specially made for her by her beautician in Paris. 'The last of that sort of luxury then,' she thought sullenly.

It wasn't clear quite how bad things were yet. There was a meeting at God's scheduled for noon. The lawyers and new accountants were coming to give them an 'extensive update on their financial affairs'. All the family were to attend. She had texted Jake to ask him to come too.

He hadn't replied.

She went back to bed with the eye mask clamped to her face. She wasn't expecting much of a result – her face was beyond repair ... even with the acclaimed Parisian 'wonder-mask'.

She tried to calm down and think rationally; would her contract with Fabulous hold up when she and her family was mired in all this shit? God! She wasn't sure. Who the hell should she ring for damage limitation, now that Lucien was gone?

She thought desperately, 'Why, why, why didn't I listen to Jake? I should never, ever have let that scum back into our lives. What was I thinking?'

But she knew what she had been thinking ... she'd been thinking about her career, power and money. That's what she'd been thinking.

She deserved this. She felt that strongly. She deserved this and worse for what she had done. What a fool. What a greedy, selfish fool. She started to cry again, tears of remorse and not a little self-pity.

'This eye mask is fucking useless,' she muttered petulantly, as she hurled it to the floor.

Then she noticed something on the massive TV screen on her bedroom wall – it was her mother! On the news, waving gaily at the cameras at an airport and then there was some more footage of her ... on top of Everest! Zelda looked again. Bloody hell, her mother was wearing that Chanel snow-suit!

She sniffed, laughed and went downstairs to make herself a

cup of coffee. She knew she was going to have to start doing a lot of things for herself from now on. Everything, in fact.

Anyway, if her mother could climb bloody Everest she could get through all this shit, surely? Couldn't she?

Jake had taken Ed, Dusty and Willow back to Hollywood Road to collect some gear. They had spent ages dismantling the cot. Ed turned out to be far more useful at that stuff than his father.

They had loaded the old Mercedes with so many things that Ed couldn't fit himself in. He volunteered to walk back to the Mews.

Dusty turned to Jake as they drove home, and said seriously, 'Thank you for letting us come to stay with you. It feels horrible at Hollywood Road without Mum. I didn't want to stay there – I'm glad it's got to be sold.'

'Well, we don't know that for sure yet, Dusty darling. But what I do know is that you and Willow live with me now – that's official. The Mews is just as much yours as mine.'

'Oh my God, Jake. I still can't get my head around this – I mean . . . no wonder Mum wanted to keep it a secret – her and Valentine. It's disgusting!'

'Well, they had taken a lot of – you know – drugs and everything. I'm sure Georgia didn't know what she was doing . . .'

'No. Don't make excuses for her, Jake. What she did was wrong.' Now that Dusty knew the extent of Georgia's drug use she was beginning to have doubts about everything, and she felt very confused and extremely angry with her mother.

'Of course, you're right, darling, it was – it was very wrong. But at least we have Willow, and there is nothing, absolutely nothing, wrong with her.' He reached into the back of the car where Willow was squidged into her seat among God knew what things, which Dusty had described as essentials. He squeezed the baby's knee and she squealed and laughed and said, 'Da Da Da.'

Jake looked pleased.

'She didn't say Dada, Jake, she does that all the time. It's just a noise, OK? I think she's trying to say Dusty.'

'Yeah, right!' Jake smiled at his lovely niece as they pulled into the Mews.

'Anyway, she'd have to say Grand-da-da-da.' Dusty smirked.

Jake jumped out and replied wryly, 'Step-grand-da-da-da, I think you'll find! And still uncle too?' He looked baffled. 'Shit! OK. Hurry up.'

He called out to Ed as he saw him walking towards them, down the cobbled street. 'Come on! We've got to get this lot unloaded. We have to be over at God's at noon.'

Zelda had set up the dining table in the west aisle for the lawyers' meeting. There would be far too many people to fit around the boardroom table in her office.

This was the first time the big table had been used in ages. In fact they never used it, she realised. What had happened to all the huge, jolly, Italian-style family meals she had imagined when they designed and converted the place? Lack of food perhaps? She couldn't remember when they had last sat down for a proper meal together. Christmas, possibly – then again no, now she thought about it Christmas was always at Max's. They had it here once, surely, hadn't they? God, how ridiculous. What had she been thinking? This huge house – what was the point of all this grandeur? Just a ghastly sort of showing off, she admitted to herself.

Max came in through the garden door and Zelda felt reassured to see him. At least her father knew how to have a party; he was the only one who ever organised any big family gatherings. Zelda realised sadly that she had always been far too busy to organise anything. 'But busy doing what?' she asked herself. 'Oh yes, important stuff, very time-consuming – maintenance: hair and makeup, manicures, facials, Botox, waxing, tanning, massages, meetings with stylists, designers, personal trainer!' Now she really felt depressed.

Max was looking rather cheerful under the circumstances. 'Just spoke to Cleo, darling ... she'll be back at two. Haven't told her anything over the phone about all this. Don't want to rain on her parade yet. You don't mind me sitting in on your meeting, darling, do you? This is going to affect all of us one way or another. I have told my people to start talking to your people. I can't believe my trustees have been so naïve.'

Max went to ring his butler Jamie on the house phone to ask him to bring cafetieres of coffee, and some biscuits for the meeting. Something told him Zelda would not have thought of that stuff. He had a feeling that they'd all be needing something a lot stronger than coffee by the time this day was done.

Zelda ran upstairs to try to make herself look a bit more presentable, and shuddered when she saw her ugly, swollen eyes staring back at her. She wondered if the lawyers and accountants would think she had been crying over her financial losses. How shaming, when in fact it was all the other losses that were causing her such pain. She took a deep breath. What did it matter what they thought anyway? They were just professional people doing their job. She was sure they had seen it all before.

But they hadn't. Hugo and Giles and the accountants had never seen anything like it before. No one had. It was larceny and mismanagement on an unprecedented scale, a reckless, runaway train of financial malfeasance. The losses ran into hundreds of millions. Dark Artists managed many of the most successful arts and entertainment people in the country. Some of their clients were the most successful in the world. It was hard to imagine how Lucien Dark had got away with it for so long.

Hugo and Giles were dreading this meeting, the first of many. They were exhausted. All their staff, in all their offices, had been working on it night and day. At this stage they weren't even sure how they would be paid. But they were pretty certain they would be able to find a way; they usually could.

Valentine was the first to join Max and Zelda in the Great Hall, followed by Hugo and Giles and their team, too many to count. Then three more arrived, from the new accountants' office.

Either there was an awful lot of bad news to deliver, or none of them had anything more amusing to do than to see the

Spenders brought low. Zelda could see the headlines now: 'LAST of the BIG SPENDERS' and so on. Her name had always been both a blessing and a curse.

Zelda had just got everyone sitting down when Ed and Dusty arrived. Ed was carrying Willow. Max was solicitously handing out coffee.

Jake arrived last, apologising politely, and introducing himself to everyone he didn't know. Max noticed that his son-in-law looked different. He couldn't think how exactly, but he definitely looked different.

Zelda could hardly breathe. She daren't look at Jake as she felt his eyes on her. Oh God, she was mortified, she knew she looked like such a monster today.

Hugo began to speak . . .

When he and the others rose from the table – an hour and forty-five minutes later – the Spenders' world had changed forever.

There was plenty of detail. But the bottom line was that they were broke.

Jake and Zelda already knew most of it, but it was painful to hear it again.

Hugo explained that since everything belonging to the family had been inadvertently signed over to Dark Artists (the lawyer was tactful enough not to look at Zelda when he said this) all that they had ever owned was now in the hands of the SFO and their administrators: the house in the South of France; the apartment in New York; God's and all its contents, the art, jewellery, even the clothes.

'How ridiculous!' Zelda thought. 'Who the hell would want our old clothes?' Then she remembered. 'Plenty of people. Designer labels with the provenance of famous people equal money.'

The same applied to all of Georgia's assets too, even her back catalogue.

The family were told that they would have to leave their houses by noon the following day. They could leave in the clothes they stood up in and take basic essentials. Basic essentials sounded promising, Zelda thought, but she was to discover that they weren't really very promising at all.

The accountants seemed pleased that they had managed to avoid any individual members of the family going personally bankrupt. The family's minds wandered a bit while this was explained to them. They sort of understood what they were being told – everything they had ever owned was gone, but they could keep whatever they earned in future.

This was good – apparently.

Hugo reiterated that Georgia had purchased the Mews in a way that protected it for Jake, via an offshore company that lay beyond the jurisdiction even of God.

So not everyone was homeless.

Hugo and Giles's assistants handed out official-looking folders to each and every member of the family, outlining their position. Folders that Hugo suspected, correctly, none of them would ever look at. For a moment an assistant appeared undecided as to whether or not to leave one for Willow too. In memory of her lost heritage perhaps? He decided against it, sliding the document back into his briefcase. He might keep it for himself, as it was a pretty historic document after all.

Everyone sat in stunned silence for a moment.

The lawyers and accountants were just getting up to leave, with lots of subdued thanks, hand-shaking and good lucks, when the house phone rang. Ed answered it. It was Jamie, to announce that Cleo was back.

Jamie said he would bring her out into the garden and he suggested they could all greet her there.

The family all rushed for the garden door, glad of a reason to run from all this hideous, unbelievably bad news.

Jake herded all the lawyers and accountants out into the garden too. After all, Cleo liked a crowd. Then he ran back to fetch David from the front of the house, and as an afterthought he beckoned to the two photographers at the gate. They couldn't believe it – they had never been allowed across the threshold of God's before. Jake called to them, 'Come on, hurry up or you'll miss it!' He felt they had earned this, these two dogged old faithfuls. Then he yelled downstairs for the house-keepers: 'You two, get up here to the garden, now!'

Cleo was very put out to find no one at home to welcome her. Jamie had congratulated her, very enthusiastically, and asked if he could get her anything. She was a little sharp with him. 'No! I think I'll go upstairs to my room, alone. I am quite tired, as I'm sure you can imagine.'

He gently suggested that Cleo might want to come into the garden, saying he thought she'd find Max there. She sighed and thought crossly, 'Max and that bloody garden.' She did want to see him though. She had missed him really, quite a bit.

Jamie opened the French windows and Cleo stepped outside.

When she appeared there was an almighty roar, from across the lawn.

There they all were: her family! They were all shouting and hollering. 'Bravo, Cleo! Hurrah!' Dusty and Ed ran towards her and hugged her, and everyone was shouting.

Ed yelled, 'Granny!' And Cleo muttered, sharply, 'Less of that!'

Max was shaking his fists in the air and bellowing, 'I knew you could do it, my darling. I knew it!' He kissed her and gave a little skip. 'I am so proud. So, so proud!'

The photographers spun around them. Zelda wished she had put her sunglasses on, to hide her puffy un-Fabulously made-up eyes, but then she thought 'sod it' and just forgot about how she would look in their shots. She soon found herself completely caught up in the moment, her marvellous mother's wonderful, extraordinary moment.

This spectacle was an unexpected bonus for the accountants and lawyers. They were whooping and hollering too. One of them was so young he didn't even know who Cleo was. He was pretty bloody impressed when he heard what she had just done though; he wouldn't be forgetting her in a hurry.

These people were fighters. Hugo couldn't help feeling that somehow they were going to be alright.

Max asked everyone to pop over to his place for a quick

glass of champagne. But the legal and money men said, regretfully, they must decline, they were late for their next meeting already. They still had a lot more bad news to deliver that day.

The photographers looked keen, but David had clearly decided they had had their moment and smartly ushered them back out through the Great Hall – they both managed to get a couple of good snaps of that magnificent room too. This had been a great day for them. They felt slightly overwhelmed.

So the family trooped over to Max and Cleo's. They were all laughing, slightly hysterically, patting their heroine on the back and firing millions of questions at her.

Jake went back to the house to speak to David and the housekeepers. They had to be told the bad news. He knew it was his job to do it.

Jamie opened the champagne to the sound of cheering and 'Bravo!' Cleo took hers up to her room, calling out to no one in particular, 'Just have to brush my hair, darlings. That beastly mountain made such a mess of it!' She gestured to Zelda to follow her. Zelda was still carrying Willow, so the baby went too.

Cleo closed her bedroom door firmly behind her daughter.

She lowered her voice conspiratorially. 'Darling, I just want you to know that I dealt with Milo. I found your text, by the way, Zelda – rather rude, darling! Anyway, don't worry. I deleted it. The thing is, I found out that little shit was planning to shop us all to the gutter press. So, um, I sort of let him slip off the mountain. For an awful moment I thought he'd been killed. But a Sherpa found him and somehow got him down.

Apparently he was quite beaten up.' Cleo hesitated for a moment, stopped arranging her hair, and looked at herself in the mirror. She still liked what she saw. Turning to look at her daughter she went on, 'But I couldn't let him bring us all down, darling. After I deleted your text it occurred to me that might not be the end of it . . . to cut a long story short, I thought Milo had got his phone back. But miraculously, when I returned to camp, on the way back down, I was crawling into my little old tent – and I found his phone! Half-buried in the snow outside my tent door. Can you believe the luck? So I got rid of it for good then!' She looked triumphant. Then something that was almost a frown crossed her face. 'Why are you carrying Willow around, darling? Where's the nanny?'

'Oh, Mummy – you have missed so much. I really don't know where to start!' But Zelda knew, sure as hell, she couldn't start now. She felt as if she was having a heart attack. She had to get to her phone. What fucking text was her mother talking about?

'Let's go and join the others – they'll be missing you!' Zelda suggested, smiling wildly as she rushed downstairs, gave the baby to Ed and ran over to God's. She dived into her bag, rummaging frantically until she found her phone, and then pulling it out she raced back over to Devil's – she daren't stay at God's in case she bumped into Jake. She smiled maniacally at everyone as she passed, then she locked herself firmly in the downstairs loo.

She plonked herself onto the closed mahogany seat. There she sat, amid the hundreds of photographs of her mother that lined the walls. Cleo with Bill (thereby hung a tale), Cleo with Tony, Cleo with David and Nick, Cleo with Elvis, Cleo with Frank . . . and so on.

She pulled out her phone.

Just when she'd thought this day couldn't get any worse, it had. She started scrolling madly through her texts. What text was her mother talking about? She couldn't remember communicating with Milo at all . . . she'd forgotten all about him the moment he left. Or . . . or – oh no! The night she was drunk? She thought desperately, was a deleted text gone forever? E-mail – there for always? Oh God, no! Had she e-mailed or texted his BlackBerry? Cleo wouldn't have known it but there was a difference. And it was a big one. Zelda scrolled down, almost blind with panic. No, she hadn't e-mailed him. Phew! Texts . . . oh God, there it was . . . she had sent this? This? 'Rather rude,' her mother had said. It was disgusting – insane! How drunk had she been? she asked herself. Very drunk indeed, clearly. She pressed delete. Was that it, deleted and gone forever? She was crying again. What had she done? It was all closing in on her now. The guilt and the horrible shame – not just about this Milo thing, but Elliot too . . . all of it.

Zelda put her hands together and prayed to the God she had never believed in. She prayed, she begged, she wept. She promised she would never, ever do anything like those things, ever again. If she could only be given a second chance . . . there was a knock on the door.

'Zelda, are you in there?'

It was Jake.

'Coming!' she sniffed. She unlocked the door and went out.

Jake was standing there, looking ridiculously handsome. 'Are you OK?' he asked kindly.

'No!' She burst into tears again. 'I am so, so sorry, Jake.'

He held her then, softly. He pulled up her beautiful hair and blew on her neck, the way he used to, when they were first together, and it had made her laugh then. But she wasn't laughing now.

'Tiger. Listen. It was all a very long time ago.'

She sobbed more.

'No, no, come on, darling. It was in another lifetime and neither of us were angels then, were we?'

This was news to her. What did he mean?

He looked into her swollen, bloodshot eyes. 'We both made mistakes. For God's sake, Tiger, you have had to put up with the most useless drunkard of a husband for years. For far too long.' He looked at her firmly. 'We are putting that all behind us now, OK? It's over. Done. We are, as they say, moving on. Together, I hope. If you still want me?'

'Oh Jake. I do. I am so sorry. I do.'

'OK, that's settled. Now you can stop saying you're sorry. I'm sorry too – we're even. Let's go and join your magnificent mother. Then we'll nip back home to the Mews to change into "The Clothes We Stand Up In" . . . I think we will find that we can stand up in quite a lot, don't you? So, soon as we're done here, pick out a few armfuls of your favourites and we'll load up the Merc.'

Zelda gave one last, very impressed, sniff. Then she smiled

at her new husband, although she didn't feel they could ever really be 'even', unless she found out he'd slept with her mother or something! In fact, what had he meant, neither of them had been angels? No, no, she told herself firmly, don't even think of going there. As Jake so wisely said, yesterday's gone. Or was that Paul McCartney? Or the Carpenters ... ? Anyway, she decided to accept his proposal gratefully and graciously.

As they walked back down the passage to the morning room, she resolved never, ever, to make such stupid mistakes again.

Later on that afternoon, they loaded the old Mercedes with everything they could fit in – and then some.

Zelda was surprised to find that, when it came to choosing, there was quite a lot of stuff she could live without. She easily weeded out a rail of her favourite things. Then there were a couple of Louis Vuitton suitcases, full of handbags, a lot of jewellery and shoes. That was it ... oh, and the little Warhol was tucked away too. Fuck it, Zelda had thought. It's so small they'll never miss it – and she knew that somehow she just would.

Jake didn't seem to have packed much at all, just his guitar and one suitcase. He had found himself standing in his immaculate dressing room unable to decide about anything. So he randomly grabbed some shirts, jeans and shoes and threw them into a bag. He carried them downstairs and into the car.

David helped him to bring down Zelda's stuff, which took considerably more effort.

Jake had asked the two tame photographers not to take pictures of this particular part of the day. He felt it would look rather undignified to be seen loading up the car like a pair of refugees.

They were leaving the kids at God's until supper. Jake told them to get their stuff together and David had offered to help bring it all over to the Mews later. Dusty and Ed wanted to watch one last 'Fantasia' on the big, big screen; they reasoned that Willow would enjoy it too. Valentine was gagging to break the news to Cleo that she was a great-grandmother, before anyone spoilt it for him

So Zelda and Jake went down to the front gate at God's, possibly for the last time, to tell the photographers that they were going to have to say goodbye.

They shook hands. Jake said, 'Bye Terry, bye George.' He had always got their names right.

Zelda looked confused. So she kissed them both warmly. Terry and George were very thrilled, embarrassed but thrilled ... and anyway, they all knew perfectly well that it wouldn't be long before they saw each other again.

As they drove off, waving, Zelda said, 'They're called Tony and John, Jake, not whatever you called them.'

'Really, darling, crikey, how embarrassing. Have I been calling them both the wrong names, for all these years?' Jake smiled to himself.

'Yes, you idiot, you have.' She poked him in the leg.

'Zelda?'

'Yes?'

'No more hitting or poking or hair-pulling, OK?'

'What, never? Not even when we're ... ?' She laughed.

'Well, there might be some exceptional circumstances ...'

Jake couldn't wait to get his lovely wife home ... to their old home.

It would be a squeeze, with all of them in there. But a squeeze was nice, everyone would agree on that. The way things were going they were bloody lucky to have a roof over their heads at all.

And, it was hardly a shack.

Much later that night David quietly loaded up all the photographs that lined the walls of Zelda's office, and her awards too. Then all of the family's personal albums and film archives. He would deliver them to Zelda at the Mews the following day – he understood how much they meant to her.

CHAPTER THIRTY-FOUR

Despite everything, things were very festive at Max and Cleo's that night. Max insisted on calling it 'the Last Supper' and saying things like 'the band kept playing as the ship went down!' The entire family sat around the dining-room table. Willow was dangled precariously on Valentine's knee, just for a minute or two, before Dusty whisked her away from him. Jamie had made a few bowls of pasta, so it was almost the Italian feast that Zelda had been fantasising about earlier.

Cleo was still reeling from all the information that Max had given her. She couldn't believe that, while she was climbing that hideous mountain, they were all back here falling over a bloody precipice.

'Never mind, Granny, at least you're not homeless yet!' Ed offered brightly.

'Oh darlings, I'm not worried. Anyway, let's not forget I just earned a million pounds this week. We'll hardly be on skid row!' Cleo looked cheerful.

Dusty piped up, 'But I thought that was for the AIDS orphans.'

'Well it was, darling. But everyone is always giving them money. They've got lots really. They'll never miss it.'

Jake couldn't help pointing out that Cleo had built all her press around 'climbing for AIDS orphans'. Wasn't it going to look a bit off?

'Oh, don't worry, I'll give them some of it.'

'How much?' Dusty asked sharply.

'I don't know, darling. Five per cent? After all, there is a recession on. Everyone knows that!'

'I don't think that has anything to do with anything,' said Jake. 'Anyway, Cleo, you'll have to give at least half of that to the tax man, so you might as well give at least that much to the charity.'

Cleo looked aghast. 'What do you mean, give half of it to the tax man? I didn't notice the tax man climbing fucking Everest with me!'

Valentine joined in. 'It doesn't really work like that, Cleo.'

'How do you know?' Cleo was getting quite upset. Why were they all ganging up on her when she was trying to be helpful and generous to her family?

'I know, Cleo. Because, firstly, I'm studying Politics and Economics at Oxford, so I'd be an idiot if I didn't know it – it's pretty basic stuff. I'm fairly sure everyone knows it,' Valentine replied, languidly.

'Really, is that so?' Cleo turned to Max. 'What do you think, darling?'

'Oh, my love, you know perfectly well I have made it a habit never to think about money. It's just too ghastly. Let's change the subject. Jamie, for God's sake stop hovering about and pull up a chair to join us. The old life has gone. We're all in this together now.'

Cleo knew Max was right to keep Jamie on side. They'd never manage without Jamie. Max understood these things. He was so clever. They were going to be all right. She just knew it. Tax man, AIDS orphans and all!

Jamie looked very embarrassed and tentatively pulled up a chair, near the table, but somehow not quite at it. He didn't dare eat anything though and nobody noticed that he hadn't.

On the way home, all of the children were squeezed into the back of the Merc: Valentine, Ed and Dusty, with Willow on her knee. It wasn't far and Jake hadn't been drinking. Zelda turned the radio on and they all sang along.

Back at the Mews, Zelda helped get the younger ones to bed, while Valentine and Jake drank coffee together downstairs.

When they had settled down at the kitchen table, Valentine asked tentatively, 'Jake, I wanted to talk to you about something. Um, the drug thing. I don't like who I am when I'm taking stuff now. It seems to get out of hand and I don't know how I've got where I've got. I behaved really badly towards Kate. I think I need to do something about it.'

'Well, I'm only just starting with my own stuff so I'm hardly the expert. But I'll ask around if you like – see what they recommend, you know, for someone your age. Good for you, Val. I wish I'd dealt with this shit a long time ago ... Kate who?'

'PA Kate.'

'What, you're kidding – Zelda's Kate?'

'Zelda's ex-Kate.'

'I hadn't noticed you were ...'

'With all due respect, Jake, you hadn't noticed lots of things.'

'Really, like what else?'

'Nothing, Dad. Go to bed, it's been a long day.'

It had been a bloody long day. Jake went up to bed.

Then Zelda came downstairs.

'Val darling, you're good with IT stuff, aren't you?'

'Ish.'

'The thing is ... I sent some e-mails about the DNA thing to Dr D'Angelo and I have just realised that they might be dangerous in the wrong hands. Well, in Milo's hands actually. Cleo says he was planning to sell us all out to the press! I was just thinking he might have access to my e-mail ...'

'Really, Mum, why would he have access to your e-mail?'

'Oh you know ... nothing's very secure these days.' She looked vague but she knew she wasn't fooling her son. Perhaps this wasn't such a good idea.

Valentine took her BlackBerry out of her hands. 'What do you need me to do, Mother?'

'Well, you see this account here?' The secret account Milo had set up for them, which thankfully she had never used to communicate with him after all. But she didn't want him getting his hands on the DNA stuff – it didn't give away much of course, but it could kick-start an investigative journalist and they were bloody good at tracking down all sorts of secret info. It could be a disaster, particularly when there was going to be so much shit hitting the fan already.

'Yep. Just tell me what you want me to do.'

'I want to cancel the account. Delete anything at all that's there, then cancel it. Oh, and all my texts too – just in case.'

'OK. What's the password?'

Shit. The password, oh God, no … Zelda grimaced. She squirmed. She had realised too late … she said it in a tiny whisper: 'Fuck me.'

'What, Mum? If you've forgotten it, I can't do what you want me to do.'

Zelda whispered, 'No, the password. It's "Fuck me"!'

'Jesus, Mum!'

'The expletive, not the command … it was a joke,' Zelda offered, unconvincingly.

'Yeah. OK.' Valentine pressed a few buttons and handed back her phone. 'Done.'

'Really, darling? You are brilliant. Are you sure?'

'Yes, I'm sure. And Mum?'

'Yes, darling?'

'Don't ever do anything that stupid again.'

'Oh darling, I won't. I can assure you of that. I really, really won't.'

They kissed each other goodnight.

It was lucky that Zelda hadn't tried to spare her blushes that night. Because, the following morning Lana visited Milo in hospital and, for the first time since the accident, he had access to a computer.

So it looked like Milo and Lana would have to scrape by on the accident insurance money. It was nearly a million, after all. In fact Milo was quite pleased; he'd almost done as well as Cleo out of their trip. Apart from his accident, obviously. He was surprised not to have heard from her though; he knew she must be back by now. Perhaps he should give her a ring?

He had put in a few calls to the producers of Cleo's show as he wanted to discuss some more ideas for a show of his own. They hadn't called him back.

He was determined that he wouldn't be in a wheelchair for long. He was certain he had a television career to look forward to. With his charisma and charm he could pull anything off. And who knew? Once he got this temporary paralysis out of the way ... with Milo, anything was possible.

CHAPTER THIRTY-FIVE

When Zelda and Jake woke the following day, the sun was shining brightly into the new bedroom of their old home and they both felt content and happy, for the first time in years.

They made love quietly, with a depth of feeling that had eluded them for so long. They had almost forgotten what it felt like, to make love for love's sake. Not as some sort of trade-off or in a drunken, drugged-up fever, but just because they loved and desired each other. Despite everything they felt connected again.

Zelda lay with her head on Jake's shoulder, her arm resting lightly across his chest. 'Jake.'

'Mmm.' Jake was snoozing contentedly.

'You know what's nice about being here at the Mews again?'

'Mmm?'

'I will always know where you are.'

'Er, OK?'

'No, I don't mean to check up on you! I just mean at God's I could never find anyone – I spent my whole day asking where everyone was. It was lonely, and fucking annoying!'

'You're right, it was. Well, we are not going to be lonely any more, are we?' Jake put his arms around Zelda and hugged her tight.

'I think I'm going to cook dinner here, for everyone, the family, tonight. What do you think?' she said brightly.

'Great, Zelda, great. We will all muck in to help. Don't want to run before we can walk, do we ... ?' he smiled teasingly.

Zelda bashed him with a pillow.

'I thought we'd agreed, no hitting! I wasn't running you down, Tiger. It's just that ... I've never seen you cook – ever, in fact. I'm sure you'll be brilliant at it. But I think we should all help, learn together, you know?' Jake tried to look serious.

'OK, yes, OK. I know. But I just want us to be a proper family and I thought we could start by sitting down to eat together occasionally. It would be nice, wouldn't it?'

'Lovely. Good idea. Now shall we have another crack at something you really are very good at already?' He flipped Zelda onto her back and kissed her, just as she seemed to be mumbling something about scrambled eggs.

Luckily no one in the household was up very early that morning. Even Willow slept in.

It was the beginning of what promised to be a surprisingly beautiful day.

Max thought that things were looking up. His trustees had arrived to inform him that although a vast amount of his trust's assets had been lost, he did still have a small amount in an offshore fund which should provide for Cleo and him to have a relatively comfortable old age.

'Old age!' Cleo responded, furiously. 'What are you talking about? We are quite young and fully intend to go on living indefinitely. So what constitutes relatively comfortable anyway?'

One of the trustees spoke up, nervously clearing his throat. 'Um, it should be possible to create an income of approximately £250,000.'

Cleo looked incredulous. 'A month?'

The trustee looked shifty. 'No, Lady Spender – a quarter of a million a year.'

'Don't be ridiculous, nobody can live on that! Are you sure you haven't made some mistake?' Cleo looked genuinely shocked.

'No, Lady Spender. I'm afraid not. There has been no mistake.' The trustee looked pale, but he continued optimistically, 'At least you will be able to keep this house. We are happy to have been able to establish that – you will definitely be able to keep your house.'

'Well, thanks a bunch. We can keep our house! You have just lost my husband's entire fortune and you sit there and tell me we can keep our house. As if you were doing us some kind of favour. Max ... Max, tell these idiots to leave now, tell them to go. I can't believe this ...' Cleo leapt up and stormed out of the room.

Max looked vaguely after her, then, without saying another word to the men who had lost him almost everything, he turned and wandered out into the garden.

Jamie saw the trustees out.

Cleo was already on the telephone to her agent asking when the fees for her Everest job would be coming through. Also, she had some ideas for her next project.

She certainly wasn't going to be retiring any time soon. Old age! The bloody cheek of it! She would show those idiotic bastards. Comfortable old age! Ha!

CHAPTER THIRTY-SIX

Zelda came down to find Dusty hurriedly giving the baby her breakfast.

She smiled at her aunt. 'Hi, Zelda. I know everything is still a bit chaotic, but I really need to get back to school today. Do you think you and Valentine could manage Willow till we can get someone to replace Lana?'

Zelda desperately tried to think of an excuse – look after a baby? All day? She wasn't sure that she'd ever done such a thing, even when her own boys were small.

Ed appeared in his school uniform, followed by Valentine. They had both heard what Dusty was saying.

Valentine spoke first. 'I can help later – sure. I just have to be somewhere,' he glanced at his Cartier watch, 'five minutes ago! I'm going back up to Oxford in a couple of days so ...' He looked apologetic.

Ed was stressed. 'Dusty, if you're coming, we have to go now. We're really late.'

Dusty handed the baby bowl full of disgusting mush to

Zelda, grabbed her school bag and flew out of the door before her aunt had time to protest.

Valentine kissed his mother noisily on both cheeks. 'You are the most wonderful, beautiful mother in the world and I love you.' And then he left too.

Zelda couldn't believe what had just happened. She was about to yell for help but then she remembered – they had all gone. That had all gone.

She slumped down on the kitchen chair, and Willow smiled a gooey, beautific smile at her. Zelda smiled back at her grandchild. Her grandchild! Was any of this really happening? She took a deep breath – how hard could this be?

Jake came downstairs to find Zelda tentatively trying to feed the baby without getting her favourite Paul Smith shirt covered in gunk.

'Ah, domestic goddess already. Bravo!' And he kissed her hair as he put the kettle on to make tea for them both.

Willow smiled at Zelda then put her lips together and blew food all over her – laughing joyfully as Zelda jumped back, in absolute horror.

Christ! Domestic goddess! Zelda grimaced. 'Jake, we need to get a nanny now that Dusty and Ed are back at school.'

'Oh, I thought you looked so adorable feeding her, when I came down just now, I was thinking . . .' he teased.

'I said I'd change, Jake. I didn't say I'd become a completely different person!' Zelda flicked baby food at him. An accidentally good shot, it hit him on the lip. He licked it and said,

'Yum ... no – yuk, what is that? Are you trying to poison that poor child, Zelda? God, that's disgusting.'

Willow had her mouth open like a baby bird. Zelda put another spoonful in. 'Well, she thinks it's lovely, don't you, Willow? She doesn't think I'm trying to poison her. Look, she thinks I'm lovely too.' The baby was grinning toothlessly at her. Zelda was pleased with herself, something she realised she hadn't felt for quite a long time.

'That's because you are lovely, Zelda.' Jake put a mug of tea down in front of his wife. 'You are very poor – but you are also lovely.' He looked at Zelda seriously for a moment. 'Are you sure you are OK? You have lost a lot, you know.'

'So have you!'

'Well, I never felt any of it was really mine, to be honest. I mean all the art and stuff – you loved it so much.' He looked sympathetic.

Zelda grinned. 'I think I'll be able to stagger on without it somehow. Anyway I'll be earning plenty, so will you, maybe we'll get ourselves some new stuff.'

Jake laughed and shook his head. She really was incorrigible.

Zelda started peering into the empty fridge. 'I was going to ring Daylesford to get them to deliver food for dinner. I'll ring Max and Cleo to tell them to come over ...' Zelda was taking her new role seriously.

Jake didn't feel it was the moment to point out that a trip to Tescos was more the sort of way they should be getting their groceries. He hadn't the heart to tell Zelda that yet. Baby steps, baby steps.

They needed to make plans; there was much to be done. Zelda would need a new agent and so would he.

He had been rereading his novel and it wasn't as dire as he had thought. In fact, with a bit more work he hoped it might be OK. If he could get it out there soon … who knew, he might even be able to get an advance?

Then, if Zelda could hold onto her Fabulous contract … it was more likely now, since the Lucien thing had blown up so hugely a lot of press attention had been drawn away from their family. Among the many superstars caught up in the collapse of Dark Artists were Scarlett's parents, and they were kicking up a fuss, creating a huge media storm around themselves. The press were camped out on their doorstep now, and on many others all over the world.

So just for today, Zelda and Georgia were yesterday's news. Jake only hoped they could remain that way while they tried to get back on their feet.

CHAPTER THIRTY-SEVEN

Valentine had been trying to reach Lily. She had not responded to his calls or his increasingly needy text messages. He couldn't believe what was happening to him. He had never ever felt like this about a girl before. Lily was driving him completely fucking crazy. He was not happy.

He thought that there must be something wrong with her phone. She had promised to meet him that day, but he wanted to know when and where, and he wanted to know now. He decided to go to her house, Johnny's house. He knew it wouldn't be cool but he had to see her. He could pretend he had a message for Johnny. In fact he did have something to talk to Johnny about: he could let him know that he was not Willow's father, once and for all. He might even tell him who was ... no, no, on second thoughts that wouldn't be good. Lily would hear about it and, something told him she wouldn't be impressed.

Actually Lily wouldn't have been in the least bit interested in the recent complex developments in Valentine's life. She was a free spirit, as Valentine was about to discover.

When Valentine reached Johnny's vast house in Richmond no one answered the doorbell. It chimed loudly with a riff from one of the Bastards' most famous songs.

Valentine found himself knocking loudly and calling Lily's name.

As he was standing on the drive, about to start throwing gravel at the upstairs windows, the front door suddenly swung open. A middle-aged woman greeted him suspiciously. 'What do you want?'

Valentine composed himself, and hiding his fistful of gravel behind him he said, 'Um, I was looking for Johnny ... and Lily. Wondered if they were at home?'

'They left last night. Who are you anyway?' The woman looked fierce.

'Oh, just a friend. Where ... When will they be back?' he stammered.

'His US tour is about to begin. Don't expect them back for months. You'll have to ring them if you need to speak. Goodbye.' She shut the door firmly.

What? She'd gone on tour with Johnny! He thought she had too many modelling assignments to go on tour. But, she'd just buggered off without a text or a word – even in fucking French!

Valentine was devastated. He wandered back into the street and walked until he could find a cab. He couldn't believe it. He felt bereft – a new sensation and a very unpleasant one too. He rummaged in his pockets for a fag, found a couple of pills he didn't know he had and swallowed them before lighting up and taking a deep drag. He felt his first flash of anger towards Lily.

His gut tightened and he found he was so livid that he started to imagine all the creative ways he could punish her. But she was far away, beyond his reach. As were all the women he had hurt before.

As he began to experience the familiar rush from the pills he had taken, he suddenly felt frightened, anxious and even a little paranoid. Nothing was going right for him.

He tried to calm down, concentrate; he needed to find out why Lily had gone off with that filthy old geezer Johnny. He could hardly bear to think about them together. Surely she couldn't put up with that for long? No, no, she'd be back soon – she'd be missing him, he was sure of that.

Lily would be back with him in no time, and everything would be fine.

Valentine's mood had swung again, and he began to feel a bit better. He hailed a cab and headed home.

In fact, Lily was having a blast on the road with Johnny. She was happy locked in her own self-gratifying little world. She had hardly given Valentine a moment's thought since leaving England. There were a couple of heavenly groupies on the road with the band and they had taken a particular shine to Lily, so she had plenty to occupy her whilst Johnny was working.

The thing she had always liked most about Johnny was that he let her live exactly the way she wanted to. He never told her she was beautiful either, which was such a relief. Because usually, wherever Lily went, whoever she met always gushed all over her about how beautiful she was, so dazzled by her looks and fame that they saw nothing else – just this famous face. She certainly couldn't see the charm in it herself, and people's reaction to her often made her feel like a freak. It was exhausting and repetitive when people congratulated her, as if it were something she had achieved rather than a genetic accident – her parents were both quite ordinary. She had always felt that she was just a marketing and fashion phenomenon, a fluke.

But Johnny was one of the few people she knew who didn't acknowledge the way she looked at all. He found her funny and he was so easy-going that she could just be whatever she felt like with him. He was almost old enough to be her grandfather, and yet he was more like an older brother – albeit an incestuous one.

Which was why she'd decided to go on the road with him and leave that pretty boy Valentine far behind.

The newspapers were rife with speculation. Another big story had broken.

The headlines screamed:

'LUCIEN DARK TO FACE FURTHER CHARGES!'

The story continued:

'In an even darker twist, more sensational details emerged today concerning Lucien Dark, the head of Dark Artists International. In addition to the charges brought by the Serious Fraud Office, the "Agent to the Stars" is to face further charges from the CPS. It appears that certain "material" has been found on the home computer of Mr Dark, uncovered in the course of the ongoing investigation by the Serious Fraud Office into the financial position of his company . . .'

The press weren't saying, or even suggesting, what that might mean. But everyone knew. There was only one kind of problem on a home computer that you got arrested for . . . wasn't there?

The police and Crown Prosecution Service were confident they had enough to charge him with.

Particularly since a young schoolgirl had contacted them that afternoon. She had seen the newspapers and thought she might have something of additional interest to tell them. She had already been in contact with the publicist Mick Silver.

It turned out that what the SFO had found on Lucien's computer was very, very serious stuff indeed: the most distressing images of pornography involving underage girls. Some of the detectives who had seen it would need counselling for shock.

The Crown Prosecution Service was delighted when the information was turned over to them by the SFO. They hadn't had anyone high profile to be made an example of for a very long time. Now they had the computer evidence and a young witness – they couldn't have asked for more.

When Lucien was formally charged he went berserk. 'What the fuck are you talking about? I'm in here for financial, um, irregularities. Child pornography – how fucking dare you?'

Then the young lawyer came back to confirm that the CPS

had his computer with all the images on it, 'and evidence from a schoolgirl?'

For once, Lucien was temporarily rendered speechless.

The lawyer looked smug as he continued, 'I'm afraid our firm won't be able to handle this case. I think you will need to apply for legal aid and use a state-appointed lawyer. Good day, Mr Dark.'

'Good day ... good fucking day?' Lucien tried to jump over the table after the lawyer to hit him ... to kill him.

He knew he had his faults. But he had never, ever downloaded an indecent image of a child. It wouldn't even have occurred to him. He told them ... told those stupid police bastards ... but they just replied. 'Well, you would say that, wouldn't you, sir?' Very sarcastically.

'But I haven't done any of this shit. What's going on? Get off me ... !' Two large police officers had stepped forward and restrained him.

He was handcuffed and placed on suicide watch.

CHAPTER THIRTY-EIGHT

Zelda was still trying to find an agency that would supply her with a nanny for the baby. When she told them that she needed a girl to start *now*, well, tomorrow at the latest, the agent would not be moved. In fact she sounded particularly insincerely apologetic when she insisted that they were unable to help. If Zelda had only known it, the agent's sister had been a makeup artist on a film that Zelda starred in and she had taken serious umbrage when Zelda snapped at her for 'poking her fucking eye out'. The makeup artist subsequently told anyone who would listen that Zelda was the most difficult bitch of an actress that she had ever worked with. The employment agent got a real kick out of this reprisal on her sister's behalf and she just couldn't wait to tell her all about it.

Jake emerged from his study to say that he'd heard from Hugo and Giles, who wanted a meeting mid-morning the following day to discuss more of the financial repercussions of Lucien's fraud. Then, looking apologetic, he said he needed to get to a meeting and promptly left the house.

She really needed to find a nanny.

Her phone rang: it was Cleo. 'Darling, I got your message. Max and I would love to come over to you tonight. The Mews! What fun. A trip down memory lane!'

Zelda thought of something. 'Cleo, Mum, I'm in a bit of a fix. Jake and I have to see the lawyers tomorrow and I haven't found anyone to replace Lana – any chance you could take Willow for me, just for a few hours?'

'Darling, you haven't told me yet, what did happen to Lana?' Cleo sidestepped Zelda's request neatly.

'It's a long story – I'll tell you later. It involves that shit Milo.'

'What? No, darling, not Lana too! Surely not.'

'Yep – the only difference being, he was married to her!' Zelda couldn't help laughing.

'No! What, all that time with us and none of us had a clue?' Cleo sounded incredulous.

'Well, maybe we just weren't paying much attention to the stuff going on around us . . .' Zelda left it at that.

Cleo changed the subject adroitly. 'Anyway, darling – supper. Can I bring anything? Jamie perhaps?'

'No, no. We'll manage. Not room here for . . . Mummy, we're fine, just come over at about eight.'

They hung up. Zelda suddenly realised she had missed an opportunity – she should have asked if Jamie could look after Willow! Damn. Well, she could ask again later, after her parents had knocked back a few drinks. She knew her mother was never going to volunteer to look after her great-grandchild herself. What if she found herself in a position where she had to tell someone who the baby was? She would be mortified – not by the baby's unconventional genetic history but that she, Cleo, was Willow's great-grandmother. That piece of information would always have to be withheld.

Zelda listened upstairs to see if the baby was awake yet. All was quiet, so she got on with unloading the groceries that had just been delivered by Daylesford Organic.

When she had rung them earlier that day, to place her order, she just told them to send over enough food for supper for ten people. She was amazed when the delivery arrived. It seemed like so much – enough to feed an army, coming from a life where the only things usually stored in the fridge were milk, wine or vodka, with endless loaves of sliced bread kept in the freezer for making toast. The only food that had ever been delivered to God's was either takeaway, or Zelda's daily rations of organic diet vitamin-shake supplements; but not any more.

The shop had sent a delicious little almond cake, which Zelda definitely couldn't remember ordering. But she found herself opening it, with the intention of giving some to Willow when she woke up. Having tasted a little corner of it, then another, half an hour later she was mortified to see that it had all gone.

She felt furious. That was why she never kept food in the house. How on earth was this new life going to work? She felt panic rising . . . she could see it now, the future stretching out before her: she would be fat and out of work and they would be on skid row then, skid row proper.

When Jake got back to the Mews, he found Zelda in a funk

about food. She had bags of Daylesford goodies strewn all over the kitchen but had obviously been unable to decide what to tackle next.

She had given up completely when Willow started crying, demanding to be rescued and fed. Zelda still hadn't been able to find a nanny and so she didn't need to tell Jake she was feeling pretty disgruntled. That was plain.

Jake took Willow from his wife just as Ed arrived back from school. Dumping his backpack onto the floor he scampered off upstairs, calling out to tell them that Dusty had gone off to meet a new friend.

Jake called after him, 'Who?'

'Alex? I think,' Ed answered, as he disappeared.

'Alex – male or female?' Jake wondered idly.

By now Jake and Zelda had heard about the other appalling charges that had been brought against Lucien, which made them very distressed and uncomfortable. They were shocked that he could be capable of such hideous stuff, but not particularly surprised. After all, apart from his history with Georgia, he had destroyed all his clients and friends seemingly without any remorse – perhaps he really was capable of anything. Zelda and Jake certainly didn't want to discuss it openly while Ed was in the house. So they muttered and hissed about it quietly as they set up the table for the evening and put the food into dishes.

Jake gave Zelda a warm hug and she began to cheer up. Everything looked lovely. A simple tablecloth and candles decorated the kitchen table. Food was laid out on the island. Drinks were in the fridge.

Dusty gave them a round of applause when she got home just before supper. She apologised for missing out on helping to set up and promised she'd be in charge of washing up. Jake noticed that Dusty looked happier – her cheeks were pink. So he guessed, correctly, that Alex must be male.

When Max and Cleo arrived they were impressed to find everyone looking very relaxed and happy in their new home. Willow had been bathed and was asleep already, which Cleo was very relieved to hear. Out of sight was, happily for her, out of mind.

Valentine appeared with Charlie and Art. There was more than enough food for everyone. The wine flowed, though not into Jake, and they all had a very jolly evening.

Lucien's name was mud.

Cleo regaled them with Everest stories, although she deftly avoided the part that everyone was burning to hear, Milo and the accident. She raved on about how gorgeous Bear was and how much the director loved her, indeed how very kind everyone had been to her.

She was justifiably proud of herself and she told them triumphantly that her agents' phone had not stopped ringing with fabulous and lucrative offers of new work. Max was obviously very pleased for her too and frankly relieved – maybe she could start keeping him for a change! He had made that joke earlier but Cleo had pretended not to hear him.

Her agents had told her, enthusiastically, that they expected even more work offers when the show went on air for the first time the following week. The final touches were being put to it in the editing suites right now. Cleo had asked for a preview but she was told that, due to time restraints, it would be aired almost the moment it was completed. So she would have to wait to see it at the same time as her public.

She was confident that she had nothing to worry about. After all, the entire expedition had been a triumph. She had seen the rushes and she looked great.

This family was getting back on its feet again fast. The press would be turned around and positively lovely again in no time.

Zelda was seeing a new agent tomorrow. As long as they could all stay out of the shit for a while, she was hopeful that her Fabulous contract could be saved.

Cleo might have been a little less confident if she had been in the editing suite, with the director, that very day. One of his assistants had drawn his attention to a random piece of sound recording he'd come across. He played it to the director a couple of times – they couldn't quite believe what they had.

The director listened to it again. There it was . . . a very faint 'Help!' followed by a strange bouncing, scraping noise, then Cleo's unmistakable voice could be heard softly hissing, 'Oh, Milo . . . you can kiss and tell – from hell!'

When Dusty finally got into bed that night she found it impossible to get to sleep. The events of the day kept spinning around in her head.

She had spent the afternoon with her new friend Alex, who had been texting her since the funeral. At first she was very reticent about meeting him, as she had learnt the hard way to be cautious about people she didn't know.

She had gone onto his Facebook. He looked very sweet and his friends seemed nice too. Of course she couldn't have a Facebook page of her own – the press would have been all over it. In fact she didn't really have close friends at all outside her immediate family, with the exception of Scarlett, and truthfully they had little in common apart from the fame of their respective families.

Alex had been really warm and friendly, and she had been feeling so very low and lonely that she had eventually agreed to meet him after school.

They had tried to go for a walk but it was impossible because people kept recognising her and trying to speak to her – not unkindly, but Alex soon realised it was going to become too much for her and he hailed a cab. He jumped in after her and exclaimed, 'Shit, that must be so weird! Are you OK?'

Dusty replied flippantly, 'Yes, I'm fine – I'm just far too fucking famous!' then she grinned at him. 'Are you sure you want to be friends with me? It's shit!'

Alex just laughed his friendly laugh, which Dusty found very reassuring.

He took her to his parents' house in Notting Hill. It was modest and homely and Dusty thought it was the cosiest house she had ever seen.

Alex made her a cup of tea and they sat at the kitchen table.

When Dusty looked at him somehow the kindness in his handsome face made her want to tell him everything that had been happening to her. She hadn't meant to at all – God no! She didn't want to scare him off with talk of her crazy family and she knew never to trust anyone, tell anyone, anything. So she was amazed when it all came pouring out.

She talked about her mother a lot, told him how much she missed her, but also how angry she was about the drugs and the deception about Willow.

She looked down sadly and said, 'I don't think I really knew my mother at all.'

Alex reached across the table and held her hand, without saying a word.

Dusty found herself blurting out her suspicions about Lucien too: all the vile things he was accused of and how he must have given Georgia the drugs that killed her. She told him about the syringe and that she had handed it into the police.

Anguished, she said quietly, 'I wish I hadn't done that now, because if there isn't any evidence on it, then it means she might have . . .' She burst into tears. 'You see, I can't bear not knowing, not knowing if she did it to herself – because, if she did, then she chose to leave us, and I just can't believe she would do that.'

Then Alex told her what she wanted to hear. 'She wouldn't have left you on purpose, Dusty, no way, no way. What has happened to you is the most horrible thing, and now that man is in prison he can't do anything to hurt you or your family any more.'

She had looked up at him, her eyes smudgy with tears, and she realised he was right. The worst had been done.

They talked for what seemed like hours. He played his music, made her a wonky sandwich, told her about his life and made her laugh. Then his parents came home and they were very kind and funny too. They didn't seem to know who she was, which was a relief, and they treated her like a normal girl. So did Alex and by the time she left that evening she felt like a normal girl. She smiled all the way home in a cab.

She had a friend – someone who wasn't in her family, or working for her family. She felt she had a real friend of her own, at last.

Chapter Thirty-Nine

Valentine offered to look after Willow, which surprised everyone when they came down to breakfast in the morning. He pointed out that she was his daughter after all and, as he was going back up to Oxford the following day, he would like to spend time with her. The others were in shock – this whole responsible, caring Valentine thing really was going to take some getting used to.

Zelda and Jake went off to their meeting.

Hugo and Giles were there to greet them when they arrived at the impressive offices of Peterson de Winter. They had taken a black cab up to the City, and Zelda was surprised to find that she attracted far less attention from the public without the car-driver-security thing.

It felt a bit weird to wander around in the real world without the trailing whispered wake of 'You know who? ... did you see? ... fuck! That was ...' A couple of people recognised her, so she was relieved not to be completely invisible. The familiar annoying public behaviour was something that had always defined her, as it was who she had been since her early twenties; it made her feel real. Could it stop just like that? She doubted it. Maybe it was because she hadn't glammed up all that much today, or perhaps it was because movie stars and celebrities were hardly ever spied in the City? Yes, she reassured herself, maybe that was it.

In fact, the people who passed Zelda and Jake on the street that day were far too preoccupied with their own lives to notice anyone or anything, hanging onto their jobs with white knuckles as everything around them folded into the dust. The markets were in catastrophic free fall. The fear in the City of London offices and on the streets was palpable. The promised recovery had never materialised. Now it was each man for himself, and each man, and the occasional woman, was scared shitless.

The news that Hugo and Giles had for them was not good. It was becoming increasingly certain that all the assets of every client at Dark Artists had been lost. The accounts systems that were operated by Lucien were so convoluted that it might never be possible to uncover where their fortune had gone. Huge chunks of money were unaccounted for and no trace of it could be found. It was likely that Lucien had salted some of it away, but as yet that could not be established.

Some of Dark Artists' clients were clubbing together to bring a class action against Lucien personally, in the hope of recovering some of their losses. Lucien had instructed his lawyers to issue a statement on his behalf claiming that he had little, or nothing, to do with the financial systems and controls of the

company, insisting that they were all designed and adminis-
tered by Craig Sanderson. The allegation was hotly refuted by
Craig Sanderson's colleagues, on Craig's behalf, as he was
clearly unable to defend himself.

Lucien had also emphatically stated, through his lawyers, that
he was completely innocent, and that he utterly refuted all these
disgusting, defamatory trumped-up charges. He intended to
have them set aside imminently, if his press statement was to be
believed.

Hugo warned Jake and Zelda that this was the kind of case
that could drag on for years. He said that if Lucien had hidden
large amounts of money somewhere, it was probably in
Switzerland, as that was where he was heading when he was
arrested – allegedly, according to the press.

Hugo continued grimly, 'Frankly, while he is locked up there
won't be a way of locating it, unless he gets out and is tailed, literally and electronically. I am sorry to say, the chance of anyone's
money ever being recovered is very remote.' Then Hugo smiled.
'Unless, that is, he decides to divulge its whereabouts himself!'

They all knew that was never going to happen.

Jake was impressed with the way Zelda had dealt with all
the disastrous news they had been given. He had to admit that
although she was appalling in someone else's crisis, when it
came to her own she really was rather magnificent. She never
ceased to amaze him.

They shared their plans and schemes on the way home in a
black cab. Both tried to be quite upbeat about their impending
period of austerity – in fact, they felt quite fired up by the

challenge. Jake was going full tilt at his novel and Zelda was confident of being able to keep her career on track. The new agents were gagging to sign her this afternoon.

An employment agency had left a message on Zelda's phone to say that they had found a live-out nanny who was able to start the following day. She had excellent references.

Valentine seemed determined to turn over a new leaf. Jake had had a really good, open talk with him before they'd gone to bed the night before. He and Zelda were pleased that their golden boy had turned a corner – they were both very proud of him. Jake felt a small twinge of pain at their familiar expression 'golden boy', as it had different connotations now. He thought he might stop using it.

They both agreed that Ed was doing brilliantly; he had never been troublesome, and his affection for Dusty and Willow made their assimilation into the family easier for all of them. They took his goodness for granted, they realised, so they both sincerely resolved to make more effort to acknowledge how proud they were of him too.

And last, but by no means least, Zelda pointed out how thrilled she was that after all these years she was no longer living in the pockets of her parents. Specifically, the pocket of her mother.

They grinned at each other.

Jake said, 'I s'pose this means we're grown up!' He reached across and pulled his wife towards him.

They kissed and Zelda found herself wanting to say, 'I've always been grown up.'

But for once, she decided against it. She remained silent and gazed out of the cab window at the streets and the public that she loved.

Their cabbie was impressed! He would go on to regale all his fares for years to come with the news: 'You know who I had in my cab the other day? Only that Zelda Spender and her husband! They were the most loved-up couple I 'ave ever driven – fan-fuckin-tastic!'

If Zelda and Jake could have heard him, they would have had to agree. They really couldn't wait to get home.

Lucien had been moved to a high-security unit that afternoon. The terrible reality of his situation was beginning to bite. He found himself in a small cell with no window. Unlike the police station, which was filled with noise – albeit clanging and yelling – the room he was locked in now was eerily silent, soundproofed. No one could hear you scream.

Lucien felt he was losing his mind. He was becoming confused. Why did they keep accusing him of that – child pornography? No, no, no!

They were making a mistake. He had never done stuff like that, well ... the schoolgirl? He did remember her, and his blood ran cold.

He had been desperately trying to think who had access to his computer. The staff? Kristina – God, no! He knew she was far too stupid. No, he was convinced it must be some sort of espionage, a professional fit-up – by one of his disgruntled ex-clients? The questions just kept coming and coming, but where were the answers? Lucien was frantic. What was happening? He had always had an answer for everything, until now.

CHAPTER FORTY

Kristina had used her old passport to leave London, which was in her maiden name – Kristina Sergevich.

She wore a slightly mysterious air, in her dark Gucci sunglasses and an exquisitely cut Burberry trench coat. The guy at passport control looked at her twice – but only because she was so remarkably beautiful. She was very relieved to board the plane without a hitch.

Now here she was, carrying baby Ivan along the concourse at Geneva airport. She turned to her 'brother' Dmitri and kissed him warmly on the mouth. In fact the handsome man Zelda had seen in the BMW outside the police station was not Kristina's brother at all. Nothing like. He was her lover, and father to the baby, Ivan. They had known each other since they met at the orphanage where they'd grown up, in Uzbekistan. Kristina and Dmitri had always been a formidable team of two.

Dmitri was a genius. Not only as a computer programmer but also as a hacker too.

Originally, he and Kristina had come to England to look for

an investor to help them get started with a business venture back home, as they needed to raise some capital. They weren't looking for a huge amount but it soon became obvious that the ordinary fundraising channels were closed to them. So they began looking for someone who might, inadvertently, invest some of their funds in Dmitri and Kristina's little company.

They did their research diligently, choosing Lucien after reading an interview with him entitled, 'Is This the Most Powerful Man in Show-Business?'

They made their first move on him by hacking into his phone and address book – a task that took Dmitri barely half an hour. Then Kristina joined an escort agency that Dmitri discovered Lucien was using regularly. They planned to work from inside and out, in a two-pronged attack. How hard could it be?

But, with Lucien, they soon realised they had bitten off more than they could chew, or more than Kristina could tolerate anyway. Life with Lucien was as abusively hellish as anything she had experienced back in her homeland.

Until, that was, the thrilling day when Dmitri discovered Lucien's secret Swiss bank account and all the millions it contained: funds that vastly exceeded anything they would have needed to start up their originally modest business.

Dmitri and Kristina had always harboured altruistic ambitions: to run a company that could provide safe, clean, civilised orphanages in their homeland. Now their plans looked far more attainable than they could ever have dared hope, even in their wildest dreams. They had access to funds that could dramatically change the lives of the most desperate, vulnerable children back home forever.

Originally, their idea was to just take the money and run. But as time went by they saw what a dangerous, vindictive and ruthless person Lucien was. They began to realise that they would have to get him out of the way completely, to feel safe in the knowledge that he would not be able to come after them.

Dmitri, in all his brilliance, came up with the perfect plan.

And so the day that the Serious Fraud officers had come calling at the house was just a happy, helpful coincidence. Kristina had been scheduled to put Lucien's computer in for repair that very day. Their original plan was that the repair company would find the images that Dmitri had placed there. They would then report Lucien to the police, and he would have been arrested and charged.

But then the Serious Fraud officers had confiscated Lucien's computer, inadvertently dispensing with the repair plan. This was an unlooked-for bonus to their scheme, as it distanced Kristina completely from Lucien's 'crime'.

Kristina would help the police with their enquiries as the distraught, shocked, vulnerable wife. Then she and Dmitri could leave the country. The tens of millions of pounds from Lucien's accounts had already been transferred to an offshore account of their own, on the very day that Lucien was arrested as he tried to leave for Switzerland.

So, Zelda might have felt differently if she had known that while she was kissing, pitying and, some might say, patronising Kristina on the steps of the police station, all her worldly goods were already nestling comfortably in Kristina and Dmitri's new bank account.

To be honest, the dynamic duo didn't know, or even wonder, where the money that Lucien had stolen and stashed away had come from. But, would they have cared that some of it might have belonged to Zelda, Georgia and all the other newly impoverished clients of Dark Artists International? The answer would have to have been no, they would not. They wouldn't have cared a damn.

Redistribution of wealth was something they believed in, quite passionately. They certainly didn't care that Lucien was going to be disgraced and sent down for something he didn't do, as well as the things he had done. After all, Kristina had seen the very darkest side of Lucien Dark. Neither she nor Dmitri felt the tiniest grain of compassion for him. As far was Kristina was concerned it was the retribution he deserved.

They had both suffered a great deal of cruelty and deprivation in their lives. But they wouldn't be suffering any more, and now they would have the resources to make sure that other children in their position could be protected and saved. They were going home and they intended to make some serious changes in their old country when they got there.

The director of 'Cleo Climbs Everest' had woken to a clear head. Having decided to sleep on the dilemma of what to do about the sound-bite, he found he was confident and clear on the best course of action. Although it was incredibly tempting to include it in the programme he knew that to do so would overshadow everything else that he had achieved with the show. Cleo would be vilified and possibly even face prosecution for attempted manslaughter. Then the director would have to wave goodbye to the other two programmes that were being commissioned for Cleo 'to face other challenges'. The budgets and fees being discussed for these shows were huge.

He told himself that he was doing the right thing. He admired and respected Cleo and God knew what sort of provocation that manipulative shit Milo was capable of. When the producers had told him about Milo's self-promotion plans the director had felt quite indignant on her behalf. OK, maybe that wasn't enough of a justification for burying the sound-bite, but frankly, he couldn't afford to screw up this career opportunity. Among other things he had a huge mortgage to pay.

So, that was it, he had made his decision – he was leaving the incriminating recording out.

The show must go on.

CHAPTER FORTY-ONE

An Inspector McVeigh arrived at the Mews asking to speak to Georgia Cole's family, just as Dusty was about to leave for school.

Jake let him in and invited him to sit down at the kitchen table where Dusty joined them. Tom McVeigh could see that she was anxious and apprehensive. He gratefully accepted Jake's offer of coffee.

Jake couldn't help noticing that the inspector looked somewhat the worse for wear – a look that Jake knew well.

He was right. Inspector McVeigh was feeling pretty rough, as the pub quiz had turned into a very long night, and this morning he certainly wasn't looking forward to delivering the news he had for this unfortunate family.

He felt particularly unsettled in the presence of these two people. They had been staring at him every day out of the tabloids, for what seemed like weeks – years even. The girl looked younger than in her pictures, but just as fragile and very pretty. The inspector was acutely aware of what a horrible time she had had.

Feeling a bit hangover shaky, he decided to address himself to Jake, which seemed more appropriate somehow. He found it hard to know where to start.

Taking a sip of coffee he plunged in. 'I'm afraid I have news that will be, er ... disappointing. I am informed that we, the police, and the CPS do not intend to proceed with a criminal charge against Lucien Dark for any involvement he may have had in events that led to the death of Georgia Cole.' He stared hard at his coffee cup; the air felt heavy.

He pressed on. 'Firstly, although the CCTV footage did show that Dark had visited Miss Cole twice that evening, it also showed Valentine Robinson's visit, as Mr Robinson said it would when he volunteered his statement. The difficulty is that it would be impossible to proceed with charges against Dark, even for intent to supply, as he was not the only visitor to the house that night.'

Dusty looked stricken. 'But what about the syringe?'

Tom McVeigh could not meet her eye. 'Yes, yes, the syringe. I was coming to that, um, I am afraid ... because the syringe was removed from the scene of the crime, it was therefore deemed vulnerable to contamination – it just wouldn't be allowed in evidence. Sorry.'

Jake was incredulous. 'What, so that's it?'

Looking increasingly uncomfortable the inspector continued, 'I can see, personally, that Mr Dark's behaviour appeared extremely suspicious, and he is clearly a very unpleasant piece of work, but, as I said, on the existing evidence there would not be a strong enough case to prove that he had a hand in the circumstances that led to the, um, tragedy. I understand that the pathology report confirmed that Miss Cole had died of an overdose of various substances, but that those did not include heroin. Even if the original pathology report was incomplete and another toxicology report was to be ordered, it seems there would be little to be gained in this case. So, without further hard evidence . . .' He realised he didn't need to say more, and it all sounded formal and frustratingly final. On days like these he really hated his job.

In an attempt to leave the family with some positive news, McVeigh pressed on. 'I have made some enquiries into the other charges pending, and I understand that the CPS case against him for the computer . . .' He suddenly felt it would be inappropriate to mention the indecent images in front of Dusty. 'Um, well, that case is very strong. I believe there is a witness. So that will result in a long and, I think I can say with confidence, very unpleasant prison term.' He tried to look encouraging. 'Although the fraud case will take longer to come to court, what with that and his other crimes, well, I don't imagine Lucien Dark will be seeing anything but courtrooms and prison walls for many years to come.'

Inspector McVeigh realised that he had probably said more than he should. He was feeling quite hot and bothered.

As he rose to leave, Dusty looked up at him and said quietly, 'However long he goes to prison for, he will still be getting away with murder.'

Dusty had finally realised that she did know – she had always known – that Lucien supplied her mother with drugs, she just couldn't bear to face the truth. Whether he had used the syringe, or Georgia had, it made no difference now. Lucien had supplied her, kept her where he wanted her, and he had killed her.

Tom McVeigh glanced down at the motherless girl. She looked so vulnerable. His professional guard slipped further and he found himself blurting out, 'I'm afraid you would be surprised by how many people get away with murder. There are suspicious so-called accidents all the time: a fall, faulty electrics, a suicide. I am sorry to say the most common is an overdose – very difficult to prove, very difficult indeed.' Tom McVeigh sighed wearily. 'In many of these cases the law is ineffectual, but I always like to think that where the law fails there is still the possibility of divine retribution. If it's any consolation, in my experience, you would be surprised how often that proves to be the case.'

He left then, feeling that he had done his best, but that his best wasn't good enough at all.

As Jake closed the door behind the dejected policeman he thought to himself, indignantly, 'Perfect, a hungover cop who believes in karma – just the man for the job!'

But he couldn't help hoping that what he said was true.

With nothing to distract him Lucien was increasingly unsettled by his memories of the last night of Georgia's life.

He went over everything again, for what seemed like the thousandth time.

He and Georgia had knocked back a few drinks together before Lucien had encouraged her to take a few lines of his coke and indulge in some ketamine – never a hard sell where Georgia was concerned. He'd even snorted quite a bit of the coke himself. The cocktail of drugs he had supplied her with was very pure and she was soon incoherent.

Then he had left her to it, slyly pocketing the front-door keys from the hall table as he went, intending to return later to execute his plan: he'd whizz back to Hollywood Road during the film premiere, by which time he was confident that she'd be 'off her silly face!' Next he'd photograph her crashed out amid the detritus of a drug binge and then he could use those pictures to keep her quiet.

This was one of Lucien's most favoured weapons in his formidable arsenal for client control.

But when he'd returned later, what he found was the kind of nightmare scenario he had never anticipated, and things had got very weird for Lucien. The drugs and shock had kicked in and . . . he'd suddenly heard it – a baby crying. Jesus! That had freaked him out – it hauntingly reminded him of the little ghost from their past. He'd panicked then and run stumblingly downstairs. He had somehow managed to muster the foresight to scoop up from the table all the drugs he'd supplied, shoving them into his pockets before he flew from the house as if the hounds of hell were at his heels.

Now here he was in a prison cell. He couldn't believe everything had gone so awry, so fucking fast. He felt himself beginning to lose his grip on his sanity. He really needed to pull himself together, to rest, but he daren't sleep. His dreams were full of images of Georgia and the sound of a baby crying constantly in his ear like a terrifying, tearful tinnitus.

Lucien felt befuddled, weak, beaten – and he could murder a bloody drink.

CHAPTER FORTY-TWO

Valentine was merrily driving up the M40 to Oxford, the sun was shining and music blared out of the brilliant sound system. He was relieved to be getting away. He wasn't sure how much longer he could've kept up the Mr Perfect act.

He had felt a bit sorry for Dusty when he'd overheard the policeman's news that the syringe had been disallowed as evidence against Lucien. He told himself he hadn't been that worried about it; Lucien had supplied it after all.

He had been standing quietly out of sight, on the staircase at the Mews, when the inspector came to call, so he knew that there weren't going to be any more enquiries into Georgia's death. This was very good news. He'd always felt confident that the police would be perfectly happy to accept his version of events. People usually were. But nonetheless he was still relieved – it was over.

That night had been such a fuck up! If only Georgia hadn't told him about Willow. At first he'd thought she was making it up to piss him off, she was so off her face. But he realised that she was serious when she told him threateningly that it could easily be proved. DNA? Didn't he know it! He'd asked her why she was telling him, when she had kept it a secret for so long.

She had slumped back onto the sofa then, looking terrible, old and deranged, and screeched accusingly, 'Because I can see the way you've started to look at my daughter and I want to make fucking sure you never lay a finger on her, so your secret is safe with me as long as you keep your filthy hands off Dusty!' Then she had passed out cold.

He had found himself standing over her. What he saw filled him with disgust and contempt – he really didn't want it getting out that he had fathered a child with this grotesque old bag. He had always thought their relationship might end badly, but this was far worse than anything he could have imagined.

He could never, even in his wildest dreams, have anticipated that he would find himself sticking a needle into her arm and pumping her full of the heroin overdose that would kill her.

But that was what he had done, and it had proved grotesquely simple.

From the moment that the syringe caught his eye he'd known what he was going to do. He had even had the foresight to put on those ridiculous customised rubber gloves that Dusty used for washing up, so he knew there wouldn't be any incriminating prints to worry about.

Then he had carried Georgia up to her room, which was quite a feat, seeing as she was bloody heavy, he'd thought, adding a small insult to a fatal injury.

He had even considered removing the syringe before he left

but then it dawned on him, as he watched Georgia's breathing become more shallow, that the syringe would still be there if she had actually OD'd, so he'd casually placed it on her bedside table. It couldn't have occurred to him that Dusty would take it, either to protect her mother's reputation or to hand in as evidence to the cops later – for all the good it had done her!

Then, as Valentine was leaving Hollywood Road he had narrowly missed being hit by Lucien's car. He'd hastily jumped into Georgia's Mini, using her car keys that he had swiped as he left the house. 'After all,' he'd reassured himself fiendishly, 'she's hardly going to miss her car now!'

He had watched with interest as Lucien went up to the front door and let himself in – Valentine instantly realised that on the CCTV cameras it could appear that Georgia had let him in herself. To all intents and purposes, at that moment, Georgia was still alive. So Lucien's arrival had been timely indeed.

Valentine had to admit that he really was a very lucky bastard.

The stupid thing was, between his mother's sleuthing and Georgia's bloody letter, his embarrassing little secret was out anyway. Ironic too, that the news hadn't even proved to be that much of a problem for him or anyone else in his crazy family. Then again the press hadn't got wind of anything yet.

Valentine almost felt a little twinge of something that might have been guilt, but he took a deep breath and swiftly banished the unfamiliar feeling by reminding himself that nothing could be done to change things now. 'And frankly Georgia was self-destructive enough to have stuck that fucking needle in her arm herself,' he thought spitefully. He knew he was being callous but he resolved not to beat himself up about it any more.

He turned the music up a little higher and put his foot down. Georgia's Mini had a lot of oomph and no one in his self-involved family had even noticed that he was still driving it around. The girls at Oxford would like it. Yes, he really was glad to be getting back there and he hadn't thought about Lily all day.

There was so much to look forward to.

Kate left her lawyer's office with very mixed feelings that morning. Things had not turned out as she had expected at all and their advice had thrown her into confusion.

Her original intention had been to apply for a very reasonable settlement from her ex-employer. So she had been justifiably upset and furious when her lawyer informed her that she was not eligible for any compensation. It seemed that her terms of employment were with a company, which had been liquidated with the demise of Dark Artists International.

She was understandably devastated by this news, Until, that is, her lawyer explained to her that the confidentiality agreement that she had signed also rested with that company and therefore its legality had expired with it.

He went on to inform her, with some relish, that she was therefore free to tell, or indeed sell, her story to anyone she chose – presumably to the highest bidder.

So Kate walked out into that fresh sunny morning feeling

slightly sick with anxiety and what might have been elation. She decided to walk home and try to think everything through calmly.

She was still extremely hurt and angry about all the injustice and cruelty that she had suffered at the hands of the Spender family. She knew that she had done a good and loyal job for them and in return she had not received a glimmer of kindness or gratitude. They deserved to pay for what they had done to her, and she felt panic rising when she thought about money – she really was so broke. Perhaps she could write a book; wouldn't that be divine retribution?

She narrowly avoided being hit by a black cab as she carelessly crossed the road and stepped into St James's Park.

The more she thought about it, the more a book seemed like a good idea – less tacky than a straightforward kiss and tell to the press. Of course she realised there would be serialisation rights with a popular daily paper as well. Yes, a book, that was it. The Spenders Lose It – the story of how Britain's favourite family lost their money, dignity and some might say decency and morality too.

Kate wondered what sort of people they would become now that they weren't rich any more. She realised that they would certainly wish they were dead if she aired all their dirty little secrets in public. Kate smiled to herself. Dead Rich – there it was, she had the book's title. After all, she had seen (and scanned) the contents of Zelda's safe and she knew far more about her ex-boss's life than anyone else – the book would cause havoc. Kate felt a pang of anxiety and guilt at the prospect of hurting Jake, since she had always had a bit of soft spot for him and for Dusty and Ed too. She tried to push them from her wavering conscience.

Inevitably, her racing mind strayed to Valentine. In truth he had never been far from her thoughts since she'd left God's on that final day, but Kate found that her anger towards that malevolent egomaniac was also mixed confusingly with feelings of loss and, very disquietingly, desire.

Kate stopped to take a few deep breaths, attempting to quell her turbulent emotions. As she looked out across the park, she spotted a young couple tightly clasped together, kissing passionately and completely oblivious to the fact that a Royal Parks lawnmower was being driven recklessly towards them. Kate was about to shout out a warning, when the young guy on the mower swerved at the very last minute, laughing wildly as he careered on. Kate's heart was pounding and she suddenly found that she was sobbing, gulping in the sweet smell of freshly cut grass that would forever remind her of this moment.

She felt an overwhelming urge to speak to Valentine. 'Just once more,' she told herself weakly, and then she would make up her mind.

Yes, that was it. She needed to speak to Valentine just to be sure, before she finally burnt all their bridges ...

Valentine noticed the Mini's speedometer hit 90mph. With the music turned up to brain-shattering volume he almost failed to hear his phone ringing as it lay on the empty passenger seat next to him. He glanced over and picked it up.

The screen read 'Kate'.

He hesitated for just a few moments – then he dismissively pressed 'ignore'.

But, in those careless seconds, Valentine sealed his fate.

The Mini hit the central reservation with a sickening bang. Then it bounced off and spun across the dual carriageway where it disappeared into the path of a vast, thundering juggernaut.

The last thing that Valentine Robinson heard, as sparks flew blindingly around him, was the terrible, deathly sound of tearing, screeching metal.

The Mini ground to a halt with one final earth-shattering jolt.